THE LAST MRS SINCLAIR

T. J. EMERSON

Boldwood

First published in Great Britain in 2025 by Boldwood Books Ltd.

Copyright © T. J. Emerson, 2025

Cover Design by Lisa Horton

Cover Images: Shutterstock and George Fairbairn/Arcangel

The moral right of T. J. Emerson to be identified as the author of this work has been asserted in accordance with the Copyright, Designs and Patents Act 1988.

Every effort has been made to obtain the necessary permissions with reference to copyright material, both illustrative and quoted. We apologise for any omissions in this respect and will be pleased to make the appropriate acknowledgements in any future edition.

A CIP catalogue record for this book is available from the British Library.

Paperback ISBN 978-1-80549-040-1

Large Print ISBN 978-1-80549-041-8

Hardback ISBN 978-1-80549-039-5

Ebook ISBN 978-1-80549-042-5

Kindle ISBN 978-1-80549-043-2

Audio CD ISBN 978-1-80549-034-0

MP3 CD ISBN 978-1-80549-035-7

Digital audio download ISBN 978-1-80549-037-1

This book is printed on certified sustainable paper. Boldwood Books is dedicated to putting sustainability at the heart of our business. For more information please visit https://www.boldwoodbooks.com/about-us/sustainability/

Boldwood Books Ltd, 23 Bowerdean Street, London, SW6 3TN

www.boldwoodbooks.com

PROLOGUE

Château Clairvallon is home to many ghosts. Soon there will be another.

A woman teeters on the edge of the château's roof terrace. Poised between life and death. In a few seconds she will fall. As she falls she will let out one final, terrible scream. Her body will hit the flagstones of the terrace below and, instantly, her life will be over.

Rumours about her death will soon spring up. People will whisper about her demise.

Did she fall or was she pushed?

Was it an accident or was it murder?

PART I

1

LEAH

May, London

All relationships are based on power, not love. My mother told me that. *Don't make the same mistake I did with your father. Don't fall in love with men. Use them. Take what you can get from them. Step up and claim your power and, once you've got it, never, ever give it away.*

I'm twenty-four now and experience has taught me she was right. That's why I'm in the bar of the Mandarin Oriental Hotel in Knightsbridge on a Tuesday evening, perched on a high stool at the horseshoe bar, a vodka martini in front of me.

It is just after 6 p.m. and outside a bright spring evening awaits. In here the lighting is low and discreet, the dim room illuminated by the molten glow from the gold ceiling. This is a plush and sumptuous space, panelled with dark wood and filled with clusters of low chairs and leather sofas. Candles flicker at the centre of glass-topped tables. It is a decadent drinking spot for the wealthy, but I'm not part of that clientele. Payday is over a week away and money is tight. Money is always tight. I ordered my martini an hour ago and I am making it last. Sipping on the glass of tap water beside it when thirsty.

Before leaving my poky, depressing flat in Tooting, I found my flatmate, Gemma, slumped on the sofa in the living room with Damien, her stoner boyfriend, sharing a bottle of cheap red wine and munching on leftover pizza. Gemma looked me up and down, taking in my black Max Mara dress, black stockings and black Louboutin stilettos. Disapproval came off her in waves. That stung, but I told myself I didn't care. My social life is none of her business. I never bring the men back to the flat.

'Can I get you another drink?' The barman – a short, attractive guy with a goatee beard – holds out the leather-bound cocktail menu.

I glance at the name badge pinned to his black shirt. 'Thanks, Josh. I'm still waiting on my friend.'

Fortunately, Josh is new at the Mandarin Oriental. I've been hitting this bar every Tuesday for the past six weeks and Josh's predecessor was starting to give me knowing, judgemental looks.

'Well,' Josh says, with a shy smile, 'if she doesn't turn up maybe you and I can—'

'You're wanted.' I point to the other side of the bar, where an elderly man in a grey blazer is waving his gnarly hand in an effort to get served.

Josh and I share an eye roll before he saunters over to his customer. I wonder what his story is. Student maybe, doing bar work on the side. An aspiring writer or actor or musician. Despite my dire financial situation, I'll have to tip him. I've worked in plenty of bars and hotels and know what a tiring, thankless side hustle it can be. Those days are in the past for me. I have a new side hustle. One that usually includes someone else paying for my extortionately priced drinks.

I swivel round on my bar stool, intending to survey the room and weigh up my options, but instead I catch two women staring at me. Middle-aged and stick-thin, with gold bracelets that look heavy enough to snap their bony wrists. Diamonds and jewelled gold bands sparkle on their ring fingers. Wives. Their suspiciously smooth faces wear expressions of pure distaste.

Back round the bar stool goes. I examine myself in the mirror behind the gleaming optics. Trying to see what they see. Checking I don't look like *that* type of woman.

My aim is always to appear elegant and understated. My dress is a simple, wraparound design that hugs my curves. Low-cut enough to hint at what is on offer but modest enough to suggest I have standards. My olive skin still has a healthy glow from my recent holiday in Antigua. My hair, black and thick and wavy, hangs loose down my back. No fancy styling. My face is free from Botox and fillers. My make-up is subtle. A thin layer of foundation. A muted palette of eyeshadow to enhance my green eyes. My red lips the only dramatic flourish.

No. I don't look like *that* kind of woman. I don't have sex with men in exchange for money. I am a woman who knows her own value. A woman who knows how to make men give her what she's worth. I don't see anything wrong with that.

I keep an eye on the wives. As soon as they get up to leave, I check out the bar, which is filling up with new arrivals. The noise level is rising. Nothing too raucous but the strong, over-priced cocktails are working their magic on the early evening crowd. Tongues looser. Laughter louder.

A young man in a navy suit sits in a low armchair on the other side of the room. Tall and lean with close-set eyes. A hotel key card lies next to his glass of red wine. He smiles in my direction.

Tempting. I've given up one-night stands, but the rooms here will be amazing, and he looks like a businessman, and they usually leave early in the morning. I could call work and say I'm sick and stay in the room until checkout. Eat a room-service breakfast and take a long, hot bath I don't have to pay for.

He has a cold, arrogant look about him. The sex could be good, a little dangerous. It could also end unpleasantly, as one-night stands with men like that sometimes do. Boundaries crossed. A sense of being used, or worse.

I turn my back on him. My casual sex days are over. I'm playing a different game now. I'm on the hunt for a more permanent arrangement.

To deter him from coming to talk to me, I take my phone out of my black Chanel handbag and check my messages. The bag, like most of my wardrobe, was a gift from one of my men. When I first decided to use the opposite sex for my own ends, I didn't know how to ask for what I wanted. Luckily, YouTube and Instagram are full of influencers and vloggers keen to share their top tips on how to take your power back from men. How to become the prize they want to keep.

Since arriving at the bar, I've had two new messages.

Call me. I miss you.

Are you ghosting me?

Both from James, the man who took me to Antigua. James is a forty-two-year-old divorcee with no kids. A successful hedge fund manager with a big disposable income. I thought he had potential. After four weeks of dating, he asked me to go on holiday with him. I thought the invite signalled a move into something serious, but Holiday James turned out to be very different from London James. When our flight from Heathrow was delayed, he raged at the poor woman behind the British Airways information desk. *Listen, you silly bitch.* I was mortified. At the hotel in Antigua, he made racist remarks about the staff. *Christ, these people.* I ditched him as soon as we landed back at Heathrow.

I delete his messages and open up Instagram. My private account has hardly any followers, and I use it to spy rather than post. Mostly to spy on Freddie, my ex from university. Sweet, sensitive, wealthy Freddie. I loved him and he loved me. Until he didn't. Until he dumped me on graduation night.

The familiar stab in my guts as I click on his profile. Tears clamour in my throat as I see a new post about his upcoming wedding to his girlfriend, Florence. Freddie and Florence. Shoot me now. I stare at a picture of them taken in the gardens of his parents' Berkshire mansion.

Not long until I marry this one! #blessed

It should have been me with Freddie in the photograph. That was the life I'm meant to be living. Instead I'm stuck in London, working long hours in the human resources department of Pillar Assurance – a job I hate – and paying extortionate rent to live in a dump of a flat. No savings. No prospect of buying a place of my own.

The last time I moaned to Gemma about the unacceptable state of my life, she said I shouldn't complain about first-world problems. That kind of dishonesty infuriates me. I don't believe for one moment that Gemma, drained by her primary school teaching job and used by Damien the loser, is happy with her lot.

Unlike her, I want more from life and I'm not ashamed to

admit it. I like luxury. I like vast, plump beds in five-star hotels. Silk pillowcases and Egyptian cotton sheets. The caress of expensive lingerie next to my skin. I was born for that kind of life. If my father hadn't screwed everything up and transformed my fairy-tale childhood into a riches-to-rags story, a life of luxury would already be mine. That's why I work so hard at this game. That's why I'm hanging around this bar in the hope of having a life-changing encounter. As the last warm dregs of the martini slip down my throat, I wonder if I'm wasting my time.

'Excuse me. Is this seat taken?'

I turn to see a tall middle-aged man looking down at me. *Is this seat taken?* A familiar opening chat-up line. One I've heard many times. I look up at him through lowered lashes. 'Help yourself.'

As he settles onto the bar stool, I realise it is in fact the only one left available. Maybe he isn't hitting on me after all? I wait for him to start talking to me but instead he waves Josh over.

'Please could I have a bottle of the Dom Perignon?' he says. 'The 2013. With two glasses.'

A man with good taste in champagne. A man with manners too, although he's already assumed I'll join him for a drink, which could be seen as arrogant.

He removes his navy jacket, hangs it on one of the hooks on the underside of the bar. The soft fabric brushes against my thigh. He tucks the back of his crisp white shirt into his dark jeans. I wait for him to start the small talk, but he says nothing. As he stares into the distance, I take the opportunity to check him out. He must be at least fifty. He has grey, neatly trimmed hair. A full head of it, although it's thinning at the sides. Quite handsome. Not in George Clooney's league, but he still has his looks. Strong jawline, broad shoulders. A slight paunch sags over the waistband of his jeans.

A silver fox. Easy prey.

His watch is a Rolex. A gold signet ring gleams on the little finger of his right hand. Old money?

When he rests both of his manicured hands on the bar, I clock his wedding ring. Should have known. He's waiting for his wife, not hitting on me. As well as giving up one-night stands, I've also renounced married men. I've had flings with several and, although they were fun and the men were always generous as well as grateful, the last affair I had ended messily. The guy, who called himself Nick, suddenly declared he wanted to leave his wife for me. Crazy. We only ever met for sex in hotel rooms, and he never even told me his real name. Not wanting to be a homewrecker, I ended it. He took it badly. Phoned and messaged me every day for weeks until he eventually gave up. After that, I decided my time is better spent dating available prospects.

Josh returns with the champagne in an ice bucket and two narrow flutes slotted between his fingers. 'Would you like me to pour, sir?'

The man nods. Josh fills the glasses with the amber, fizzing liquid. With a resigned look, he pushes one of the glasses in my direction. When I shake my head, he discreetly withdraws it and edges it towards the man. Then he flashes me a smile both relieved and hopeful.

'Just the bill,' I say to him.

Time to call it quits. Time to cut my losses and head back to my sad little flat.

The man beside me drops his head and makes a strange choking sound. Is he crying?

'Are you okay?' I ask.

'Sorry.' He wipes his eyes. 'Sorry.'

'No need to apologise. I just—'

'It's my wife's birthday.'

Why would that make him sad? 'Don't tell me,' I tease, 'you forgot to get her a gift?'

He turns to look at me. He has striking eyes. Deep blue with amber flecks. A haunted look to them.

'She's dead,' he says.

'Oh. I'm sorry to hear that.' A widower. Interesting. 'Recently?' I say.

'Just over a year ago.'

I shake my head. 'That's tough.'

A year. This man must still be raw. Vulnerable. Is that a good thing?

'This was her favourite champagne.' He gestures at the glasses, their bubbles losing their fizz. 'I thought I'd take her for a birthday drink.' A short, pained laugh. 'Stupid idea.'

'It's a lovely idea.' His grief is moving. His wife was lucky, to have been loved like that. If I died tomorrow, who would mourn me?

'And now I'm stuck with a bottle of champagne I'll never finish by myself,' he says. 'Or at least I shouldn't.' He stares at me as if seeing me for the first time. 'Will you help me out?'

'I don't want to intrude.'

'You'd be doing me a favour. Unless you have plans?'

'I was supposed to be meeting a friend, but she stood me up.'

He pushes a glass of champagne towards me.

'I've got a better idea.' I flutter my hand at Josh. When he comes over, card machine at the ready, I tell him I've decided to stay and ask him to bring me another champagne flute. He frowns and backs away. 'What was your wife's name?' I ask the man.

'Riley.' His face softens. 'Her name was Riley.'

'Unusual name.'

'Yes. She was American.' He smiles. 'When we first met, she told me she'd always had a crush on Hugh Grant. We always joked she fell for my accent, not for me.'

'I'm sure that's not true.' He looks nothing like Hugh Grant, but he does have some of the actor's self-effacing charm.

The smile falls away from his face. His eyes take on that haunted look again.

'Well,' I say. 'I think Riley should still have her birthday drink.'

'You're very sweet.' He sighs. 'Thank you.'

'My pleasure.'

His eyes flick down to my chest and up again. A tiny movement, but an important one. Even in the midst of his grief, he can't resist checking me out. When I tuck my hair behind my ear, he watches me do it. Little gestures like that always capture a man's attention. I wonder if he has kids and if so, what age they are.

Josh brings me a glass and fills it. His eyes move from me to my drinking companion and back again. He radiates disapproval, just like Gemma, and also something else. A flicker of repulsion in his eyes.

Shame prickles across my chest. In the mirror behind the optics I can see the man and I make an odd pair. The age difference obvious. So what? I've always found older men attractive. I'm sure a therapist would tell me I have Daddy issues but what girl doesn't?

I meet Josh's judgemental gaze. What does he have to offer me? A trip back to a messy room in a shared flat. Mediocre sex.

A lacklustre relationship where I put all my energy into making him feel good about himself and helping him find his direction in life. No. I don't want to gamble on a man's potential. I'd much rather profit from a mature investment.

I pointedly turn my back on Josh and raise my glass. 'I'm Leah,' I tell the man beside me.

'I'm Miles.'

We clink glasses. A light tinkling sound.

'To absent friends,' I say.

His smile returns. 'To new acquaintances.'

2

THE PICARDY DAILY

WIFE OF LOCAL CHÂTEAU OWNER FOUND DEAD

Police have confirmed that Riley Sinclair, wife of Miles Sinclair, has been found dead at Château Clairvallon, the family's property near Montreuilac. No details have been officially released, but Mrs Sinclair is believed to have fallen from the château's roof terrace. Police have declared the death accidental.

Mr and Mrs Sinclair were spending the Easter holidays at Château Clairvallon. They had just celebrated their seventh wedding anniversary the day before her death.

Her husband has released the following statement:

It is impossible to put into words the grief that myself and all those close to Riley are experiencing at this moment. To lose her so suddenly is a terrible shock and while a verdict of accidental death is in some ways a relief, it is also inconceivable to think she was taken from us by a tragedy that could have been avoided.

3

LEAH

Six Weeks Later, July

My hair whips around my face as the silver Lexus convertible zips along narrow country lanes, the roof down. The sky overhead is clear and blue. Almost 6 p.m., but the sun is still a warm caress. Hard to believe that here, deep in the peaceful Picardy countryside, with vast fields spreading out either side of us, we're only an hour and a half away from the chaotic bustle of Paris.

Miles sits beside me in the driver's seat of the hire car, his eyes fixed on the road ahead, his experienced hands commanding the steering wheel as we approach a tight bend. We take it at speed and, as the car straightens up again, he turns to me with a self-satisfied smile, as if impressed by his own skills.

I smile back and rest a hand on his thigh. I'm a good driver and would love to try out the Lexus, but I'm more than happy to be chauffeured around and, in this game, it pays to let the male ego take centre stage.

Miles looks relaxed behind the wheel. When we left Paris this morning after our night at the Ritz, he seemed on edge. Not surprising considering where we are headed and the memories it will bring back for him.

When he first suggested a trip to Château Clairvallon ten days ago, I was surprised. We've only known each other six weeks. Does this trip mean our relationship is heading into serious territory? Since we met at the Mandarin Oriental, I've been steering him in that direction. On our first date, I told him I was seeking a genuine connection, not casual sex. We dated for over two weeks before I slept with him. Since then, I've spent most nights at his apartment in South Kensington, the bachelor pad he purchased after selling the Chelsea town-house he shared with Riley. I haven't taken him to my flat in Tooting, and he has never asked to see it. I have let him believe my life and my past are uncomplicated and that seems to have put him at ease. No family for him to deal with. No ex-husbands or children. As far as he knows, I'm a woman with no baggage.

We turn right onto a narrower road. Tall, interlocking beech trees on either side of us make a cool green tunnel of the road. I tilt my head back and watch the sunlight glinting through the leaf canopy.

A few minutes later, Miles pulls the Lexus over into a passing place at the side of the road.

'There.' He points through a gap between two thick, smooth beech trunks. 'Can you see it?'

I remove the oversized Celine sunglasses he bought me in Paris yesterday and narrow my eyes.

'Can you see it?' A hint of impatience in his voice.

I can see the château clearly but keep him waiting a little

longer. I've learned not to praise the possessions or achievements of wealthy men too enthusiastically.

You are the prize, Leah. Always remember that.

My mother was right. In this game, you have to believe *you* are the trophy, and you have to make the men believe it too.

'Leah?' Miles says.

'I see it now. How beautiful.'

Even from a distance, the château impresses. No fairy-tale turrets or towers, but the white, two-storey building is still imposing. It fits with the picture I've built up of Miles and what he has to offer. Solid wealth. I'm not a bimbo in search of a billionaire. That's a whole other game. Miles is old money. A multi-millionaire heir to a lucrative, privately owned commercial property company, three generations old. A company he hopes to sell for a large profit to a pension fund in the near future. A life with him would mean financial security and just the right amount of luxury.

We look the part. Miles in his navy linen trousers and white linen shirt. Me in my floral Isabel Marant maxi dress with its short, ruffled sleeves.

'Most of the building was constructed in the late eighteenth century, but it wasn't completed until the early 1800s.' Miles lifts my hand from his thigh and kisses my palm. 'The original owners, the Dumonts, were farmers who made a fortune from sugar beet.'

'Oh,' I say, nodding in all the right places as he launches into a lengthy explanation about the Napoleonic wars and France needing to produce their own sugar when they couldn't import it from the Caribbean.

'Sorry,' he says eventually, 'I know history's not really your thing.'

'It's fascinating,' I say.

History is a subject close to my heart. I've tried to find out as much as possible about the man I've set my sights on. I've read articles online about the Sinclair family. I've seen pictures of Miles' now deceased parents, Sir and Lady Sinclair, at various charity events.

Information about the château's recent, more tragic history has been much harder to come by. One small article on a local news website called *The Picardy Daily*.

Miles places my hand back on his thigh. Traps it beneath his. 'Thank you. For coming here.' His eyes have that haunted look I saw the first night we met. His grief comes over him sometimes, when we're together. I always respect it, and he knows I understand his pain. At the same time, I have no intention of letting a dead woman get in the way of what I want.

Coming back to where Riley died is bound to be weird, but I think it's positive he wants to share this part of his life with me. Maybe he's ready to move on from the past now. Accidents happen. People die in tragic circumstances and those left behind have to get on with their lives. Another thing my mother taught me.

The car engine thrums beneath us. 'Are you okay?' I say.

'Of course.' The haunted look vanishes. 'When I'm with you, it's almost like the past doesn't exist.'

If only I could move on as easily. Last month, Freddie married Florence in a lavish ceremony at a villa in Tuscany. I cried myself to sleep after seeing the pictures on Instagram and still feel sick when I think about it.

Miles pulls me to him. His kiss is hard and deep, as if he is claiming something. My hand escapes his and roams across his thigh. He lets out a low moan.

'Behave.' He captures my hand again. 'I have to arrive looking semi-respectable.'

'Aren't you the lord of the manor?'

'Very funny.' He checks the Rolex watch that once belonged to his father. 'Right. Come on. We're late enough as it is.'

Before we left Paris, I heard him on the phone to Vivienne, his cousin. She's been staying at the château and acting as housekeeper since the recent death of her husband. After telling her we wouldn't reach Clairvallon in time for lunch as arranged, Miles promised we'd be there by mid-afternoon. I hope 'good old Viv' as he calls her won't mind our late arrival.

When I first accepted the invitation to come to the château for a week, I didn't realise I'd have a grieving widow for company. Still, Miles' kindness towards her says a lot about him. The more I get to know him, the more fond of him I am. Hopefully this holiday won't expose a dark side, like my trip to Antigua with James did. Looking back, there were red flags about James from the start. So far, Miles has been nothing but courteous, gentle and caring.

He presses his foot down on the accelerator and the Lexus roars away from the verge. Since leaving the village of Sacy-le-Petit and turning onto this road twenty minutes ago, I haven't seen another vehicle. We're still the only car on the road when Miles turns right at the entrance to the château.

Up ahead is a pair of tall metal gates. They look new. Not like the old wrought-iron ones you might expect with a property like this. Miles stops the car, jumps out and punches a code into the keypad fixed to the side of the gate. By the time he is back in the driver's seat, the gates have swung open.

When we are halfway through them, Miles brakes.

'What's wrong?' I say.

'Sorry.' That haunted look in his eyes again. 'I'm just wondering if it was right to bring you here.'

'It's okay,' I say. 'I know you had a life before me.'

'It's not that.' He sighs. 'Maybe I should turn around and take us back to Paris? We could be at the Ritz in time for cocktails.'

'Look, if you really don't feel like—'

'Ignore me.' He drums his fingers on the steering wheel. 'It's too late now. Vivienne will be waiting.'

He presses his foot on the accelerator and we surge ahead.

The iron gates clang shut behind us.

4

LEAH

July

Gravel crunches beneath us as the Lexus pulls up in front of the château, next to a red and white 2CV convertible that has seen better days. Behind us is the meandering driveway flanked by towering lime trees. Green lawns slope away from the driveway on both sides, bordered by colourful flower beds. When Miles cuts the engine, birdsong floods my ears. The high-pitched chirp and chatter of smaller birds and, underneath it all, the soft coo of wood pigeons. When I inhale, the scent of freshly cut grass fills my nostrils.

A set of stone steps leads from the driveway up to a long terrace in front of the château. The balustrade surrounding the terrace is spotted with moss and lichen. Up close, the exterior of the building looks slightly worn. Here and there, patches of sandy stone peek through flaking white paint. Some of the pale green shutters have missing slats. It's more rustic than I imagined, but still beautiful. A pair of arched double doors with glass panes mark the entrance to the château. Above them is an ornate carving of a lion's head and above that, set into the stone, is the date 1814. That must be the year the château was completed.

I glance up at the grey mansard roof with its slate tiles and the arched attic windows set into it. Similar to the old buildings in Paris. Where is the roof terrace? I scan along the château. On the far left-hand side is what looks like an extension to the original building. Small, the size of one room, it covers the ground and first floor and has a flat roof surrounded by wrought-iron railings. Is that it? Is that where Riley fell from? Did she land on the flagstones below? Her body twisted and broken beside the blue ceramic flower pots?

I glance at Miles, but his unflinching gaze stays straight ahead.

My stomach knots. I'm not only disturbed by thoughts of Riley, I'm also anxious about meeting Vivienne. Until now, Miles and I have been too wrapped up in each other to make our relationship official in any way. He hasn't expressed a desire to meet any of my friends, and he hasn't introduced me to any of his. Vivienne, at fifty-two, is just over a year younger than him, and is the only family member he has left. His father's sister's daughter. The only one he's close to. She knew Riley too. Up until now I haven't had to deal with anyone who knew Miles' dead wife.

I have a sudden feeling of not belonging. Of not being good enough.

I take a deep breath. Main character energy. That's what I need right now. This is my story. I deserve to star in it.

'Well,' Miles says, 'here we are.' He pushes open his door and attempts to exit the Lexus in one smooth move, but the car is too low for him. He grips the door and, with a low grunt, hauls himself out. I glance at my lap to hide my smile. Don't want him to think I'm mocking him.

I stay seated, while Miles strides around the car and opens the passenger door for me. 'Thank you.' If you expect men to treat you like a queen, they will.

As the wedge heels of my Chloé sandals strike the gravel, the doors to the château open and a woman steps onto the terrace.

'Hello, Viv,' Miles says.

Cousin Vivienne is not what I was expecting. I'd pictured a tall, horsey woman. Broad-shouldered and strong. Instead, the woman on the steps in front of me is small and thin, her face ghostly pale. Her strawberry blonde hair is pinned up in a messy bun. A single white streak runs through it at the front. A black shirt dress smothers her small frame. Her hands are hidden in the pockets of a black apron.

'Miles,' she says. 'You managed the new gate okay?'

'Yup. All in working order.' He points at the rusty 2CV. 'I can't believe Dolly's still going. She looks like a death trap. Are you sure she's safe to drive?'

'She's perfectly fine. Stop fussing.' Vivienne opens her arms. 'Come here, you.'

He bounds up the steps into her embrace. 'Great to see you.'

They kiss on both cheeks, the French way. When they part, Miles slings an arm around her shoulder. She stands beside him, an arm around his waist. They look down on me from the top of the steps, as if they are a couple about to welcome me to their home.

'Great to meet you, Vivienne.' I walk up the stairs towards her, my hand outstretched. 'Miles has told me a lot about you.'

From her startled expression, I can see Miles hasn't told her about the thirty-year age gap between us. My twenty-four to his fifty-four. She looks from me to him and back again. A quick succession of judgements flashes across her face. *Too young. Gold-digger. Not Riley.*

Being with Miles is bound to provoke the first two criticisms. And anyone who knew Riley is bound to compare me with the dead woman. Not much I can do about that.

'Hello, Leah.' She releases Miles and takes my hand. Her palm is rough and dry against my smooth, pampered one. Her wrist doll-like. I'm scared to shake her hand too hard in case I break her. 'Welcome to Château Clairvallon,' she says.

She is well-spoken. Her voice firm and clear. She has Miles' deep blue eyes. Her eyebrows and eyelashes are so fair they appear almost non-existent. Deep lines fan out from the corners of her eyes and make ridges across her forehead. The only colour in her pale face comes from the freckles scattered across it.

'Sorry about missing lunch,' Miles says. 'Leah insisted we make the most of the Paris shops before heading down here.'

Nice one, Miles. Great way to confirm Vivienne's first impressions of me. It's true that one of my conditions for coming on the holiday was a night in Paris on the way so I could stock up on summer outfits. I knew Miles would offer to pay for the clothes so I made the most of it by taking him to Samaritaine, a new department store on Rue de Rivoli. A store renowned for its selection of designer brands.

'It's his fault,' I say. 'He spoils me.'

'Miles has always been generous,' Vivienne says. 'It's both a blessing and a curse.'

I hope she won't be the one unloading our luggage. Suddenly my stash of ribbon-tied bags seems shameful.

She takes a black vape pen out of her apron pocket, puts in between her thin lips and inhales.

'Really?' Miles says. 'I thought you were giving up?'

'Don't nag.' Smoke trails from her nostrils. 'At least I'm off the cigarettes.'

Seems Vivienne is in need of a crutch at the moment. Not that I'm judging. She has just lost her husband.

'Everything is organised for dinner,' she tells Miles. 'Just as you requested.'

'Good. Lovely.' Miles flashes me a quick smile. 'Viv will be cooking for us while we're here, but tonight we're having a picnic. All local produce. You'll love it.'

'Sounds great,' I say.

'You don't have any allergies or intolerances?' Viv asks me. 'Miles said you didn't, but people your age always seem to be avoiding something.'

'No,' I say. 'I eat everything.' I enjoy my food and can easily polish off an eight-course Michelin-star tasting menu with paired wines. Miles likes that about me. He says I'm a pleasure to take out to dinner.

'I had trouble extending the table in the pergola,' Vivienne says. 'Maybe you could do it, Miles, and I'll show Leah to her room.'

Miles hesitates. 'If you're sure?'

'Of course.' She gestures towards the château doors. 'Leah, shall we?'

5

LEAH

July

The château's entrance hall is a bright, warm space. The black and white tiles underfoot are spotless but worn. A glass chandelier fitted with candle bulbs hangs overhead. Ahead of me is an arch leading to a staircase. To the left of the arch is a tall grandfather clock and beside it a tall, narrow table with a black seventies dial phone on it. To the right of the arch are two wooden coat stands – one with a variety of coats and jackets heaped upon it, the other decorated by a large collection of caps and sun hats.

'We leave our outdoor shoes here.' Vivienne points to the floor between the coat stands, which is strewn with a jumble of flip-flops, trainers and wellingtons. 'The flooring in this château is very old, so we do all we can to preserve it.' She points to the classic black espadrilles on her narrow feet. 'We wear these indoors.'

I slip off my sandals and place them neatly next to the other shoes. The tiles are cool beneath my feet. Vivienne glances at the shiny red polish on my pedicured toenails. A perfect match for my manicured fingernails.

Ignoring her, I take in my surroundings. To my right, the tiled hallway gives way to a gleaming parquet corridor that seems to lead through several rooms. Same on the left. 'Well?' says Vivienne. 'Not quite the fairy-tale castle you imagined, I suppose?'

'It's charming.'

'These types of châteaus are more like large manor houses than castles. People often get the two things mixed up.'

'Guilty,' I say, noting the smirk that flits across Vivienne's face. Best to play dumb and let her think she's in control. She's obviously taken an instant dislike to me, but I can't afford to let her get under my skin.

The grandfather clock gives one solemn strike for half past the hour as Vivienne leads me through the archway. Next to the staircase, a half-open door gives me a glimpse of what looks like the kitchen.

Somewhere up above us, another clock marks the half-hour. My bare feet are silent on the wooden staircase as I follow Vivienne up it. A strange clinking sound accompanies her as she moves. I catch a glimpse of her pale, freckled calves.

The wooden stairs are polished smooth from centuries of use. A dip in the middle of each one where most of the footfall has landed. At one point I almost slip and have to grab the banister for support.

Random objects adorn the walls. A toy drum. Framed letters in elaborate handwriting, the sepia-coloured paper ragged at the edges. Three paraffin lamps perched on a shelf.

'My aunt and uncle wanted to honour the lives of the château's original owners,' Vivienne says. 'They were fascinated by the history of the building and the area.'

'Wow. Really interesting.'

When we reach the first-floor landing, Vivienne stops to give me a brief orientation.

'East wing rooms that way,' she says, pointing to her right. 'West wing rooms the other way.' Her arms move mechanically as she speaks, like an air stewardess pointing out emergency exits in a safety demonstration.

'I can't wait to explore,' I say. 'These old houses must have some really quirky bits.'

'Most of the east wing rooms are closed.'

'Why?'

'An old building like this costs a fortune to maintain.' Vivienne's tone is condescending. 'It's easier to close sections off from time to time.'

'Makes sense.'

'I, however, am in the east wing. I've always had my room there.'

I attempt a friendly smile. 'You must know this place so well?'

'I've been coming here every summer since I can remember.' She doesn't smile back. 'And the summers before that. Since I was a baby.'

I follow her into the west wing. Red, hexagonal tiles line a narrow but bright corridor. At the far end is another tall grandfather clock. Early evening sun pours in through tall arched windows that overlook the gardens and driveway. On our right, a succession of doors, all painted pale green.

'How many rooms does the château have?' I ask.

'Eight bedrooms, four bathrooms, two reception rooms, a study, the kitchen, the dining room and a utility room.' She stops by one of the green doors. 'This is where you and Miles will be sleeping.'

She removes a large set of keys from her apron pocket. That explains the clinking sound as we climbed the stairs. She unlocks the door and pushes it open, revealing a bright, spacious room. Golden light streams through the tall rectangular window. The window is open, the shutters folded back. White muslin curtains hang limp from the pewter curtain rail. A large oriental rug partially covers the varnished floorboards. The furniture looks antique. The artwork on the walls – pastel landscapes of the French countryside – is uninspiring.

A four-poster bed dominates the room. Peach drapes hang from the mahogany frame, tied up with cords of gold rope. A chintzy floral bedspread covers the wide mattress and matching cushions decorate the plump nest of pillows.

Did Miles once share this bed with Riley? I brush the thought away. No point being childish and sentimental.

'They slept in the east wing,' Vivienne says, as if reading my thoughts. 'I would never give you their room. That wouldn't be appropriate.'

Even though Riley has been dead for over a year? Still, I'm relieved not to be sharing my bed with a ghost.

Vivienne clears her throat. 'The marriage bed is sacred.'

Great. She's obviously a traditionalist. A staunch believer in the sanctity of marriage. The chances of us hitting it off are getting even slimmer.

'Death doesn't change that,' she adds, twisting the wedding band on her ring finger back and forth. She must be thinking about Dom, her late husband. He's only been gone five months. I need to cut her some slack and remember she's still grieving.

'Let me show you the en suite,' she says. We go into the adjoining bathroom. The walls are a calm, pale blue. The curtains are made of the same gaudy material as the bedspread. Not my taste at all, but I like the broad, old-fashioned sink with its gold taps and the freestanding bath with its gold claw feet. I imagine myself reclining amongst fragrant bubbles, staring out at the pine trees framed by the window opposite.

'The bath is out of bounds,' Vivienne says. 'We have to keep the water bills down.'

'Oh. I see.' She doesn't look like the kind of woman who treats herself to long, indulgent baths.

'There's a shower room next door. You'll find it perfectly adequate.'

'Okay. No worries.' I bet I can persuade Miles to overrule her on the bath ban. Especially if I suggest he and I take one together.

Vivienne points out the fresh white towels she's hung on the wooden towel rail and the Fragonard soap in the clam-shaped soap dish on the sink.

'Thanks,' I say, thinking of the chambermaid job I had while at the University of Edinburgh. Long shifts at the five-star Balmoral hotel. Picking up used, soiled towels from the bathroom floors. Thank God those days are behind me. 'It's good of you to do all this.'

'I want to make myself useful while I'm here.'

Miles told me he was letting Vivienne stay at the château as a favour. She has a house of her own, a large cottage near Sevenoaks in Kent, but she can't bear to be there since her husband died. She has a son, Nathan, but he recently moved to New York to work as a stockbroker. Vivienne works as an English teacher at a private school near Sevenoaks but, according to Miles, she is currently taking a sabbatical. Her husband died in a car accident. Brutal and sudden. No chance to say goodbye. Miles knows how that feels and I'm sure their similar losses have brought them even closer together.

Vivienne tuts and scuttles over to the towel rail. She lifts the towels off and starts rearranging them, aiming for a standard of symmetry invisible to me.

I leave her to it and return to the bedroom. When I sit on the four-poster bed, the mattress springs squeak beneath me. A framed photograph on the bedside table catches my attention. Riley looks out at me from the frame, her face split by a wide smile. Her cropped chestnut hair gleams. Her khaki shorts and white T-shirt show off her tanned, athletic body. I'd recognise her anywhere, even though I've only ever seen one picture of her. The head-and-shoulders shot that accompanied the brief and uninformative online obituary I discovered.

After I started dating Miles, I naturally trawled the Internet searching for information about his first wife. I found nothing for Riley Sinclair, apart from the obituary and the *Picardy Daily* article. I don't know her maiden name, so I can't do a deep dive on her life before Miles. Still, that one photograph was enough to imprint her face on my mind. With her close-set grey eyes and hawkish nose, she isn't conventionally beautiful but she is undeniably attractive. Even in a photograph she gives off energy and charisma.

Miles hasn't spoken much about her, but I know she was from Portland, Oregon. They met when Miles and some friends visited a skydiving facility near Las Vegas. Riley was working as an instructor there and took Miles for his first ever tandem skydive. She was fourteen years younger than him so it's not as if he hasn't dated younger women before. Maybe not one thirty years younger but, as they say, there's a first time for everything.

'Miles always had that picture in the bedroom.' Vivienne

stands in the bathroom doorway. 'I thought I should move it here.'

Her eyes are on me, looking for a reaction. 'If the photograph bothers you, I can take it away,' she says.

'It's all good. Miles doesn't need to hide his past from me.' In this game, you have to accept that older men come with baggage. It's the price you pay for their life experience, money and protection. 'Riley looks like a force of nature,' I say.

I mean this. She sounds like a huge character.

'She was unique. I've never met anyone like her.' Tears spring to Vivienne's eyes. 'I still can't believe she's gone.'

I feel myself softening towards her. Miles isn't the only person grieving Riley's death. 'The two of you must have been close?'

Vivienne nods. 'Very close.'

'Well, I'm sure—'

'He'll never get over her.' Vivienne's expression hardens, her display of emotion over. 'You're too young to understand but that kind of love, real love, can never be replaced.'

6

LEAH

July

Just before 7.15 p.m., I return to the bedroom after taking a shower in the next room along. No sign of Miles, but he has left me a note on the antique mahogany dressing table.

See you downstairs at 8. Outfit on the bed. Don't be late.

Earlier, when he brought our luggage up to the room, he seemed nervous. When I asked what was wrong, he told me he wanted our first night here to be perfect. Maybe I'm imagining it but he seemed distant. Distracted.

Was he thinking about Riley?

Vivienne shouldn't have put that picture of her in here. Miles removed it from the bedside table as soon as he saw it. Without saying a word, he left the room and then returned five minutes later empty-handed. We didn't discuss the matter. I'm glad the picture is gone. Open-minded as I am, I don't want his dead wife watching us in bed together. A threesome with a ghost doesn't appeal to me.

As I pad across the rug, a thick white towel knotted at my chest, I inhale the scent of his aftershave. Bleu de Chanel. I bought it for his birthday in June. His previous aftershave did nothing for me, and I wanted to see if he was willing to change. To let me change him. He hasn't worn any other aftershave since.

Shopping bags cluster in front of the tall walnut wardrobe. The spoils of our Paris shopping spree. Lying on the bed is one of my purchases – a Saint Laurent slip dress in bronze silk. Miles likes to choose what I wear sometimes. Whenever we're in public together, he also likes to know what I'm wearing under my clothes. It turns him on. For tonight, he's picked a black mesh bra with a matching thong. The shoes he has left up to me. Amidst the huddle of shopping bags, I find the one containing the Alizé slides by Chloé. I lift them out of the box, savouring the softness of the cream-coloured goatskin leather and the shine of the brass buckles on the two wide straps. Perfect.

I bought far more than I need for one week's holiday. Thanks to Miles' generosity, I've got enough new clothes to see me through most of the summer. I don't feel guilty about spending so much of his money. I had to take a week's unpaid leave to come here and Olivia, my line manager, wasn't happy about me disappearing at such short notice.

Vivienne would, I'm sure, disapprove of this kind of excess. After she finished showing me the room earlier, she said she hoped I had everything I needed to enjoy my *holiday*.

My holiday? Yes, I've come here on holiday, but I sensed more beneath her comment. She was suggesting I was nothing more than a guest. Temporary. One of many women Miles has brought to the château over the years.

Maybe she's right. How do I know if this relationship with Miles will last? I should focus on the present. Get as much out of this experience as I can.

That kind of love, real love, can never be replaced.

In my experience, love is totally replaceable. After losing all of my mother's money, my father left and replaced us with another family. Freddie replaced me with Florence and will one day probably replace her with someone else.

I let my towel drop to the floor and stand in front of the open window, inviting the warm evening air to caress my bare skin. Our room overlooks the back of the château. Green lawns slope away from the building and, in the distance, a small lake glitters in the evening sunlight. Twisting my head to the right, I look between the trunks of four tall Austrian pines and catch a glimpse of the swimming pool. How much land surrounds this place? Maybe Miles will give me a guided tour before dinner.

We're cocooned in our own private world here. So peaceful and secluded. The non-stop opera of the birds the loudest distraction. So different from London's deafening soundtrack of sirens and traffic.

I should take some pictures of the château and put them on Instagram. A few of the girls I knew at uni who follow me on there are still in touch with Freddie, so I make sure to only post snaps that show me living my best life. However, I'll only put up pictures of Clairvallon if Miles doesn't mind. When we first started dating, he seemed relieved I wasn't someone who splashed every moment of my private life across social media. In this game, it pays to be discreet. Having private social media accounts and posting sparingly makes me seem more mature than other girls my age.

A swallow darts past the window and swoops down to the terrace at the back of the house. It perches for a moment on the long wooden table at the centre of the terrace and then hops onto the back of one of the white canvas chairs before taking off again. On this side of the house, the terrace is less well kept. The flagstones are patchy with lichen and weeds have sprouted up between them.

The windowsill digs into my stomach as I lean out. Blood thunders in my ears. It is more of a drop from up here than it seems when you are safely on the ground. I twist my head and look to the left. The extension at the end of the château goes higher than this floor, but there is still a drop between the attic level and the roof terrace. Several of the railings surrounding the terrace are missing and some of the stone they were once secured to has crumbled away.

Is that the place where Riley fell? It has to be. When I first read about her death, I wondered if she might have committed suicide. Judging by the crumbling masonry and missing railings, it looks more likely to have been an accidental fall.

An image flashes into my mind. Riley's strong, muscular body lying twisted on the unforgiving flagstones. Bones snapped. Eyes lifeless and staring up at the sky.

Miles has never shared any details of the fall that killed her, and, seeing as the subject clearly upsets him, I've never pushed him for any. If I tell him I know she fell from the roof, he'll know I've been snooping around online. Never a good look.

I shiver and turn away from the window.

7

LEAH

July

The grandfather clock in the entrance hall strikes eight as I descend the staircase. Remembering Vivienne's orders, my feet are bare and I'm clutching my Chloé slides in one hand. My hair is blow-dried, my face made-up. Pearl earrings dangle from my ears – a gift from James before the Antigua holiday turned everything sour.

Miles is waiting for me in the hallway. His smile is strained, the lines around his eyes etched deeper than usual. Is he just tired or is being back here too much for him?

I sashay through the archway at the foot of the stairs and give him a twirl. 'Ta-da.'

Tonight, instead of his usual exaggerated wolf-whistle, he nods and says, 'You look great.'

He doesn't sound convinced. 'You like the dress?' I say.

'The dress is knockout. Really.'

It *is* knockout and I look great in it. I'll put his lack of enthusiasm down to fatigue. 'You look good too,' I say. 'I was right about the shirt.'

This morning, during our shopping spree, I convinced him to buy a blue floral shirt from Paul Smith. He thought it might be too young for him, but it looks good with the navy Ralph Lauren chinos I also made him buy.

'Come on,' he says. 'Let's get going.'

He picks up his tan leather deck shoes from the pile by the coat stand and slips them on. I do the same with my slides and then we head out of the front door and turn left onto the terrace. We pass a circular wrought iron table with three matching chairs. The white paint has flaked off the surface of the table, leaving spots of bare metal and rust.

'We're eating down by the lake tonight,' Miles says. A casual comment, as if everyone has a lake in their back garden.

'Is Vivienne joining us?' I ask.

'Not tonight.'

'I don't think she's my biggest fan.'

He stops and sighs. 'She's... she's had a rough ride lately.'

'Totally. I get that.'

'We've known each other all our lives,' he says. 'She's very protective of me. She's more like a sister than a cousin in some ways.'

'Yes. Of course.' Note to self: Don't say anything negative about Vivienne. 'She's lucky to have you.' She is. Not every woman in her position would have someone like Miles looking out for her.

He grips my hand tighter, and we march along the terrace and around the side of the château. Ivy smothers the gable end wall, almost obscuring the attic window there. Miles glances up at the roof.

'There's been a house here since the fourteenth century,' he says. 'The original was knocked down, of course.'

He talks fast. Is he using ancient history to cover up the memory of more recent events?

'Amazing,' I say. Owning a place like Château Clairvallon must feel like owning history. The stories of the past yours to tell.

We cross the terrace I looked down on from our room, past the table I hope we'll be eating breakfast at tomorrow. We set off across the lawn at a brisk pace. I'm glad to be in flats and not heels.

Glancing back, I glimpse Vivienne in one of the east wing windows. As soon as I catch sight of her, she disappears. My eyes stray to the roof terrace above the extension.

'Come on, Leah.' Miles pulls at my hand.

When we pass the tall Austrian pines, I glimpse the pool again and ask if we can take a look.

'Maybe later,' he says.

We march on, his sticky palm clamped against mine. I fight back a surge of irritation. Why the rush? On our left is the entrance to a walled garden. Beyond the red-brick walls are the roofs of what might be outbuildings. I don't ask Miles for clarification. He doesn't seem in tour guide mood.

Maybe he's hungry? The only time he gets grumpy is when he needs something to eat. Or drink. He does enjoy a drink most nights. Not that I ever criticise him for it. I'm careful not to play that kind of role in his life.

The lawn dips below us and there, up ahead, is the lake. The setting sun glints on the surface. Tangled rushes surround it and, on the opposite side, three willow trees weep their leaves into the water.

'Wow,' I say.

'It is pretty special.' Miles squeezes my hand. Some of the tension seems to drain from him.

I see the pergola up ahead – a round wrought-iron structure with a white canvas canopy above. 'How gorgeous.' I drop Miles' hand, take off my shoes and hurry across the grass towards it.

Underneath the canopy, a red-and-white-checked tablecloth is laid over a long trestle table. On it sits a wicker picnic hamper, the two sides of the lid splayed open. Beside it, a bottle of champagne nestles in an ice bucket.

'The food is all from my favourite delicatessen in Montreuilac,' Miles says, when he catches up with me.

I pick out a jar from the top of the hamper and read the label. *Terrine au Maroilles.*

'It's a regional speciality,' he says. 'A sort of pork pâté with soft cheese. Much nicer than it sounds.'

'You know me. I'll eat anything.' Now that there is food in front of me, I realise how hungry I am.

'I'll get us started with some olives. Or maybe some of the tapenade?' Miles plucks jars from the hamper, then puts them back again. When he removes two plates from the hamper's lid, they slip from his hands and clatter onto the table.

'Is something wrong?' I ask.

'We should have a drink first.' He yanks the champagne from the ice bucket. 'This is from one of the local champagne vineyards. Not many people know this is a champagne region.'

As he pours us each a glass, I notice his hand shaking.

'Here,' he says, his hand still unsteady as he passes me my drink. When we clink our glasses, I smile at him, but his eyes are avoiding mine.

An anxious knot in the pit of my stomach.

He drains his glass in two gulps. 'I needed that.' He takes

my untouched champagne from my hand and puts both our glasses on the table. 'Let's take a look at the lake.'

I follow him as he dashes across the grass to the water's edge. What's wrong with him? Something is off; I'm sure of it.

We stand by the lake. The setting sun is bathing everything in a deep pink light. Despite the beauty of the moment, an awkward silence blooms between us.

'I was going to wait until after dinner,' he says, 'but I can't.' When his amber-flecked eyes meet mine, they are full of sadness. 'There's something I need to talk to you about.'

The anxious knot at my core tightens. *There's something I need to talk to you about.* The exact words Freddie said before he ended our relationship.

Just as Miles is about to now. I steel myself against what is to come.

'Leah,' he says.

I look across the garden to the château. The grand building looms in the distance. Everything was fine until we came here. The house, his memories of Riley; it's all too much. Maybe here, he's realised how unsuited we are. Maybe he's seeing me through Vivienne's eyes and doesn't like the view. Has she said something to him?

I brace myself. I can take it. There will be other men. Other opportunities. Even as I think this, I realise I've grown used to having Miles around. The security and solidity of him.

He could have at least waited until the end of the holiday. What will he do? Drive me back to Paris tonight? In the morning? Will he pay for me to get the Eurostar home? Maybe I should ask him to put me up in a hotel in Paris for a couple of nights. At least then I'll get some kind of holiday out of all this.

'Leah.' Miles drops to the grass. Is something wrong with him? Is he having a heart attack? He is down on one knee, the

other leg stretched out in front of him in an odd lunging position. He winces as he shifts his weight onto the knee on the
ground. He's got issues with that knee. An old rugby injury.

'Have you hurt yourself?' I say.

He reaches into the pocket of his trousers and produces a
small black velvet box. When he opens it, the setting sun
makes the diamond ring inside it glitter.

'Leah Rose Williams,' he says. 'Will you marry me?'

8

LEAH

July

I am the first to wake. Sunlight creeps in through the half-open window. A light breeze stirs the thin muslin curtains. Miles snores gently beside me, the flesh-coloured strip of fabric across his nose keeping the worst of the noise at bay. I hold out my left hand and examine my engagement ring. An elegant platinum band with a large rectangular diamond mounted on it. An emerald-cut stone, Miles informed me last night. It is designed by Boucheron, one of the most prestigious jewellery houses in Paris. I did sneak a look at their website last night to find out how much the ring cost but next to an image of it were the words *Price on Demand*.

Expensive as well as stunning.

Seven faint chimes ring out from the grandfather clock downstairs, shortly followed by seven louder ones from the clock outside our room. Still early. Last night, as Miles slept, the clock kept me company as the night's events whirred in my brain. Did Miles really propose to me? Did I really say yes?

Now I understand why Miles was so distant and nervous. He was anxious about proposing, not troubled by thoughts of Riley.

Beside me, he snorts loudly enough to disturb himself. He turns on his side. In a few minutes he will be awake. I slip out of bed and tiptoe across to the en suite. The ancient floorboards creak beneath me, but Miles doesn't stir. Is he really asleep or just pretending so I can carry out this part of our morning routine?

Once in the bathroom, I close the door softly. After lifting the toilet lid, I lower myself onto the seat and empty my bladder as slowly and quietly as possible. I think about how Miles caught me off guard with the proposal. I was certain he was going to end the relationship. After asking me to marry him, he told me to wait before giving my answer.

'Sorry,' he said, sweat beading on his forehead. 'I've done this the wrong way round. The speech should come first.' He shifted his weight forward, probably trying to relieve his dodgy knee. I considered telling him to stand up, but decided he wouldn't like me pointing out one of his frailties, especially at that moment.

'I love you, Leah,' he said. 'You've made me feel alive again in a way I never thought possible.'

After flushing the toilet, I pull my ivory silk nightdress over my head and drape it over the side of the bath. I soak my pink flannel in the deep sink and then wipe my face and armpits. As I freshen up between my legs, it occurs to me that at no point, even after I accepted the proposal, did I tell Miles I love him. Is that not important to him? Maybe not. Maybe he feels what we have is enough. I've come to care about him and, with time, that could become a kind of love.

All relationships are based on power, not love.

My mother's words come back to me. Her voice from beyond the grave, warning me not to blow this opportunity. Isn't this what I've been working towards? A guarantee of life-long comfort and security?

The ring on my finger proves I've achieved my goal. Getting a rich man is a competitive game, and I've almost sealed the deal. Despite Miles blindsiding me with the proposal, I held myself together. No gasping or squealing or crying, and I made him wait a fraction too long for my answer. Long enough for uncertainty to cloud his eyes. Long enough for relief to flood them when I said yes. When he slid the ring on my finger, I felt overwhelmed and almost thanked him, but I didn't. Instead, I subjected the diamond extravagance to a long appraisal before declaring it stunning. As if such a ring was exactly what I expected and deserved.

You are the prize, Leah.

After rinsing the flannel, I apply a quick lick of deodorant and clean my teeth. Miles has never seen me first thing in the morning without a freshen-up. Will I really have to do this every day for the rest of our time together? I feel a pang in my chest as I recall how Freddie and I would reach for each other as soon as we woke in the morning. The long, hot, dirty kisses we shared. Neither of us ever thinking to clean our teeth first.

I add a dab of pink lip gloss to my lips and pinch my cheeks until some colour floods into them. I never put make-up on first thing in the morning – Miles likes a natural look. Or he thinks he does. Every day I wear at least light foundation and basic eye make-up. I don't need much more at my age but that will one day change.

Doubt snakes up from the cool floor tiles into the soles of my feet. A sudden tightness squeezes my chest as I realise what I've committed to. Marriage. Until death do us part.

Tragedy aside, death will come to Miles first. Not that I want to think like that. With his money and resources, he could live at least another thirty years. I could be his age now before I find myself a widow.

No advice from my dead mother about that eventuality.

I put my nightdress on again, take a deep breath and open the bathroom door.

* * *

When I enter the bedroom, I find Miles sitting up in bed, peeling the snore strip off his nose.

'Good morning,' I say, surprised by the hesitancy in my voice.

'Hello, you.'

He scrunches up the snore strip and drops it on the bedside table. An icky shudder runs through me. I tell myself not to be childish. We've never openly discussed his use of the strips – his snoring another frailty I thought best not to point out – but surely they show his willingness to make adjustments for me? He cares about me getting a good night's sleep. That has to be a mark of decency.

'When I woke up and you weren't in bed I thought you'd left,' he says.

'Were you relieved?' I aim for a light-hearted tone but can't rule out the possibility he's changed his mind about marriage during the night.

'Of course not.' He pulls back the chintzy bedcover. 'Get in here.'

On my way back to bed I take a detour, pull aside the curtains and open the window wide. Warm, sweet air rushes in. A morning haze hangs over the sun but that will soon clear.

Birdsong is again the only disturbance to the deep silence that cloaks the château.

As soon as I climb into bed beside him, Miles takes my left hand. My smooth palm rests against his creased, ageing one.

'Diamonds suit you,' he says.

'Feel free to buy me more.'

He laughs. 'I really surprised you, didn't I?'

'You did.' When we first arrived in Paris, Miles told me he was going out for a jog while I took a bath. That's when he picked up the ring from the Boucheron store on Place Vendôme. I had no idea he was so good at keeping secrets.

'It feels right, doesn't it?' he says. 'Me and you.'

I lean in and kiss him.

'I know it sounds corny,' he says, 'but as soon as I saw you in the bar that night, I just knew.'

As far as I recall, he spent our first hour together talking about his dead wife and how much he missed her. No point spoiling his fantasy, though.

'Did Vivienne help you plan it all?' I ask.

He shakes his head. 'No. She doesn't know yet.'

Great. I'm sure she'll be thrilled. Miles must be thinking the same thing because a grave expression comes over his face. To distract him, I slide my left hand beneath the covers and let the diamond ring gently graze the tip of his cock. It doesn't take him long to get hard. He grasps the back of my neck and pulls me close for a kiss. His stale breath is tinged with garlic from last night's dinner and the odour of sour sweat clings to his body.

I pull the covers aside and straddle him. He likes it this way in the morning. Easier on his stiff back. I move my hips. Gently at first. He gasps and a familiar look appears on his face. A mixture of gratitude and surprise.

We've only been having sex for just over a month and Miles is still high on the thrill and novelty of it all. I'm the first person he's slept with since Riley died.

Sex with him has been satisfying so far. Miles was a bachelor until his mid-forties so he's had plenty of experience. I've been testing his limits. How far will he go if given permission? I've subtly given him chances to reveal any kinks and fetishes. Not to judge him but to decide if his idea of kink and mine will be compatible in the long term. His tastes have turned out to be fairly vanilla. Either that or he's decided to keep any dark desires to himself. Casting me as Madonna rather than whore. More proof I've played the game correctly.

Once we're married, I'll have to manoeuvre him into a more sustainable routine. One that combines the excitement of having a lover with the stability of having a wife. Tricky, getting that balance right. I don't want him going in search of either more or less sex.

'You're so beautiful,' he says.

The bright morning light shows up the deep creases on his forehead. Grey stubble covers his cheeks and, with his head pressed back against the pillow, his double chin is pronounced. I close my eyes and move faster. My hands grasp at the rough, silver hairs on his chest and the soft flesh beneath them. I think about Freddie and his firm, smooth, hairless chest. His long, muscular legs and his toned arms. We couldn't keep our hands off each other. Sex was an adventure we were on together, discovering ourselves and each other for the first time. Always his warm whispering breath in my ear. *I love you.*

When I heard him say those words, I thought my troubles were over. The troubles that began when my father abandoned my mother and I and left us bankrupt. We had to swap our large country house in West Sussex for a council house in Hastings. My exclusive private school for a rundown state school. After the initial shock of the transition had worn off, I realised only hard work would get me back to the life that was meant for me. I worked hard at school and got myself to the University of Edinburgh. Once there, I neglected my studies and focused on targeting the rich English boys, just as my mother told me to. When I met Freddie and was accepted into his circle of privileged friends, I thought I'd made it.

I love you.

Back then I thought love was enough. I didn't understand I had no power. I was no more attractive than lots of other girls my age and I had no money or status to bring to the party. I didn't think Freddie cared about stuff like that.

Now, here I am, engaged to a man I've only known for six weeks. A man who is digging his fingers into my waist as I writhe on top of him.

'You're incredible,' Miles says, his deep blue eyes misty with adoration. A hot shivering sensation deep in my belly. Sometimes with Miles, I don't know if I'm getting off on the sex itself or on his desire for me.

When he can't hold back any longer, he screws up his eyes and tilts his head back. It looks painful and ugly. I remember Freddie again, the way we held each other's gaze during the most intense moments. How that always made me cry.

I have tears in my eyes when Miles eases me off him. I lie beside him and put my head on his chest, the way he likes me to. His warm, sweaty arms encircle me. I listen to his hammering heartbeat settle. Birdsong drifts in from outside. Unable to move my head, I stare at the bland landscape picture on the wall between the windows and think about the night of my university graduation. Freddie held a party at his flat in Edinburgh's New Town. Not long after midnight, the pair of us snuck away to the communal gardens that belonged to his grand, sweeping crescent. He said he had something to talk to me about and, when he said it concerned our future, I stupidly thought he was about to ask me to marry him. Instead, he told me our relationship was over. We had a new era of our lives ahead of us, he said, and we should be free to do whatever we wanted. He also said he wasn't sure we were compatible. I understood then that he didn't see me as an equal and never would.

All of this came flooding back to me last night when Miles proposed. The irony of it. Miles down on one knee holding out a diamond ring when I thought he was about to dump me and Freddie dumping me when I thought he was about to propose.

Maybe that's why I said yes.

Miles kisses the top of my head. 'I was so scared you'd say no.'

I make a non-committal noise. Somewhere between a laugh and a grunt.

'You're not having second thoughts, are you?' he asks in a quiet voice.

'No.' A fluttering unease in my stomach. Are my thoughts that transparent?

'I've got a lot of baggage,' he says. 'Sometimes I think it's too much.'

I can hear the fear in his voice. A sign of the power I have over him. With Miles I've got my youth to bargain with. Life has given him experience and wisdom but it has also broken him a little and that damage makes him more malleable. He doesn't have the endless options available to younger men, and he doesn't have their swagger. He will look after me and give me the life I want.

'Everyone has baggage,' I say.

'I just need to know you really want this. No second thoughts.'

I glance again at the expensive ring on my finger. I look up at the high ceiling with its elaborate cornicing and at the vast window letting in sunlight and clean air. I picture my boxy room in the tiny flat in Tooting. One small window, opening onto a view of a brick wall. Boiling in the summer and freezing in the winter. My earlier doubts vanish. Of course I want this life.

I lift my head and plant a trail of kisses from the silvery hairs on his chest to the silvery hairs around his navel. 'No second thoughts,' I say. 'None at all.'

9

LEAH

July

The château's numerous clocks have already struck nine-thirty by the time we leave the bedroom.

'We're late.' Miles hurries ahead of me along the corridor, hands in the pockets of his salmon pink shorts, his pale blue Polo shirt half untucked at the back. Before we left the room he shoved his feet into a pair of black espadrilles, but I'm still in bare feet. We didn't have time to shower. I barely had time to pull my red cotton maxi dress over my head and drag a brush through my hair. I wonder if we smell of the sex we were still having fifteen minutes ago.

'Nine is early for breakfast,' I say, 'when you're on holiday.'

'Breakfast has always been at nine here.'

Jangling bell peals echo through the house. When they first started up half an hour ago, I couldn't figure out where they were coming from. Then Miles explained about the bell at the back of the house, outside the kitchen. Vivienne is ringing it to tell us breakfast is ready. It is apparently the way mealtimes have been announced for centuries.

History and tradition. That's what I'll be marrying into. I'll either have to get used to it, or, over time, find ways to make changes.

In the château's entrance hall, Miles stops and rummages in the jumble of shoes between the coat stands. He pulls out a pair of red espadrilles, shakes the dust off them and holds them out. 'You can't go into the dining room barefoot,' he says.

I stare at the shoes.

Who did they belong to? Riley? Miles wouldn't expect me to wear his dead wife's shoes, would he?

'Leah?' His tone bristles with impatience. Reluctantly, I take the espadrilles and put them on. The soles feel damp. They are at least half a size too small and there are indents at the tip of each shoe, where someone else's toes have been. My own toes instinctively curl up.

A shrill ringing noise intrudes on us. It's coming from the chunky black telephone. Miles stares at it.

'Shouldn't you get that?' I say.

'No,' he snaps. 'It'll just be a call centre.'

The ringing stops.

'Right,' he says. 'Breakfast.'

* * *

The dining room is a formal space. Gilt-framed portraits hang on walls panelled with dark wood. The château's former inhabitants, I assume. A young boy with a starched white collar and embroidered black jacket. A man with a handlebar moustache and a golf cap. A young woman with a high lace collar on her white blouse and a pompadour hairstyle.

A dusky pink tablecloth covers the long, oval table and hangs over its solid dark-wood frame. Doors open out onto the terrace at the back of the house, but the summer air can't disguise the room's musty smell.

'Why don't we eat outside?' I ask, looking longingly at the empty wooden table on the terrace. 'It's gorgeous out there.'

Miles stares at me, puzzled. 'Breakfast is always served inside.'

For now.

Two places are set at opposite ends of the table. Miles claims one, leaving me with the other. I pull out a high-backed chair. Is this where Riley sat? As I settle into the seat, I imagine her here. As I touch the china cup in front of me, I imagine her picking it up and blowing on the hot coffee or tea inside before bringing it to her lips.

The bell is silent. I wonder when Vivienne is going to appear. I wish Miles had given her some warning about the proposal. He assured me she'll be fine once she gets used to the idea. He likes to see the best in people, but I'm not so optimistic.

'Let's make a start on the cold stuff,' he says. He guides me over to the long sideboard at the back of the room where a buffet awaits us.

'This looks great,' I say. There is a large glass bowl of fresh fruit salad and, beside it, a silver bowl filled with thick, creamy yoghurt. There is a platter of various cheeses and another of charcuterie. An uncut white baguette sits on a wooden bread-board. Croissants and pain au chocolat fill a woven rattan basket.

'Viv went to pick up the bread and pastries this morning from the shop in Grandfresnoy,' Miles explains. 'We get them fresh every morning.'

He pours two glasses of freshly squeezed orange juice from a crystal jug and takes them back to the table. I fill myself a small glass bowl with fruit salad and yoghurt.

Framed photographs hang on the wall above the sideboard. A teenage Miles, dressed in a blue Adidas T-shirt and tight white shorts, looks out at me from a family snapshot taken in front of the château. Behind him are his parents. Sir and Lady Sinclair. She is elegant in a floral summer dress that dates the photograph to the eighties because it makes her look like a young Princess Diana. Her husband is smart in a beige linen suit and has an air of superiority about him. They were both dead by the time Miles married Riley. If they were still alive now would Miles have proposed to me? I doubt they would have approved of his choice. Next to Miles is his older brother, Bruce. Miles doesn't talk about him much. Bruce died in a skiing accident when he was nineteen, and I haven't been able to find any information about the incident online. In the picture, he wears a sleeveless black T-shirt and denim shorts. He is taller than Miles. More muscular. He has a thick mop of black hair and a cocky expression on his handsome face.

'I was hot in the eighties, wasn't I?' Miles says.

I turn and smile. 'Smoking.'

'Bruce was a hard act to follow.'

'You're much more my type.'

'That's sweet, but maybe I should be glad he's not here to make you prove that.' Sadness flits across Miles' face. 'Joke. Obviously.'

Poor Miles. The Sinclairs have certainly suffered a lot of tragedy. Let's hope the family's run of bad luck ended with Riley. As I fill another bowl with fruit and yoghurt for Miles, I glance at the other pictures. All of them are taken on the steps in front of the château. In one, Miles and Bruce stand either side of a young girl. Vivienne. No mistaking that hair and her pale, narrow face. She's in the next photo along, between Miles and Riley this time, the three of them holding up cocktail glasses to the camera.

'Thanks,' Miles says when I hand him his fruit and yoghurt. I take my seat at the opposite end of the table. He puts on his black rectangular-framed reading glasses and takes his phone from the pocket of his shorts. 'Sorry,' he mutters, as he scrolls through his emails. 'Just need to check in with everything.'

'No worries.' I'm used to him being on his phone. He rarely takes a full day off from work. Sinclair Properties has a full-time manager, Chris, who handles a lot of the day-to-day running of the company, but, as CEO and the major share-holder, Miles is still in charge of everything.

I never look at my phone during mealtimes. Mindless scrolling in front of Miles might make him feel neglected. It's important for me to appear available at all times.

'That's interesting,' he mutters, staring at his phone.

'What?'

'Heritage Capital might be ready to show some serious interest in buying Sinclair Properties.'

'That's good, isn't it?'

'Nothing to get excited about at this stage. I've had interest from them before and it didn't come to anything. That's how these pension funds operate.'

'What happens next?'

He doesn't reply, too busy typing an email to tell me any more. I get on with my breakfast. The fruit is fresh and delicious but the too-tight espadrilles are pinching my feet and distracting me. Have I really got a dead woman's shoes on my feet?

'Done for now.' Miles pushes his phone to one side and

removes his glasses. 'I've just got engaged, for Christ's sake. I think I can justify a morning off.'

I glance at my engagement ring. 'I still can't believe it.'

'Me neither.'

We smile at each other and continue eating. The sound of our spoons scraping the glass bowls fills the sombre room.

'This is delicious,' I say.

'Isn't it? The yoghurt's from a local dairy. I'll have to take you there.'

'Sounds interesting.'

We're talking like an old married couple who have nothing to say to each other. It's ridiculous to be sitting this far away. Usually, we eat breakfast in bed together or sitting side by side at the kitchen counter in Miles' apartment.

Now and then he glances nervously at the dining room door. Is he thinking about Vivienne and how he's going to share our good news with her?

'Is it just me or is this weird?' he says eventually.

'Totally weird.'

'So not us.'

I laugh. 'So not.' Relieved, I pick up my bowl and glass of juice and move to sit on his left, with my back to the doorway.

'That's better.' He leans in and kisses me. 'Getting engaged doesn't mean we have to act like grown-ups.'

I stroke his cheek. 'Glad to hear it.'

We kiss again.

'You're up.'

I turn my head. Vivienne is standing in the dining room doorway, clutching a silver coffee pot.

'Yes.' Miles clears his throat. 'We had a lie-in.'

She fixes us with a cold disapproving stare. 'So I gathered.'

I press my lips together, not daring to smile. With the

bedroom window open, Vivienne must have heard everything we got up to. I peek at Miles. His neck is bright red. Under the table, I squeeze his thigh playfully, but he brushes my hand away.

Vivienne moves silently across the room. She's dressed in the same black shirt-dress as yesterday, with the black apron cinching her in at the waist. Her hair is pinned up again, red wisps of it framing her narrow face. She looks like a historical figure dressed in modern clothing. Like a ghost of one of the château's former inhabitants. She wouldn't look out of place in one of the portraits on the dining room walls.

When she reaches the table, she holds the coffee pot out ceremoniously in front of her. 'Granny Sinclair's coffee pot,' Miles tells me. 'She picked it up at one of the local brocants. Haggled until she got the price she wanted.'

'A brocant is a car boot sale, flea-market-type thing,' Vivienne explains. 'They have them in all the villages here in spring.'

'Fascinating.' Christ. Does every object here have a story attached to it? If so, this is going to be a very long and dull week.

'Coffee, Leah?' Vivienne says.

I prefer tea to coffee in the mornings but, not wanting to annoy her, I pass over my cup. As I do so, she spots the diamond ring glinting on my finger.

'Miles?' She places the coffee pot on the table with a thud. 'What have you done?'

Beneath the table, his leg presses against mine. 'Leah and I are engaged,' he says. 'I proposed last night.' He picks up my hand and kisses it. 'And she very kindly did this old wreck the honour of saying yes.'

'I see.' Vivienne's eyes travel over me with an even greater intensity than yesterday. As though the engagement ring means I deserve a more thorough inspection. I see a different word in her eyes now.

Whore.

I ignore the prickle of shame inside me. Let her think what she wants. I'm no whore. I'm a modern, independent woman taking control of my life and my future. I don't need anyone's approval for that. Especially Vivienne's.

'It's a bit sudden, isn't it?' she says.

Miles glances at the empty seat opposite him. 'She's been dead for over a year.'

Vivienne flinches. I can't help feeling sorry for her. She was close to Riley, and I suspect that even if I was the same age as Miles, she would find it hard to accept him moving on. And she's a widow herself. I imagine she can't bear to think of being with anyone except her husband right now.

That doesn't excuse her malevolent expression. I didn't steal Miles away from his wife. I'm not a marriage wrecker. My last relationship with a married man ended precisely because I didn't want to play that role.

'Have you told your parents yet?' she asks me. 'They must be delighted?'

She is digging for information. Trying to work out what kind of person she's dealing with.

'My parents are dead,' I say. Not a total lie. My mother is dead, and my father is dead to me. Most days that feels like the same thing.

'Shame,' Vivienne says, although she doesn't sound like she means it.

A hollow ache in my chest. My mother would have been delighted about the engagement. *Marriage is a financial arrange-*

ment, Leah. Marrying for love is a ridiculous idea. I married your
father for love and look where that got me.*

'No brothers or sisters?' Vivienne asks.

'No.' I was an only child. My parents' little princess.

'I know this is a bit of a shock for you,' Miles says to Vivienne, 'but I need this and I'd like it if you could be happy for
me. You're all the family I've got left.'

Tears shimmer in her deep blue eyes. I wait for her to relent
and congratulate us, but she says nothing.

'From what I've heard about Riley, she was someone who
loved life.' I put an arm across Miles' shoulders. 'I think she'd
want Miles to live his life to the full and be happy.'

A loud clattering sound from outside startles me. We all
turn and look towards the open terrace doors.

A large slate roof tile lies shattered on the flagstones.

Vivienne gasps. When she turns to look at me, she has a
thin, cruel smile on her lips. 'Would she really?' she says.

10

LEAH

July

Late morning. I enter the dining room, my straw fedora hat in one hand, my Chloé basket bag slung over my shoulder. The table and sideboard are empty. No sign of the breakfast we finished in a hurry. I leave the château through the open doors and pause on the terrace. No trace of the roof tile that fell and smashed on the mossy flagstones.

The incident startled Miles. He rushed out to where I'm standing now and knelt down beside the broken tile. He gathered the fragments of slate together tenderly, before looking up to the roof terrace at the end of the château, his face drained and haunted. At that moment, I knew for certain that was where Riley fell to her death.

Lifting up my sunglasses, I glance up at the roof terrace and wonder, not for the first time, what Riley was doing up there. I thought the roof tile might provide a way in for Miles and me to discuss her death, but when I asked him if he was okay, he suggested I take myself to the pool while he made a few work calls.

I drop my Chloé slides onto the flagstones, slip my feet into them and set off across the lawn, my sunhat dangling at my side. The air around me hums with birdsong and is filled with the scents of roses and lavender and other flowers and herbs I cannot name. My multi-coloured Missoni kaftan stirs in the warm breeze.

As I head towards the tall pine trees that mark the entrance to the pool, I see Miles down by the lake, talking to Vivienne. Or are they arguing? She is up close to him, her finger jabbing at his chest. When she turns to walk away, he follows her. They stop and the conversation continues.

They're too far away for me to hear anything. Not wanting them to catch me spying, I carry on towards the pool. I bet the château's roof is always in a state of disrepair, but from the way Vivienne reacted, you'd think Riley had sent the tile hurtling to the ground as a message from beyond the grave. Vivienne could, at this moment, be trying to convince Miles he's made a mistake by proposing to me, but surely him doing so is a sign he wants to move on from the past?

The pool is larger than I expected, and the aqua-blue water looks inviting. Cream-coloured paving stones surround it and form a patio at one end. A border of trees keeps the pool private and secluded. I can just glimpse the upper storeys of the château through the tall Austrian pines.

Four white plastic sun loungers with olive green cushions are arranged in a line on the patio. I claim one with my hat and drop my bag on the ground. After pulling my crocheted kaftan over my head, I put my hat on and stretch myself out on the warm cushions. I untie the straps of my black halter-neck bikini top and pull my high-leg bikini bottoms up over my hipbones. I feel drained and slightly disorientated. No wonder. After less than twenty-fours at the château I'm engaged – amazing – and dealing with my future husband's hostile relative – not so great.

I need this. When Miles said that to Vivienne, I assumed he meant he needs this fresh start with me. Maybe he thinks my youth will protect him from the past and give him a future. I need this too, but for different reasons.

My engagement ring sparkles on my finger. I'm still not used to the weight of it. What if I lose it? Luckily, it's a snug fit. Miles judged the size perfectly.

The sky is cloudless like yesterday, and the temperature is already rising. Despite the sun's warmth seeping into my limbs, I can't fully relax. I can't stop thinking about the shattered roof tile.

Was it an omen? A sign of some sort? I've never believed in ghosts, but anyone who did might think Riley clearly doesn't want Miles to move on with his life and be happy.

Take control, Leah. Don't let a dead woman get the better of you.

Unsentimental advice as always from my dead mother.

I learned the hard way not to ignore her advice. When I met Freddie at university, she was delighted. After all, she was the one who had urged me to set my sights on the wealthy boys there. When I told her I'd fallen in love with Freddie she was appalled. *Power, not love, Leah. Haven't you learned anything?* She warned me if I gave my power away to Freddie, he would break my heart. That was the start of the rift between us. I stopped going home in the holidays, preferring to stay with Freddie instead. I didn't want her to embarrass me in front of him or to meet his family. She was a washed-up, bitter drunk and I wasn't going to let her ruin the love of my life.

If she hadn't gloated when he dumped me, our relationship

might have recovered. Instead, to avoid her making my heart-break worse, I moved to London after graduation, and we only saw each other occasionally. Then came the pandemic. We spoke more often on the phone at the start of it and saw each other a few times when the first lockdown ended, but she died during the winter of the second lockdown. A heart attack. Her body lay undiscovered for three days until a neighbour found her.

Like Miles and Vivienne, I know how it feels to lose someone suddenly. To never have the chance to say a proper goodbye. Miles knows my mother died of a heart attack, but I've never told him the circumstances. In this game, it pays not to expose your weaknesses. Another of my mother's rules.

Keep your pain close, Leah. Men say they want to hear all about your suffering but they don't. Not really. And if you do tell them your deepest fears and your darkest secrets, they'll use them against you at some point. Trust me.

These days, I listen to her advice. It is one way to keep her memory alive.

'Leah.'

I open my eyes and see Miles walking towards me. His dark Ray-Bans make his face hard to read but his body language speaks of sadness and resignation.

A tremor of anxiety runs through me. What was he arguing about with Vivienne? What did she say to him?

I sit up and fish my suncream out of my bag. When he reaches me, I hold it out to him. 'Put some on for me?'

'Leah, I—'

'Please.'

With a sigh he takes the suncream and perches on the edge of my sun lounger. He snaps open the lid of the bottle. When the cool cream makes contact with my stomach, I gasp.

His hands are hesitant at first but it doesn't take long for desire to overpower them. His fingers pull down my bikini top and he massages my breasts slowly, making me flinch when he pinches each nipple in turn. The more aroused he becomes, the less anxious I feel.

It doesn't take long for his fingers, greasy with suncream to invade my bikini bottoms. I part my legs so he can slide his fingers inside me. I don't make a habit of faking pleasure, but it's getting unbearably hot with his body so close to me and, even though the pool is secluded, I can't help worrying that Vivienne might be somewhere nearby.

'Fuck,' I say and moan and shudder as if I can't control myself.

Swearing is reserved for sexual activity only. I never swear when we're out in public, or even when we're alone. Men like Miles don't like to be embarrassed when out in company or in exclusive surroundings. He does like it when I swear during sex. As if he's responsible for bringing out my bad side. For getting me so turned on I can't help myself.

When he slides his fingers into my mouth, I suck on them greedily, watching him closely. Worry replaces the desire in his eyes. I reach out and caress his exposed thigh.

'Leah.' He takes his fingers from my mouth and lifts my hand from his thigh. 'I've been thinking.'

This doesn't sound good. My heart knocks against my ribs with a dull, defeated thud. Is this it? With Vivienne's help, he's reached the conclusion that marrying me would be a bad idea. Did he just make sure he got one last bit of fun, knowing he's about to cut me loose?

I peek at my beautiful diamond ring. Will I get to keep it?

'Let's get married here,' he says.

'What?' I sit up, my breasts still exposed.

'Why not?' He gently lifts my bikini top back into place for me. 'It won't take long to sort out. We'll have to register with the town hall first and then I think we need to have been in residence here for a month, but we could have it done before the end of the summer.'

'This summer?'

He laughs at my confusion. 'Yes. This summer.'

'What about your work?'

'I can work from here.' His fingers trace spirals across my stomach. 'If I need to pop back to London for meetings that's easy enough.'

'What if something happens with Heritage Capital?'

'Even if they're serious, nothing will happen for a while. It's a long game.'

'Okay,' I say, trying to keep up with this turn of events. 'What about my work? There's no way my manager will let me take that long off.'

'Then quit.'

'Quit?' My pulse quickens. 'Are you serious?'

He smiles. 'From now on you don't have to work unless you want to. And you can certainly take a summer off.'

Is this really happening?

'What about my flat?' I ask. 'I'll have to pay rent or Gemma will—'

'I'll cover it. We'll pay the rent until the end of September. That will give you plenty of time to move out and she can get someone else in.'

'Move out?'

He laughs. 'We're getting married. When we get back to London, I want us to live together.'

'Okay.' Tears sting my eyes. 'This is all... It's so sudden.' I stare down at his neat, manicured hands. 'It's not just the rent I'm concerned about. I need to keep paying off my—'

'Student loans? Credit card bills?'

'Both.' We've never discussed money as openly as this before. Better to get it out of the way now. Test how far his generosity extends.

'Let's pay everything off now,' he says. 'No point the banks getting all that interest.'

An ever-present tension inside me begins to uncoil. The permanent anxiety about money.

Use men. Take what you can get from them.

'You've really thought all this through, haven't you?' I say.

He smiles. 'I may have done a little plotting and scheming.'

This is what I want, isn't it? A clean slate. No more money worries. Then why do I feel guilty?

'Let me look after you, Leah.' Miles tilts my head up and looks deep into my eyes. 'What do you say?'

How safe and solid he seems at this moment. With him, my life could get back to how it was meant to be.

I nod. 'Okay.'

He pulls me to him and holds me in a tight embrace. 'You make me so happy,' he says.

Looking over his shoulder at the pool, I imagine a wedding here at the château, a three-day extravaganza to rival the nuptials of Freddie and Florence. Guests lazing by the pool before and after the ceremony. Not that I've got that many people to invite. Some of my work colleagues might turn up for a free party and Gemma might come out of morbid curiosity but that would be it.

'I do have one request,' Miles says when he finally releases me.

'Shoot.'

He hesitates. 'Do you mind if we keep it small?'

'The wedding?'

'Small and private. I don't want to deprive you of a proper celebration, but I have done it before and I want this time to be different.'

It sounds as though his marriage to Riley was the opposite of small and private. I imagine them standing on the steps of a church in a quaint English village, surrounded by a vast gathering of friends and family. Riley in a long white gown and Miles in top hat and tails.

'Leah,' Miles says, 'is that okay?'

'It's fine.' I fight back a surge of disappointment. 'I understand.'

Relief floods his face. 'We could get married at the town hall in Montreuilac and then perhaps have a lovely meal here.'

I've never given much thought to what my wedding day might be like, but I've always expected something grander than that. I smile. 'All that matters is that we're together.'

All that matters is getting the gold ring to go with my engagement one. All that matters are the official documents joining us together and what they might entitle me to. Keeping the wedding small and doing it here means less time for anyone to put him off the idea.

'And there's no rush to tell anyone about the engagement,' he says. 'Apart from the people you need to.'

'Oh,' I say. 'Okay.'

'Not because I don't want people to know. I just think we should get used to the idea ourselves first.'

It occurs to me he may have another reason to keep his good news to himself for a while. 'Is this because of Riley's family?' I ask.

He frowns. 'What do you mean?'

'I suppose you'll need to tell her parents you're getting married again. Out of respect.' He's never spoken of Riley's family, but I imagine her relatives would rather hear about his fresh start directly from him.

'That's so thoughtful, Leah, but I never met her family.'

'Really? But you were married for seven years.'

'Riley never knew her father and she was estranged from her mother and younger sister. She was mostly brought up by her grandmother, Lucille.'

'You didn't meet Lucille?'

'She died when Riley was nineteen.'

'That's sad.'

He shrugs. 'Riley had come to terms with her family. As much as any of us ever do.'

It seems Riley and I have much in common. Like me, she had no family around to support her and I obviously share her taste in older, wealthy men.

'All that's in the past now,' Miles says. 'This wedding is about us and our future. We can have fun sorting it all out. Just the two of us.'

'Sounds perfect.'

'We'll need two witnesses for the ceremony,' he says. 'Obviously Viv will do it and we'll find someone else.'

'Have you told her about this?'

'She's fine with it all.'

'Miles.' I stroke his cheek. 'I saw you arguing, down by the lake. Were you telling her about your wedding plans?'

He looks away. 'She'll come round. She's not herself just now.'

'I'm sorry she doesn't like me.'

'It's not that.'

'She doesn't approve of the age gap?'

He takes my hand from his face and kisses it. 'Look, after Dom died she had a breakdown. She had to leave her job.'

'Oh.' So she's not on a temporary sabbatical then.

'I can't send her away. Not now. Not with her son in New York and only an empty house to go back to.'

'No. That wouldn't be right.' Pity. 'Anyway, it's good she's here. I'm no domestic goddess.'

He laughs. 'I'm not marrying you for your housekeeping abilities.'

'Good. You won't be disappointed.'

I'm a capable cook and have cleaned for a living plenty of times, but I don't want Miles to know that. I've no intention of signing up for a life of domestic drudgery.

'Vivienne won't be the only one to think we're crazy,' I say.

'I'm sure we'll get plenty of beauty and the beast comments.'

'Don't say that.'

'It's true.'

'I think it's the gold-digging whore comments we need to worry about.'

He kisses my forehead. 'Anyone who says anything like that will have me to deal with.'

We lie back on the sun lounger together, Miles wrapping me up in his strong, safe arms. Everything I've worked for is paying off. For once in my life, everything is going according to plan.

11

LEAH

July

The town hall in Montreuilac is more impressive than I'd imagined. Its Gothic facade boasts ornate stonework and intricate carvings, including several solemn bishops and a number of snarling canine gargoyles. A belfry tower rises high above it, the spire at the top slightly crooked. The gardens in front of the building, where I'm walking now, combine symmetrical rectangles of grass and neat, colourful flower beds packed with cornflowers and red poppies.

There are worse places to get married.

Miles is inside there now, getting advice on what we need to do to set our wedding plans in motion. Is it really only yesterday he suggested we get married as soon as possible? He seems keen to get the arrangements made quickly. I did offer to go in with him, but he urged me to enjoy the gardens. No point me having to deal with all the boring admin. According to him, we'll need to sort out some basic paperwork first and he wanted to come here and get more information on the process.

Don't marry in haste. That's what I did, Leah, and I'm bloody well repenting now.

My mother's favourite moan after she'd had several strong gin and tonics. Miles isn't like my father. Miles is a solid prospect. My father was, in many ways, a con artist. A convincing salesman with grand ambitions. All of his business ventures funded by my mother's inheritance and all of them failures.

I think she would approve of my hastiness in this instance.

Only eleven in the morning and the sun is already fierce. I'm glad of my fedora and the long sleeves of my Zimmermann floral minidress.

Between the flower beds are information plaques in English about Montreuilac. It is, apparently, a market town dating from the seventeenth century and it now has a population of around 30,000.

I sit down on a wooden bench and tilt my face up towards the sun. I wonder what everyone is doing at Pillar Assurance, the company I no longer work for. Olivia, my ex-manager, will be sitting in her cubicle office with its view over Liverpool Street station, sipping on her second black coffee of the day. She wasn't thrilled when I called her on Monday afternoon to tell her I wasn't coming back. She is thirty-six now and a committed career girl. First one into our department every day and the last one out. She was even less thrilled when I explained I was giving up work to get married.

I feel uneasy knowing there won't be any money going into my account at the end of next month, but, as Miles reassured me, I don't have to worry about money any more.

I haven't told anyone else about the engagement yet. I understand what Miles said about us taking time to get used to the idea but can't help wondering if he is putting off dealing with the disapproval of others? If that's the case, I get it. I haven't called Gemma yet to tell her about the wedding and about moving in with Miles for exactly the same reason. She is bound to be a total buzzkill.

Cheers erupt at the entrance of the town hall. A couple emerges into the sunshine, hand in hand. The woman in a pale blue mini dress with spaghetti straps, the man in an electric blue tuxedo. A small group of family and friends follows them outside. When the couple kiss, everyone claps and cheers. I put my fingers in my mouth and let out a loud wolf whistle, which makes the couple laugh.

Someone in the wedding party throws confetti into the air. This will be me soon. I have to put the doubters and the naysayers out of my mind. Soon, I'll have the life I've been dreaming of and nothing is going to get in my way.

* * *

When Miles finally comes out of the town hall, he has another man with him. Short and slim, his black hair peppered with grey. Well-tailored suit in navy linen. Dark eyes behind round wire-framed glasses.

'Leah, this is Monsieur Lecomte,' Miles says. 'The mayor of Montreuilac.'

The mayor's eyes flick over me. 'Philippe, please.'

I hold out my hand. 'Lovely to meet you, Philippe.'

He takes my hand, dips his head and kisses it. Cheesy.

'Congratulations on your engagement,' he says when he lifts his head and releases my hand. 'This is wonderful news.'

'Thank you,' I say.

'Miles is a lucky man,' the mayor says. 'Very lucky.' He

mutters something to Miles in French. Locker room banter has the same tone in any language.

'Your town hall is amazing,' I say. 'Really beautiful.'

'It is, yes.' The mayor smiles, showing neat white teeth. 'This year we had some work done, some restoration on the tower.' He points up at the spire. 'Your fiancé was one of the donors who make this possible. Very generous.'

'It was nothing,' Miles says. 'Happy to help.'

'We have a special connection,' Philippe says. 'Miles and I.'

'The mayor is a distant relative of the family that used to own the château,' Miles explains.

'I see,' I say.

'A cousin on the side of my mother married a Dumont many, many years ago.' The mayor lays a hand across his heart. 'The château is a very special place to me. I am very happy to see joy is coming back to it after the sadness. Very happy.'

He means the sadness of Riley's death, I assume. At least someone is positive about my impending nuptials.

'And now you must excuse me,' Philippe says. 'I have a committee meeting to attend. Always a committee meeting.'

He shakes hands with Miles but wraps his arms around me in a tight embrace. 'Very beautiful,' he says.

* * *

'Think you've got yourself an admirer there,' Miles says as the mayor disappears inside the town hall.

'He's only human.' I say it jokingly, but it doesn't hurt for Miles to see other men admiring me. Yes, it's important to make Miles feel like the centre of attention, but it's also crucial to keep him a little on edge. Sometimes I show him texts from former lovers, asking to see me again. I always tell them no, but I want Miles to think I have other options. To think I can walk away whenever I choose and someone will snap me up.

'Philippe's a good guy,' he says. 'He's certainly helped me through some difficult times.'

He must mean Riley's death.

'Let's grab a coffee,' Miles says. 'I'll fill you in on everything.'

He leads me over the busy road and down a street lined with low, solid buildings made of sandstone. Almost every shop is either a delicatessen or a pâtisserie or a chocolaterie.

'This town is famous for being a foodie's heaven,' Miles says.

We end up in a small, cobbled square that contains the entrance to a cavernous food market I will have to explore at some point, as well as several cafés and restaurants and a florist's shop with tall buckets of sunflowers either side of the entrance. *Esprit Fleurs.*

Miles selects a café called *Le Paradiso* and we settle at a table beneath a green awning. When a waitress appears, Miles orders white coffees for both of us.

'Bugger,' he says. 'I left my reading glasses in the car.' He takes his phone from the pocket of his short-sleeved white shirt and checks his emails, holding his phone at a distance so he can see better.

The outfit he has on today is not one of my favourites. Beige chinos with the white shirt and tan suede loafers. To add insult to injury, his white trainer socks are visible inside his shoes. A look that always gives me the ick. Once we get back to London, I'll have to get him a whole new wardrobe.

I remove my hat, rest it on my lap and shake out my hair. A pleasant buzz of chatter fills the square. Our café and the ones nearby are busy with people getting their mid-morning caffeine injection. A few people sitting alone, several couples and a few families.

Miles puts his phone away. 'Sorry, darling,' he says. 'Pressing work issues, unfortunately.'

Darling. He started calling me that yesterday. As if I'm in a different category now we are engaged. Did he call Riley that? Did she find it slightly condescending too?

'So,' he says, 'it looks like we'll be able to get married before the end of August. I've booked in a provisional date.'

'That's amazing. When?'

'August the twenty-sixth. There is some paperwork to sort out,' he says. 'We need to go online and get copies of our birth certificates, that sort of thing.'

The waitress brings our coffees. We pause the conversation while we both take our first grateful sips.

'And we'll have to go up to Paris to the British Consulate,' Miles says when he puts his cup down. 'They need to approve the paperwork, apparently. Luckily, I have a contact there. Guy called Hugo. Son of my old friend, Hugo.'

I'm guessing Hugo and his son are old money, like Miles. These families always seem to pass on their names from one generation to the next. If I have a son with Miles, will he have to be called Miles too?

'I'm going to give young Hugo a call,' Miles says. 'See if he can speed things up a bit for us.'

'That would be amazing.' Miles has contacts everywhere. I like that about him. 'I can get my wedding dress in Paris.'

'Will it be a surprise or can I help you choose it?'

'Maybe it should be a surprise? We need to do at least one thing traditionally.'

'Whatever you want, my darling.' He picks up my left hand and studies the ring he bought me.

What I want is a grand wedding at the château filled with loving family and friends. What I want is enviable Instagram posts to rival Freddie's.

'Can we have a photographer?' I ask. 'I know we're not having a traditional day, but if we get a professional set of pictures done, we'll at least have some proper memories.'

'Of course,' he says. 'That's a lovely idea.'

I may not be able to compete with Freddie's grand wedding, but I can put a few stunning shots of myself out into the world. Unlike Florence, who documented almost every second of her wedding preparations, I shall hold off doing any social media until after I'm married. Then I will put up a single post with a number of elegant, tasteful pictures of my day. If anyone who knows Freddie shows him the post, my restraint will make Florence's approach look tacky.

Miles kisses my hand. 'Once we get all the boring legalities done, we can relax and enjoy ourselves.'

'What about the prenup?' I say. 'I assume we need to get that out of the way?'

A startled expression crosses his face.

'It's okay,' I say. 'I know someone in your position will need me to sign a prenup and I'm okay with it.'

Not that I have much choice. In this game, prenups are the norm. As long as Miles is fair, I'm prepared to sign one.

'Thank you for bringing that up.' He sighs. 'I wish we didn't need one, but my lawyer will insist.'

'I understand. I want to be with you, Miles.'

He gives me a sad smile. 'Sometimes it's hard for me to believe that.'

'Well, believe it.' I lean in and kiss him. A display of affection that will make him feel good in front of anyone watching.

'Whatever twist of fate brought you into my life, I'm very grateful for it,' he says.

'Same.'

At that moment, a young couple with twin toddlers arrive in the square and claim a table at the café opposite us. The twins, two adorable girls with dark ringlets draw fond glances from everyone, including Miles.

'I really want kids, Leah,' he says. 'I always have.'

I force a smile. 'Me too.' I do, or at least I've always assumed I'd be a mother one day. If I marry Miles, it looks like I'll be having them sooner rather than later. Understandable, given the age difference between us, but I'd rather wait a year or two.

If he's so keen on starting a family, why did he and Riley never have kids?

A loud jangling noise. Miles' phone vibrates on the table. He checks the screen and tuts.

'Sorry, darling,' he says. 'Have to take this.' He picks up his phone and jabs at the screen with his forefinger. 'Chris.' He presses the phone against his ear. 'No,' he says to his company manager, 'it's fine. I'm here.'

I drain the last of my coffee. Miles is conducting his business with Chris in a booming, embarrassingly loud voice. My gaze wanders to the florist's shop in the corner of the square.

Miles frowns when I nudge him. I point towards *Esprit Fleurs*. 'Back in a minute,' I say.

12

LEAH

July

The interior of the shop is dark and cool and fragrant. Flowers press in on me from all sides – roses, gerberas, chrysanthemums and white lilies. Pot plants hang from the ceiling in wire baskets.

While Miles deals with work issues, I might as well do some wedding research. It would be nice for me to carry a beautiful bouquet on the day. I also want to pick up a bunch of something for Vivienne as a thank you for all she's done since my arrival. Flowers won't miraculously transform her into a friend, but she's not going anywhere soon, so I should try to get on with her. I suppose Miles getting married means she'll be losing her biggest companion in grief. No wonder she's finding it hard to get her head around the wedding.

'*Bonjour.*' The florist behind the counter smiles at me. A middle-aged woman with grey, bobbed hair and bright pink lipstick. Her shiny name badge introduces her as Sondrine. '*Puis-je vous aidez?*' she says.

'I'm just looking,' I say, wishing I'd paid more attention in my school French lessons. I only have the most basic of French phrases. '*Merci.*'

'Okay. No problem.' She wipes her hands on the front of her pink apron before continuing to snip the stems of the tall white roses laid on the counter in front of her.

So much to choose from. If I was having a proper wedding, a big one with lots of guests, I'd have to decide on flowers to decorate the tables for the meal. Flowers for my bridesmaids as well as myself.

No point thinking about what might have been. This is the game I'm in now. Still, there's no reason why I shouldn't have flowers all over the château as well as a stunning bouquet. Miles can at least give me that.

I pick out a bunch of light pink roses for Vivienne. Pale, ethereal blooms. '*Merci,*' I say as I had them to Sondrine. She pushes aside the roses she's working on and lays a sheet of cerise paper flat on the counter. 'Do you do wedding flowers?' I ask.

'*Bien sûr.*' She tears the sheet of cellophane in half. 'Is for you?'

'I'm getting married. Yes.'

A figure appears in the doorway behind the counter. A woman about my age, the sunflowers in her arms a bright contrast to her black T-shirt. Her bleached hair is scraped into a high ponytail. A silver stud glitters in her nose. According to her less shiny name badge, her name is Naomi.

She mutters something to Sondrine in French before moving around the counter and pushing past me. Empty buckets clatter as she fills them with the sunflowers.

'You marry here?' asks Sondrine.

I nod. 'At the town hall. But we're having the reception at Château Clairvallon.'

Sondrine freezes, the blades of her scissors open in mid-air.

'Château Clairvallon?' Naomi says behind me. 'The Sinclairs?'

'Yes.'

She steps closer, clutching a lone sunflower, and stares at my engagement ring. 'Who is it you marry?'

'Miles. Miles Sinclair.'

Her dark eyes widen. '*Merde.*'

'You know him?'

She looks me up and down. 'Not any more.'

'How did you know him?'

'I sometimes worked at the château. As a cleaner.'

'But you don't now?'

'*Non*. After Riley... after Madame Sinclair died, he said no more work.'

'He let everyone go?'

Naomi nods. 'And now, he is marrying again? Very soon, *n'est-ce pas*?'

My shoulders tense. 'He needs to move on.'

A rustling sound from the counter as Sondrine swaddles the pale pink roses in the cerise paper.

'You should be careful,' Naomi says.

Dread creeps up my spine. 'Why?'

Naomi gives me a sly half-smile. 'Some people around here think Madame Sinclair's death was not an accident.'

13

LEAH

July

'Engaged?' Gemma says when I finally get round to calling her. 'It's... it's only Friday. You haven't even been there a week.'

'When you know, you know,' I say.

'You're kidding, right?'

'I'll take that as congratulations.' I'm sitting on a wooden swivel chair at the antique walnut desk in the study next to the sitting room, my phone on speaker, staring out of the window at the château's extensive front lawn. The study windows are open but bring no hint of a breeze. It is early afternoon, but the temperature hasn't dropped since lunchtime. Even with only my bikini and kaftan on, I'm sweating.

'Was the proposal romantic?' Gemma asks.

'Very.' I describe the moment by the lake, Miles on one knee. The champagne waiting for us on ice.

'Old-school,' she says, a brittle note of envy in her voice. 'Nice, I guess. If you like that kind of thing.'

Maybe the proposal was a bit cheesy, but it's more than Gemma will ever get from loser Damien.

When I tell her Miles and I are getting married here this summer, she gasps.

'Are you mental?' she says.

'Your support is touching.'

'Maybe it is a good idea to do it soon. He's not getting any younger.'

'He's fifty-four, not seventy-four.'

'Classic age for a heart attack.'

'Fuck off, Gemma.'

'Are you pregnant? Is that what this is all about?'

'No.'

'Bet you will be soon.'

A ripple of panic runs through me when I think about impending motherhood. Miles and I haven't discussed it since our trip to Montreuilac three days ago. At least I had my contraception injection before I came here. That means there's no chance of a honeymoon baby.

'What about work?' Gemma asks.

When I tell her about handing in my resignation, she says nothing but I can imagine the disapproving look on her face.

'And I'll be moving in with Miles when we get back to London,' I say.

A terse silence. Then: 'I didn't think you'd be shacking up with him here,' she says.

'I've just transferred two months' rent into your bank account. That gives you until the end of September to find someone new for my room.'

'Tell Miles thanks for the money.'

Snarky cow. She's just jealous because her boyfriend is a taker who never pays for anything.

'Actually,' she says, 'there's a woman at work looking for somewhere to rent. I'll offer her the room.'

I'm relieved Gemma won't have to search too long for a flat-mate but also a little stung at being so swiftly replaced. I didn't expect my life to be so easy to dismantle.

'I bet he makes you sign a prenup,' she says.

'Well, duh. We've already discussed that.'

Yesterday Miles informed me his lawyer was drafting a document and would have it ready for me to read soon.

While Gemma lectures me about the perils of giving up my financial independence, my gaze wanders around the study. The small square room with its bright yellow walls has windows facing front and back. On one of the walls hangs an old wooden tennis racket with a long handle and a small head. On another hangs a collection of black-and-white photographs of the château's former owners. Stern-faced women in corseted dresses. Men with handlebar moustaches and straw boaters. Little boys in sailor outfits. Next to these historical images is a corkboard crammed with snaps of the Sinclairs here at the château.

'What will you do with yourself if you don't work?' Gemma says.

I look out of the window in front of me, hoping to see Miles' car coming up the drive. He's gone into the village of Grandfresnoy to pick up a few supplies for Vivienne. Last time I saw her she was upstairs cleaning, so I decided to stay out of her way.

'Leah?' Gemma says. 'Are you even listening to me?'

'Not really.'

'Fine. Well, congratulations,' she says. 'If this is what you really want.'

After hanging up, I feel drained. Pity I don't have any close, supportive female friends to call. Gemma and I only know each other because I rented a room in her flat. I've never been good at female friendship, and my recent mission to find a man like Miles isn't something I can openly discuss with most women. Sometimes, when out in hotel bars, I spotted others on the hunt like me. Attractive girls sitting alone, eyes scanning their surroundings. I often considered talking to them. They at least would understand my goals. But these girls could not be my friends. They were the competition.

Beneath the table, I slip my feet out of the pale blue espadrilles I bought in Montreuilac. No need for the red shoes that may or may not have belonged to Riley. I press the heels of my hands into my eyes and yawn. Last night, unable to sleep, I lay next to Miles' hot and restless body and thought about Riley.

Some people around here think Madame Sinclair's death was not an accident.

As soon as Naomi said that to me, Sondrine intervened in the conversation.

'Do not listen to her,' Sondrine told me. 'This is a silly rumour.'

An agitated exchange in French between the women followed. A sulky expression settled over Naomi's face.

'People around here, they gossip,' Sondrine said as I paid for the flowers. When I left the shop, I glanced back and saw Naomi staring at me, her expression a mixture of curiosity and pity.

Gossip. Nothing I should pay attention to. I haven't mentioned it to Miles. He probably had to deal with those kinds of rumours when Riley died and I don't think he'd appreciate me dragging up the past again.

On top of the desk, next to Miles' laptop, is a blue cardboard folder containing printouts of the paperwork we've been putting together for the marriage documentation. Everything must be in order before Miles can take it to Hugo, his contact at the consulate in Paris.

I open the folder. Inside is a copy of my birth certificate, which came through yesterday. The sight of my father's name triggers the usual dull ache in my chest. I don't regret telling Miles he was dead. My father and I are estranged; it's hardly as though he's going to be walking me down the aisle. I could probably track him down if I tried hard enough, but what's the point? When my mother died, I half-expected him to get in touch. I thought he'd somehow know. An ex-husband's telepathy. I thought he might send condolences in a card or in floral form but nothing came.

Many times I asked my mother why she was stupid enough to marry my father. She would look at me and say she loved him. She loved him and because of that she gave away all her power. She always said that while she couldn't undo her mistake, she would make sure I didn't repeat it.

I sift through the other papers in the folder, uncovering a copy of Miles' birth certificate and what looks like a utility bill linked to the château.

Beneath them is another document I haven't seen yet.

Certificat de Décès.

I don't need Google translate to tell me this is Riley's death certificate. Miles must need it so we can get our Certificate of No Impediment. So we can prove we are both single and eligible for marriage.

There, on the left-hand side is Riley's name. Her *maiden* name. Riley Johnson. Adrenalin shoots through me at this unexpected discovery. Below her name is her date of birth and the date and estimated time of her death. On the right-hand side are a number of questions with Yes and No boxes beside them that have been ticked. With the help of my phone, I manage a rough translation of the questions. The one that jumps out as interesting translates roughly as: *Is it necessary to search for a cause of death and therefore transfer the body to a forensic institute?* The *No* box has an emphatic tick inside it.

There is no cause of death anywhere on the certificate, but a quick Google search tells me that the French don't record the cause on the certificate. Instead it is filed separately with the French Regional Health Agency.

I close the folder and open the Facebook app on my phone. I hardly use it. My Facebook profile, like my Instagram one, is set to private with only my profile picture available for public consumption. I type 'Riley Johnson' into the search box and scroll through the profiles that appear. Just as I'm about to give up, I find her.

When I click on her picture and open up her profile, I see immediately that the account hasn't been used for years. The most recent entry was made the same year she married Miles. There are only a few posts available to view and around thirty photographs. I search through the images, hungry for insights into my predecessor.

In all the pictures her hair is long and mostly tied back in a ponytail. When not in her skydiving gear, she dresses in jeans and T-shirts. Her single life looked like fun. There are shots of her jumping out of planes, a parachute strapped to her back. Records of skydiving trips to Spain and Portugal and Belize. Campfires on beaches. Rowdy nights in bars. In most of the social shots she has a bottle of beer in one hand. She is sometimes pictured with women, but often she is the only female in an all-male group. When she looks into the camera her gaze is direct. She was clearly a woman happy to live on the edge. A woman unafraid to take everything she could from life.

Nowhere on the profile have any of her friends commented on her death. This is not a memorialised account. Maybe she lost touch with everyone she knew when she married Miles.

I put down my phone and take a deep breath. My pulse is thrumming. My senses are overloaded with all this new information. The tips of my fingers fizz and tingle, and I find myself opening the deep drawer on the right-hand side of the desk. I'm not normally one to pry but having just discovered this new information about Riley, I'm itching to know more. After all, I have now agreed to marry Miles. Surely I should find out as much about his past as I can?

Knowledge is power, Leah. Another of my mother's favourite mantras.

Inside the drawer, I discover several Bic biros, a small stapler and a round metal sweet tin filled with paperclips.

When I touch the handle of the drawer on the opposite side of the desk, a dark vibration passes through me. Dread.

The drawer is stiff on its runners and opens slowly. The first item I encounter is the framed picture of Riley that was sitting on Miles' bedside table when I first arrived. This must be where he stashed it. Underneath I find three loose photographs. All of them of Riley. In the first, she is floating on a white Lilo in the château's pool, a flute of champagne in one hand, her tanned, toned body on display in a skimpy white bikini. Her hair is cropped and sleek. Seems her appearance changed when she married Miles. Gone are her long hair and her casual clothes. I don't blame her. I too will make the most of marrying into money.

In the second picture, she is sitting at the table on the terrace at the back of the château, dressed in a white bandeau cocktail dress, her skin a luminous rose-gold from the setting sun. She has what looks like a martini in one hand and she is laughing, her head tilting backwards. Diamond studs sparkle in her ears. The third picture must have been taken somewhere in the château's gardens. Riley, clad in khaki hot pants and a white T-shirt that reveals the lack of a bra underneath, is kneeling next to a vegetable patch packed with lettuces of different types. She is holding a bunch of freshly picked lettuce leaves and smiling up at the camera. Behind her is an apple tree laden with fruit.

Who took the pictures? Miles? All of them have a tiny hole top and centre where a drawing pin must have been. Perhaps these images were pinned to the corkboard in here. Did Miles take them down because he didn't want them to offend me or because he couldn't bear looking at what he has lost?

After putting the photographs back, my tingling hand plunges further into the drawer. I pull out a blue envelope with a name on the front. *Miles.* The neat, angular handwriting is unfamiliar, yet I know instinctively who it belongs to.

The envelope is open. A neat slit across the top made with a letter opener. I tell myself the envelope's contents are private. This is correspondence between Miles and his dead wife.

I reach into the envelope and pull out the card inside. I'm only human.

The white card has a single red heart on the front. My stomach twists. My breath sticks in my chest.

When I open the card, a photograph falls out and lands on the desk, image side down. I read the card first. A simple inscription.

Miles, baby. All my love, always. R xxx

Miles, baby. Those two words bring her voice alive in my head. A generic American accent that probably doesn't resemble her real voice at all but now it is there.

Miles, baby.

What is it I'm feeling right now? Not jealousy. Not exactly. Riley is dead and gone and even if she and Miles adored each other, that doesn't mean it would have lasted forever. Look at Freddie and me. We were always saying how much we loved each other and what did that mean, in the end?

I place the card and the envelope on the desk and turn over the photograph that lies beside them. 'Oh.' My trapped breath escapes me in a gasp. Riley looks up at me, her grey eyes sultry and inviting. She is sitting, naked, on a red velvet armchair with her legs apart.

A creaking sound makes me snap my head up. Just as the study door opens, I brush the card, envelope and photograph off the desk and onto my lap.

'Leah.' Vivienne stands in the doorway. 'There you are.'

14

LEAH

July

Vivienne enters the study, a glass of cloudy liquid in one hand and her vape in the other.

'Fresh lemonade?' she says. 'It's Miles' favourite.'

'Thanks,' I say cautiously. 'Looks great.' Does this gesture mean Vivienne is thawing towards me? Now it's clear I'm going to be a permanent fixture in her life, she might have decided to change her attitude towards me.

Her keys jangle in her apron pocket as she scuttles across the room. I cover the contents of my lap with my hands when she places the glass on the desk. She then retreats and stands with her back to the window.

I take a large gulp of the lemonade. I'm thirsty, drained from the excitement of so many new discoveries. The lemonade is good. Sweet and sour at the same time. Cool and refreshing. 'Delicious,' I say.

'Riley gave me the recipe.'

I smile. Of course she did.

'It's an old Oregon recipe,' Vivienne says. 'Her grandmother used to make it.'

'It's a classic.' I take another sip.

Hey, baby, how about some of Grandma's lemonade?

Great. I've got Riley's voice in my head and a naked picture of her nestling in my lap.

'Miles told me Riley was brought up by her grandmother,' I say casually. As though I'm not fishing for information on my predecessor.

'So I believe.'

Vivienne turns her head towards the open door. In the distance, the telephone rings in the hallway. She frowns. Every day that phone rings at least once and no one answers it.

When the ringing stops, she peers at the corkboard with its array of Sinclair family pictures. 'Gosh. There are some real blasts from the past here.'

Neat change of subject from Riley's background.

I place the glass of lemonade back on the desk. 'You must have so many great memories of this place.'

'I do.' Vivienne sucks on her vape pen. 'My parents got divorced when I was eight years old. That's why I spent so many holidays here. Mum was always busy and she was desperate to get rid of me so she could work and I could have some company.'

'What did your mum do?' My head is too full of Riley to care about Vivienne's mother, but as this is the first information Vivienne has offered up about herself, I feel obliged to take an interest.

'She was a professor of feminist studies at Cambridge University.' Viv slides a hand into her apron pocket. The hidden keys clink as she toys with them. 'Even though we came from money, she taught me the importance of having my own career and my own identity. My own financial security.'

Miles must have told her I've packed in my job. Bet she's horrified. Last thing I need is a lecture on second-wave feminism. Especially from someone with Vivienne's privilege.

'I worked hard to build the life I had,' she says. 'I worked hard at my teaching career, at being a wife, at being a mother.' She stops and pinches the bridge of her nose.

'Sounds exhausting,' I say.

She tilts her head defiantly. 'It was challenging at times. But I *did* have it all. My career, my son and a marriage of equals. A marriage based on love.'

Did she really have it all? Sounds like she was *doing* it all, rather than *having* it.

I want the having without the doing.

'I certainly didn't put anything about obeying in my wedding vows,' Vivienne says. 'Nor did I take my husband's name. Couldn't see the point of it.'

Miles and I haven't discussed surnames yet. The subject hasn't even occurred to me.

'I suppose you'll be taking his name?' she asks, a scornful edge to her voice.

'Leah Sinclair,' I say, just to wind her up. 'I do like the sound of it.'

Her nose crinkles as if she's just smelled something rotten.

'Look, Vivienne,' I say. 'I know Miles and I are not an obvious match and maybe I'm not what you imagined for him, but I honestly think I can make him happy.'

Another puff on the vape. She turns her head to the window. The sun catches her light red hair, making it appear almost translucent. 'It's brave of him to come back here,' she says. 'I'll give him that.'

The menthol scent of her vape liquid fills the room.

'He's been through so much,' she adds. 'Riley's death was so sudden.'

'Like your husband's.'

Her head snaps round. Her expression is unreadable.

'Miles told me what happened to Dom,' I say. 'I'm sorry.'

'Why? Did you kill him?'

'What?'

'I'm sick of hearing sorry. It's all anyone ever says, and it's meaningless.'

I open my mouth to say sorry, then close it again.

Vivienne sighs. 'None of this is easy for me.'

'I know. I understand.'

'You really don't.' She pinches the bridge of her nose again. 'I only want what's best for Miles.'

Clearly, I'm nowhere near the best in her opinion.

'Well,' she says, 'at least the wedding isn't happening tomorrow. You've got plenty of time to really get to know one another.'

With that she turns and marches out of the study, slamming the door behind her.

What did she mean by that? Did she simply mean Miles and I have never lived together for any length of time and now we'll be seeing one another as we really are? Or that none of this is a done deal until I have the ring on my finger and that Miles still has time to change his mind? Does she intend to use the weeks before the wedding to sabotage me? So far, she's attempted to make Riley a constant presence. It's up to me to keep Miles in the present. To keep him headed towards the future.

To do that, I need to forget about Riley too.

Despite the open window, the heat in the study is oppressive. I lift the card, envelope and photograph from my lap and lay them on the desk. I stare at the photograph. Is it me or is there a challenge in Riley's gaze? I tuck her back inside the card, return the card to the envelope and put the envelope back in the drawer, taking care to leave it exactly as I found it.

From now on, I won't investigate my future husband's past. From now on, Riley can rest in peace.

15

LEAH

July

Monday morning and Miles and I are in the dining room, having breakfast. In the glass bowl in front of me, fruit salad nestles beneath a heavy dollop of yoghurt. Exactly like yesterday. Miles is once again in his salmon pink shorts and blue Polo shirt, and I have on my red maxi dress. Through the terrace doors, warm, scented air drifts in. The sky is blue and cloudless. Everything is exactly as it has been every morning since I arrived here. An idyllic Groundhog Day. We've been here just over a week now and were due to travel back to London today. I would have gone back to my shabby flat in Tooting and my boring job. Instead, I'm a lady of leisure hanging out at a French château. Life could be worse.

Miles puts down his phone and leans over to rearrange my hair, making sure the bite mark he left on my neck this morning is covered. 'Sorry,' he says. 'I'll try not to get carried away in future.'

I smile. We spent a lot of this past weekend in bed. At one

point, I jokingly reassured him we would still have plenty of sex after we were married, but he remained insatiable. During each intimate moment, I couldn't get the naked photograph of Riley out of my head. The confident, seductive way she looked at the camera. How at ease she seemed in her own skin. As I writhed and contorted myself into various positions for Miles' pleasure, I couldn't shake the idea I was competing sexually with a dead woman. I couldn't help wanting to outdo her.

Part of me wishes I'd never looked in the drawer and found that photograph. Or the others of Riley at the château. I can't get any of the images out of my mind. Serves me right for snooping. My mother would have called it research. She said I should always find out everything I could about a potential partner's exes. That, she believed, would tell me everything I needed to know about the man. How did the relationship end? What baggage did it leave him with?

Yesterday, even though I promised myself not to obsess about Miles' past, I crept into the study while he was taking a nap and Vivienne was in her room. I wanted another look at the photographs, but the desk drawer was locked. For a moment I worried Vivienne had seen me prying, but Miles probably locked the drawer to protect his privacy. To protect his memories of his dead wife.

Afterwards, I couldn't resist doing more online research about Riley using her maiden name. All I found was a staff profile of her at a skydive centre in San Diego, where she worked as an instructor a few years before she met Miles.

Vivienne appears with Granny Sinclair's coffee pot. We exchange pleasantries about the weather as she fills my cup, but I haven't forgotten our encounter in the study. Her words have also been on my mind.

You've got plenty of time to really get to know one another.

I haven't come this far to let either Riley or Vivienne sabotage me.

'Could we go out somewhere this morning?' I ask Miles,
once we are alone again. 'Just for a few hours.' Lovely as the
château is, I'm starting to feel a bit cooped up. Some time away
from here and away from Vivienne would be great.

'Sure,' he says. 'We'll take the bikes out and I'll show you
the local dairy. Beautiful place. We'll pick up some fresh milk.'

'Thanks.'

He pushes his empty glass bowl aside and reaches for the
blue cardboard folder at the middle of the table. 'Just need to
go over a bit more paperwork,' he says.

I expect him to produce another legal document to do with
the wedding ceremony, but instead he lays in front of me a
thick paper document held together with a paper clip.

Kingsley Law

Miles Sinclair and Leah Rose Williams

Prenuptial Agreement

'Sorry, darling,' he says. 'I thought it best to get the bloody
thing out of the way.'

'Sure. Of course.' I'm alarmed to feel the hot sting of tears in
my eyes. I blink them away. Why would I be upset by this? I
expected it, didn't I? Any rich man with his wits about him
would make me sign one of these. I resist the temptation to ask
if Riley had to sign one too.

'Obviously you can get a lawyer to look at it,' Miles says. 'If
you feel you need to. I can recommend someone, but we do
need it done soon.'

'Yes. No problem. I know a lawyer who can help me.'

'Great. I'll forward an email copy to you.' He gives me a

tentative smile. 'I hope you'll find it fair. I want you to be confident you'll be well looked after.'

He looks so earnest. So eager not to offend me.

'I'm sure it will all be fine,' I say. 'I'll ask my lawyer to look it over so we can get it signed and done with as soon as possible.'

'Thank you.' He strokes my arm. 'Your co-operation tells me everything I need to know about you.'

16

LEAH

July

'How did it go with your lawyer?' Miles asks when he comes upstairs after finishing his work calls.

'She was very helpful. I've forwarded the document to her and she said she'll look at it as soon as possible.'

I don't have a lawyer and can't afford one, but I have identified several websites offering useful advice about prenuptial agreements as well as endless YouTube videos by legal professionals and vloggers. I'm sure I'll be able to find out what I need to know.

'Excellent.' Miles appraises the outfit I've chosen for our morning's excursion. Navy Chloé culottes, a sleeveless top in cream linen and white Veja trainers. 'Very nice. You all good to go?'

I jam my straw fedora onto my head. 'Good to go.'

At the front of the château, two bicycles with wooden baskets lean against the building.

'I've checked them over and pumped up the tyres,' Miles says.

We set off down the drive. When we reach the château's gates, Miles rides his bike up to the keypad and punches in four numbers.

'What's the code?' I ask as the gates swing open.

'The code?' He looks at me, confused.

'For the gate.' I have no idea how to get out of this place. Nor do I possess any keys.

'It's 1814,' he says. 'The year the château was completed.'

We set off along the narrow country road, shaded by the beech trees overhead. We soon reach Sacy-le-Petit, a small, neat village of solid sandstone cottages. We pass an old church and a modern primary school. On the outskirts of the village we stop and Miles points out a sugar refinery in the distance across the vast fields. A sprawling steel monstrosity, glinting in the sunlight.

When we set off again, I surge ahead, pedalling fast. It feels good to get my body moving and the wind in my hair is exhilarating. After a while I realise Miles is lagging behind and slow down. When he catches me up, I try and ignore how red his face is and how hard he is panting. Don't want to embarrass him.

The dairy farm is a small, family-run operation, accessed by a bumpy, rutted driveway. When we arrive, a tall, bulky man greets Miles like an old friend.

'This is Pierre,' Miles says, introducing us. 'He owns this wonderful place.'

Pierre's grubby jeans are tucked into muddy wellingtons. By contrast, his white overcoat is pristine. When Miles tell him about our engagement, Pierre's bloodshot grey eyes subject me to an intense inspection. His interest isn't sexual, like the mayor's. Instead he's examining me as if I'm a cow for sale at an auction. He grunts and nods to himself, as if satisfied with what he's seen.

'Congratulations,' he says. 'Very happy for you.'

He leads us into a nearby barn filled with large white cows. The air in here is earthy and pungent and the dominant sound is the cows peacefully munching hay. Miles and I stand near one of the stalls while Pierre settles on a milking stool and with firm, rhythmic movements coaxes milk from the teats of a patient cow into a metal bucket. Miles explains that Pierre will bottle this fresh milk for us.

'It's the best taste ever,' he says. 'I promise you.'

When we emerge from the barn, Pierre leads us across the courtyard, the bucket of milk sloshing at his side.

'Monsieur Sinclair.' A woman's voice, rough and husky. 'Miles.'

I turn to see a short, stocky woman in a paisley dress hurrying across the courtyard towards us.

'Estelle.' Miles says. '*Bonjour.*'

'Poor Estelle,' Pierre says. 'Very sad.'

When the woman reaches us, she is older than I first thought. Red clips hold her straggly silver hair back from her lined face. Her wrinkled hands clutch the purple bum bag that rests on her stomach.

'Miles.' Estelle's face lights up. '*Mon petit.*' She grips him in a tight hug. 'Such a big boy now.'

'Madame Framboust was our housekeeper at the château for many years.' Miles eases himself free of her embrace. 'It's good to see you, Estelle. We miss you at Clairvallon.'

'She has... how do you say it... dementia,' Pierre tells me. 'Very sad. Her daughter, Béatrice, looks after her. Very hard for the family.'

'Yes. I can imagine.'

Pierre excuses himself and strides across the courtyard to one of the outbuildings, clutching the bucket of milk. I glance around the courtyard. There must be someone with Estelle?

The old woman turns her attention to me. Her smile vanishes. Confusion clouds her dark eyes. '*Où est Riley*?' she says, her voice taut with anxiety. '*Dis-moi.*'

Even with my poor French, I know she is asking where Riley is. On her tongue, the dead woman's name sounds like *Reeley*.

'*Où est-elle*?' she says. 'Where is she?'

She clearly expects to see Miles and Riley together. No wonder she's confused.

'Maman.'

I turn and see a man walking in our direction. He is about my height, his lean, muscular body dressed in dark jeans and a grey T-shirt. One hand clutches a plastic bottle filled with milk, the other he runs through his black shoulder-length hair. I guess him to be in his early thirties.

'Maman,' he says, '*tu ne peux pas partir comme ça.*'

Maman. He must be her son.

'*Jacques.*' Relief softens her face. '*Jacques, c'est Monsieur Sinclair. C'est Miles.*'

Miles tenses beside me. Jacques stares at him, as if lost for words. Is it me or does this encounter feel awkward?

'Jacques.' Miles holds out his hand. 'Good to see you. How are you?'

After a slight hesitation, Jaques accepts the handshake. 'I am well,' he says. 'You?'

'Very well indeed.' Miles lands a manly, almost paternal slap on Jacques' back before releasing his hand. 'I thought you were working in Marseilles?'

'Yes. I am,' Jacques says. 'But Béatrice, she needs a holiday, so I am here to help Maman.'

Jacques glances at me. Beneath his thick black eyebrows are his mother's dark, soulful eyes. My heart rate quickens. He is good-looking, no doubt about that. I wait for Miles to introduce me but instead he tells Jacques he is sure Estelle must be delighted to have him at home.

'I am not back for good,' Jacques says hurriedly. 'It is a visit and then I will be gone.'

Estelle is looking from Miles to me and back again. Terror crawls across her face.

'*Tu vas me mettre dans une maison de retraite?*' she says.

Jacques slips an arm around her shoulder. '*Non,* Maman.'

'No, Estelle,' Miles says. 'No one is going to put you in an old people's home.'

Poor Estelle. I don't have much experience of dealing with people with dementia, but her condition seems pretty advanced. It must be scary, not knowing where you are half the time. Not knowing if you might be carted off to a care home at any moment.

'*Merci, Monsieur Sinclair,*' Estelle says to Miles. '*Merci.*' Then she looks at me and her expression changes. '*Qui êtes vous? Où est Riley?*'

'I am sorry,' Jacques says. 'She is not well.'

'Please, don't apologise,' I say. 'It's totally fine.'

He nods and, gripping his mother's hand firmly, leads her away to a black Hilux parked near the cowshed.

'Where is Riley?' Estelle shouts as Jacques opens the passenger door for her. 'What have you done with her?'

17

LEAH

July

Before dinner, we go for a walk around the château grounds, leaving Vivienne in the kitchen preparing an Ottolenghi recipe that involves dicing a mountain of aubergines. I did ask if she wanted help but was relieved when she refused my offer. Will she eat with us again like she did last night, or will she eat alone in her room, as she seems to prefer?

'Routine is good for her,' Miles says as we stroll across the back lawn. 'Staying busy keeps her mind off things.'

Vivienne has been in a strange mood since Miles and I returned from the farm. When Miles told her about our encounter with Estelle and Jacques, she looked startled.

'Jacques is back home?' she said. 'I thought he was off doing labouring work somewhere?'

'He's just helping out while Béatrice is on holiday,' Miles said.

'Béatrice must be desperate for a break if she's allowed Jacques to take over. The two of them are more or less estranged.' Vivienne sucked on her vape pen. 'When is she coming back?'

Miles shrugged. 'I don't know exactly. But when she does, he'll be off again.'

'I should hope so,' she said. 'He's hardly ideal carer material.' She glanced at me. 'Sorry if I sound harsh, but Estelle is very dear to us. Miles and I have known her since we were infants. And of course, she and Riley adored each other.'

'Of course,' I said. Trust Vivienne not to miss an opportunity to mention Riley. I thought Jacques seemed very tender with his mother at the farm, but I kept that opinion to myself. Miles didn't mention Estelle's concern about Riley's whereabouts. Her confusion and distress. I decided not to bring the subject up with him. He must have found Estelle's words upsetting.

Where is Riley? What have you done with her?

Now, as we meander across the lawn, the early evening sun gilding everything around us, Estelle's haunting words seem like nothing more than the ramblings of a senile old woman. She has probably forgotten Riley is dead.

I should forget about Estelle. I should forget about her son and his dark, brooding eyes. To distract myself, I focus on the beauty around me. This is fast becoming my favourite time of day at the château. The sun has lost its sting and the flowers and herbs that grow all over the property are at their most aromatic.

'Let's take a look at the outbuildings,' Miles says. 'I haven't checked on them yet.' He is still withdrawn, the remnants of a dark mood upon him. Seeing Estelle like that today and hearing Riley spoken about was bound to be hard for him. Before we came for a walk, when I showed him my dinner outfit – a Dior maxi dress in pale blue linen with thin white straps – a brief smile was his only comment. He looks a bit dishevelled, his white linen shirt in need of ironing and a small stain from last night's dinner on the front of his beige chinos. Details he would normally notice and rectify. Are these the kind of things I'm supposed to deal with now, as a prospective wife?

The smooth lawn gives way to a dusty weed-choked path. I wish I'd worn something more practical than my Chloé slides. The path leads us eventually into a courtyard of unkempt grass and patches of gravel. To our right is a stone barn with a slate roof. Ivy has taken over almost all of the building's exterior. Smaller buildings huddle at the far end of the courtyard – several sheds and a long, low tumbledown cottage. Beyond the barn, a line of pine trees marks the start of the woods that border the château.

At the centre of the courtyard lies a red wheelbarrow tipped on its side. Next to it lie clear plastic sacks filled with grass and leaves and a tangle of green hosepipe. Rusted cogs and bolts hide amongst the grass and weeds. This must be the working area of the château. The messy reality behind the idyllic facade.

'Christ, what a shambles.' Miles kicks away a paintbrush lying in the grass in front of him. 'That's the problem with these old places. The maintenance is a bloody nightmare.'

Where he sees a nightmare, I see renovation potential. 'That cottage could be so cute,' I say. 'You could do it up and make it into two rental properties.'

He shrugs. 'Maybe I'll get round to it one day.'

Maybe *I* will, after we're married. As much as I'm going to enjoy my lazy summer here, I'll have to do something with my time eventually. Even I would get bored without some kind of project and kids alone won't satisfy me. If I could persuade

Miles to let me make a business of this place, it could help cover the running costs.

'Can we look inside the barn?' I ask, already envisioning it as some kind of yoga studio.

'Another time.' He turns and marches back towards the path, leaving me to follow. 'I'll show you the potager,' he says.

'The what?'

'Potager. It means a kitchen garden.'

When we reach the lawn, he turns right and leads me into the walled garden. This too, has fallen into disrepair. An apple tree, low and sprawling, stands at its centre. Four soil beds radiate out from it, divided by planks of wood.

This garden was in one of the photographs I found in the desk. The one with Riley kneeling by a vegetable bed, displaying an armful of colourful lettuce leaves. I wonder if this garden was her project? If so, she would be sad to see what has become of it. Nettles and weeds have replaced the vegetables and fruits that once grew here. I imagine her, dressed as she was in the picture in her hot pants and T-shirt, kneeling beside the neglected vegetable beds and shaking her head in dismay.

Miles crouches down by one of the beds and pulls out a handful of weeds. 'I should never have let it get into this state.'

'Don't you have a gardener who could come and sort it out?' The lawns were freshly cut when I arrived, so I assume he must have used someone recently.

'No.' He tosses the weeds aside and savagely rips out another handful.

Irritation pulses through me. Minding what I say all the time and treading so carefully around the past is exhausting. Why can't we discuss everything openly? 'You must have had one?' I say. 'Before you let all your staff go.'

'Who told you about the staff?' He drops the weeds on the ground and straightens up. 'Viv?'

'No. Naomi.'

'Naomi?'

'She works at that florist in Montreuilac but she used to clean here.'

'I don't remember her.'

'Blonde hair, pretty,' I say. 'Around my age. Lots of earrings and a nose stud.'

'I never paid much attention to the women who came in to clean,' he says dismissively.

Really? I would have thought that as the château owner he'd know everyone he employed. Maybe he knew Naomi better than he's letting on. I think of the way she looked me up and down when I asked if she knew Miles.

Not any more.

Did that mean she once knew him intimately? Miles wouldn't be the first boss to sleep with one of his employees. I wouldn't judge him for it. Or Naomi. Having slept with a married man myself, that would be a touch hypocritical.

'In the past, Estelle did most of the cleaning,' he says. 'When it got too much for her, she hired extra staff to help. Eventually, Riley took over the management of the staff.'

'Why did you let them all go?' I ask.

'I shut the place down after... after Riley. I couldn't bear to be here. I even considered selling it.' His eyes narrow. 'What else did this Naomi say?'

Heat creeps into my cheeks. I don't want us to slide back into the past, but I am about to marry this man. I should be able to share what's on my mind. If it's only a silly rumour, what does it matter? 'She said some people think Riley's death wasn't an accident.'

The birdsong stills around us. That tortured look creeps into Miles' eyes.

'Sondrine, the other florist, she said it was just gossip.' My voice sounds strange – high and breathless.

Miles steps closer to me. His pupils are dark pinpricks in the white mask of his face. 'Is that what you were doing? Gossiping about me?'

'No. Of course not. I—'

His hands grip my shoulders. 'What else did they say about me?'

'Nothing.'

'Christ.' His fingers dig into my flesh. 'As if your wife dying in a tragic accident isn't hard enough.'

'Miles, I—'

'Do they think she jumped? Is that it?'

'They didn't—'

'No, that wouldn't be enough for them, would it? Murder at the château sounds much more thrilling. Château owner throws his wife from the roof. Is that what they said?'

I gasp as his fingers dig deeper into me. 'No, of course not.' Hearing him say those words aloud, the idea sounds ridiculous.

'How dare they talk about her for entertainment? As a distraction from their shitty little lives.'

'Miles, you're hurting me.'

He lets me go, startled, as if he didn't even realise he was holding me. 'God, Leah. I'm sorry.'

'No. I'm sorry.' Sore red petals are unfurling where he gripped me. 'I shouldn't have brought it up.'

He presses his forehead against mine. His breathing is fast and shallow. 'I shouldn't have shouted at you. That was unacceptable.'

'It's okay.' Maybe Vivienne is right. This engagement is too much too soon. Miles clearly has difficult memories to deal with. Buried feelings to address.

'Leah,' he says. 'I'm afraid I haven't been honest with you.'

'About what?'

He hesitates. Then, placing his hands gently on my shoulders, he turns me so I'm looking at the east wing of the château.

'I should have told you everything when you first arrived,' he says, 'but I couldn't face talking about it.' He points towards the extension and the small terrace on top of the flat roof. 'She fell from there.'

'Oh,' I say, as if this is news to me.

'You can climb down onto that bit of roof from the attic window. We were forbidden to go up there, but Bruce and I used to do it all the time as teenagers. Vivienne too. We would sneak out there and smoke or drink some stolen wine.'

I can almost see them up there, three teenagers at sunset, passing a cigarette between them.

'Riley loved it up there. Being a skydiver, she had no fear of heights.'

'It doesn't sound like she was scared of anything.'

'Yes, she was fearless.' He sighs. 'She could also be reckless at times.'

A tingle of something. The strange thrill you get when a partner says something negative about their ex.

'She would often go up there for a cigarette,' he says. 'Or a joint.'

'You smoke weed?'

'No, not me. I'm an old square. But she did sometimes.' He presses himself against the back of my body. 'That's what we think happened the day she died. She went up there for a smoke and must have been standing by the railings. They gave way, you can see where the stonework crumbled, and that was that. I was away in Paris for the day. I found her when I got back. Lying amongst the rubble.'

'I'm so sorry.'

'That's all it takes,' he said, a note of strangled wonder in his voice. 'One stupid accident and it's all over.' He turns me round, tilts my face up to his and kisses me. 'Anyway. I'm sorry. My past is not your problem.'

Another note to self: Do not bring up anything connected to Riley again. Keep your head down. Get through the remaining weeks until the wedding without messing up so you can both enjoy the future together.

'Do you really want to be with me, Leah?' he says.

'Yes.' I press myself against him. We kiss again. His hands slide down my back and gather up my dress in tight fistfuls.

The only way to push Riley further into the past is to make new memories. To block her out of his mind. That's what Miles is trying to do. He doesn't need me reminding him of what he's lost.

I lead him over to the wall. To a bare patch of red brick between two thick tongues of ivy. He watches as I lean against it and, with both hands, reach under my dress and pull off my underwear. Lust fills his eyes as I tease him by touching myself. 'Come here and get down on your knees,' I say.

'No.' He unbuckles his belt and unzips his trousers. 'I can't wait.'

When he lifts me up, I wrap my legs around his waist. When he pushes himself inside me, I gasp. I'm not quite ready and it hurts but it's a good pain and he is in pain too and with every thrust I sense something dark leaving his body. With every thrust, I think of Riley, kneeling by the vegetable patch, watching us. With every thrust I tell her it is time for Miles to finally move on.

18

LEAH

July

The next morning, I wake to find the bed beside me empty. The clock on Miles' bedside table tells me it's almost nine. Seconds later, the grandfather clock in the hallway outside chimes a confirmation.

I throw back the sheet. 'Miles?'

He's not in the en suite bathroom. I quickly brush my teeth and my hair before throwing my turquoise silk robe over my nightdress. I push my feet into my espadrilles before leaving the bedroom. When I find the shower room empty, I head downstairs.

'Vivienne?' Miles calls. 'Hurry up, I'll be late.'

Miles is in the entrance hall, smartly dressed in a crisp white shirt, navy chinos and his tan suede loafers. He has a brown leather satchel slung over one shoulder and his sunglasses tucked into his shirt pocket.

'There you are.' He holds out his arms. 'I didn't want to wake you.'

'Where are you going?' I step into his embrace. We kiss. His cheeks are freshly shaven and he smells of soap and aftershave.

'Paris.' He runs his fingers through the tangled ends of my hair.

'Now?'

'I was up early and when I checked my phone I found a voicemail from Hugo, my contact at the British consulate. He has a cancellation for a lunchtime appointment and he offered it to me so I can get all this paperwork sorted.'

'You should have woken me. I'm meant to come with you.'

He kisses my forehead. 'We'll go dress shopping another time, I promise. I just want to get there and get this sorted. I'll be back this afternoon.'

A sudden longing to be in Paris comes over me. Or is it an urge to get away from the château?

'Have a lazy morning by the pool,' Miles says.

I shrug. 'Yeah. Whatever.'

'I'll bring you something nice back,' he says, his tone placatory, as though I'm a sulky child. 'Vivienne?'

'I'm coming.' Vivienne clatters down the stairs, untying the straps of her apron from around her neck.

'If I miss the fast train I won't get there in time,' Miles says impatiently.

'You're not driving to the station?' I ask.

'Viv's taking Dolly to the garage for a check-up,' he says. 'She's going to drop me off on the way.'

'Nearly ready.' Vivienne disappears into the kitchen. A crashing sound, followed by muted swearing. She reappears, clutching a black tote bag and car keys. 'Let's go.'

A shrill ringing sound fills the entrance hall. Miles and Vivienne glance at the black telephone and then at one another. Why don't they just answer it?

'Bloody thing.' Vivienne marches over to the phone and yanks the lead out of the wall socket.

'Goodbye, darling.' Miles kisses me before striding out of the château into the sunlight.

'I haven't had time to lay any breakfast out,' Vivienne says to me as she follows him. 'Just help yourself from the kitchen.'

'How long will you be?' I ask.

She shrugs. 'Couple of hours. Tops.'

I step out onto the terrace and watch as they pile into the rickety 2CV. The engine needs three attempts before it sputters into life and they set off. Miles waves from the passenger window and I wave back, feeling like a teenager left at home by her parents. As if the two of them have conspired to stop me going to Paris.

As soon as the 2CV is out of sight, I return indoors and kick off my espadrilles. Two whole hours. This is the most time I've had to myself since we got here. My shoulders drop and I let out a deep sigh. I often find myself doing that when Miles and I part company. Not that he's stressful to be around, but when alone again, I become aware of the role I play for him. That's normal, though. Everyone plays different roles for different people.

I saunter across the cool tiles to the kitchen. The first time I saw this room, it surprised me. I'd expected an airy, refurbished space with an Aga and a large kitchen island, like some of the châteaus I've seen on TV renovation shows, but this kitchen, with its one small window, is dark and cramped. Old pans with blackened bases hang from an overhead rack. A dusty wooden dresser houses cups and plates and a blue ceramic dish piled with plump peaches. The room hasn't been updated for years. The oven and hob look like they were installed in the seventies. The bulky, white fridge hums and shudders. The square wooden table at the centre of the room is covered with debris from the prep for last night's dinner – onion skins and carrot peel, the brown flesh of aubergines. Vivienne does not keep an immaculate workspace. The patches of table not covered with food waste and dirty pans bear scratches and burn marks. The air is infused with garlic and onion and a sour smell seeps in from the small anteroom that contains the sink, the rubbish bin and the overflowing compost bin.

Back in the kitchen, I open the juddering fridge. What to have? I spot the leftovers of last night's apricot flan on the top shelf, uncovered. I pull out the flan dish and cut myself a huge slice. This will be heaven with a pot of coffee.

As I wait for the kettle to boil, I examine the corkboard on the wall next to the oven. Scraps of paper, business cards and leaflets are pinned to it. A collage of local information. A piece of blue paper covered with sprawling handwriting grabs my attention. *Estelle Framboust, Les Arbres, Rue des Bois. 07454665832.* The address and phone number of the château's former house-keeper. Maybe all the contact details for former staff were kept here? I search through the layers of paper and card on the board for Naomi the florist but find nothing. If I wanted to speak to her, I could easily ring the shop. Not that I need to. Not now I've resolved to leave the past alone.

I turn my back on the noticeboard, only to notice Vivienne's black apron hanging on the back of the kitchen door. I look away and distract myself with a bite of the flan, pretending to myself I have no intention of checking the apron's deep front pocket for Vivienne's keys.

Who am I trying to kid? I hurry over to the apron and thrust my hand into the pocket. No keys. She might have left them in her room. Why not check? I've been waiting for a chance to look in the east wing.

Munching on the apricot flan as I climb the stairs barefoot, I tell myself I will only go as far as the first-floor landing. A peek in Vivienne's room. Nothing more. When I get to the landing, I glance up at the next flight of stairs. They ascend into darkness. No need to go up there. After what happened with Miles yesterday, I shouldn't go poking around in the past. Him confiding in me about Riley's death forged a new tenderness between us. I felt it last night when we had sex again before falling asleep. Slow, tender sex, so different from our urgent coupling in the garden.

Yet part of me still wants to see the scene of the accident close up. To understand for myself how it could have happened.

After swallowing the last mouthful of flan, I flick the light switch at the bottom of the narrow staircase, casting the wooden steps in a sickly yellow glow. I climb the stairs slowly. At the top, I turn to the door on my left. A strange green light creeps through the cracks in the frame. A sudden chill grips me. I shiver. This château, like all old buildings, must be prone to draughts. Especially up in the attic.

I reach for the doorknob and twist it. The door is locked. Of course it is. No one in their right mind would leave it open. Miles must be thinking of safety above all else.

The door on my right is locked too. I give up and return to the first floor.

The east wing corridor contains five doors. I start with the one at the far end of the corridor. It is locked. I bet this is the room Miles shared with Riley. So frustrating not to be able to get inside. The door beside it opens onto an empty double bedroom. The next room is a dingy kitchenette.

The fourth door along reveals a bathroom I assume Vivienne must use. In the cabinet above the sink, I find an array of

inexpensive skin products and numerous packets of pills. Zopi-
clone and clonazepam. Seems Vivienne needs more than a
summer at a French château to help her get over her
breakdown.

The final door leads me to Vivienne's bedroom. It is a poky,
cluttered space. Against one wall is a small double bed with
muslin drapes screening it off from the rest of the room. Lying
on top of the messy bed is a copy of *Jane Eyre*. I guess as an
English teacher, Vivienne will be familiar with all the classics.
Jane Eyre probably resonates with her notions of a grand love
that can never be replaced. That must be why she approved of
Riley and disapproves of me, even though Riley and I are in
some ways quite similar. Younger than Miles, no family to
speak of, and both able to enjoy the finer things in life. But
Riley and Miles married for love, a claim I can't make for my
own relationship with him.

In front of the window is a small wooden school desk. Did
the children of the château's original owners sit at this desk to
do their lessons? A pair of binoculars lies on the scratched
surface. A shudder runs through me. Does Vivienne use them
to keep an eye on the château grounds? On me? I pick them up,
hold them to my eyes and twist the focus knob back and forth.
The clarity is amazing. I can see right down to the lake and the
pergola. Did Vivienne see Miles proposing to me? Why would
she? She had no idea it was going to happen. To my left, I can
see the roofs of the outbuildings and the woods and to my
right, through a gap in the pines, I glimpse the pool. I can also
see right into the walled garden, which makes me uneasy. Or
maybe it's a good thing if Vivienne saw us having sex in there
yesterday evening. It will have showed her Miles is determined
to move on from the past and so am I.

A banging sound from downstairs distracts me. Has Vivienne come back early? I put the binoculars back where I found them and hurry out of her room. On the landing, I wait, ears straining.

Did I imagine the noise?

'*Bonjour.*' A high, singsong voice echoes in the downstairs hallway. '*Je suis là!*'

Footsteps on the staircase below. Light and brisk. Energetic humming.

'*Bonjour. Monsieur Sinclair? Riley?*'

19

LEAH

July

It is Estelle Framboust, the château's former housekeeper. Climbing the stairs towards me, a red bucket filled with cloths and bottles of cleaning fluid in one hand, and a large, jangling set of keys in the other. Keys. She must have forgotten to give her set back when she stopped working here. Her gaze is fixed on the stairs, and she doesn't look up and see me until she reaches the landing.

'Ah.' She stops and inspects me with dark, wary eyes. '*Qui êtes-vous?*'

'*Bonjour*, Estelle.'

Her expression falters. A deep line appears between her eyebrows as she tries to place me. She wears white sandals with Velcro straps across the front and white ankle socks. Both are covered with dust and flecks of mud, as are her sturdy calves. She must have walked here. She still has the same purple bum bag strapped to her body. She looks like an overgrown child who has got herself grubby after going out to play.

'I am late,' she says. 'Sorry.'

She thinks she still works here. Maybe seeing Miles at the farm yesterday muddled her already fragmented memory, jolting her back into a once familiar routine.

'Who are you?' she asks, her voice edgy with suspicion. If I'm not careful she might kick off like she did yesterday. If I tell her Riley is dead, I'll disrupt this temporary delusion she's living out and upset her.

'Leah, I'm a friend of Riley's.'

She shifts from one foot to another, unconvinced. I sense she is hovering on the edge of her delusion. If I'm not careful I might lose her.

'Riley's gone to the bakery,' I say. 'She'll be back soon. She wanted me to ask you to clean her room first.'

'Okay.' Estelle's face brightens. She feels safe again. 'I can do that.'

I follow her down the east wing corridor to the room at the very end. As she searches through her keys, my heart thumps against my ribcage.

Estelle laughs. 'So many keys.' She finds the one she is looking for, slides it into the lock and pushes the door open.

Darkness greets us. Estelle steps inside and flicks on an overhead light.

'*Quel désordre!*' she says, staring at the untidy room. '*C'est bon. Estelle est là.*' She strides over to the window, pulls aside the red velvet drapes and opens the shutters. Sunlight streams into the room. The window squeaks in protest as she wrestles with the latch, but she wins the contest and flings it wide open.

Then she places her hands on her wide hips and surveys the room. 'Big mess.'

I look around at the room Riley and Miles once shared. It is larger than the one he and I sleep in. At its centre is a modern canopy bed with a divan base and thin muslin curtains hanging down from the pale wooden frame. The bedspread is a rich red velvet. Nothing like the chintz in my room. The artwork here is colourful and impressionistic. Much nicer than the drab rural scenes I have to endure. My skin prickles as I realise the room still looks lived in. A black silk kimono lies crumpled on the unmade bed. A glass of murky water sits on one of the bedside tables. On the ivory damask seat of an antique wooden chair is a pile of tangled women's clothes.

No sign of Miles anywhere. It is as if he removed all traces of himself and then locked the door for good.

Is this exactly how the room looked the day of Riley's death?

The keys Estelle clutches in her hand look identical to Vivienne's. When she catches me looking at them, she unzips her bum bag, drops them inside and zips the bag up again.

'Okay.' She takes a deep breath in, as if steeling herself for the work ahead. First she picks up the black kimono and adds it to the pile of clothes on the chair. Then she picks up the bedspread, lifts it into the air and lets it settle again on top of the white duvet below. Dust swirls in the sunlight. I can't help imagining microscopic fragments of Riley's skin mixed in with it.

'You are Riley's friend?' Estelle asks me.

'*Oui*. Yes.'

'She has many friends. Many friends.'

In Estelle's mind, Riley could walk back into this room at any moment. So strong is her conviction, I begin to believe Riley will walk in and greet me and ask me what I'm doing in her château.

I should call someone. I remember the kitchen noticeboard and the piece of paper with Estelle's contact details pinned to it. I should try that to begin with. I should, but I feel caught in a time warp. One where the present doesn't exist.

As Estelle smooths the bedcover, I edge into the en suite bathroom. The shutters are open in here. I realise this room must be part of the extension at the side of the château. Above me is the roof terrace Riley fell from.

I shudder. That sudden chill again. Another of the château's random draughts?

The bath is positioned next to the window, overlooking the back lawn. Three bottles of aromatherapy oil are lined up on the windowsill and a loofah hangs on a string from the bath's brass taps. Seems like Riley didn't heed the rules about water wastage.

I open the mirrored cabinet over the sink. No trace of Miles inside, but I do find an assortment of La Roche-Posay face creams and serums, as well as a Chanel lip balm in a shiny black case. Unable to resist, I apply the balm to my lips. It tastes of coconut. It feels like a kiss from a dead woman. I put the lip balm in the pocket of my silk gown. A little piece of Riley.

Back in the bedroom, I find Estelle placing the kimono on freshly plumped pillows with reverence. The air is now a strange blend of musty staleness and summer fragrance, like two weather fronts colliding. Isn't that when storms happen?

'Estelle,' I say. 'Does Riley have a lot of male friends?'

'*Les hommes*?'

'*Oui*. Men.'

A coy smile creeps over Estelle's face. 'Men, they love her.'

'But she loves Miles?'

The smile vanishes. Estelle retrieves a cloth from her red bucket and starts polishing the bedside table that once belonged to Riley. '*Oui, bien sûr,*' she says. 'She loves him very much.'

Unwilling to push her, I turn to the dressing table in front of the window and find a small glass bowl filled with make-up. Black eyeliner, a sparkling silver eyeshadow and a red Chanel lipstick. Next to the glass bowl is a bottle of Chanel Cristalle.

The glass lid comes off with a pop. Without thinking, I spray the bottle into the air and dip my nose into the cloud of scent that settles around me.

Estelle gasps and clutches her cloth to her chest. 'Riley?' Her eyes, brimming with tears, dart about the room, as if she has suddenly snapped out of a trance and is surprised at where she finds herself. '*Où est Riley*?' she demands. 'Where is she?'

My trance-like state is broken too. I'm in a room I'm not supposed to be in with a woman with dementia. What the hell am I playing at?

'Shall we go downstairs?' I say. 'I can make us some coffee and—'

'*Non.*' She sits on the bed, arms folded. Her lower lip trembles.

A burst of classical music fills the room. I glance around me. Is there a phone in here somewhere?

Estelle hears it too and, with a bemused expression on her face, she opens her bum bag and pulls out a small, old-fashioned Nokia phone. She holds it up and examines it, as if she has no idea what it is.

I hold out my hand. 'Estelle,' I say in a commanding voice.

She drops the phone on the bed. I snatch it up and press the green call button. 'Hello.'

A pause. 'Who is this?' A man's voice. His English heavily accented. 'You are with my mother?'

'With Estelle?'

'*Oui*. Yes. Estelle.'

'Yes.'

'Thank God.'

It's her son. The man who was with her at the farm yesterday. 'Is this Jacques?'

'Yes. Who are you?'

I tell him my name and remind him of our encounter yesterday.

'Leah?' he says. 'You were there with Miles, *non*?'

Part of me feels pathetically pleased he has remembered me.

'Maman is at the château now?' he asks.

'Yes.'

'*Merde*.'

'You'll have to come and get her. I don't have a car or—'

'Who is there? At the château?'

'Just me.'

'No one else? You are alone?'

'Yes, it's just me.'

'Okay,' he says. 'Tell Maman I come now.'

20

LEAH

July

Eleven minutes later, the buzzer in the hallway sounds and I punch in the entry code. Soon I see a black Hilux speeding up the driveway, kicking up dust. How often do Estelle's children have to come and rescue their mother? It can't be easy, looking after her.

A sharp crunch of gravel as the Hilux brakes and comes to rest next to the Lexus. Jacques jumps out of the truck. His hair is tied back today and he wears a black T-shirt with his jeans, instead of a grey one. I'm still in my nightdress and robe. I didn't want to leave Estelle alone while I got changed in case something happened to her.

Jacques casts a worried glance at Miles' car.

'He's not here,' I say. 'Vivienne drove him to the station.'

Fear flits across Jacques' face. 'When is she coming back?'

'Not for a while. I think.'

'What about her husband?'

'Oh.' Jacques obviously hasn't heard the news. 'Her husband died. Five months ago.'

'I am sorry to hear that.' He tucks a stray strand of hair behind his ear. 'He was a nice guy. The best of them.'

He gazes at the ground for a moment, as if absorbing the news. His tied-back hair has exposed a black ink tattoo of a swallow on the right-hand side of his neck.

'Where is my mother?' he says, when he looks up.

'Upstairs. She wouldn't come down.' When I told Estelle her son was coming to pick her up, she snapped back into her delusion, insisting she had work to finish first.

He follows me into the château, pausing for a moment in the entrance hall.

'She thinks she still works here,' I say. 'She's obviously confused.'

He nods. 'Seeing Monsieur Sinclair muddled her up. Before then she was not thinking about this place.'

'I hope it didn't upset her too much.'

'You say she is upstairs?'

'Yes. In Riley's room.'

He sets off ahead of me. On the first-floor landing, he doesn't hesitate before moving down the east wing corridor towards Riley's room. No directions needed.

He stops in the doorway.

'What's wrong?' I ask.

'Nothing.' He steps into the room. His expression is neutral as he glances around, but his jaw muscles are clenched tight. Riley's perfume hangs in the air. He closes his eyes. Inhales.

'Jacques.' Estelle appears in the bathroom doorway, a cloth in her hand. She hurries over to him and swaddles him in a tight hug, as if she is the one who has been worried about him.

When they part, he glances down at her dirty shoes and socks. 'Maman. Look at you. *Quel état!*'

She giggles like a girl.

'She walked here through the woods,' he says. 'Her cottage is on the other side of them. She used to walk to the château all the time.' He shakes his head. 'A care worker was supposed to come this morning for two hours, but she did not. I had to leave Maman alone a little while. I thought she would be okay.'

I recall Vivienne's reservations about Jacques as a carer. Again, I don't want to judge. It must be impossible to keep an eye on her twenty-four seven.

'My son, he is the gardener here,' Estelle says proudly. 'He makes the château look so beautiful.'

'You're the gardener?' I ask Jacques.

He shakes his head. 'Not any more.'

Estelle smiles up at him. 'So clever.' She walks back towards the bathroom.

'Maman,' Jacques says. 'Time to go.'

'I finish in here,' she says. 'Then we go.'

Jacques sighs. 'Can we wait? She may get angry if I make her leave.'

'It's fine,' I say. 'No rush.'

In the bathroom, Estelle hums. A tap gushes, then stops. Birdsong floats into the room. Jacques stares at me. I stare back. His eyes travel over me, as if taking in my half-dressed appearance for the first time. He has a wolfish air about him. A hint of danger. He definitely belongs in the bad-boy category.

He bites his lower lip. 'So.' He reaches for my left hand, lifts it up and examines my engagement ring. 'You are engaged to Miles?'

'Yes.' His thumb presses into my palm. 'Aren't you going to congratulate me?'

'Should I?' His dark eyes probe mine. A spark ignites low in my belly.

'That would be the polite thing to do.' The black swallow on his neck beckons me closer. I step towards him. My heart thumps against my ribs. A sudden urge to kiss him overcomes me.

Before I can give in to the urge, he drops my hand and steps away.

'Maman,' he says. 'We have to go.'

From the bathroom comes the sound of a toilet flushing. Estelle bustles into the bedroom, carrying her red bucket.

'Okay,' she says. '*Je suis prêt.*'

I feel dizzy. Disorientated. Overcome in a way I don't understand.

Estelle nestles into her son. He wraps a protective arm around her and kisses the top of her head.

'Don't tell anyone about us coming here,' he says. 'Please.'

'I'm sure Miles would understand. He knows your mother's ill.'

His expression hardens. There is an edge about him, despite his tenderness with Estelle. 'Please,' he says. 'I don't want anyone to know I was here.'

He takes his mother's hand. She looks suddenly tired. She looks as if she might cry.

'Goodbye, Leah,' he says.

'Wait. Your mother has a set of keys. In her bag.'

'Keys?'

'For the château. I'll have to take them back.'

Jacques murmurs an instruction to Estelle in French. She sighs, opens the bum bag and passes him the keys. When I hold out my hand for them, he hesitates.

'It wouldn't be right for her to keep them,' I say.

He shrugs and dangles the keys in front of me. When I take them, his fingers circle my wrist, trapping it tight. My pulse jolts. 'Good luck, Leah.' He says good luck as if he thinks I will really need it and also as if he knows luck will be no use to me.

'*Au revoir*,' Estelle says as Jacques leads her to the bedroom door.

At the last moment, he turns to look at me. 'Be careful,' he says.

21

LEAH

July

'Viv, this looks delicious.' Miles heaps his plate with couscous and pomegranate salad. 'Doesn't it, Leah?'

'Yes. Amazing.' I smile at Vivienne, who gives me a cool nod in return.

A rush of guilt. Vivienne didn't return to the château until an hour after Jacques and Estelle left, but my conscience is playing tricks on me. Making me think she knows I'm hiding something.

It is almost eight-thirty at night, and we are eating out on the terrace. The air is balmy, the daylight fading all around us. Thin streaks of pink sunset cloud split the sky. A colourful spread decorates the table in front of me. Numerous different salads, bowls of olives and artichokes and a platter of charcuterie.

Miles only returned from Paris an hour ago. After dealing with the paperwork at the consulate, Hugo took him out for a late lunch followed by cocktails at the George IV Hotel. Then he went shopping. The Chloé wraparound dress I'm wearing now, a black, silky number, is one of the gifts he brought back for me.

'Allow me.' Miles spoons couscous salad onto my plate. As he does so, some of it drops onto the napkin on my lap. 'Sorry, darling.'

He is drunk. Not unpleasantly so. I've never seen Miles nasty drunk. He is talkative, enthusiastic, expansive. He insisted on fetching a dusty bottle of Pinot Noir from the cellar beneath the kitchen. A 1980s vintage from a vineyard in the Loire. It's supposed to be special. When we all took our first sip we made appreciative noises, but to me it tastes musty and harsh.

'So,' he says, after sampling his first mouthful of the salad. 'Tell me everything. What did you girls get up to today?'

I concentrate on gathering a forkful of salad. No need for me to share the events of my day with Miles. Not only did I promise Jacques I wouldn't say anything, but I doubt Miles would like the thought of me being in Riley's room. He certainly wouldn't like to hear about Jacques taking my hand in his. Or of the strange urge I had to kiss him.

'Not much,' Vivienne says. 'When I got back from the garage with Dolly, I did some cleaning. Then I sat outside and read this afternoon. Shame Leah had such a bad headache. We could have gone for a walk in the woods. It's always so cool in there on a hot day.'

The mention of the woods makes my stomach lurch. As if Vivienne is hinting she knows who walked through them earlier today.

'Yes, how is your head, darling?' Miles asks me.

'Better now. Thanks.'

'Just as well you slept it off,' Vivienne says. Her lips are stained red with wine. She doesn't usually drink, but when Miles presented us with the Pinot Noir, she said it would be rude to refuse such a good vintage.

By the time she got back from the garage, I was already in bed with the shutters closed against the sunlight, claiming a possible migraine. I wasn't lying. A crushing headache gripped my temples, forcing me to lie still with my eyes closed. Each time I thought of Jacques, the pain intensified, but I couldn't stop. I thought about the black swallow tattooed on his neck and his dark eyes and the way he bit his lower lip when he looked at me.

Before Vivienne returned, I restored Riley's room to its former disorder, messing up everything Estelle had tidied. As I picked up the black silk kimono from where Estelle had left it perfectly folded on the pillow, I couldn't resist holding it to my nose and inhaling. It smelled musty, although I did detect a trace of the Chanel Cristalle. A scent I haven't been able to get out of my nostrils since. On my way down to dinner, I thought I caught a hint of it on the first-floor landing.

'So,' Vivienne says. 'Everything went smoothly at the consulate?' She pushes her couscous around her plate with her fork. No wonder she is frail as a bird; she eats like one.

'Absolutely.' Miles squeezes my thigh beneath the table. 'The documents are all approved.'

'I can't believe it's come together so quickly,' I say. 'The government website made it look so complicated.'

'Miles has a knack for sorting things out,' Vivienne says.

'I have the odd useful contact or two,' he admits.

This could be my reality from now on. All of life's problems and bureaucracy dealt with efficiently by a man with knowledge and contacts. Guilt fizzes beneath my skin at the memory of how tempted I was to kiss Jacques this morning.

Why would I risk sabotaging a potentially great future with Miles?

Don't screw this up, Leah.

My mother's voice in my head. I can't disagree with her. Yet I also can't stop thinking about Jacques wishing me luck when he left. As if he felt sorry for me.

'Talking of contacts,' Miles says, 'I called Philippe on my way back from Paris and, after pulling a few strings, our mayor friend got our initial booking for the ceremony moved forward to Wednesday the sixteenth of August. One o'clock in the afternoon.'

'Well,' Vivienne says, a strange smile on her face. 'It's really coming together, isn't it?'

'That's only three weeks away.' I take a swig of wine. 'I thought this whole process would take longer.'

Miles shrugs. 'Philippe is a handy friend to have.' He squeezes my thigh again. 'No point us hanging around, is there, darling?'

'It's not like there's a huge amount to organise,' Viv says.

'There's my dress,' I point out, 'and the photographer and—'

'Wedding rings?' Miles picks his phone up from the table and, after some clumsy tapping and scrolling, shows me a photograph of two matching platinum wedding bands, nestled on a background of blue velvet. 'I went into the Boucheron store this afternoon and ordered these for us. They had your ring size from the engagement ring.'

'They're beautiful,' I say. The rings are stunning, but it would have been nice to have been involved in choosing them. In this game, however, the man always needs to feel in control. I get that. Money gives Miles power and, if I want to enjoy that money, I will have to get used to him calling certain shots.

Miles picks up the dusty bottle of wine and refills our glasses. 'I think we should do photos here on the morning of the wedding,' he says, 'before the ceremony. Then we'll head to the town hall and, after we're married, we'll have a late lunch at that lovely place near the old church.'

'Café St Honorè,' Vivienne says. 'Yes. I love that place.' She gulps her refreshed wine. 'I'll stay the night at a hotel in Montreuilac. Let you lovebirds have this place to yourself.'

Lovebirds? She is either more drunk than I thought or she's being sarcastic.

'There's no need for that,' Miles says.

'None at all,' I add.

Viv shakes her head. 'I insist.'

'Right,' Miles says. 'That's settled. Wedding day planned.' He clinks his glass against mine. 'Cheers, darling.'

'Cheers,' I say. Seems like my input to my wedding day will be minimal.

Vivienne's keys are lying on the table, next to her vape pen. I hid the keys I took from Estelle in the internal compartment of my empty suitcase. Possessing them at least gives me a morsel of power. The locked rooms of the château are no longer solely under Vivienne's control.

She puts down her cutlery, picks up her vape pen and takes a deep inhalation. 'So how was young Hugo?' she asks Miles.

'Smart, funny and a social animal. Just like his father.' Miles swigs his wine. 'The place he took me to for lunch was the same one Hugo took us to that summer.'

'Summer 1985?' Vivienne says. 'The night we ended up in that club in Montmartre?'

'Yes,' Miles says. 'That night.'

Vivienne laughs. A sound I realise I've never heard before. Girlish laughter that still carries a hint of breeding. Maybe it's the wine. If she's taking a concoction of those pills I saw in her bathroom, she probably shouldn't be drinking at all.

'How did we even get into that nightclub?' Miles asks. 'You were only fourteen.' He turns to me. 'We used to drag Viv out with the boys back then.'

'They were a bad influence,' she says. 'Especially Bruce.'

The pause is tiny but unmistakeable. A nanosecond of remembrance for Bruce that vanishes when Vivienne dissolves into more peals of laughter.

'Do you remember that girl who followed you around the club the whole night, trying to get off with you?' she says.

Miles groans. 'The one in the—'

'White mini skirt and pink, fluorescent boob tube. Total Eurotrash.'

'She was terrifying.'

'Miles was so shy,' Vivienne tells me. 'Girls always fancied him, but he was rubbish at chatting them up.'

He winks at me. A gesture that makes him look like a naff uncle. 'I was too much of a gentleman.'

'Yeah right.' Smoke trails from Vivienne's nostrils.

Miles gasps. 'Wasn't that the night Hugo met that older woman and she took us all back to her flat in the Marais and fed us onion soup?'

Vivienne gasps even louder. 'Oh my God, yes.'

More laughter. They continue to reminisce about that night, sharing stories that happened before I was even born. I zone out and listen to the frilly tweeting of the small brown skylarks that flit about the lawn and peck around for crumbs on the patio. I conjure up the photograph of Riley, taken here on the terrace. I imagine her sitting with us now, in her white, strapless cocktail dress, a large glass of the Pinot Noir in her hand. Looking across the table at me with a coy smile on her face. As if she knows exactly what I wanted to do to Jacques.

I press my lips together. Beneath my pink lipstick is a layer of her lip balm. After applying it, I hid the lip balm in my suitcase next to my keys. Silly, but it makes me feel as if I have a connection to her.

I glance up at the window of her bedroom. It will once again be dark and silent in there. I recall how Jacques knew exactly where the room was. I remember Estelle telling me that men liked Riley. Do I really think Riley had an affair with the gardener? Bit cliché, isn't it? Jacques is a former employee here and he must have also visited the château many times with Estelle over the years. He probably knows this place inside out.

'Leah?' Vivienne's voice, clear and sharp, jolts me out of the past. 'What do you think?'

'Sorry.' I look from her to Miles. 'I missed the question.'

'Not to worry.' Miles leans towards me and kisses my cheek. 'I have a feeling eighties music trivia is not your forte.'

'Don't be so sure,' I say. 'I grew up with eighties music. My mother loved it.'

Another tiny, unmistakeable pause.

Vivienne snorts. 'Your *mother* loved it. That's priceless.'

'Sorry,' I say. 'I wasn't meaning...'

A wry smile from Miles. 'It's not your fault, darling. We *are* old.'

Vivienne knocks back the rest of her wine. 'You're old enough to be her father.'

Miles tenses beside me.

'Oh come on,' Vivienne says. 'We might as well laugh about it. When you're married, people will say stuff like that to you all the time.'

Miles sighs and softens. 'You're right.' He slips an arm around my waist. 'Pour this old man a drink, would you?'

'I don't know if I should,' I say teasingly, playing along. 'We need to look after your health at your age.'

'Leah Williams. She's a lover and a carer.' Vivienne's tone is as playful as mine.

'I'm not quite ready for the carer part.' I kiss Miles' cheek. 'I'm hoping to get a bit more life out of him before then.'

'You will, darling.' Beneath the table, his hand lifts my dress and slides up my thigh. 'I promise you.'

'Stop groping, old man,' Vivienne says. 'It's unbecoming.'

Miles rolls his eyes at her. 'Spoilsport.' We all laugh as he removes his hand from my thigh with a flourish.

In terms of atmosphere, this is the best meal we've had since I arrived. Maybe now the date for the wedding is set, Vivienne knows she must accept the situation.

Darkness creeps up on us. Vivienne lights the thick white candles at the centre of the table. For dessert, we eat baked peaches with crème fraiche. Miles insists on making coffee. As soon as he disappears into the château, Vivienne leans across the table, her pale face ghoulish in the candlelight, her lips stained a deep red.

'I assume you've sorted your prenup?' she says.

'Prenup?' I say, caught off guard. 'Yes. I mean, we're on to it.'

'Don't be embarrassed.' She leans back in her seat and sucks on her vape pen. 'Prenups are standard for this family.' She sighs. 'They're supposed to be, anyway.'

Supposed to be. Who in the family didn't have one? Miles and Riley?

'My lawyer's looking it over,' I tell her. 'For due diligence.'

By that I mean I will soon be ploughing through the legal

advice I've found online to ensure my marriage to Miles will leave me richer than I am now.

'Very wise,' says Vivienne. 'Pity they don't have adultery clauses in UK prenups like they do in America.' Her face is in shadow, her expression unreadable. 'Not that a legal clause stops people,' she continues, her words beginning to slur. 'Didn't stop my husband.'

Okay. I did not see this coming. 'Your husband had an affair?'

'He did. Not long before... before the end.'

'That's awful.'

'I found out, naturally.' A sucking sound. A trail of smoke from her nostrils. 'I confronted him, we fought and then he drove away. I never saw him again.'

'Vivienne, that's awful.'

'It is what it is.' She leans into the candlelight again, a gaunt apparition. 'Have you ever slept with a married man, Leah?'

'Me?' An echo of my earlier headache stirs at my temples. 'No.' Not a chance I'm going to be with honest with her about that. Even if we are having some kind of sharing, bonding moment. 'I've never needed to take someone else's man.'

I think about Nick, the last man I had an affair with. Shy and sweet and so grateful just to be wanted.

'That's good to know.' Vivienne's eyes drill into me. 'I hated the woman he had the affair with. Still do.' She sighs. 'I know Dom was equally responsible and I know I'm a bad feminist for blaming the woman, but I can't help myself.' She sinks back into the shadows. 'To be honest with you, Leah, I wanted to kill her.'

PART II

22

VIVIENNE

Two Months Earlier, May

Love is the foundation of all relationships. People who don't understand that need to learn. People who don't respect love need to be taught a lesson. People like Leah Williams.

On the night he first met with Leah, Miles arrived at my flat in South Kensington shortly after 11 p.m.

'Well?' I said, after I'd ushered him into the living room.

'I got my driver to take her home.'

'Ever the gentleman.'

He cleared a space for himself on the book-strewn sofa and sat down. I'd inherited the two-bedroom flat from Mum and had never cleared out any of her extensive library. Nathan lived here when he was studying at the London School of Economics, but this is the first time I've stayed here for a while. Anything to avoid rattling around the house in Kent by myself.

'Whisky?' I said.

He held up both palms. 'I'm good. We... I've already had quite a few.'

'You paid the bill, I suppose?'

'I could hardly—'

'Don't make me drink on my own.'

'Fine,' he said, 'if you insist.'

Too weak to say no to a drink. What chance did he stand with Leah Williams?

I poured us both a shot of the 1972 Brora from the bottle on top of the gold Art Deco drinks trolley. As I handed him his crystal tumbler, I smelled perfume. Something musky and slutty. Her scent all over him already. Marking her territory. 'Cheers,' I said.

'Cheers.' He clinked his glass against mine.

I sat in the brown leather armchair opposite him. 'This was Dominic's favourite whisky,' I said after the first bracing sip.

Miles nodded solemnly. 'He had great taste in whisky.'

Tears clawed at my throat. I cauterised them with another sip of alcohol. That girl had made me cry far too many times. No more.

I lit a cigarette.

'You said you were going to give up,' Miles said.

'Don't nag. I will. Soon.' I'd only started smoking again after losing Dom. Who could blame me during such a crisis?

'How's Nathan?' Miles asked. 'Still loving New York?'

I shot him a withering look. One that made it clear we weren't doing small talk tonight. 'What was she like?'

'Nothing special.' An involuntary smile, brief but unmissable, betrayed him. Why did people think they could get away with lies?

'You were there long enough,' I said.

'We talked for ages.' He sipped his whisky. 'She was very easy to talk to.'

'Of course she bloody was. She was trying to hook you in.'

Just like she had with my husband. A gnawing sensation deep in my belly as I pictured Dom in bed with her. Pillow talk. *I wish I could speak to my wife like this.*

Miles looked crestfallen. As if he believed Leah had actually taken a genuine interest in him. Yes, he still had his looks, but only just. Riley's death had aged him. It wouldn't be long until that soft belly of his became unmanageable and his distinguished grey hair fell out. As if someone as stunning as Leah Williams would bother with him if he wasn't rich.

Another inequality of the sexes that infuriated me. Men with money didn't have to worry about preserving their looks. Women would always pay them attention. Take Dom for example. I'd always found him handsome, but he was actually quite ordinary to look at. Average height, very thin thanks to his passion for endurance running, wide hazel eyes and mousy brown hair receding at the temples. His sensitivity, intelligence and good listening skills made him popular with women, but I'm sure it was his willingness to splash out on five-star hotels and expensive meals that attracted Leah Williams.

'What was she wearing?' I asked.

'Wearing?' He looked perplexed. 'I don't know... some sort of black dress.'

I'd looked at pictures of her so many times that I could easily imagine her in a number of different black dresses. She existed like some kind of Barbie doll in my mind. One I could dress and undress at will. In some of the photographs I'd seen on my husband's phone she was naked.

You're so fucking hot. Nick x

Nick. Dominic was known as Dom to those who loved him.

Not Nick. She didn't know him. Not really. Yet he still wanted to leave me for her.

'Did you ask to see her again?' I said.

He shot me a wary look. 'She's very young.'

'More than aware of that, thank you. That's why my husband was fucking her.' I summoned the image of Leah's naked body. Her smooth décolletage. Those buoyant breasts. My hand touched the dry, crinkling skin on my chest and fluttered away again, repulsed.

'She's only twenty-four,' he added.

'She's an adult. Old enough to know the difference between right and wrong.'

'It's just...' Miles rubbed the tip of his nose with his thumb. 'She seemed... nice. Warm even.'

'Nice? Warm?' My bitter laughter filled the room. 'My husband is gone and it's all her fault.'

'Well, I'm not sure—'

'Let me guess.' I took a slug of whisky. 'You saw a vulnerability in those big green eyes of hers. You saw a lost soul in need of love and protection. A delicate flower waiting for her knight in shining armour.'

From the way he shifted in his seat, I could see I'd hit a nerve.

'Was she easy to talk to, Miles? Did she listen to all your woes?'

He glanced at my glass and then at the bottle of whisky. Trying to gauge how much I'd had to drink. Too much and yes, I knew what a cliché I was. The wronged wife, drunk and spiteful and out for revenge. At times my obsession with Leah Williams scared me. What if I was losing my mind? Grief could do that to a person.

'She behaved in a perfectly acceptable manner.' Miles put

his empty glass on the table. In a minute he would get up and go.

'We have to stick to the plan,' I said. 'That's what we agreed.'

He rubbed his palms together slowly. 'Are you sure she doesn't know who I am?'

'No. She doesn't.' Dom insisted that at no point during the affair had he told Leah his real name or any details about his family. Despite all his lies, I believed him. The evidence I saw on his phone appeared to back him up. He seemed to think the fact he'd kept Nathan and I separate from his sordid behaviour made him somehow honourable.

Miles opened his mouth as if to speak and then closed it again.

'Tomorrow you'll have two dozen red roses delivered to her flat,' I said. 'You can tell her you got the address from the driver.'

'Just a few dates?' he said with a baleful stare. 'That's what we agreed.'

'Just a few dates.' I opened the whisky and poured him another dram. 'String her along a bit. Nothing sinister.' I smiled. 'The whole thing will be over in a couple of weeks.'

23

VIVIENNE

June

Two weeks after Miles approached Leah at the Mandarin Oriental, he and I met for drinks at an obscure wine bar near Covent Garden. One of those chain ones I wouldn't be seen dead in normally. It was early evening on the first day of June. Freakishly warm weather meant that the tables outside the wine bar were packed with after-work drinkers making the most of the sunshine. Miles and I sat indoors in a booth with red velvet seats. He kept casting nervous glances over his shoulder, in the direction of the door, which amused me. We weren't spies involved in some dangerous, high-stakes operation. We were two lonely, grieving souls indulging our bitterness and I, for one, was enjoying the experience.

Miles sipped on a large glass of Chablis. I'd ordered a soda and lime. Being involved with Leah had given me a sense of purpose I'd lacked since losing Dom. I wanted to keep a clear head. I didn't want to miss any details.

'Dom once took her to the Sky Lounge at the Shard,' I said.

'You'd think he would have picked somewhere anonymous like this but no, he took her to one of the flashiest places in town.'

'Vivienne.' Miles brushed a speck of white fluff from the sleeve of his navy blazer. 'I'm not sure I—'

'Do you think he got a kick out of it?' I said. 'Maybe the possibility of getting caught was a turn-on for him?'

My cousin's already ruddy cheeks turned burgundy. 'I don't know.'

'She didn't wear any underwear under her dress when they met,' I said. 'I read it in their texts.' A raw knot of emotion throbbed in my chest. 'Tacky, don't you think?'

Miles said nothing. Had she pulled a similar tarty trick on one of their dates? Bet he didn't feel so special now. Or maybe she hadn't suggested it and that had made him feel worse.

'Well?' I said. 'Tell me everything.'

Miles twisted the stem of his wine glass round and round. 'To be honest, there's not much to tell.'

'To be honest.' I resisted the urge to roll my eyes. 'People always say that when they're lying. Dom used to say that all the time.'

To be honest, Viv, I've got such an early start tomorrow I might as well stay over in London tonight.

'Have you screwed her yet?' I said.

'Christ, Vivienne.'

'I assume that's a yes.' I sighed. 'So predictable.'

'Actually, we haven't... we haven't slept together yet.'

'Really?'

'Really. Like I told you, we mostly talk.'

He explained how keen she seemed for them to get to know one another. He said she wanted a deep connection with a partner, not a one-night stand.

'Don't be weak, Miles.' I fixed him with what I hoped was a

penetrating stare. 'We've both been hurt by people we loved. We said we wouldn't be those people any more. Remember?'

I first brought up my thoughts of revenge on the anniversary of Riley's death. Miles and I were drowning our sorrows together in the lounge of his luxurious, sad bachelor apartment. We were two drunk, broken people trying to come to terms with our losses. Miles was reminiscing about his dead wife. The good times they'd had together.

The bad times too.

When I suggested it might feel good to make careless people face up to the consequences of their actions, he agreed. In fact, he loved the idea. I could tell he wanted to do it not just for his own satisfaction but also to make me feel better. The two of us had always shared a strong and special bond.

Now, in the wine bar, Miles looked less certain about our plan. 'Leah comes across as very genuine,' he said, a sweet, earnest expression on his face.

Poor Miles. He'd always been useless with girls. Despite his good looks and charm, he'd always lacked confidence. I blamed Bruce. His bullying of Miles started at a young age and didn't stop until he died. That combined with the bullying Miles suffered at boarding school really dented his self-esteem.

'She's grooming you for a commitment,' I said. 'It's obvious.'

When he refused to believe me, I took out my phone and showed him one of the videos I'd found on YouTube. In it, a thin blonde influencer from New York called Stacey offered women tips on how to bag a rich man. The video I showed him was called 'When to have sex for the first time' and in it, Stacey told her followers to do exactly what Leah had been doing to Miles for the past fortnight.

As he watched the video, I saw a mixture of hurt and stubborn disbelief in his eyes.

'You've made your point,' he said and then reluctantly added, 'I'll stop seeing her.'

Panic rippled through me. 'No. You can't do that.'

'But I thought you—'

'We need to make her think she's winning the game.'

'The game?'

'Yes. It's a game to these girls. Only this time, Miles, it's a game you and I are going to win.'

For a brief moment, his eyes glinted with anger. 'How?' he said.

I reached into my handbag and took out a square black box with silver letters imprinted on the lid. Cartier.

'Very nice,' he said when I opened the box and showed him the exquisitely fine gold chain with the small diamond pendant attached. Simple, elegant and expensive. I didn't tell him I'd found it when packing up Dom's belongings. My husband, I assumed, had bought the gift for Leah. No point it going to waste.

'I'm willing to bet,' I said, 'that if you give her this rather expensive token, you'll get her into bed in no time.' The necklace was the kind of gift that would motivate Leah to progress to the next stage of the game. One that hinted there could be other, more expensive gifts to come.

Miles snapped the lid of the box shut and pulled it across the table towards him. 'Fine. You're on.'

24

VIVIENNE

June

I won the bet. No surprise there. The Cartier necklace got Leah into Miles' bed less than an hour after he gave it to her.

'Fine,' Miles said when I called him the next day to check in. 'You were right.'

Why did I feel like he was the one who had won something and not me?

'Satisfied?' he said.

'Were you?'

A brief silence. 'I'm not going to discuss details.'

'Such a gentleman.'

'Vivienne, please. You've had your fun.'

'As have you.'

He said nothing but even over the phone I could sense the post-sex glow radiating from him. His chest and ego puffed up after a night with someone thirty years his junior.

'Don't pretend it was a chore,' I said.

'It certainly wasn't that.'

It hurt to hear the satisfaction in his voice, but part of me wanted to feel that pain. One of the most disorientating consequences of discovering my husband's affair was realising that while I'd thought our life had been carrying on as normal, he had been deceiving me. Instead of feeling angry and sad, I had been going about my life as usual. A blissfully ignorant idiot. Now I was almost getting to relive that time, only now I was in control and feeling all the appropriate emotions. It was, in some respects, cathartic.

'I think you should keep seeing her,' I said.

'What?'

'If we want to hurt her and humiliate her, we need to—'

'I never said I wanted to hurt her.'

'Don't be weak, Miles. We both know what happens when you're weak with someone you love.'

He sighed.

'It will hurt her much more if you end it when she thinks she's got her feet under the table,' I said.

'Okay. Okay.' He sounded harassed and weary, but I knew deep inside he was delighted at the thought of sleeping with her again. 'If that's what you really want,' he said.

25

VIVIENNE

June

Manipulating Leah Williams brought me both pleasure and pain. Pleasure in knowing I was controlling her life at a distance, just as she, consciously or unconsciously, had once controlled mine. Pain in thinking about the pleasure Dom must have experienced with her.

During the first week Miles and Leah were having sex, I found it hard to sleep. I couldn't stop thinking about the two of them together. Lying in bed at night, I was overcome by a violent urge to touch myself. The resulting orgasms were quick and shameful. The most enjoyable I'd had for a long time.

Manipulating the woman who had wronged me also gave me power, and power is addictive. As the days passed, I became more and more dependent on it. I needed it to keep me on the right side of sanity. To keep my anger under control.

Sometimes, strange as it was, I felt angry she hadn't targeted my husband as a potential sugar daddy, the way she was targeting Miles. Instead, she trashed my marriage just for sex. A fling that, to my husband, became anything but casual. In that last, terrible argument we had at the house before he drove off, when I confronted him with all my evidence about the affair, he'd looked crushed when he told me Leah didn't want a serious relationship with him. He showed me the texts she'd sent him, asking him to leave her alone. Telling him never to contact her again.

Yet he still wanted to leave me. He said Leah had woken him up and shown him how unhappy he was in our marriage. She may not have wanted him, but she still took him from me.

One afternoon, Miles and I met for a debrief at a coffee shop in Chelsea. As we took the first sips of our cappuccinos, I inspected his appearance. He looked younger. His eyes had a shine to them and his face looked leaner. Less puffy. Had he lost a few pounds? A haze of aftershave hung around him. Something zesty and fresh.

Leah had exerted a similar de-ageing effect on my husband. As if she had the elixir of youth between her legs.

When I asked Miles how the situation with her was going, he shrugged.

'It's okay,' he said. 'I mean, we don't have much in common. Because of the age gap.'

'But you have a good time together?'

'Sure. I mean... nothing special.'

I wasn't so sure. I'd paid the same private investigator who'd brought me evidence of Dom's affair to keep tabs on Miles. As a result, I had photographs of Leah and Miles strolling hand in hand in Regent's Park. Leah laughing, or pretending to laugh, at something Miles had said. The pair of them having a long, boozy brunch in Notting Hill. Leah entering and leaving Miles' apartment block, where she had stayed four nights in the past week.

'Mind you, we never run out of things to talk about,' Miles said.

'Fascinating state-of-the-nation debates, no doubt.'

'She's not stupid,' he snapped, 'she went to the University of Edinburgh.'

'Where she only just scraped a pass in business and marketing.'

He frowned. 'How do you know her grades?'

'How do you think? I paid someone to investigate her background.'

His eyes narrowed. Was he angry with me? He surely didn't think this girl liked him for himself? Typical Miles. Even during his decades of bachelorhood, he always ended up lovesick over the women he was supposed to be casually involved with. He didn't seem able to help himself.

'I'm not sure we should be doing this, Viv,' he said.

'Don't chicken out now.'

'She's young and she's also vulnerable. Both her parents are dead and—'

'No, they're not.'

'What?' Deep lines appeared on his broad forehead. 'Her mum died recently and her dad died years ago.'

'Her father is still alive.' I took my phone from my handbag. 'Let me show you.' I searched through my emails until I found the one from my PI with the report on Leah's family background. I opened the report and handed my phone to Miles. I sipped my coffee while he read about Alan Williams' life in Toronto with his new family, as well as the few details my PI had gathered about his failed business ventures in the UK. 'The mother inherited money from her father's business,' I said. 'Some kind of engineering company. They were new money. Looks like Leah had an affluent childhood before the father lost it all. The poor mother died in a council house, with hardly anything to her name.' I sighed. 'They do say it's much harder to have had money and lost it than never to have had it at all.'

'Whatever.' Miles handed me back my phone. 'I'm only using Leah to get my confidence back.'

I hoped that was true. He was certainly angry now; I could tell. His neck flushed red. A vein pulsed in his left temple.

'I've thought of a way we can take this to the next level,' I said.

'How?' he said, wariness replacing anger.

'You need to propose to her.'

'What?'

'It's what she wants. It's what all these girls want.'

'Are you out of your mind?'

'Possibly.' The thought had occurred to me. Grief and anger were a heady mix. Even the cocktail of medications my GP had prescribed me couldn't drown out my desire for revenge. Teaching Leah Williams a lesson would do her good and it was the right thing to do for womankind. What would happen if every young woman turned her back on all the progress feminism had made? All the sacrifices of the women before us would mean nothing.

'No.' Miles thumped his fist on the table. My cup shook in its saucer. 'I will not propose, Vivienne. Absolutely no way.'

26

VIVIENNE

June

My cousin's vehement refusal to propose to Leah worried me at first, but after a couple of days to dwell on the idea, he changed his mind. He knew I only had his best interests at heart. We'd always looked out for each other. Always would.

Coming to the château was his idea. I was surprised and, at first, uncertain. Did we really want to come back so soon, after the drama of Riley's death? If the shock of it was still raw for me, how on earth did he feel? The accident itself was upsetting enough, but dealing with the aftermath was stressful and complicated. My memories of that time are not ones I wish to revisit.

'I need this,' he told me, as we sat together on the sofa in my flat, drinking more of the 1972 Brora. 'Either I go back and face up to what happened or I sell the place. I don't want to lose the château. I won't let Riley's death take that from me as well.'

The more I thought about it, the more I realised what a good idea it was. What girl could refuse a proposal at a French château? There was even a time in my teenage years when I'd fantasised about getting married at Clairvallon.

'Yes,' I said, 'that will work. Give her a taste of the life she could have. She'll have more to miss when you end it with her.'

Soon, we were both fired up, the ideas flowing. Miles and I had always enjoyed a synergy. A meeting of minds. I suggested he should ask her to stay all summer and pretend they would get married at the end of it.

'Okay,' he said, 'but only if you're there too.'

'Of course.' I had no desire to spend the summer in my empty, echoing cottage in Kent. Mooching about, haunted by memories of my husband. My son had made it clear he had no intention of coming back from New York to visit me.

'We need to make it look real,' Miles said. 'Like, actually book the wedding. Make it official.'

I nodded. 'And I'm sure you can persuade her to give up her job.'

'Offer to look after her?'

'Yes. She'll love that. Promise her money she's never going to get.'

'I bet I could get her to give up the flat she lives in.'

'She'd leave that dump in Tooting in a heartbeat,' I said.

'You can't let her know who Dom really was,' Miles said. 'You do know that?'

'I know.'

'I'm serious, Viv. At no point can she know it's a set-up. Even after I end the relationship.'

'Yes. Fine. I get it.' As much as I loved the idea of a grand revelation and a final confrontation, Miles was right. I would have to settle for watching Leah's dreams crumble. At least at the château I'd have time to properly observe her. To dismantle the myth of her that lived in my head. To see she was just a normal person who defecated and had body odour and bad breath in the morning. All this might kill my obsession. 'This will really help me move on,' I said.

I was still trapped in that awful argument with Dom. The two of us saying things we could never take back. Terrible things that would live with me forever. Sometimes I kicked myself for not handling it differently. If I hadn't confronted him so aggressively, been so vicious and unforgiving, he might not have left that night. If he'd stayed at home instead of driving off into the darkness, we might have been able to talk, calmly. Everything might have turned out differently.

'It will help you too,' I said.

He drained the last of his whisky. 'What if she susses us out?'

'She won't. She'll think she's stepped into a fantasy. You'll be the rich man who is going to make all her problems go away.'

'And what about you?'

I close my eyes. I see myself standing in the driveway of the cottage, watching my husband's VW Golf screech away. Eyes fixed on the angry red tail lights until they vanished. 'I'm your poor cousin, Vivienne, aren't I? Grieving the loss of her husband in a tragic car accident.' I open my eyes. 'Surely even someone as heartless as her will have to feel sorry for me.'

Miles looked at me, his expression a blend of pity and fear. 'Maybe this is a bad idea,' he said. 'Maybe you just need to accept the situation and try to get used to life without Dom. Wouldn't that be healthier?'

'No.' I shook my head. 'This is what I want.' I reached out and grabbed his hand. 'I'd do the same for you, if you asked me to,' I said. 'You know I would.'

He squeezed my hand. 'I know.'

Of course he knew. My loyalty to him could never be in doubt.

'What if something goes wrong?' he asked.

My eyes filled with tears. 'Dom is never coming back.'

'I know, but—'

'You of all people should understand how that feels.'

He sighed and let go of my hand. For a moment I thought he would change his mind and say no to the whole plan.

'Okay,' he said finally. 'Just promise me there won't be any trouble.'

'Trouble?'

'Promise me.'

'Fine. I promise.'

Trouble. Honestly. As if he had something to worry about. As if I would hurt her.

PART III

27

VIVIENNE

Now. August

It is the first day of August. A week has passed since Miles went to Paris. A week since the arrangements for the wedding that will never take place were finalised.

I'm in the bedroom my cousin shares with Leah, lying on my back on top of the four-poster bed. The two of them have gone for a drive to a winery where they will eat lunch and purchase some wine for the château's collection. They won't be back for ages. I'm taking a well-deserved break after cleaning the en suite bathroom. Scrubbing out the toilet. Mopping the floor and cleaning the sink. After finishing, I made good use of Leah's expensive toiletries. What on earth does someone so young need with anti-ageing serum? My dry, 'mature' skin soaked it up like a sponge. Whenever I can, I take the opportunity to smell the lotions she puts on her face and body. The perfume she uses. When I inhale, I imagine Dom with his face buried in her neck, drinking her in.

My arms and legs are killing me. I'm starting to regret

casting myself in the role of temporary housekeeper. I've always prided myself on keeping a tidy house, but this place is big and dusty, and I miss having cleaning staff. Still, Miles was adamant about letting them all go after Riley died, and there was no way we could invite them back with Leah here. Our plan requires privacy if it is to succeed.

When I first got here, a week before Miles and Leah arrived, the château hadn't been opened for almost a year. I had to hire a company to come from Amiens to do the bulk of the cleaning and tidy up the gardens. The four burly Serbian men who turned up did their best to tackle the château's grime and neglect. After they left, I aired all the rooms, dusted ornaments and, of course, made sure to remove all traces of my husband from the place. I hadn't realised how much of him would be here. I had to remove some of the family pictures from the walls and I even went as far as searching through all the old photo albums in the west wing of the attic. I put all the evidence into a cardboard box and stored it under my bed.

I got a security company in to fit a new gate too. The old one had needed replacing for a while and I thought it best to keep our guest as safe and secure as possible.

Leah, I have to say, appears more than happy to be waited on hand and foot. Spoilt little madam. My Nathan always had to do his fair share of housework growing up. I was determined to raise a good man and, in many ways, he is. Yet he always preferred his father to me. Always thought Dominic the superior adult in the household. Even now, with Dom gone and me all alone, Nathan only graces me with one phone call a week. It has taken all my willpower not to tell him about his father's affair. Nathan still thinks of his dad as a great, upstanding guy. He may have found my mothering skills lacking at times, but it would have been so easy to destroy his image of his father. To poison him with my own bitterness. I deserve some credit for not doing that.

Must get moving soon. I've yet to strip this bed and change it. More sex-stained sheets to deal with. I close my eyes. A power nap will set me up for the rest of the morning's work. Rolling onto my side, I press my face into Miles' pillow, seeking out his scent. There it is. When you've known someone your whole life, you carry their smell with you always. It is a primitive bond. One you never escape.

Just as I'm starting to relax, a pattering sound above my head startles my eyes open. I glance up at the ceiling. Mice probably, although I can't shake the thought of Riley tiptoeing across the attic floor.

When I first opened the château up again, I half-expected to find her here waiting for me. It is still hard to believe someone with her vitality could actually die. She had such magnetism. An almost animal charisma, as well as a filthy laugh that made everyone around her laugh too. No wonder Miles fell so hard for her. No wonder he was so blind to her faults.

I sit up and rest back against the plump pillows. I can't believe Leah has only been here a couple of weeks. She's certainly made herself at home. Clothes strewn everywhere, the contents of her make-up bag spilled out over the dressing table. As far as she's concerned, this place will be her home once she and Miles are married. One of her homes. Over the past few days, I've often seen her staring into the distance, a dreamy expression on her face. I bet she's imagining the cushy life ahead of her. She didn't need much persuading to give up her job. Sometimes I catch her admiring her engagement ring. I'm glad, considering the effort I put into choosing it. The diamond had to be large enough to entice but not obscene enough to repulse.

So far, everything is going according to plan. Miles has done a brilliant job sorting out all the wedding admin. I was apprehensive about him asking the mayor for a favour. My husband and I attended several drinks parties at Philippe's house over the years and, although Philippe is very well meaning and has been useful to us in the past, I don't need his pity. Also, the fewer people we have poking around in our business before the wedding day the better.

Miles handled it well. When Philippe asked after Dom and me, Miles shared my sad news and told him I was keeping a low profile at the château. Taking time to come to terms with my loss. A loss I wished to keep private. The mayor said he understood.

The only random factor to unsettle me so far, is the return of Jacques. Miles assured me he isn't staying for long, which I can only hope is true. It's hardly surprising I don't trust him. How could I, after what he put everyone here through? Me in particular. He's bad news.

Miles told me to forget about him, so I'm doing my best. Good old Miles. His performance of the role of enamoured fiancé is Oscar-worthy. He did have one wobble. That first morning here, after his proposal the night before, he almost chickened out. The roof tile smashing on the terrace like a sign from the afterlife really got to him. Afterwards we argued. He said he should end everything there and then. Tell Leah the proposal was a mistake. He was convinced she might report us to the police if she worked out what was going on. Could we be charged with luring her here under false pretences?

'Only if we were planning on committing an actual crime against her,' I said.

'Christ,' he said, 'you've actually looked into it?'

'I'm just saying, we're not planning on doing anything criminal. Are we?'

I calmed him down, eventually. Reminded him of everything we've been through together. Convinced him we can easily triumph in a silly little game like this.

Let's be honest; he's hardly having a terrible time. You'd think he'd never had sex before, the way the two of them are going at it. I suppose he knows his time with her is finite. He might as well make the most of every opportunity he gets.

One evening last week, I was at the desk in front of my bedroom window, binoculars pressed against my eyes, watching them shagging in the kitchen garden. Leah up against the wall, Miles thrusting away like a madman, trousers round his ankles, his buttocks glaring white. She looked like she was enjoying herself, but I'm sure she's a pro at faking it.

As I watched, I wondered if my husband had ever screwed her like that. His lewd texts to her did give away some clues.

> I want to tie you up and make you mine.

> Your lips on my cock. I've never experienced anything like it.

For a long time, I couldn't stop myself imagining what the two of them had got up to. No need to imagine any more. I've seen the real thing live in front of me.

I don't think I've ever been wanted the way men want her. Sex with my husband was loving and affectionate at the start and routine and scheduled as the responsibilities of marriage, work and parenthood consumed us. A familiar story and, thanks to my husband's inability to keep his dick under control, it had a familiar ending.

When I think back to that last terrible argument he and I had, that's what hurts the most. She turned us into two characters in a cliché-ridden drama. She made a turgid soap opera out of our lives.

Sometimes the effort of concealing my real emotions from her is exhausting. Sometimes I'd like to break down and cry and let her see the pain she has caused me. I came close last week over dinner, when I told her about Dom's affair. When she told me to my face she'd never had an affair with a married man. Liar.

I'm not the only one struggling to control my feelings. Before Miles and Leah treated me to a sex show in the garden last week, the two of them were arguing. Miles looked very threatening, towering over her like that, shaking her by the shoulders.

The next day he told me Leah had heard some gossip about Riley from a girl who used to do the cleaning here. I reminded him we always knew there would be rumours. People are like that around here. I told him he has nothing to worry about. However bad he still feels about it, Riley's death is last year's news.

He can't let petty gossip get to him like it did that night with Leah. He will have to watch himself. My cousin is a gentle soul, but there have been times in the past when his temper has got the better of him.

Like all of us, he has his limits. Like all of us he can be pushed too far.

28

LEAH

August

It is mid-morning and I'm alone by the pool. Stretched out on a sun lounger, at the mercy of another hot morning. The long-range forecast for August is one blue, cloudless sky after another. The only sign of time passing is the grass growing longer on the lawns. Patches of it are turning brown from where the sun scorches it daily.

My wedding will take place two weeks from today. On my lap is the printed copy of the prenuptial agreement Miles wants me to sign. I'm reading through it one last time before I do so, just in case I've missed anything. My diligent online research has reassured me the prenup is fairly standard. As I expected, he has ring-fenced his existing assets, including Sinclair Properties. If he does sell the company, none of that money will come to me. If we get divorced, my settlement will reflect the length of the marriage. The longer I stay with Miles, the more money I get. After five years, I will get half the marital home, after ten years the whole property is mine.

That's not so bad. Whatever happens, I could come out of this with a house.

The prenup also hints at major bonus points for providing Miles with children. If there are kids involved, any alimony payments will increase vastly. The prenup, which will be revised every five years, also gets revised every time I have a child.

This document also makes it clear that if Miles dies, my inheritance will be consistent with the prenuptial agreement. His existing assets will not pass to me. Our children, if we have any, will be entitled to that money. They will inherit almost everything.

More bonus points for embracing motherhood.

Vivienne was right about British prenups not having an adultery clause. I guess a man with Miles' power could still find ways to make life difficult for me if I did cheat on him. Not that I'm planning to.

A hot spark ignites low in my belly as I picture Jacques' face. I shove the prenuptial agreement into my Chloé basket bag and stare at the pool's still, aqua-blue surface. I'll sign the document later. It seems like a pretty good deal, and I'm hardly in a position to negotiate. I remember the photograph of Riley in the pool and suddenly there she is, floating beneath the sun on her white Lilo, her skimpy white bikini leaving little to the imagination. She raises her glass of champagne in my direction.

What kind of deal did she get in her prenup? Did she sign hers as willingly as I'm about to sign mine?

I blink rapidly. As soon as Riley vanishes, Miles and Vivienne appear, deep in conversation. I'll discuss the prenup with Miles later, when we're alone.

A black kaftan swamps Vivienne's small frame. A black

bucket hat and oversized black sunglasses shield her face from the sun. Miles is in his salmon pink shorts, his pale blue shirt undone to his waist.

'I think the Heritage deal sounds hopeful,' Vivienne says. 'All you can do is talk to them again and see if they're serious about making an offer.'

'Maybe.' Miles tosses his towel on the sun lounger beside me. 'I didn't plan on them moving so quickly.'

A few days ago, Miles had a call from someone at Heritage Capital. A call he described as 'very positive'. A call that makes me think the sale of Sinclair Properties might happen sooner than I hoped. I may not ever directly receive any of the money from that sale, but I can help Miles spend it.

I tilt my fedora hat back and look up at him. 'Everything okay?'

'Work stuff, darling.' He bends down to kiss my forehead. 'Nothing for you to worry about.'

Nothing for me to worry about but clearly something for Vivienne to advise him on.

She opens the umbrella between her sun lounger and mine, putting both of us in the shade. 'Be careful you don't burn, Leah,' she says. 'The sun can be deceptive here.'

She sounds almost maternal. I keep forgetting she is actually a mother. Now that I know her husband had an affair, it's hard not to feel sympathy for her. Her pain and fury were still so present when she told me about it. Not only does she have that hurt to deal with, but the family life she once enjoyed has fallen apart. No wonder she hasn't been on her best game since I arrived. Last night in bed, I thought again about my affair with Nick. I feel bad for not considering his family when we were together. I hope our fling was a one-off mistake he put behind him. I hope he and his family are happy now.

'I was thinking about photographers for the wedding day,' Vivienne says. 'I believe I might have found someone suitable.'

'Oh.' I sit up. 'Thanks.'

'There's a Facebook group for ex-pats in the area.' She takes off her hat. 'It's dreadful, like all these groups are, but it does have some useful information.'

'Thanks, Viv,' Miles says. 'You're the best.'

'Her name's Anne-Marie Lebrun,' she says. 'British woman married to a local.'

'Amazing. Thank you.' I flash her a smile. 'I appreciate that.'

Vivienne has certainly been warmer towards me the past few days. Her choice to confide in me about her husband's affair and this gesture about the photographer feel like signs she and I are making some progress.

I bet she was enthusiastic about Miles and Riley's wedding from the start. I can just imagine her helping Riley with the preparations. I bet she had a special role to play on the day. A bridesmaid, perhaps? Or, more likely, an unconventional best man to Miles.

'Darling.' Miles, who has stripped down to his navy swimming shorts, perches on the side of my sun lounger and passes me a bottle of suncream. 'Will you do the honours?'

While I massage suncream into his pink, sunburned shoulders, Vivienne lifts her kaftan over her head. The outline of her ribs is visible through her black tankini top. The tops of her thin white legs are covered by her black tankini shorts. Even when swimming, she is dressed for mourning. She must have still loved her husband when he died, even after he'd cheated on her. How awful for them to have argued just before his death. How sad they never had a chance to try and save the marriage. No wonder she's finding it hard to watch Miles moving on when her grief is still so raw. One day, she might find someone new and move on too. That will mean also moving on from her husband's infidelity and getting her confidence back. With some new clothes, a decent haircut and a bit of make-up, Vivienne could be stunning. She needs to start believing in herself again.

'Come on, cousin dearest,' she says to Miles. 'Let's cool off.' She turns to me. 'It's a good job you're keeping the wedding simple. Can you imagine trying to organise a big extravaganza in this heat?'

Her flip-flops slap against the flagstones as she makes her way to the deep end of the pool. She casts her footwear off and lowers herself into the water using the metal steps.

'Bugger.' Miles, tackling the hot flagstones in bare feet, hops and stumbles to the poolside. 'Bombs away,' he yells as he jumps into the air, tucks his knees into his chest and hits the water with a loud thwack, spraying water everywhere.

Vivienne squeals. 'You idiot,' she says when he resurfaces.

Watching them splash one another like feuding infants, I wonder how many times they must have played in this pool together as kids, as teenagers and then as adults.

I settle back on my sun lounger. Only my legs are in the sun, thanks to Vivienne's umbrella. Her comment about my simple wedding has left me deflated. If I had a big extravaganza at the château to organise, I wouldn't be lying around by the pool. I'd have a million things to do. Part of me feels sad not to have that kind of stress and anticipation. No 'big day' to get excited about. All I have to do is find a dress and get this photographer organised. Miles has booked the lunch on the day for us and our wedding rings will be arriving by courier in a few days. I hardly have a say in any of it.

And it's all happening sooner than I expected.

I tell myself that's a good thing. This is what I want, isn't it? My grand plan is coming together.

My fingers trail across my stomach, my skin glistening from a generous application of suncream. I close my eyes and see Jacques' face. I remember the feel of his fingers around my wrist. I remember how much I wanted to kiss him.

Since that day, I haven't been sleeping well. At night my imagination turns the sounds of the château shifting and settling in the cooling temperatures into something more sinister. The creaking noises above my head turn into footsteps. The footsteps of someone pacing back and forth across the attic floor.

Now, baking beneath the unrelenting sun, my nocturnal fears seem foolish. I need to pull myself together and put Jacques out of my mind.

Be careful.

His final words to me. It is hard now to recall his exact intonation when he spoke them. Was he trying to warn me he was someone to be wary of? Or was he hinting at some other danger that might befall me?

29

VIVIENNE

August

'Race you,' Miles says.

We're treading water in the deep end of the pool, the sun beating down on us. I spy a patch of pink scalp through his thinning hair. He should really have a hat on. These glimpses of him ageing shock me almost as much as the changes I see in myself. Whenever we're together, especially here at the château, it's easy to forget how old we are. I see the boy in him and he sees the girl in me. I suppose we always will.

'Viv?' he says. 'Race?'

'Why? You'll win.'

'Indulge me.'

We set off. My cousin is not an elegant swimmer. His front crawl is lopsided and splashy. He inhales huge gasps of air between each stroke. Still, it's nice to see him at home in the water. When Miles was nine years old, Bruce held him underwater here, in this pool. Held him under long enough for Miles to panic and flounder. Long enough for an adult to have to intervene. After that, Miles lost his confidence in the water for quite some time.

That was typical behaviour for Bruce. More than once he pushed me into this pool when I wasn't expecting it. More than once, he grabbed my bikini bottoms and pulled them down, just so he could make some pathetic joke about my red pubic hair. His sense of humour was one of the many warped features of his personality.

When I complete my length of the pool, Miles is waiting for me in the shallow end, arms raised in triumph.

'You're such a dick,' I say.

'A triumphant dick.'

'Whatever.'

He interlaces his fingers and extends his meshed hands. 'Push-off?'

'Let's do it.'

He puts his hands beneath the water, and I place my feet into them. My hands rest lightly on his shoulders. He squats down and counts to three. As he rises up, he lifts me into the air and propels me backwards.

I scream as my back hits the water. When I surface, my shoulder grazes the side of the pool.

'Miles.' Leah sits up on her sun lounger. 'Be careful. Vivienne nearly hit her head then.'

It was a bit close, but Leah is worrying for nothing. Miles would never hurt me. He is my protector. Always has been. The one man I can always rely on.

'I'm fine,' I tell her. Miles and I roll our eyes at each other and grin like naughty children.

He tips onto his back and floats towards the middle of the pool, letting out a deep, contented sigh. Leah reclines again on her lounger, stretching out one long, inviting leg then another.

I clamber up the steps out of the water, retrieve my flip-flops and make my way back to the shade of my umbrella. Leah has her sunglasses on, and I can't tell if her eyes are open or shut. She yawns and tilts her head away from me. An ill-disguised attempt to avoid conversation. Fine by me.

My lounger creaks as I settle myself on it. I put on my sunglasses and steal a glance at the woman lying next to me. She is undeniably an attractive specimen. Golden-skinned to my milky white. What would be like to have skin that plump and smooth? These days my skin is thin and dry. My chest an alien landscape of skin tags and sunspots. She does have a large, dark freckle on her stomach. It looks sexy now, but she will have to keep an eye on it as she ages.

Her clavicles are fleshy mounds, not bony ridges like mine. Her shoulders are round and soft-looking. I have an urge to sink my teeth into them until she screams.

I look away, heart racing, my fists clenched tight. She is so close we could be lying in bed together. Did my husband reach for her in the night, like he once reached for me? Did he grip her long, dark hair in his hands as he entered her?

Deep breaths, Vivienne. Deep breaths. I console myself with the knowledge all her scheming is for nothing. She thinks she's getting married soon. What a shock it will be when Miles tells her to pack her bags and get out of his house. Especially since we've made the whole charade so convincing. Over the past few days, I've been putting phase two of my plan into action. Having been cold and unwelcoming and doing all I can to make her feel inferior to Riley, I'm now trying to be kinder. I want her to feel comfortable. The more accepted into the family she feels, the bigger her humiliation will be.

Miles had one of his wobbles yesterday. He told me he feels bad about lying to the mayor about the wedding and taking advantage of his good nature. Understandable misgivings, but I'm sure we'll come up with a story to deflect all blame away from Miles. He can tell Philippe he had to call the wedding off after discovering something unsavoury about his young fiancée. He can say Leah was only after his money, which, let's face it, is true.

If this deal with Heritage Capital comes together, Miles will have more money than ever. He had opportunities to sell Sinclair Properties in the past but had to keep putting it off. Now there is nothing standing in his way.

A warm hand lands on my upper arm, making me jump.

'Vivienne?' Leah says.

I turn my head to look at her. She is lying on her side, her firm, young breasts pushed together. 'What?'

'About the photographs.' She flicks her hair over her shoulder. 'I've been thinking.'

Thinking? Steady. Don't want to tire yourself.

'It would be lovely to have some taken on the front lawn,' she says. 'With the château in the background.'

'Of course. That will look gorgeous.'

Except it's never going to happen, you silly little girl.

'Well, it would look gorgeous if the grass wasn't getting so overgrown.' She flashes me that smile she must think is winning. One that must work on men but does nothing for me. 'It really needs cutting.'

'I'm sure we—'

'What about getting in the gardener you used before? You did have one?'

'Yes.' Nerves tingle in my fingertips. An image of Jacques sweeping leaves from the poolside flashes into my mind. His strong, tanned forearms. His insolent eyes. I glance at the pool. Miles has resumed his noisy front crawl, churning up the water. Showing off for Leah. 'Yes, we did. The housekeeper's son.'

'Oh, yes,' she says casually. 'The guy who was with Estelle at the dairy farm that day.'

As if she's only just remembered him. Jacques was never my type, but most women seem to swoon in his company. 'Yes, that was him,' I say, 'but Miles had to let him go.'

'Like all the other staff?'

'No, Jacques was fired before Riley died.' No harm in telling her the truth. Jacques won't be at his mother's for long and there's no way he'll show his face here again. Not after everything that happened.

'Why?' Leah asks.

'Miles should never have taken him on in the first place.' In a low voice, I explain that Jacques was always a difficult boy. Always in trouble. 'When he was in his early twenties he did time in prison for burglary.'

'Wow. Okay.'

'Miles took Jacques on here as a favour for Estelle. She thought the gardening job would keep him out of trouble.'

'But it didn't?'

'No.' I sigh. 'He just couldn't stop taking things that didn't belong to him.'

30

LEAH

August

The grandfather clock in the hallway outside the bedroom strikes eleven-thirty, echoing the clock on the ground floor. Miles has gone for a shower. I'm already dressed for bed in the silk baby-doll pyjamas Miles brought back from Paris for me.

The room is airless and warm. I'm standing by the open window, my forearms resting on the windowsill. A sharp crescent moon casts a dim silver light over the terrace. I imagine Riley in her white cocktail dress, gazing up at the sky. I imagine her dead body lying smashed on the concrete beneath the roof terrace. How strange it is that earlier we ate dinner only metres away from where she died.

Turning my head to the left, I look beyond the château and past the walled garden to the outbuildings. Behind the roof of the barn, I can just make out the silhouette of the tall pines that mark the start of the woods. Beyond them lies Estelle's cottage. What is Jacques doing now, right at this moment? Is he even there?

Vivienne didn't exactly give him a glowing character reference. She told me that Miles, keen to reward Estelle for her hard work and loyalty to the Sinclair family, gave Jacques some gardening work at the château when he came out of prison. At first, Jacques seemed grateful for the opportunity and worked hard. Eventually he fell back into his old ways and stole money from the château, as well as some jewellery that had once belonged to Lady Sinclair. After that, Miles fired him. According to Vivienne, this all happened about a month before Riley's death. She asked me not to mention any of this to Miles as it would only upset him.

Both times I saw Jacques with his mother, the close bond between them was clearly visible. Yet I sensed his bad-boy aura too. A hint of something wild. No wonder he didn't want me to tell Miles about his visit. Is that why he was hesitant to hand over Estelle's keys? He could have been coming to the château while it was supposed to be locked up.

This afternoon, while Miles was working in the study and Vivienne was at the pool, I snuck into the kitchen. After finding the scrap of paper containing Estelle's contact details on the corkboard, I added her address and mobile phone number into Contacts on my phone.

Back in my room, I called the mobile number, but it was no longer in use. Must have been the phone she used before she got ill. What would I have said if she'd answered? *Hi, can I speak to your son?* What would I have said to him? That I had questions to ask about Riley? That I'd heard rumours her death wasn't an accident, and I wondered if he knew anything about it? The whole thing is ridiculous. A girl who used to clean here, a girl who lost her job because of Riley's death, has shared some gossip with me. Nothing more. People who don't have money or power like to make up stories about those who do. Fact. Added to that, an old woman with dementia inferred that Riley was popular with *les hommes* and her ex-convict son looks like the kind of man any woman would enjoy attention from.

What exactly do I think happened? Riley had an affair with Jacques, Miles found out and, jealous and angry, pushed her to her death?

I lean out of the window and strain my eyes against the gloom, looking up towards the roof terrace where Riley lost her grip on life.

'Leah.' I gasp as firm hands grab me around the waist. 'What the hell?' Miles pulls me back from the window and turns me to face him. 'These window frames are centuries old. You can't... You need to be careful.'

That tortured look in his eyes.

'I'm sorry. I was just—'

'Please.' He cups my face in his hands. 'Promise me you won't do that again.'

'I promise.' His palms are clammy against my cheeks. I stand on tiptoes and kiss him. 'I promise.'

He shakes his head and releases me. 'If only to spare me a heart attack.' He turns away and begins to tidy up the clothes he left lying on the bed when he went for his shower. His pink shorts, his blue shirt. He stuffs his awful white trainer socks into his brown deck shoes. He is wearing a short white robe that only reaches his mid-thighs. I notice how rough and wrinkled the skin on his knees is.

Am I inventing drama about Riley just to cover up my doubts about this marriage? Maybe that's why people have such big weddings. With so much to do they don't have time to let their misgivings get out of control.

Before dinner, I signed the prenuptial agreement. The

comfortable life I want is now within reach. Miles looked so happy and relieved once I'd signed it.

'That was nice of Vivienne to organise the photographer's visit,' he says as he disrobes and climbs into bed.

'Yes.' I get into bed beside him. 'It was.' At dinner, Vivienne announced she'd called the photographer recommended by the Facebook group and arranged for her to come for a visit tomorrow. Apparently, Anne-Marie wants to scope out backdrops for photographs and get an idea of the kind of look I want to achieve.

'Vivienne can be very thoughtful.' Miles rests back against his pillows. 'It's her birthday next week. On Monday.'

'Really? She never said.'

'It's her first birthday without Dom. She doesn't want to make a big deal of it.'

I hesitate. 'I know,' I say, 'about what her husband did.'

'What?' Miles sits up again. 'What do you mean?'

'She told me he had an affair.'

'What else did she say?'

'Nothing.' His intense gaze is making me uncomfortable. 'Only that she found out about it just before he died.'

'I still can't believe Dom did that to her.' He sighs. His intensity vanishes. 'Losing him nearly broke her. She even tried to take her own life.'

'That's sad to hear.' And hard to imagine. Vivienne seems as tough as they come.

'That's why I want to keep such a close eye on her this summer.'

'Totally. I get it.'

'Just to make sure she's really recovering.'

'We should do something nice for her birthday,' I say. 'Make her a special meal or something.'

He lifts my hand and presses it against his lips. 'You are a sweet girl.' He reaches over to his bedside table and grabs his laptop. 'We'll do something lovely for her.'

When he settles back against his pillows again, I snuggle closer. He opens his laptop and taps at the keyboard. A website appears. *Beaumont Estates: Luxury London Properties.*

'What's this about?' I ask.

'We'll need a home once we're married.'

I sit up. 'What about your place in South Kensington? I thought we'd be moving in there.'

'Into that soulless shell? Not a chance.' He smiles. 'I want to make a proper home for you. Look.' He clicks on one of the properties. 'Most of these aren't on the market yet. A friend of mine runs this agency. He can give us a heads-up on the best stuff around.'

The first link he clicks on is for a four-bedroom modern penthouse in Dulwich Village. Its vast windows have panoramic views over to central London. I can't see a price, but this property must be worth millions.

'Not quite us,' he says, 'but I think Dulwich would be a perfect location. We could have the best of both worlds. Relative peace and quiet, in London terms. Perfect for me work wise and you won't be isolated. You'll be able to get a job, if you still want one; you can see your friends. Have a life.'

I spy uncertainty in his deep blue eyes, as if he is worried what he's offering might not be good enough.

In this moment I feel safe and cared for, in a way I haven't for a very long time.

'Wait until you see this next place,' he says. 'This won't be on the market for a few weeks but it's pretty special.'

The next property he brings up almost makes me squeal. A Grade II listed Georgian mansion with six bedrooms and huge gardens, sealed off from the outside world by secure gates. The interiors have been fully restored. Tasteful, off-white walls. Luxurious bathrooms gleaming with expensive marble.

I am overwhelmed but mustn't show it. *You are the prize.* Yes, I want comfort and security from this marriage but I didn't expect anything as grand as this.

'This definitely has potential,' I say. 'Obviously we'd need to view it and see how it feels when we're in there.'

'And it's a great area for schools.'

A brief silence, punctured by a burst of birdsong.

'You do want a family, don't you?' he says.

I nod. 'I've always thought I'd be a mother one day.'

'I don't want to force you into motherhood,' he says, 'but I've learned the hard way that a couple needs to want the same thing when it comes to kids.'

A creaking sound overhead.

'Riley didn't want children?' I ask.

'When we met, she told me she wanted to settle down and have a family,' he says. 'We tried and finally got pregnant about a year after we married. Four months into it, she had a miscarriage.'

'I'm sorry,' I say. 'That must have been hard?'

He nods. 'It was terrible for both of us, but of course she suffered the most. After that she said she needed a break before trying again and I agreed.' He looks out of the window. 'I thought she meant a few months, but even then she said she wasn't ready. She started skydiving again. Eventually she said she didn't know if she wanted kids any more.'

'That must have been tough for you?'

'It was, but what could I do? I loved her, and I didn't want to be without her. I thought she might change her mind. She was in her late thirties by then, but she was fit and healthy. She still had time to have a safe pregnancy.'

'Sounds like the miscarriage really affected her?'

'It did, but there were other issues. Her mother for one.'

'I thought they were estranged?'

'They were. Her mother had mental health issues. Serious ones. When Riley was a child, her mother was often violent. Brutally so. I think Riley was secretly scared she might not be a good mother herself.'

'That's sad.' Sounds like Riley was carrying a lot of dark and heavy baggage.

'She didn't tell me any of this until after we were married,' he says.

'Did you ever think about a divorce?'

'No.' He looks shocked. 'I think she truly believed she wasn't cut out for motherhood and I had to try and respect that. When you love someone, you have to love all of them, don't you?'

'Of course,' I say, even though loving someone that completely sounds like hard work. The cynic in me would say Riley could have tricked her way into the marriage and used Miles for her own ends, but maybe that's because I could be accused of the same thing.

Miles taps the laptop's mousepad and brings up the details of the Georgian house again. I watch as he scrolls through the images of the pristinely decorated, empty rooms. This would be a great home for a family. Two kids, maximum. I will probably have a nanny to help me out with them. The very best of schools for them to attend. My experience of motherhood will be one of comfort and ease rather than drudgery. My children will be grown up before I'm fifty and this house, according to the prenup, will be part of my settlement if Miles and I do divorce in the future. He is showing me I will be taken care of, whatever happens. I doubt any man is going to give me a deal as good as this one.

'I thought my life had ended when Riley died,' Miles says, 'and now here you are. You've given me a future I never thought would be mine.'

And Miles can give me the future I once thought would be mine. I think about how far I've run from my past and how I intend to keep on running. I need to think about the future he could give our children. They won't be born into privilege only to have it snatched away. He won't let them down and abandon them, like my father abandoned me. They won't want for anything, and he will be so grateful to have them he'll ruin them with love.

I can think of far worse situations to have a child in.

'You really want this to work between us, don't you?' I say.

'So much.' He dips his head and kisses me. 'Trust me, all I'm thinking about right now is how you and I can enjoy the rest of our lives together.'

31

VIVIENNE

August

Anne-Marie, the real photographer I've booked for the fake wedding, has arrived at Château Clairvallon. It is just after ten in the morning and Leah, Anne-Marie and I are on the terrace at the front of the château, having coffee and macaroons at the wrought iron table. Macaroons. How nauseatingly bride-like. The kind of sweet treat Leah would eat on a hen night if she actually had any friends. Soon we will commence the charade of looking at charming locations for the wedding photographs that will never be taken.

'My husband, Charles, has an antiques business in Paris,' Anne-Marie says to Leah and me. 'He commutes, which is perfect, and we've got a lovely farmhouse just outside Montreuilac.'

Anne-Marie, with her long limbs, sleek blonde bob and red lipstick is one of those annoying Francophile women desperate to be labelled chic. I wonder if her sleeveless navy linen pantsuit is her work uniform. Part of her *signature look*.

Leah looks sickeningly fresh in one of her designer floral dresses. I can't seem to wear anything else apart from my black shirt dress.

'Paris property is *so* expensive,' Anne-Marie continues, 'and we're planning on starting a family soon so we needed a bigger place.'

'I can totally imagine,' Leah says.

Can she? I doubt she's got any idea how much property in Paris costs.

'Miles and I are actually looking at a place in Dulwich.' Leah picks up the cafetière and tops up Anne-Marie's coffee. 'That area offers such a good quality of life.'

Pretentious little cow. And since when have she and Miles been looking at property? I did suggest a while ago he should throw in a morsel like that to keep her on her toes, but I didn't know he'd taken my advice.

'I adore Dulwich,' Anne-Marie says. 'My bestie from school lives there.'

Leah's green eyes widen. 'No way.'

'Her youngest is in this incredible nursery and she says the other mums are so friendly.'

'Sounds amazing.'

'Listen to me,' Anne-Marie says, 'just assuming you'll have kids. Sorry if that was presumptuous.'

'It's fine.' Leah waves her apology away. 'Yes, we both want kids at some point.'

At some point. That's what Riley said to Miles when they first married. Didn't take her long to change her mind.

'I can't wait to be a mum,' Anne-Marie says. 'We're going to start trying next year.'

'Macaroons, ladies?' I offer the plate of colourful confections to each of them.

'Thanks. I literally cannot get enough of these.' Anne-Marie nibbles at the periphery of a pink macaroon before discarding it onto her plate. 'So, Leah,' she says. 'Tell me about the wedding. How many guests? What sort of theme are you going for?'

'Well.' Leah dabs macaroon crumbs from her painted lips. 'It's going to be very intimate. A small ceremony at the town hall with our witnesses and then a meal in Montreuilac. We thought we'd do the pictures here, before the ceremony.'

'Great.' A tight smile on Anne-Marie's face. 'Intimate weddings are much more authentic, aren't they? Especially when it's a second marriage.'

Leah's cheeks flush. So, Anne-Marie has heard the local gossip. I should have known dabbling with that Facebook group was a mistake. She probably knows a number of people in this area.

'And for that kind of day the photographs are *doubly* important,' Anne-Marie says. 'You'll have treasured memories you can enjoy together and share with other people.'

'Morning, ladies.' Miles saunters out of the château and onto the terrace. He has a white suit shirt on with his pink shorts. His top half smart and ready for a Teams business meeting shortly. 'Anne-Marie, welcome to Château Clairvallon.'

'Thank you,' Anne-Marie gushes as Miles bends down to kiss her on both cheeks. 'This place is beautiful,' she says as he steps away and rests his hands on Leah's shoulders. 'I've heard so much about it.'

A flicker of pain in my cousin's eyes. He knows what she will have heard. *Wife of Local Château Owner Found Dead.*

'Actually, we have mutual friends,' Anne-Marie says. 'Pauline and Colin Forsyth?'

Miles glances at me. We both know exactly who she's talking about. That dreadful couple from Norwich who own an old cottage near Sacy-le-Petit.

'Of course,' Miles says, playing the gracious host. 'Pauline and Colin. Great folk.'

Riley met them in Montreuilac one summer and then invited them for drinks a few times. I think she knew Miles didn't like them, but she could be obtuse if the mood took her. If she was bored. I met the Forsyths twice. On both occasions Dom was with me. I wonder if Anne-Marie will be on the phone to Pauline as soon as she leaves here. Giving her the gossip on Miles' child bride. I'll have to be careful what I say to her. Once she leaves here today, it won't matter. She won't be coming back. There will be no bride and groom to photograph. That will give her and Pauline something to talk about.

'Such an old building. So much history here.' Anne-Marie glances around her, as if it is really distant history that interests her.

'Well, make sure these girls give you a full tour,' Miles says. 'I'm afraid I have to work this morning, but Vivienne will stand in for me. She knows just as much about this place as I do.'

I meet his eyes and nod to reassure him. I'll make sure Anne-Marie gets no fodder for the local scandal machine.

'Before you go, Miles, can I grab a picture of you and Leah in front of the château here?' Anne-Marie asks. 'We'll definitely use that as one of our backdrops.'

'Of course.' Miles kisses the top of Leah's head. 'Happy to oblige.'

While Anne-Marie fetches a camera with a long lens from the boot of her Range Rover, Leah and Miles wander over to the front door of the château, hand in hand.

'Yes, let's try in front of the door there.' Anne-Marie loops the strap of her camera over her neck. 'These are just to give me some idea of the two of you together and what I'll be working with.'

Leah and Miles wrap their arms around one another and gaze into each other's eyes. Someone pass me a bucket.

'Gorgeous.' Anne-Marie snaps away. 'Now try standing a little distance apart and holding hands. That's it. Super.'

As she guides them into a number of different poses, I think of my own wedding photographs. At the house in Kent, I have an album full of memories from my wedding day. Since losing Dom, I can't bear to look at them any more. The pictures of us smiling at each other, just as Miles and Leah are doing now, make me sad. So much hope in our faces, so much love, but he's gone now, and – thanks to Leah – my memories of my marriage are tainted.

'You guys are *so* cute,' Anne-Marie says.

She wouldn't say that if she knew what Leah really is. The damage she has done. Bet she wouldn't want her in her home, sniffing around her husband. *Enjoy this moment, Leah Williams,* I think as Miles enfolds her in his warm, strong arms. *It is as close to a wedding with my cousin as you're ever going to get.*

* * *

Almost two hot, tedious hours later, Leah and I wave Anne-Marie off. As her Range Rover disappears into the trees at the end of the driveway, I can't help a relieved sigh escaping me.

'Thanks, Vivienne.' Leah flashes me one of her disconcertingly wide smiles. 'Anne-Marie's fab and I'd never have found her without you.'

'My pleasure.' This whole experience has been anything

but pleasurable. Traipsing around after Leah as she talked excitedly to Anne-Marie about the château that doesn't and never will belong to her. Watching her bask in the reflected glory of my family's heritage.

My body tenses as she ambushes me with a hug. This is as close as we have ever been. Her warm flesh against mine. Her breasts pressed against me. Her perfume filling my nostrils. I long to pull away. I long to punch her hard in the stomach.

'I'm going to research that dress shop Anne-Marie told me about,' she says when she finally releases me. 'It sounded amazing.'

'Didn't it just?' I say, but she is already walking away, into the château, my sarcasm wasted on her.

When we were down by the lake, which Anne-Marie insisted on seeing, she asked Leah what her wedding dress was like. What colour. What sort of *theme.* Theme, for God's sake. It's a wedding, not a fancy dress party. When Leah said she didn't have a dress yet, Anne-Marie enthused about a vintage store in Paris owned by a friend of hers and urged Leah to look at it online.

'I'm actually going up to Paris next week,' she said. 'If you want to come, we could go and visit the shop together.'

'That would be brilliant,' Leah said.

I made a mental note to make sure that girlie day out doesn't happen.

We must have walked all over the grounds, Anne-Marie insisting on seeing everywhere so she could find 'uniquely beautiful' locations. She looked relieved when I said I'd booked a gardening company to come and tidy up the grounds before the wedding. When we walked around the back of the château, I caught her looking up at the roof terrace. How drawn we humans are to tragedy. How irresistible we find it. Did Anne-Marie imagine poor Riley plummeting to her death? Did she wonder how those of us who knew Riley could carry on with our lives in the very place where she died? I wonder that myself sometimes, but the truth is, Château Clairvallon is bigger than Riley. No interloper, dead or alive, should be allowed to claim it for themselves.

When Anne-Marie suggested looking around the barn and outbuildings, I tried to put my foot down. I told her there was nothing worth seeing there, but she and Leah wouldn't be persuaded. I felt quite embarrassed when we walked into the neglected, weed-infested courtyard. I didn't want Anne-Marie telling Pauline and her cronies that Clairvallon was falling into disrepair.

'Amazing,' Anne-Marie said when we stepped inside the barn. A pigeon observed us from the rafters high overhead. Dust swirled in the warm air, trapped in shafts of sunlight from the windows in the roof. Anne-Marie was very excited by some old items she found under a dust sheet at the back of the barn. An old pram, an antique lamp with two kissing cherubs for a stand, a rotting velvet armchair. 'We could create a tableau of these random gorgeous things and put you and Miles in it,' she said. 'A sort of vintage theme that acknowledges the château's past.'

A tableau. Seriously?

'I can *so* see that,' Leah said, already mimicking her guest's speech patterns.

At that point, my mobile rang. I fished it out of my apron pocket, only to find my lawyer's name on the screen.

'Excuse me for a moment,' I said and left them in the barn, unable to put off speaking to Oliver any longer.

He sounded both relieved and surprised when I answered. I've been ignoring his calls for weeks.

'I know this is difficult, Vivienne,' he said, 'but we need to talk about money.'

'I'm not ready,' I said. 'Can't all you vultures give me time to come to terms with my loss?'

Oliver cleared his throat. 'You know we can't ignore this any longer.'

Only after I lost Dom did I realise the extent of his financial incompetence. When he left his job as an IT consultant to realise his dream of setting up a software development company, I loaned him the start-up money, never thinking I would have to bail him out several times when the company started to struggle.

'I think you'll find I can ignore it as long as I want,' I said and hung up.

A few minutes later, Leah and Anne-Marie emerged from the barn into the harsh sunlight. Arm in arm. BFFs already.

'You know,' Anne-Marie said, 'this whole place would be an amazing renovation project.'

'That had crossed my mind,' Leah said.

Really? She was already planning what to do with my family's property?

'You could easily turn the château into a business,' Anne-Marie continued. 'You could convert those cottages for accommodation.'

'And the barn would make an amazing yoga studio,' Leah said.

'God, totally.' Anne-Marie looked around the courtyard. '*So* much potential here.'

Leah nodded. '*So* much.'

'I agree,' I said. 'There's a lot someone could do here if they had the time and energy.'

Leah looked happy and surprised by my apparent enthusiasm and endorsement.

She will soon learn I can be full of surprises.

32

LEAH

August

It is almost lunchtime. I'm in my bedroom, lying on the four-poster bed, escaping the heat and thinking about this morning's visit from Anne-Marie. Her enthusiasm about the château, her numerous suggestions for staging the wedding photographs, the tiny flicker of surprise that passed across her face when I mentioned the intimate wedding. At that moment I once again wished I was planning an extravagant celebration. One filled with family and friends, like Florence and Freddie's.

Still, I enjoyed showing Anne-Marie around Clairvallon. It made what I'm about to marry into feel real. One day, I will entertain guests here. This is where my children will come on holidays. Even Vivienne seems to have accepted this inevitability. Or at least she isn't resisting it as much. She was really helpful when we were exploring the château grounds and didn't seem to mind the idea of me doing renovations here in the future. With some money behind me, I'm sure I could make a success of it. Maybe I could do the same with a few properties in London. Renovate them and sell them on at a profit. Isn't that the sort of thing the wives of rich men do?

I also really appreciated Anne-Marie's offer of helping me find a wedding dress in Paris. It would be fun to have a girls' day out.

The one strange moment of the morning came when Vivienne left Anne-Marie and I alone in the barn. I was saying how much I loved her idea of incorporating old objects from the château's history into the photographs to make them unique.

'If you're worrying about making this wedding different from his last one, you shouldn't be,' she said.

'I'm not. I'm sure his last wedding was pretty conventional.'

Anne-Marie frowned. 'He got married in Las Vegas, didn't he? All a bit of a whirlwind apparently. Hardly conventional.'

Las Vegas? 'Sure, of course,' I said, not wanting to look ignorant. 'I mean... I was talking about the age gap. Him and I. We're hardly conventional.'

Anne-Marie laughed. 'Who cares about age difference these days? What has that got to do with love? I saw the way Miles looked at you. That man *adores* you.'

Now, lying here in this chintzy bedroom with its dull, traditional paintings, I find it hard to imagine Miles getting married in Vegas. Especially when I'd pictured him and Riley having a traditional English wedding.

How whirlwind was their marriage exactly? Did they even have time to sort out a prenup?

A knock at the bedroom door.

'Come in,' I say. 'Have I missed the lunch bell?' I ask when Vivienne opens the door.

'Not at all,' she says breezily. 'Lunch can wait. I've got something I want to show you.'

33

LEAH

August

'After Anne-Marie left I had a flash of inspiration,' Vivienne says.

We're on the first-floor landing, by the staircase that leads up to the attic floor. I have no idea what she wants to show me, but when she starts climbing the stairs, curiosity and dread compete inside me.

'Come on,' she says.

When we reach the landing, she rummages in her apron pocket and pulls out her bundle of keys. I glance at the door to the east wing. The shimmering green light is still visible beneath the attic door. Once again, a chill spreads through me. For a moment I think Vivienne is going to take me in there and show me where Riley met her death, but instead she inserts a large key into the door to the west wing.

'Follow me,' she says as the door swings open.

Stepping into the attic feels like stepping into a sauna. A

dark sauna. No draughts in here. Vivienne fumbles around on the wall beside the door. A light switch clicks and an overhead light flickers to life.

Vivienne marches across the room towards a window, flings back the shutters and yanks the window open. Sunlight floods in and I get the strange sense that the space around me lets out a deep exhalation.

'Wow,' I say as I take in my surroundings. The attic has at some point been renovated. The gaps between the wooden rafters have been filled in, plastered over and painted pale green. The wooden floorboards gleam beneath a thin layer of dust. 'This is cool.'

On my left is a beige corner sofa covered in colourful cushions and throws. On the wall above it are shelves crammed with books. The low coffee table in front of the sofa is stacked with board games. Monopoly, Cluedo and Dominos and some French games in worn, faded boxes that must have belonged to the château's former owners.

In the centre of the room is a large pool table.

'That's for *Carom*,' Vivienne says when she sees me looking at it. 'French billiards.' She wanders over to the table, reaches into one of the pockets and pulls out a white ball. 'This was our playroom up here.'

'Must have been fun when you were kids?'

'Yes. We did have fun.' Vivienne lets the ball roll across the table's blue baize surface. 'What I really wanted to show you,' she says, abandoning the French billiards table, 'is this.' She beckons me over to the far right-hand corner of the room, which is occupied by an imposing antique wardrobe. When she opens the doors, the scent of mothballs rushes out. Inside, clothing in suit covers hangs from the rail. 'My aunt Louisa loved vintage clothes. She used to pick them up in Paris or at the local brocants around here.' She searches the rail, unzipping the top of each suit bag and peering inside until she finds what she's looking for. 'Some pieces, like this one, she found here at the château and kept.' She unhooks one of the items and unzips the cover. 'I remember how beautiful I thought this was when I was a kid. I think it might fit you.'

She pulls out a dress and holds it up against me. 'What do you think?'

The knee-length dress has a bodice covered with ivory lace, short transparent lace sleeves and a full, flared skirt made of ivory silk.

'It's beautiful,' I say. It is, although I had no intention of getting married in anything approaching white. The dress does, however, fit in with the theme Anne-Marie suggested for the photographs and there's no doubt it has been exquisitely made. 'It looks a bit small for me.'

'Try it on,' Vivienne says.

I'd prefer to take it back to my room and try it in on private, but she seems so eager, and I don't want to offend her. 'Sure,' I say.

When I unzip my floral dress, I expect Vivienne to turn away or avert her eyes but instead she watches, one hand stroking the bodice of the vintage dress as I strip down to my underwear. A matching black thong and bra Miles brought me back from his recent Paris trip. I wish I was wearing something more modest.

'It might be easier to step into it,' she suggests when I'm ready. She unfastens the buttons of the bodice and hands me the dress. I step into it as instructed and pull it up to my waist. It is a better fit than expected. I slip one arm then the other through the delicate sleeves.

'Let me fasten you up,' Vivienne says.

I flinch as her cold fingertips touch my back. She works quickly, fastening the bodice tight around me. Even with the air from outside coming in, the attic is stuffy and as she seals me in with the last button, my ribs push against the lace as I try to inhale.

'We can get the bodice altered,' Vivienne says.

'I think we might have to.' I shift side to side, looking for some wiggle room but the bodice offers none.

'It looks wonderful,' she says wistfully.

I look at myself in the mirror on the inside of the wardrobe door. She's right. The dress is stunning and, with a few minor adjustments, will fit perfectly.

As much as I'd love to hang out with Anne-Marie in Paris and choose my own dress, I can't refuse Vivienne's kind gesture. She is offering me a dress that once belonged to Miles' mother. It would be rude to say no.

What did Riley wear when she married Miles? I'd love to ask Vivienne about the Vegas wedding, but I don't want to give her the satisfaction of knowing how little Miles has told me about his past. I suppose in some ways, his non-traditional wedding choice made sense. Riley had no family to invite and both of Miles' parents were dead. They had no one to please but themselves. Maybe they were so in love they had to tie the knot as soon as possible. Or did Riley entice him to the altar quickly for more materialistic reasons?

'My wedding dress was very traditional,' Vivienne says. 'Long and white and it even had a train. My mother was horrified. I wanted to wear a veil, but she made such a fuss I didn't dare.'

'Mothers,' I say.

'She didn't understand how I could be a feminist and also

want to give myself away to love.' Vivienne's eyes glaze with tears. 'I believed in love. Was that wrong?'

'No. Not at all.' Vivienne's grief crowds round me, dark and clingy and sucking all the air out of the room. I reach behind me, grasping at the buttons on the bodice, desperate for release.

Vivienne comes to my rescue, nimbly unfastening one button after another so I can pull the bodice down to my waist. I suck in lungfuls of air. Looking up, I see myself in the mirror, my black bra exposed. Like a bride ravished on her wedding night. Behind me hovers Vivienne's face, pale and gloomy.

'I hardly look at myself in the mirror these days,' she says. 'When I do, I don't like what I see.'

'Vivienne, don't say that.' I step behind her and nudge her gently towards the mirror. Now my face is the one hovering over her shoulder. 'You're a very attractive woman.'

'It's okay, Leah. You don't have to lie to me.'

'It's true.' When I put my hands on her shoulders, she tenses beneath me. 'For a start, I'd give anything for your bone structure.'

She turns her head, side to side, as if looking at herself properly for the first time in ages.

'And your colouring is so unusual,' I say. 'There's a lot you can do to make it work for you.'

She smiles. 'Is that a hint I should stop wearing black?'

'I'm just saying you've got a lot to work with.' I step over to the wardrobe. 'What else is in here? Is there anything you really like?'

'There's... Well, there is one dress I've always loved but I'm not sure I could carry it off.'

'Let's see it.'

Vivienne searches through the rail. 'Here.'

She unzips the suit cover to reveal a long dress of emerald-green silk. Sleeveless with a plunging neckline.

'Are you kidding?' I hold it up against her and we both look at her reflection. 'This colour is so you.'

'Do you think?'

'Absolutely. Can I try something with your hair?'

'My hair?' Vivienne grimaces. 'If you must.'

I get her to hold the dress and release the black claw clip holding her red hair in place. 'You could totally carry off a bob.' I tuck up the ends of her hair to show her what I mean. 'Like this.'

A shorter cut would show off her bone structure, make her look less haggard.

'You might be right.' A shy smile spreads across her face. 'It actually looks quite good.'

'This style is totally you.' I watch as she dares to admire herself in the mirror. 'Why don't you get it cut for the wedding? There must be a decent hairdresser's in Montreuilac. I'll come with you.'

'I don't know.'

'Let me treat you to a haircut,' I say. 'For your birthday.'

'Miles told you my birthday was coming up?' Her smile vanishes. 'I told him I didn't want any fuss.'

'I know and maybe I shouldn't have mentioned it, but I think you deserve a bit of fuss.'

'That's kind, but—'

'You've been through a lot,' I say. 'You need to be kind to yourself.'

I know it's too soon for Vivienne to move on after her husband's death, but a change of image might give her some hope for the future.

'I'll think about it,' she says. 'I am quite keen on the dress, though.'

'Then you should wear it to the wedding. As the bride, I insist.'

'Are you having a bridezilla moment?'

'Yes. Totally.'

She laughs. 'Okay, bridezilla. If you insist.'

34

VIVIENNE

August

I'm in the kitchen, sipping on a glass of chilled Chablis and chopping a block of feta into cubes for a Greek salad when Miles wanders in, a lost expression on his face.

'Lunch is late,' he says.

'That, cousin dearest, is because I have succeeded in finding your fiancée a beautiful wedding dress.' I scrape half of the feta cubes into the glass serving bowl filled with chopped tomatoes and cucumber.

'A dress? From where?'

I remind him about his mother's collection of vintage clothes in the attic.

'You went up into the attic?' he says.

'Only into the west wing. The old playroom hasn't changed a bit.' I take another sip of Chablis.

He juts his chin in the direction of my glass. 'Bit early for that, isn't it?'

'Relax, it's lunchtime. We're in France, remember?' I stare at the salad. What is it missing? 'Can you grab the tub of black olives from the fridge?'

Miles plods over to the fridge and opens the door.

'Middle shelf, probably,' I say.

After some rummaging, he finds the olives and hands them to me. 'How did it go with the photographer?' he says.

'Lots of girly fun and excitement. It was unbearable.'

He shoots me a strange, questioning look. 'Aren't we being a bit cruel? Getting a young woman's hopes up like this?'

'Her hopes of getting your money?'

'You know what I mean.' He pinches an olive from the tub and pops it in his mouth. 'I think she's becoming fond of you. She wants us to do something nice for your birthday.'

'Yes, thanks for telling her about that.' I pick up the small, sharp knife lying on the wooden chopping board. 'Now she wants to treat me to a haircut.'

'She can be very sweet. Underneath it all.'

'Underneath all the lying and cheating and gold-digging?' I tip the olives onto the chopping board. 'None of this is real, Miles. You do remember that?'

'She says she wants to have children with me.'

'So did Riley. As I recall.'

He has nothing to say to that.

'Dearest.' I slice one olive in half, then another. 'There will be another young woman out there, yearning for motherhood. I promise you. A decent woman, not someone in it just for herself.'

'Maybe.'

'You're getting Riley out of your system,' I say, 'and I'm getting Dom out of mine. By the time this game is over, we'll be new people.'

'As long as you're enjoying yourself, Vivienne.'

'Why shouldn't I? You certainly are.'

He turns his back on me and grabs a wine glass from the dresser. Once he's fetched the Chablis from the fridge and poured himself a glass, I ask how his meetings went this morning. Best to change the subject. This scheme of ours is meant to be bringing us closer together, not causing us to fall out.

'Good, actually.' He leans against the dresser. Takes a sip of wine. 'I think Heritage Capital are serious about making an offer for Sinclair Properties.'

'Miles.' I pause, knife hovering over the chopping board. 'That's amazing.'

'Nothing's definite yet.'

'Still, it's good news.' A sale wouldn't harm my finances. My mother had no head for business and made little of her inheritance, but I still have some shares in Sinclair Properties.

'I need to go to London tomorrow,' he says, 'just for the day. Face-to-face meeting with one of their guys.'

'Of course. You must.' I scrape the olives into the salad bowl.

'I'll take Leah with me.'

I meet his gaze. Is that suspicion in his eyes? 'No need. She'll be perfectly fine here.'

'No. I'll take Leah with me,' he says.

'Take Leah where?' In she glides in her floral dress, fresh lipstick on, her hair brushed and gleaming. I think of the slutty underwear hiding beneath her elegant outfit. Did Miles choose it for her? It didn't look like the kind of underwear a woman would choose for herself.

'I've got to go to London for a meeting tomorrow,' he says. 'Just a day trip. I'll book us first-class seats on the Eurostar.'

'Actually,' she says, 'I'd rather stay here.'

He stares at her. 'Really?'

She shrugs. 'Sounds like it's a flying visit. Not much point me tagging along. I'll be spending most of the day on trains.'

Poor Miles looks a bit confused. And a bit paternal. As though he might order her to go.

'You could shop,' he says. 'Have lunch with your friends, maybe.'

Funny. He and I both know she is a friendless soul.

'No, I'm good,' she says. 'I've got my dress now, thanks to Vivienne.' She turns to me. 'We could take the dresses into Montreuilac tomorrow, maybe? Get the alterations done.'

'Good idea.' Christ. Is she going to bully me into getting my hair done?

'Can I give you a hand with lunch?' she asks me.

'If you can set the table on the terrace; that would be wonderful.'

'No worries.'

She glides off, leaving Miles and I alone again.

'Stop looking worried,' I tell my cousin. 'She's perfectly safe here.'

'We can't afford for any of this... this business with Leah to get out,' he says. 'If anyone discovers what we've been up to, if my reputation is damaged in any way, it could harm the future sale of the company.'

It hurts, him talking to me like this. As if I don't know what I'm doing. As if I, of all people, would let him get into trouble.

'Everything will be fine,' I say. 'Haven't I always been good at keeping secrets?'

35

VIVIENNE

August

There is one secret in particular I have been keeping for decades. When Miles leaves me alone in the kitchen, I top up my wine, take a hefty gulp and allow myself to think about Bruce. There's no doubt his death drew Miles and I even closer together.

It was January 1986. I was fifteen years old. Miles was seventeen and Bruce only a few months away from turning twenty.

The Sinclairs were going to Chamonix for a week's skiing holiday and they kindly invited me to join them. I was delighted, having endured a dull Christmas with my mother in Cambridge. Mum was also delighted I was going. She claimed she had student dissertations to mark, but we all knew she intended to spend the rest of the holidays with her latest lover, an Italian postgraduate student. I didn't complain. According to her own theories, Mum wasn't supposed to be constrained by motherhood, and I had to play my part in helping her prove she could have it all.

We arrived in Chamonix on the third of January. Despite his wealth, my Uncle John refused to go away for New Year due to what he called 'criminally inflated' prices. However, the chalet he'd booked for us was luxurious and close to the slopes. I had a room on the upper floor, next to where Miles was sleeping. On the flight over to Geneva, he'd told me how glad he was to have my company. He hated being stuck with Bruce on family holidays. Or rather, Bruce hated being stuck with him and wouldn't let Miles forget it. My presence didn't stop Bruce tormenting him, but at least I was another target. Someone else to absorb his brother's cruelty.

As we sat there on the plane, neither Miles nor I had any idea Bruce would be returning from Chamonix in a coffin.

On the first morning, an athletic blonde chalet girl called Natalie arrived to cook our breakfast. In an effort to show off to her, Bruce announced he intended to ski off-piste during the holiday. Bruce was a macho idiot. A gifted rugby player at school and now at university, he exemplified the 'rugger bugger' attitude that some women inexplicably found attractive. I thought he was gross.

My Aunt Louisa gasped and forbade him to do any such thing, but everyone at the breakfast table knew Bruce would do exactly as he pleased. He was reckless and had no boundaries. Failings that would be the death of him.

I hated skiing and had no aptitude for it but, as Uncle John had paid for me to have daily lessons, I felt obliged to be enthusiastic. I was, however, a big fan of après ski activities. My aunt and uncle were too busy hanging out with other wealthy businessmen and their wives to supervise us, and we were left to our own devices. Every afternoon we hit the resort's noisy and crowded bars. Bruce usually abandoned Miles and I for a pretty girl or a group of men as macho and charmless as he was. Miles, chivalrous as ever, would hang out with me. He had no problem getting served alcohol and no one ever questioned if I was old enough to be drinking the Southern Comfort and Cokes he bought me. We drank and smoked cigarettes, and I picked out women for him to chat up, but he was too shy. Like me, he was still a virgin and, like me, he felt insecure around the opposite sex. When he did pick out women for himself, they were always wrong for him. Too obviously attractive. Too vain. More his brother's type.

On the fifth night of the holiday, my aunt and uncle left Bruce, Miles and I at the chalet alone, so they could attend a gala dinner at a nearby resort. They planned to stay overnight at their friends' chalet and made it clear we were to behave ourselves in their absence. They left Bruce in charge and, in a rare fit of generosity, he bought us all tickets to see a Duran Duran tribute band at La Cave, the resort's biggest nightclub. I was excited. Like so many girls my age, I was a massive Duran Duran fan and utterly in love with John Taylor. I selected my outfit for the evening with care. Tight stonewashed jeans, a pastel pink jumper and my beloved black slouchy ankle boots.

My mum disapproved of women preening themselves for the male gaze, but Aunt Louisa, who was determined her niece should learn to be feminine instead of feminist, had bought me make-up for Christmas. Foundation, blusher, eyeshadow, thick black mascara and an eyebrow pencil she insisted would give my fair eyebrows 'a little definition'. I think she liked having a girl to play with. A daughter doll. Her gift was a kind gesture, although I sensed an implied criticism of my looks in her attempts to change them.

That night, before going out, I applied the make-up with trembling hands. When finished, I hardly recognised myself.

As I examined the mask I'd created in the bathroom mirror, I had no idea that by the next day Bruce would be dead, and that I would have played a not insignificant part in his demise.

36

LEAH

August

I have the bed to myself. I lie in a star shape, arms and legs stretched as far as they will go. Dawn sounds filter through the open window. The soft coo of the wood pigeons. Birdsong, cheerful and shrill. Beneath these natural sounds lurks the unnatural silence that cloaks the château and its grounds. The silence that once heard, becomes deafening.

Six solemn chimes from the grandfather clock in the hallway. Miles left half an hour ago to catch a train to Paris Gare du Nord, where he will then take the Eurostar into London. He'll check in at his office and then have lunch with a representative from Heritage Capital.

Yesterday, in the kitchen, when he announced we'd be going to London today, his attitude annoyed me. His assumption I have nothing better to do than accompany him everywhere he goes. Although his money does give him a certain amount of power, I have to start setting some boundaries.

A week ago, I would have jumped at the chance to get back

to a city. A week ago, I wouldn't have wanted to be at the château alone with Vivienne. Now, with her thawing slightly towards me, I think the two of us can rub along. I hope so. We're meant to be going into Montreuilac to get the dresses altered after breakfast.

To be honest, it feels good to have a break from Miles. Soon we'll be married, and I will have less time to myself than ever before in my life. Add kids and a large house to manage into the equation and my life could become time-poor very quickly.

Everything's a trade-off, Leah. You don't get something for nothing in this life.

Unsentimental advice from my mother as always.

I did suggest Miles should stay overnight in London and not tire himself with a long day of travel, but he said he couldn't bear to be away from me for even one night.

Pity. I would have enjoyed the time to myself.

Time to myself. Is that the only reason I turned down the chance to go to London with Miles? Or is it because since finding out about his Vegas wedding to Riley, I'm longing to conduct a proper search of her room? Each time I convince myself to leave the past alone, I discover something that makes me curious again.

Vivienne told me yesterday we wouldn't have a formal, sit-down breakfast this morning. She will go to the bakery at eight as usual and leave the fresh pastries in the kitchen for me to help myself. As soon as she goes out, I'll get my set of keys and check out Riley's room.

My phone pings. I pick it up from my bedside table and find a text from Miles.

On train to Paris. Will keep in touch xx

I told him he doesn't need to be texting me all day. He has far more important things to deal with.

In my emails, I find the link he sent me to the Dulwich property we're considering as a future home. I scroll through the photographs of the mansion's grand, empty rooms and try to picture myself serving dinner at the marble-topped kitchen island, or hosting a drinks party in the garden, or sitting in a rocking chair by the window of one of the bedrooms, breast-feeding a newborn. In these fantasies I look like a model from a catalogue. Someone put there to make the house look nice and represent the dream life that is supposed to be lived there.

The floor of the attic creaks above me. I think about Riley and the children she once promised to have. Miles could easily have divorced her. Unless their whirlwind wedding meant they didn't sign a prenup and that left him with too much to lose.

Or maybe he did love her enough to sacrifice his own desires. Maybe he does believe marriage is a commitment for life.

I examine my engagement ring. The large diamond at the centre catches the early sunlight creeping through the curtains. For the first time since Miles put the ring on my finger, I slowly ease it off.

My ring finger looks bare without it but feels lighter. Liberated. I had no idea how heavy the diamond was.

My phone pings again. Startled, I drop the ring. It rolls off the bed and onto the floor. I jump out of bed, drop to my knees and search with one hand under the bed until my fingers close around it.

Thank God. I climb back into bed and slide the ring back onto my finger, grateful again for its cold, weighty presence.

* * *

I drift back to sleep. When I wake it is almost 7.30 a.m. I open up Spotify on my phone and select the playlist I used to listen to on my way into the office. 'Bad Guy' by Billie Eilish fills the room. I throw back the sheet, spring out of bed and dance naked around the bedroom, feeling oddly liberated.

In the bathroom, I forgo my usual painstaking morning routine. Instead, I splash water on my face and give my teeth a cursory brush. No make-up this morning, only sunscreen. My hair could do with a wash, but instead I tether it into a messy bun with a scrunchie. Finally, I put on a pair of denim cut-off shorts I brought with me from home and a white cropped T-shirt. Not an outfit I would wear in front of Miles. I feel guilty for feeling so relaxed. So myself. I didn't realise how much I hold myself together when I'm with him.

My suitcase is tucked down the side of the wardrobe. I pull it out and open it. From the internal compartment, I retrieve Estelle's keys and slip them into the back pocket of my shorts. I also take out Riley's Chanel lip balm and apply a thick layer to my dry lips. The kiss of a dead woman.

The corridor outside my room is empty. On the first-floor landing, the grandfather clock is a few minutes away from eight. I'll wait until I hear Vivienne leave to go to the bakery.

Eight chimes later, the hallway below is still empty. No sign of Vivienne with her wicker basket over her arm.

A loud banging noise from downstairs gives me a jolt. Is that Vivienne shouting? I hurry downstairs in my bare feet. The noise is coming from the kitchen. As I approach the half-open door, Vivienne's ranting gets louder. She is standing by the window, looking out onto the back lawn, her phone pressed to her ear.

'Absolutely not,' she says, 'no way.' A pause. 'Really? Well tell them to go fuck themselves.' Another pause. 'You're my lawyer, aren't you? Then follow my instructions.'

She turns and slams her phone down on the kitchen table. As she lifts her head, she sees me hovering by the door. Her face crumples.

'Vivienne?' I push open the door and step into the kitchen. 'Are you okay?'

She rests her palms on the table and lets her head drop. 'Not really.'

I stay where I am, not wanting to move in case she spots the bulge of the keys in my back pocket. I'll have to return them to their hiding place as soon as I get a chance. 'Anything I can do to help?'

'No.' She laughs bitterly. 'Nothing at all.' She lifts her head. She's been crying, the skin beneath her eyes puffy and swollen.

'That was your lawyer?'

She nods. 'My dear departed husband wasn't blessed with business acumen. Sincerity and charm, yes, but I should never have let him set up his own venture. He had debts I didn't know about and now he's gone, I'm the one who has to suffer the consequences.'

She pulls out a chair and slumps into it. Removes her vape pen from her apron pocket and takes a desperate inhalation.

'Sorry to hear that,' I say.

She rubs her eyes. 'Bollocks – I haven't been to the bakery yet.'

'Doesn't matter. I'm sure we can manage.'

'No. We need supplies.' She gives me a pleading look. 'Would you come with me? I could do with the company.'

37

LEAH

August

Dolly the 2CV hurtles along the winding country road that leads from the château to the village of Grandfresnoy. A breeze surges in through the car's open windows, blowing strands of Vivienne's hair in front of her eyes. She is an erratic driver, a cigarette in one hand and the steering wheel gripped tightly in the other.

Charming and characterful as Dolly is, I can see why Miles labelled her a death trap. The gears crunch every time Vivienne changes them and the brakes, when she jams her foot on them, take a while to kick in. Hard to believe this car has been serviced recently.

'Don't tell Miles about the fag,' she says. 'I only smoke them when I'm driving.'

'Your secret's safe with me.'

'He's a hypocrite, you know? He gave me my first ever cigarette.'

Golden fields flash past. I press my hands against the dashboard as we career around a tight bend. As nice as it is to escape the confines of the château, this five-minute journey is beginning to feel like one of the longest drives of my life.

'Sorry,' Vivienne says. 'I'm an appalling driver, I know.'

'It's fine.'

She reaches into the pocket of her black shirt dress and pulls out her phone. She checks the screen before jamming it back in her pocket. 'My husband always criticised my driving, but he's not here to do it now.' She sighs. 'Men. Even when they're gone, they still find a way to hurt you.'

I assume she's talking about the financial mess her husband left behind. I consider telling her about my father and his business failures. We could bond over this shared disappointment, but I don't want to give away anything to her I don't have to.

A black transit van pulls out from a side road ahead of us. Vivienne, humming a tune to herself and sucking hungrily on her cigarette, doesn't slow down.

'Vivienne.' I point at the van.

She carries on humming. The car surges forward as she hits the accelerator.

'Vivienne.'

'Shit.' She slams on the spongy brakes and pumps the horn hard. We miss hitting the van by centimetres. The driver sticks a hand out of his window and flicks us the middle finger.

'Fuck you,' Vivienne yells, returning the gesture.

My seatbelt shoots out of its buckle. I grab it and jam it back in.

'Bloody French drivers.' Vivienne glances at me as I try to jam the seatbelt back in. 'That thing's knackered. It does that sometimes.'

Lucky it didn't do it when the car was braking.

We drive the remaining mile to the village at a slower speed, but my heart continues to pound. Miles said Vivienne once tried to take her own life. She didn't seem to have much regard for her life or mine just then. That phone call this morning must have really got to her.

We park outside the village store, Vivienne easing the 2CV between two round concrete pots filled with weeds and wilting purple flowers.

The main street of Grandfresnoy is uninspiring. Drab two-storey houses with dilapidated facades. A bus stop covered with graffiti. The village store is low on French rustic charm and reminds me of the Spar near my old flat in Tooting. One aisle is filled with crisps, cheap chocolate and biscuits, another is crammed with tinned goods. There is a chilled cabinet containing milk and cheap packaged cheese and, at the back of the store, a well-stocked off-licence. Only the bakery section redeems it. Large baguettes in a wire basket behind the till. Croissants and pastries in a glass cabinet on the counter.

As Vivienne wanders the aisles and raids the chilled cabinet, throwing items into her wicker basket, I stare at the front covers of the French gossip magazines. I have a sudden yearning to be back at work, swapping celebrity gossip with my colleagues.

When she's done, Vivienne hands her basket over to the stocky man with a shaved head behind the counter. They chat in French as he rings up her items. Distracted by an article about Leonardo DiCaprio and his latest model girlfriend, I forget about her for a few minutes. When I look up again, she is staring at the shop door and there, on the other side of the glass, staring back at her, is Jacques.

Heat surges into my cheeks. Has he seen me? Not wanting Vivienne to catch me looking at him, I pretend to be engrossed in the magazine, the photographs of Leonardo and his much younger girlfriend blurring before my eyes.

'Leah?' Vivienne appears at my side, her face tight with tension. 'Can you pay for the shopping?' She shoves a bundle of euros into my hand. 'I've just seen an old friend outside, and I want to say hello.'

'Sure.'

Jacques is nowhere to be seen. Vivienne scurries out of the shop and turns right, the door banging shut behind her. I smile at the man behind the counter as I follow her as far as the door. While the shopkeeper carries on ringing up our purchases, I peer to the right. There, at the end of the street are Vivienne and Jacques. The conversation between them is a heated one – Vivienne jabbing a finger at Jacques' chest, while he holds up his hands as if telling her to back off.

'Twenty-eight euros,' the shopkeeper says sullenly.

'*Oui.*' I hurry over to the till. 'Of course.'

By the time I exit the shop, Vivienne is already marching back to where the 2CV is parked. I glance up the road and glimpse Jacques turning left into a side street.

'Did you catch your friend?' I say.

'Yes.' She looks tired, distracted. 'I did.' A deep groove has appeared between her eyebrows. She takes the basket of shopping from me, unlocks the driver's door of the car and chucks the basket on the back seat.

'Do you mind if I walk back?' I say.

'Walk?' Her eyes narrow. 'Is my driving that unbearable?'

I laugh. 'Well, yes, but also I just feel like walking. I need the exercise.'

She inspects the Veja trainers I pushed my feet into when we left the château in a hurry. 'You're going to walk four miles in those?'

'These are my walking shoes.'

She shrugs. 'Okay.' I'm keen for her to get going so I can follow Jacques but suddenly the sound of pealing bells fills the space between us. Vivienne reaches into her pocket, takes out her phone and checks the screen. 'Christ's sake.' With a sigh she cuts the call off. 'Do you mind if we don't go into Montreuilac today? I'm knackered and, as you've witnessed, a little preoccupied.'

'Sure,' I say relieved. 'Fine by me.'

She manages a weak smile. 'I don't think Miles would be delighted if I killed his fiancée in a car accident.'

'No,' I say. 'Probably not.'

38

LEAH

August

I wave as Vivienne leaves. Only when the 2CV is out of sight do I hurry down the side street where Jacques disappeared. It is a narrow street, lined with a high fence on my side of it and several dingy bungalows on the other.

My pulse quickens when I see his Hilux parked halfway down the street. As I get close, the driver's door opens and he jumps onto the pavement. He's dressed in the same jeans and black T-shirt he came to the château in.

'What are you doing here?' he says.

'I want to talk to you.'

'Why?'

'I have questions.'

'Where is Vivienne?'

'She's gone back to the château.'

He looks at me warily. 'What questions?'

What do I say? That I can't stop thinking about him? That I

can't stop thinking about Riley and what may or may not have happened to her?

'Please,' I say. 'It won't take long.'

He scratches his neck. I see the head of the small black swallow that nests there. 'Fine.' He opens the passenger door of his truck. 'Get in.'

The Hilux is surprisingly tidy inside. The dashboard gleams and the floor mats are free from dirt. An air freshener in the shape of a snowflake dangles from the rear-view mirror. This car is the complete antidote to Dolly.

His hand rests in between the seats. The skin around my wrist tingles as I remember his fingers imprisoning it.

'First,' he says, 'I have a question for you.'

'Okay.'

'Did you tell Vivienne that Maman and I were at the château?'

'No.'

'Really?'

'Yes. What did she want to speak to you about just now?'

'She warned me to stay away from Clairvallon.'

'That's got nothing to do with me.'

'If you say so.'

Heat creeps across my chest. Is he accusing me of lying? 'I know you got fired from the château and I know why.'

'Who told you?'

'Vivienne.'

'You asked her about me?'

'No. I made some general enquiries about previous staff, and she told me about you.'

'She told you about the money and the jewellery?'

'Yes, she said you—'

'I stole nothing.' His hands clench the steering wheel. 'She lied.'

'Why would she do that?'

'Vivienne hates everybody. I bet she hates you. No?'

'She's not my biggest fan, but I—'

'She lied, but that didn't matter. I am a guy with a criminal record.'

'How long were you in prison?'

'Only ten months but once you have a record, life is hard. Vivienne said she would tell the police about me stealing if I didn't leave the job.'

That does sound like something Vivienne might do. 'What about Miles and Riley?' I ask. 'Did they believe her?'

He releases his grip on the steering wheel. 'It did not look good for me. I did not want trouble so I left.'

Is he lying? Either version of the story could be true. Why would Vivienne go out of her way to get him sacked?

'Were you having an affair with Riley?' I say.

He frowns. 'What?'

I can't tell if my question is lost in translation or if he understands and finds it ridiculous. 'Was Riley cheating on Miles? With you?'

'No,' he says emphatically. 'She was not cheating on her husband.'

He sounds convincing. We stare at each other in silence until my phone intrudes. I take it out of my pocket and check the screen. It is Miles, telling me he is on the Eurostar.

I put the phone away.

'Monsieur Sinclair?' he says.

'Yes.'

He peers out of the windscreen, then looks in the rear-view

mirror. 'Is that why you are here?' he says. 'You want some fun, to cheat on him and you think I am your man?'

'No.' Once again the urge to touch him overcomes me. I reach for his cheek and caress the dark stubble there.

'Don't,' he says.

I lean towards him. When I press my lips against his, they part for me. Our tongues meet. He tastes of coffee and tobacco. He pulls me close and soon we are clinging together, my hands in his hair, his dark stubble grazing my chin. When he slides a hand between my legs, I unzip my shorts and guide his fingers inside me.

His eyes look deep into mine as he explores me. Heat gathers low in my belly. My breath quickens. He seems to know exactly where to touch me.

Then, just when I'm on the brink of release, he stops and pushes me away.

'This is what I thought.' He leans back in his seat, his breath ragged. 'You have your rich old man, but you want some fun.'

'No.' My head feels light. Dark spots appear in front of my eyes.

'You people are all the same.'

'Fuck you.'

'Get out.' He slams his hands on the steering wheel. 'Go on. Get out.'

Tears prick my eyes. I zip up my shorts. 'Why did you tell me to be careful?'

'What?'

'At the château. You told me to be careful.'

'You are too young for this engagement. You don't know what you're getting into.'

'I'm an adult.'

'Sure.' He leans across me and opens the passenger door. 'Just get out.'

'Fine.' I jump out of the Hilux.

'Leah,' he says. I turn to look at him. 'Stay away from me. Please.'

39

LEAH

August

By the time I arrive at the château gates, it is almost ten-thirty. My T-shirt clings to my sweaty back, my trainers have rubbed raw patches into my heels, and a headache throbs at my temples. I can't remember when I was last this hungry and thirsty. After marching away from Jacques, I was too shocked and angry to think clearly about the logistics of my long walk home. I should have returned to the shop and bought some water and something to eat but instead I typed Château Clair-vallon into my Google Maps and set off into the hot August morning.

I punch in the code on the keypad by the gates and, after a longer hesitation than usual, they creak open for me. I limp up the drive, grateful for the shade of the tall trees flanking me. Most of the walk back from Grandfresnoy was a blur. Fuelled by adrenalin and confusion, I hardly noticed the fields on either side of me or the village I passed through. All I could think about was Jacques. What the hell was I playing at? Now, despite my hot and flustered state, I shiver as I recall the sharp, sweet shock of his tongue touching mine.

A messy mix of desire and shame runs through me. When I was with Jacques, I felt out of control. As if something or someone was urging me on. As if I wasn't myself.

Or maybe I was. Maybe all engaged people are tempted to cheat in the lead-up to their wedding. It was a classic cold-feet moment. A chance to act on impulse. To snatch something I might not have again for a long time.

When the château comes into view, I stop and stare. It looks different. The attic windows are open. As if the château can't contain its secrets any longer and wants to set them free.

When I step inside the front doors, the first thing I do is slowly remove my trainers. My red, swollen feet gratefully absorb the chill from the hallway tiles.

'Vivienne?' The kitchen door is wide open. No sign of her in there. Ignoring my empty stomach and my dry throat, I dart up the stairs to the first floor. 'Vivienne?' I say, quieter this time.

No response. Instead of the usual darkness, the staircase up to the attic floor is bathed in light. I tread gently on the stairs, quiet as I can in my bare feet.

The door to the west wing of the attic is open, but I ignore that. I already know what's in there. The door on the opposite side of the landing is open too. Wide open.

'Vivienne?' My voice cracks. I swallow and clear my throat. 'Vivienne?'

No response.

A chill at my core. Hard and icy. I step over the threshold and into the attic's east wing.

Even with the windows open on both sides, the light that fills the space is a gloomy green. The only window still closed is the one straight ahead of me at the gable end of the attic. The one above the roof terrace.

The attic stretches away from me, a long space cluttered with boxes, odd pieces of furniture and piles of random stuff. The rough wooden planks beneath my bare feet are grimy and gritty. This side of the attic hasn't been refurbished like the west wing. Here, there is exposed stone between the wooden rafters on the sloping walls. Is that why I still feel cold? Why I have goosebumps on my legs?

I stare at the sealed window at the gable end. All I want to do is open it and take a look. To see where Riley's death happened. To reassure myself how easy it would be for someone to have an accident there.

As I pick my way through the cramped space, strange objects catch my attention – a wooden birdcage, a soldier's helmet, a box filled with stamps cut from envelopes, another filled with empty jars. A stack of old newspapers up to my waist. *Les Actualités du 'Petit Journal'*. The top one is dated 13 May 1933 and on the front is a picture of a Nazi soldier addressing a crowd and another of an angry mob burning books. The other side of the attic, with its playroom and childhood memorabilia, is all innocence but here in the east wing lives the dark side of history.

A creaking sound behind me. I turn around. Nothing there but my footprints in the dust. As if a ghost has just crept up on me.

Ahead of me, the window Riley once climbed out of lures me on. I step over a mound of leather-bound books and a wooden chest filled with abandoned doorknobs and I'm there. I unfold the shutters, wrench the rusty latch loose and open the window wide.

My hands rest on the windowsill. My legs tremble beneath

me. The view is spectacular. From here I can see beyond the edge of the château's grounds to an endless spread of fields. To my left is the walled garden and the outbuildings and then the dark mass of the woods. Somewhere beyond them is Jacques. The thought of him makes me feel faint. The view in front of me blurs before coming sharply into focus again.

I pull in lungfuls of warm air. I can see why it would be tempting to come up here as a teenager. Not just for the thrill but also to glimpse the outside world.

The roof terrace is bigger than it looks from the ground. About four metres by four metres. To reach it I'd either have to jump from the window or lower myself down.

My stomach twists and plummets. The wrought-iron railings that surround the terrace would only reach to my waist. Not much of a barrier. I stare at the gap where the railings partially collapsed. There is the spot where Riley fell. From here it looks like a long way to drop. A tight pain in my chest. I realise I'm holding my breath. A strong desire to climb down there and investigate grips me. I lift one leg and swing it over the windowsill.

'What the hell are you doing?'

Vivienne is standing behind me, hands on her hips, her pale face tight and anxious. How on earth did she creep up on me like that?

My head swimming, I ease my leg back to the ground and step away from the window. 'I just wanted to see... to see this part of the attic.' I stare down at my grimy feet, suddenly ashamed. She must think I'm morbid for wanting to get close up to the scene of a tragedy.

'What if you'd fallen?' Vivienne's eyes flare wide. 'Miles would kill me if I let anything happen to you.'

'I'm sorry.'

'It's my fault.' She pulls her vape pen from her apron pocket and drags deeply on it. 'I shouldn't have left the door open.'

'No, I shouldn't have come in here.'

'The attic needed airing. I thought I would do it while Miles is away.'

'Does he ever come up here?'

'No.' Vivienne looks at me, incredulous. 'Of course not.' She sighs. 'I suppose it was inevitable you'd want to come up here. To see.'

'I just—'

Vivienne peers out of the window. 'It can't be easy competing with a dead woman. Especially one like Riley. She was in a league of her own.'

A stab of envy in my guts. 'That's not how I feel.'

'You're the sort of girl who could steal any man away from his wife. A touch harder when she's dead though.'

'Look, Vivienne I—'

'How much has Miles told you about that day?'

I should pretend Miles has told me everything I need to know. I should make a dignified exit. 'Not much,' I say. 'It's hard for him to talk about.'

She steps up to the open window and looks down at the roof terrace. 'It was a terrible day. I'll never forget it.'

'You were here?'

'Yes. I came for the Easter holidays.' She rests her hands on the windowsill. 'So much you don't know.'

I shrug as if it doesn't matter but my mind is whirring. Why didn't Miles tell me Vivienne was here too?

A fraught silence swirls around us. Vivienne sucks on her vape pen.

'Miles was in Paris that day,' she says, blue smoke shrouding her face. 'I was here until lunchtime and then I drove to Compiègne for a change of scene. I had lunch in the town and then I visited the palace. Fascinating place. Restored by Napoleon in the early nineteenth century. Incredible art collection.' She shakes her head. 'I stayed out much longer than I expected to. When I returned, I found Miles on the back terrace. There were fragments of stone everywhere and the broken railings lying in a heap. Miles had Riley in his arms. He'd called for an ambulance, but it was obvious she was dead.'

Part of me wants Vivienne to stop talking. Part of me is desperate for her to carry on. Perhaps if I hear the story of that day, I will stop inventing crazy scenarios of my own.

'Her head was hanging to one side,' Vivienne says. 'All floppy. Her neck broken.'

Her eyes have glazed over, as if she is absent from herself. As if she is down on the terrace below with Miles, reliving that awful day.

'That's enough,' I say. 'I don't need—'

'One side of her face was smashed in.' Vivienne's voice is strange and distant, as if she is in a trance. 'Miles had blood all over his shirt.'

'Vivienne.'

My voice is loud enough to jolt her out of the past. She slams the window shut and quickly folds the shutter over it.

The fraught silence thickens.

'Don't come up here again.' She steps closer to me. 'It's not safe.'

'I won't.'

'Don't worry, I won't tell Miles.' She wipes her hands on the front of her apron, as if the past can be wiped away that easily. 'As long as you don't tell him about my shocking driving and my leaving the attic door open.' A sudden smile. 'It will be our little secret.'

40

VIVIENNE

August

After Leah leaves me alone in the attic, I stand for a moment amongst the boxes of junk and piles of bric-a-brac, adrenalin and exhaustion warring inside me.

What a morning. First the phone call from the lawyer and then the incident on the way to Grandfresnoy, when I almost crashed into that van. Instead of concentrating on the road, I was thinking of all Leah and Dom had put me through. Whipping myself up into a rage.

I, like my cousin, need to watch my temper sometimes. Those flashes of anger are a familial bond we share. A legacy from the Sinclair side of the family.

Time to seal up the attic again. I start with the windows on the left-hand side, shutting out the light. My temper flared again when I saw Jacques this morning. I made it clear he should leave home again as soon as he could. His presence is a reminder of the past both Miles and I could do without. Seeing him prompted me to come back and fling open all the windows up here. An attempt to chase out the château's darker memories.

I leave the window overlooking the roof terrace until last. Unable to resist another peek, I lean on the windowsill and survey the view of the château's grounds and the fields beyond. Finding Leah up here was very unsettling. When I first saw her with her leg slung over the windowsill, I contemplated letting her climb down onto the roof terrace. I even imagined her meeting the same fate as Riley.

I couldn't let that happen. Miles wouldn't want it to end that way. Telling Leah about Riley's death wasn't easy. Thinking back to that day never is. What a mess Miles was. He was lucky I was here to sort everything out. We've always looked out for each other. Especially after what happened with Bruce.

My vape pen finds its way between my lips. I take a couple of deep drags and think back to Chamonix. To the night of Bruce's death. To my younger self, getting ready to see the Duran Duran tribute band. The stonewashed jeans, the pink pastel jumper, the slouchy ankle boots.

When I came downstairs to the chalet's living room in my finery, my aunt and uncle had already left for their night away. Miles and Bruce were lounging on the sofa. I stood there, suddenly self-conscious. Aware of the thick layer of make-up on my face and my backcombed fringe. My body tensed as I awaited the usual barrage of sarcastic comments from Bruce.

Instead, he sat up straight and let out a low whistle. 'Look at little Vivienne,' he said. 'All grown up.'

Something in his tone made me shudder.

'You look great,' Miles said. 'Love the hair.'

'Love the shirt,' I told him. Miles had a thing for stripy shirts back then. This one was red and white, and he'd tucked it into his dark blue jeans. Bruce wore his white shirt untucked. The room reeked of his Brut Musk aftershave.

Our plan was to go to Le Coin des Amis, one of our favourite bars, for a drink before the gig, but Bruce produced a bottle of Ricard pastis he claimed to have shoplifted from a supermarket that afternoon. Maybe he had. Bruce was such a bullshitter it was hard to tell.

'Let's have this before we go to the bar.' He swigged straight from the bottle and offered it to me. I was going to refuse but my bold new mask made me grab it from him and take a long gulp. The pastis burned the back of my throat, but I didn't cough.

'Go, Viv,' Bruce said.

'I wouldn't have any more,' Miles warned me. 'That stuff is strong.'

I should have listened to him. Instead, I took another swig before passing him the bottle. The alcohol lit me up from inside, making me smile. The night ahead seemed tinged with magic. I had a strong feeling that by the end of it I would be transformed in some way. I was right but the transformation was one I could never have imagined.

Despite Miles and Bruce drinking most of the pastis, I was still tipsy by the time we reached Le Coin des Amis. Bruce bought me a vodka and Coke. As soon as I took the first sip, I could tell it was a double, but I didn't care. Tonight was a special night. I wondered if I might actually kiss someone. I hadn't yet, not properly, not with tongues, and it was something I wanted to get out of the way.

Natalie, our chalet girl, was there with a few friends. Bruce was all over her, but I was pleased to see she seemed more interested in talking to Miles.

More drinks. Doubles from Bruce. Singles from Miles who

didn't realise Bruce was slipping me drinks as well and who was too busy chatting to Natalie to notice. A sweet guy called David started talking to me. He was eighteen and had thick metal braces on his teeth. He was on holiday with his parents and was hoping to study law at Oxford and he was going to see the Duran Duran tribute band and I wondered if he might be my first proper kiss. I wondered if it would be weird with his braces.

'Viv,' Miles said, interrupting us. 'Time to head to the gig.'

'Shall I walk up with you?' David asked shyly.

'Look, mate,' Miles said, switching into protective older-cousin mode, 'she's only fifteen.' He grabbed my arm and we followed Bruce and Natalie and her friends through the resort's snowy streets. The cold air made me realise how drunk I was. At one point, I stumbled and Natalie helped me up and asked if I was okay.

When we reached La Cave nightclub, we joined the queue outside. Music flooded out of the bar and into the street. 'Blue Monday' by New Order.

Once we got to the front of the queue, Bruce handed over our tickets to one of the bouncers.

'How old is she?' the stocky Frenchman asked him, pointing at me.

'Eighteen,' Bruce said.

'Any ID?' the bouncer asked me.

'She's only fifteen,' said a voice behind us. We all turned around to see David with the braces standing there.

'You dick,' Miles said, but it was too late.

* * *

The bouncer turned all of our group away, including Natalie. After summoning his best French to tell the bouncer to go and fuck himself, Bruce insisted we go back to the chalet and party there. Natalie came too, although every time Bruce tried to slip an arm around her waist on the walk there, she brushed him off.

'Shall I make you a coffee?' Miles asked me when we got back to the chalet. 'You're totally sloshed.'

'I'm fine,' I said, but my wobbly legs told me otherwise. Still, when Bruce produced a bottle of chilled champagne from the kitchen, I swigged from the bottle when it came my way.

Bruce put a cassette of *Seven and the Ragged Tiger* by Duran Duran in the stereo in the living room and turned the volume up as high as it would go. We jumped around and belted out the words to 'The Reflex' and 'New Moon on Monday'.

'Who needs a tribute band?' Bruce said.

We downed another bottle of champagne, none of us caring how much trouble we would get in tomorrow when my aunt and uncle returned. Bruce put on one of the 'Now That's What I Call Music' cassettes. Miles found a bottle of Gordon's gin and made gin and tonics. He has always made an exceptional gin and tonic.

At one point I was dancing with Natalie to Madonna's 'Get into the Groove'. Natalie was a good dancer, all sexy long limbs and shimmying hips. Yet even though I must have looked awkward and clumsy next to her, she made me feel confident. She made me feel almost beautiful.

Bruce couldn't take his eyes off her. Miles was hammered. His head kept lolling back on the sofa like he was going to fall asleep.

Shortly afterwards, when I was throwing up in the downstairs toilet, Natalie was the one holding my hair out of my face and patting my back.

'You'll feel better when it's all out,' she said.

When we returned to the living room, Miles was sitting on the floor, cross-legged, trying to light a cigarette. Bruce was sprawled on the sofa.

'Hey,' he said to Natalie when she walked over to him. 'Come and give us a cuddle.'

Natalie reached over him and fetched her red ski jacket from the back of the sofa. 'I'm leaving.'

'Don't go.' Bruce grabbed her arm and tried to pull her on top of him. 'You can stay. My parents are away all night.'

'Get off me.' Natalie wriggled free.

'Fine.' Bruce sneered. 'See you in the morning when you come back to make my breakfast. Waiting on rich guys like me is all girls like you are good for.'

'Fuck off, you prick.' She shot me a concerned look. 'Don't let Vivienne drink any more,' she said to Miles. 'She's had enough.'

Miles looked up, a cigarette hanging from his lips the wrong way round, smoke trailing from the singed filter. His expression was morose, his eyes bloodshot. 'Bye, Natalie,' he said.

I watched her go.

'Stupid bitch,' Bruce said. Miles made another attempt at lighting the filter end of his cigarette. Dizziness washed over me.

'Vivienne?' Bruce said.

* * *

That's when I must have blacked out. When I came to, I was lying on top of my bed on my back. My bedside lamp was on, but the light seemed very dim. I was struggling to breathe. There was something over my face. Something soft that smelled of cigarette smoke. My arms were trapped overhead. I realised my jumper had been pulled up over my head, covering my face and trapping my arms. I realised my jeans and my underwear had been pulled down to my ankles.

My legs had been pushed apart and a heavy weight lay on top of me. I felt a hot stab of pain as something hard and warm thrust itself inside me and then withdrew. Then came another thrust and then another, faster this time.

I screamed. Again and again. A hand smothered my mouth.

'Shut up.' Bruce's voice in my ear. 'Stop it.'

Seconds later came a crashing and slamming sound. Someone yelped. The weight lifted off me.

'What the fuck are you doing?' I heard Miles say.

I found the strength to move my arms and pulled my jumper down, freeing my face. I sat up and yanked my underwear and my jeans back up again.

'You animal.' Miles, red in the face, his eyes wild, had an arm around Bruce's neck. 'You can't do that to her.'

Bruce, taken by surprise, allowed Miles to drag him as far as the bedroom door before he retaliated. First, he drove an elbow into Miles' gut. Miles groaned and loosened his grip just enough to allow Bruce to squirm free. Then Bruce turned and punched him in the exact same place in his stomach. Winded, Miles staggered backwards.

'You're crazy.' Bruce pushed past him and ran out of the bedroom.

'Bastard.' Miles straightened up. 'I'll kill him.'

'Don't,' I said. Tears streamed down my face. I hugged my knees close to my chest. 'Don't.'

Miles turned and disappeared down the hallway. When Bruce yelled out in pain, I jumped out of bed and followed the grunting noises until I found the pair of them wrestling at the top of the stairs.

'Miles, don't,' I said, although part of me wanted him to pulverise his brother.

What happened next was an accident. I've never doubted that. The two drunk men pushed and shoved each other and, after Bruce leaned backwards to avoid a punch from Miles, he lost his balance.

His eyes opened wide with shock as gravity took over. His arms flailed around, searching for the banister but missing it. For what seemed forever, he was suspended in mid-air and then he tumbled and the first time his head made contact with the staircase I heard a sickening crack that made me freeze.

Miles and I looked down at his crooked body for several minutes without speaking.

'Bruce?' Miles whispered finally.

He crept down the stairs and I followed him, expecting Bruce to leap up and laugh at us both. One of his sick practical jokes.

Bruce didn't move. Miles nudged him with his foot.

'Stop messing around. Get up.' He was clearly clinging to the same thread of hope I was. 'Shit.' He started to cry. His shoulders shook. Snot ran from his nose.

I knelt beside Bruce and felt his neck for a pulse like I'd seen people do on TV. I didn't really know what I was doing but I couldn't feel anything beat or race beneath my fingertips.

'I think he's dead,' I said.

41

LEAH

August

The grandfather clock outside our bedroom door chimes three times. In the four-poster bed, Miles thrashes around in his sleep beside me, his sweating body entangled in the sheets. Trapped in a nightmare.

'No,' he whimpers. 'Please. No.'

'Miles.' I grip his shoulder and shake him. 'Miles.'

'No.' He wakes with a start and sits bolt upright. 'Jesus.'

'Come here.' I ease him back down and hold him in my arms. 'It's okay.' I kiss the top of his head. 'It's okay.'

He didn't return from his London trip until almost eleven. We had a quick glass of wine on the terrace before coming to bed. He didn't tell me much about his meeting, but he said everything went well. Does that mean Sinclair Properties will be sold soon?

'Were you dreaming about Riley?' I ask. The darkness makes it easier to be direct. To discuss what gets hidden in the daylight.

'Yes.'

Since Vivienne shared those gruesome details about Riley's death with me up in the attic, I haven't been able to get them out of my mind. No wonder there are times Miles can't suppress his memories.

He rolls away from me and switches on his bedside lamp, flooding us with soft yellow light. He sits up, reaches for the glass of water on his bedside table and drains it in one long gulp. His snore strip is dangling from one side of his nose, dislodged by his tossing and turning. He peels it off and drops it onto the bedside table, next to his empty glass.

'I haven't dreamt about her since we came here,' he says. 'Silly really, to think I'd get away with it.'

I rest a hand on his chest. The wiry grey hair there is slick with sweat. 'It's not surprising you would dream about her.' I glance up at the ceiling. I can't help feeling that by intruding into the attic today, I've somehow stirred up his memories of Riley. Given her permission to visit him in his dreams.

'It's probably guilt,' he says.

'Guilt? About what?'

'You and I getting married. In the dream she was wearing a wedding dress.'

'That's some very direct symbolism.'

'Very direct.' He gives me a tired smile. 'If only I could take a pill and wipe out the memory of that day forever.'

'It must have helped to have Vivienne here?'

'You've talked with Vivienne about what happened?' he says, his expression guarded.

'Not much. It came up in conversation the other day, that's all.' I have no intention of telling him about my jaunt to the attic. 'She told me she got back to the château just after the accident.'

I try not to imagine Miles with blood all over his shirt. I try not to imagine Riley's smashed-up face.

'It's a good job she was here.' He rubs his eyes. 'She helped me deal with everything. The medics, the police. All of it.'

No wonder the two of them are so close. No wonder she is so protective of him.

'It's easy to take her for granted sometimes,' Miles says. 'I need to remember how much she's done for me.'

'You've helped her too,' I say. 'You're helping her now.'

'I still feel like Riley's death was my fault,' he says. 'Like I could have prevented it.'

'Miles, accidents happen.'

'Yes, they do, and the people left behind have to deal with the aftermath.'

Disturbing as it was, going up into the attic today and seeing where Riley died reassured me of one thing. That roof terrace was an accident waiting to happen. An accident that did happen. One that still haunts Miles now.

'Are you having second thoughts about the wedding?' I say. Why shouldn't he be? Isn't that what my encounter with Jacques in Grandfresnoy was about? Second thoughts. Cold feet. At least I now know Jacques didn't haven't an affair with Riley. I can stop creating wild scenarios about the past. I can stop suspecting Miles of any sinister involvement in Riley's death.

'No,' he says, 'no second thoughts. If all goes well and I sell the company, I'll retire. We can be together, raise our family and have a wonderful life.' He lifts my hand from his chest and kisses it. 'I can see it, Leah. Our future. We could be happy together. Free of the past. Free to love each other with nothing in our way.'

Miles and I together in the Dulwich mansion. Two beautiful children. No money worries. I can see this future too. It's what I've been working for. Why then would I risk it all by making out with an ex-convict in a backstreet of a rural village?

'It will be a fresh start for both of us.' His hand strays to my breast. 'You in your white dress.'

'Ivory dress. I'm hardly a virgin.'

'How old were you when you lost your virginity?'

'Fifteen.'

He dips his head and kisses my breast. 'Early starter.'

'Not compared to the other girls in my year.'

'How old was he?'

'Nineteen.'

Miles lets out a low whistle. 'Naughty.'

'I was three weeks away from my sixteenth birthday.'

'Where did it happen?' He is getting aroused, his eyes taking on an intense, glazed look. 'I want to know everything.'

This is new. He's never asked for details of past conquests before. Most men don't want to know.

'Close your eyes,' he says. 'Tell me what you remember.'

I lost my virginity in my bedroom one afternoon when my mother was out. It was quick and disappointing but at least I'd got it over with. Not an experience I want to relive. I find myself thinking of Jacques. His dark, soulful eyes. The black swallow on his neck.

'We were in his car,' I say. 'It was summer. I was wearing shorts and a T-shirt.' I describe what happened with Jacques this morning only I carry it on further, turning reality into fantasy, the two of us ending up on the back seat with my legs around his waist.

'Christ.' Miles pushes my legs open and climbs on top of me. I keep my eyes closed. It is Jacques' face I see during the fast, urgent fuck. It is Jacques' face that lingers after Miles has rolled off me and turned off the light. Jacques' face that stays with me as, eventually, I lose myself to sleep.

42

VIVIENNE

August

Today is my birthday. Fifty-three years old. Thus far, I am not in a celebratory mood.

It is 10.30 a.m. and I'm in the back seat of the Lexus. Miles is driving with Leah seated beside him, looking as fresh and glamorous as ever in one of her designer outfits – cream-coloured culottes and a navy linen blouse. I did think about making an effort this morning but ended up in my usual black dress. Today, I am missing my husband more than ever.

We are on our way to Montreuilac. Miles is dropping Leah and I off there so we can hand in our wedding outfits for alteration and deal with some other wedding-related errands. How excruciatingly dull. To add insult to injury, Leah has booked me in at the hairdresser's for this makeover she insists I will thank her for.

The roof of the Lexus is down and, as we cruise along the main road towards town, the breeze on my face is a soothing antidote to what is already a hot, sunny morning. Miles turns his head and says something to Leah I cannot hear. She tips her head back and laughs. So insincere. I love my cousin dearly, but he isn't that witty.

When we stop at a set of traffic lights, he fondles her thigh. He is getting his kicks while he can. The wedding is supposedly in nine days' time, which means eight days from now, he will have to end the relationship. Maybe that is why he has been distant with me since his return from London. Or perhaps being so close to selling Sinclair Properties is making him edgy. If the sale goes through, he will be free of everything. Free from his memories of Riley and from the legacy he inherited when Bruce died. He always felt guilty about that. As the eldest son, Bruce would have taken over the company and Miles' life would have been very different.

As if he knows I am thinking about him, my cousin turns and glances at me. I smile but he looks away again. He can be moody sometimes. If he continues to be aloof, I will have to remind him of the secret we share. Of everything we have been through together.

The lights turn green. The Lexus surges ahead. Leah's long, dark hair streams behind her in the breeze. I yearn to grab a handful of it and pull hard. Instead, I yawn and stretch my arms overhead. I endured a fragmented sleep last night, disturbed by dreams of Riley hiding up in the attic. Dreams of Dom getting into his car and driving away into the night.

How strange it was to wake up this morning without my husband bringing me breakfast in bed like he usually did on my birthday. Leah and Miles are going to cook dinner for me tonight, but it won't be the same. A lesser woman than me might have given in to grief and taken her own life, unable to live with the pain any more. Not me. I'm made of stronger stuff. Suicide has never been an option.

* * *

Miles parks on a street near *Le Tailleur*, the clothes alteration shop. When he opens the passenger door for Leah, she steps elegantly out of the Lexus.

'I'll go in and tell them we're here,' she says, leaving Miles and I to fetch the dresses from the boot.

My cousin opens my car door for me before walking around to the boot. As I step onto the pavement, my phone rings in my black tote bag. I fish it out, heart thumping. Even though I know it won't be Dom, part of me still expects him to call. It still seems impossible my birthday will go by without me talking to him.

I stare at the screen. My son is calling to wish me happy birthday.

Miles slams the car boot shut and joins me on the pavement, the suit bag containing the two dresses slung over his arm. 'Is that Nathan?' he asks.

'Yes.'

The call rings out. I put my phone back in my bag.

Miles sighs. 'You should speak to him.'

'He always wants to talk about his father.'

'That's understandable.'

'I can't handle it. Not right now.'

'Look, Viv.' Miles puts a hand on my shoulder. 'If this business with Leah is all getting too much for you, maybe we should—'

'Call it off?' I brush his hand away. 'No, I'm fine.' I stare at him. 'Are you?'

'Totally fine.' He holds my gaze. 'I promise you I'm in this until the end.'

* * *

'Well, that was painless,' Leah says when we emerge from *Le Tailleur*. 'And it won't take them long to make the changes.'

'Yes, it went very well,' I say. The experience was indeed painless for Leah. Two seamstresses fussing around her, telling her how stunning she looked. Deciding how much they should let the dress out at the seams to accommodate her enviable curves. My consultation involved a few minutes with one seamstress. A dour elderly woman who made no comment on my figure but who tutted at the prospect of taking the dress in to fit my scrawny frame. Such an alteration would spoil the way the dress flowed, she said, but what else could she do?

'What next?' Leah asks. We have time to kill before she deposits me at the hairdresser's for my makeover ordeal. Miles has driven out to visit the Armistice Museum, not far from town, and won't be back for a while. When we parted, he told us to enjoy our 'girlie time'.

Girlie time. I'm old enough to be Leah's mother.

'Wedding cake,' I say. 'You can't have a wedding without a cake.'

I lead her to my favourite pâtisserie, *La Douce Époque*, a few streets away. Once there, I ask Marianne, the matronly owner, to show us some pictures of a traditional French wedding cake.

'It's called a *croquembouche*,' I tell Leah as she examines the pictures. 'It's basically a tower of cream-filled profiteroles. It's delicious.'

We choose a tall one, glazed with caramel and bound together with a web of spun sugar, and I arrange to have it delivered the day before the wedding.

'I can't wait to taste it,' Leah says.

She won't even get to enjoy one mouthful. I imagine Miles

and I picking at it for days after he has banished her from the château.

Outside in the street, Leah suggests we make our way to the hairdresser's. She doesn't want me to be late. I'm starting to feel nervous about this haircut. Dom liked my hair long, but, I realise, my appearance has nothing to do with him now. Funny how I still take his preferences into account. As if his gaze is still upon me.

We are walking down Rue de la Surveillance when I hear someone calling my name. I stop and turn around, a plummeting sensation in my stomach.

'Vivienne. *Je pensais que c'était toi.*'

It is Philippe, hurrying towards us, the jacket of his beige linen suit slung over his shoulder. Christ.

'Yes,' I say. 'It's me.' The mayor is the last person I want to see. Especially as I have Leah with me. A cold sweat erupts on my chest. I feel like a criminal about to get caught out. As if Leah is a kidnap victim and Philippe is about to recognise her and rescue her from my clutches.

'So good to see you.' Philippe leans in and kisses me on both cheeks. He knows nothing, of course. I just need to stay calm. 'How are you?' he asks.

'Very well,' I say.

He shakes his head. 'A sad story about your husband. I was sorry to hear it.'

Tears spring to my eyes, uninvited. I blink them away. Sympathy from others doesn't help. It only makes my loss more real.

'We're in town to get some of the wedding preparations done,' I say with forced cheeriness. 'Not long to go now.'

'Of course, of course.' He turns to Leah. 'The beautiful bride.' He steps close and subjects her to a tight, lingering embrace. Another man who can't resist her. 'How are you?' he asks.

'I'm very well.' She eases herself from his clutches. 'Excited about the wedding.'

'*Mais bien sûr.*' Philippe smiles, revealing startlingly bright teeth. He must have had them whitened since I last saw him. 'Tell Miles I will ring him to arrange *un enterrement de vie de garçon.*'

'What's that?' Leah asks.

'Literal translation is the burial of your boy life,' I tell her. 'We call it a stag do.' I smile at Philippe. 'I think Miles is a bit old for that sort of thing.'

'Me too,' the mayor says. 'I am thinking him and I can share a good bottle of wine. Nothing crazy.' He sighs. 'Miles has been through so much. I would like to make this gesture for him.'

'I'm sure he'll be very grateful,' I say, remembering how much Philippe has helped us in the past and how useful he has unwittingly been to us recently.

'And you ladies will have your own plans, no?' He turns to Leah. 'Historically, here in France, it was only the men that would celebrate before the wedding, but these days, we have the hen night too.'

Hen night. I couldn't think of anything worse.

'Don't you worry about us, Philippe,' I say. 'I'm sure Leah and I can find a way to have some fun.'

43

LEAH

August

After depositing Vivienne at the hairdresser's, I head back in the direction of the pâtisserie we visited earlier. She looked nervous when I left her, even though Talyse, the stylist I booked her in with, assured her a bob cut was going to look *incroyable* on her.

I understand Vivienne's apprehension. A new hairstyle can symbolise a fresh start, and for her that means acknowledging that a huge part of her past, her life with her husband, is over.

She looked emotional when the mayor gave her his condolences. I suppose they all go back a long way and Philippe must have known Dom as well. It was kind of him to suggest a stag do of sorts with Miles. God knows what Vivienne and I will do. Probably make stilted conversation over a couple of cocktails. Freddie and Florence both had their pre-wedding celebrations abroad – Freddie in Berlin and Florence in Ibiza. #friendship is everything. #theseguys!

I pass a café where a group of young women are sitting at

one of the outside tables, drinking coffee and laughing at a story one of them is telling. A wave of loneliness hits me. If only I had a tight group of female friends I could share my hen night with.

Everything's a trade-off, Leah. You don't get something for nothing in this life.

My mother again. A sudden longing for her presence makes my chest ache. If only I could spend the night before my wedding with her. Sure, we would spend most of it arguing but still, I miss her.

When I enter *La Douce Époque*, Marianne, the woman who served us, is surprised to see me so soon.

'Okay, I see,' she says, when I explain I want to buy a birthday cake as a surprise for Vivienne. My choice is a decadent one. An almond sponge layered with coffee butter cream and chocolate ganache and topped with a thick chocolate glaze. Marianne places a decoration on top. *JOYEUX ANNIVER-SAIRE* in gold letters. She also insists I take a packet of gold birthday candles.

After she puts the cake box in a supermarket carrier bag to disguise it, I pay and leave the shop. After checking for directions on my phone, I head towards the square where Miles and I had coffee when we first came to Montreuilac. I need to visit the food market and get supplies for Vivienne's birthday dinner. Fresh artisan pasta and the ingredients for a fresh pasta sauce. Such good quality ingredients won't be cheap. The cake was expensive too. It occurs to me that at some point soon, I will run out of money in my current account. How will Miles and I organise the finances once we're married? If I don't go back to work, will I get a monthly allowance? Will I have to ask whenever I want or need anything? As much as I love the idea of being taken care of, it will be strange not to have some money of my own coming in.

Are these valid concerns or am I sabotaging myself with doubts? I have so much to gain from this marriage. If Miles sells Sinclair Properties, he'll have even more money. We'll have the big house in Dulwich. A luxurious lifestyle. Yet even with all this to look forward to, I still find myself obsessing over Riley's death. Even though I know she didn't have an affair with Jacques and even though I'm sure Miles had no sinister involvement with her accident, I can't seem to let it go. Over the weekend, I thought about Vivienne being there the day Riley died. I thought about Miles holding his dead wife's body. Last night, I dreamt I was standing at the bedroom window looking down on the terrace. Riley was looking up at me. She was wearing the white cocktail dress and it was covered in blood.

Am I just projecting my anxieties about the future onto the past?

When I reach the square, I hesitate. The entrance to the food market is on my left but straight ahead is *Esprit des Fleurs* and, outside it is Naomi, arranging flowers in tall silver buckets.

Some people around here think Madame Sinclair's death was not an accident.

I should talk to her. Just to clear a few things up. After all, I've seen the roof terrace for myself, and I know Riley could easily have died in an accident. When I marry Miles, I'll be spending a lot of time in this area. I don't want people spreading false information about my husband's past.

I am across the square and outside the shop in no time. Naomi's bleached hair is loose today and, since I saw her last, she has added two thick blue streaks to it. Seeing her for the second time, I feel doubtful anything happened between her and Miles. She is far too alternative for his tastes.

When she sees me, she straightens up, a bunch of red roses in her arms and a defensive expression on her face.

'More flowers?' she asks. 'Or maybe you are here for something else?'

Directness is a trait I respect.

'I thought you might come back,' she says.

'Curiosity is a failing of mine.'

'Sorry?'

'I'm someone who likes to know all the facts.'

'You like facts or truth?' she asks. 'They are not always the same, no?'

'Riley's death. You said it wasn't an accident.'

'No. I said some people round here *think* it wasn't an accident.'

'If it wasn't an accident, then what did happen?' I ask her. 'Are you suggesting someone killed her?'

Naomi shakes her head. 'I did not say this.'

'You're implying it. Do you think Miles did it? Is that what people say about him?'

'Of course they say it. People say a lot of things.'

'Do you agree with them?'

'I think he loved her.' She sighs. 'I think most men loved her. She was that kind of woman.'

'What about Jacques Framboust?' I ask. 'Was he one of those men?' I didn't come here intending to speak about him, but I have a sudden need to know if he was lying to me. A need to know what kind of man he is.

'Jacques?' A pained shadow passes across her face.

'You must have worked at the château at the same time?'

'*Oui.*' A flicker of hurt in her eyes. An anguish I recognise.

'Were you and Jacques together?' I say.

'Together?' Her laugh is forced and unconvincing. 'We had a one-night stand. This is not being together.'

A one-night stand I suspect she wished had been more.

She bends over and jams the bunch of red, thorny roses into a nearby bucket.

'Did he have an affair with Riley?' I ask.

'*Merde*.' She whips her hand away from the roses. When she straightens up, I see a bubble of red blood on the pad of her thumb. She sucks at it.

'Did Jacques have an affair with Madame Sinclair?' I say.

Naomi removes her thumb from her mouth. Her lips are smeared with blood. 'Yes,' she says. 'They have an affair and I am sad and jealous and push her from the roof and she is dead.'

I watch as she licks the blood from her lips.

'Look at your face.' She laughs again, convincingly this time. '*Mon Dieu*, as if I would risk prison for *un vaurien* like Jacques Framboust. A no-good guy.'

I believe her. Jacques may have messed her around or misled her, but she doesn't come across as someone who would take revenge in such a drastic way.

'I don't know if he slept with Madame Sinclair,' she says, 'but they flirted. She flirted with everyone.'

'Is that why he was sacked?'

'No. He stole from the château.'

'You believe that?'

'It could be true. I don't care.' She sucks at the prick of blood on her thumb again. 'Anyway, he did okay from the Sinclairs.'

'What do you mean?'

'Estelle's cottage.'

'What about it?'

'It is part of the château estate. For many years the Sinclairs let her rent it. When Monsieur Sinclair closed down the château, he gave her the cottage. I heard also a small pension too.'

That sounds like something Miles would do. After all, Estelle worked for the family for decades.

'When Estelle is dead,' Naomi says, 'the cottage will go to Jacques and Béatrice.'

To me that suggests there is no bad blood between Miles and Jacques. Even if Miles didn't like Jacques flirting with his wife, it didn't stop him doing the right thing by Estelle.

'The rest of us who worked there got nothing,' Naomi says. 'No leaving bonus. No thank you for our hard work.'

'What do you really think about Riley's death?' I say, trying to get her back to the topic that really concerns me. 'Just between us. Was it an accident?'

Naomi shrugs. 'I think if they did a proper investigation at the time, there would be no rumours.'

'What do you mean?'

'They say it was an accident. Maybe it was. Maybe she just falls from up there. It is dangerous, no? But the police, they don't make any enquiries. The mayor just turns up at the scene, they all say okay is an accident and that is it.'

'The mayor?'

Naomi steps closer to me. 'The mayor is in charge of the local police. This is how it works here, but why should anyone trust him?'

'Why wouldn't they trust him?'

Naomi shakes her head. 'You do not know the system here. Our mayor he is charged with corruption before and he will be again, I tell you. This kind of thing happens all over France.'

'Naomi?' Sondrine comes out of the shop, a pair of scissors

in one hand, a length of red ribbon in the other. 'Oh, hello,' she says to me. 'You have come to talk about the wedding flowers?'

'Yes,' I say. 'Naomi was giving me some very useful information.'

'Good. When you are ready to make an order, please come and speak to me.' She leans close to Naomi and says something curt in French before hurrying into the shop. It sounds like she is ordering Naomi to get back to work.

'Goodbye, Leah,' Naomi says as she turns to go back into the shop. 'And good luck.'

44

LEAH

August

It's 6 p.m. I'm standing by the kitchen table, chopping the tomatoes for my arrabbiata sauce. Plenty of time to get everything done before cocktails on the terrace in an hour. Vivienne requested French Gimlets, which Miles is going to make. Underneath my white apron, I'm wearing my Saint Laurent silk slip dress. The one I was wearing when Miles proposed to me.

As the tomatoes bleed their seeds onto the wooden chopping board, I replay my conversation with Naomi in Montreuilac earlier today. Her accusations about the mayor disturbed me. Could she be right about him being corrupt? If so, his friendship with Miles is concerning, as is his involvement with Riley's death.

Or maybe Naomi was just complaining about the system here the way people complain about the police back home. Rumours about Riley could easily be a way for people like Naomi to vent about a system they perceive to be corrupt.

And why bring up the matter of Estelle's cottage? What business is it of hers how Miles chooses to reward his long-serving and loyal housekeeper? She sounded like a disgruntled ex-employee having a go. Whatever happened with Jacques, she obviously still feels sour about it and doesn't like the thought of him getting a financial windfall in the future.

I daren't ask Miles about the cottage. He'd be furious if he knew I'd spoken to Naomi again. I think about her wishing me good luck when we parted. She said it the way Jacques did. As if she thinks I will really need it and also as if she knows luck will be useless to me.

'Hello, darling.' Miles appears, still dressed in the pink shorts and blue T-shirt he wore out to the pool earlier. 'How's it going?'

'Good. All going to plan.'

He takes a deep, theatrical inhalation. 'Something smells amazing.'

'It's only onions sautéed with garlic.'

He hovers by the table, watching me chop the tomatoes, as if fascinated by the sight of me in a domestic setting.

'Who taught you to cook?' he said.

'My mother.' Another white lie. When we lost all our money, my mother, who had relied on Marks and Spencer's and expensive delicatessens to feed us, didn't know how to deal with our reduced food budget. I taught myself to cook so we could eat well with the money we had. The kitchen became my domain.

'Don't expect me to cook all the time when we're married,' I say.

'I wouldn't dream of it.' Miles wraps his arms around my waist. 'We'll have a housekeeper, and you can save your skills for special occasions.'

He kisses my neck.

'Pack it in.' I elbow him away. 'I need to get this done.'

He sighs and lets me go. I carry the bowl of cut tomatoes over to the hob and scrape them into the frying pan.

'Is something wrong?' he says.

'No. I'm just busy with dinner.'

'You're not annoyed about Philippe are you?'

'No.' The bowl lands on the worktop next to the hob with a clatter. 'Why would I be?'

'You don't mind him inviting me out the day before the wedding?' Miles fiddles with the neck of his T-shirt. 'When he called earlier, he said it will only be for a couple of hours in the late afternoon. I'll be driving so it will hardly be a rage.'

'It's fine. Honestly.'

'You and Viv can have a few drinks here.'

Great. The hen night of my dreams.

'It's lovely,' he says, 'what you've done for her today.'

I push the tomatoes around the frying pan with a spatula. 'It's nothing.'

'Giving her a makeover isn't nothing. She looks great.'

'I just wanted her to feel nice.'

'You're a good person, Leah. That's why I love you.'

A good person? Sometimes I'm not so sure about that.

'I should get showered,' he says. 'Viv won't be happy if her birthday cocktail is late.'

'Miles,' I say as he turns to go. 'There is one thing I want to talk to you about.'

He turns back, drums his fingers restlessly on the doorframe.

'I was doing some research about Montreuilac town hall earlier,' I say, 'just to learn a bit more about where we're getting married, and I came across some weird newspaper stories about Philippe.'

My Internet search had nothing to do with the town hall and everything to do with the town's mayor. I had to find out if what Naomi told me was true. All the newspaper stories I discovered had the same headline. *Le Maire de Montreuilac accusé de corruption*. It seems five years ago Philippe was charged with embezzlement.

'What do you mean?' Miles says. 'What stories?'

When I tell him what I found, his face relaxes.

'Oh, that.' He waves my concerns away. 'Hardly a month goes by without some accusation of local authority corruption. It's what the French do.'

'The corruption or the accusations?'

He smiles. 'Both. But in this case some journalist made a story out of an administrative error. A simple mistake that led to some regional funds going to the wrong place. Philippe is a stand-up guy. One of the good ones.'

Is he? Miles' explanation is possible. 'He seems to have been kind to you.'

'He has. He was a loyal friend when I needed one.'

How loyal a friend? I wish I hadn't spoken to Naomi today. I wish I hadn't let her fill me with doubt again. Funny how I don't want to believe her accusations about the mayor, but I do want to believe that Jacques didn't steal from the château and didn't have an affair with Riley.

Miles kisses me on the cheek. Tells me he must go and get ready.

Alone again, I stand by the hob as the tomatoes sizzle slowly in the heavy frying pan. I try to push Naomi's words about the mayor's corruptibility aside. What do all these snippets of gossip add up to exactly? That people in this area think

Miles killed Riley and that the mayor helped him to cover it up in return for money or some other mutual favour?

Get a grip, Leah. Don't let your imagination run away with you.

My mother is right. The financial security I've been working for is within reach. I can't let small-town gossip derail me now.

45

LEAH

August

'Leah, you absolutely surpassed yourself.' Vivienne pushes away her plate, which is empty apart from red smears of arrabbiata sauce. 'That was delicious.'

I've never seen her eat so heartily. Makes me feel guilty for not offering to cook before.

She sinks back in her chair and lets out a contended sigh. We are at the table on the back terrace, dusk settling around us, warm and sticky. All of us have made an effort for Vivienne's birthday dinner. Miles in a pink shirt and beige linen trousers and Vivienne, who despite wearing her usual black shirt dress, has been transformed by her new hairstyle. The chic bob, which ends just below her chin, takes years off her. As I thought, it accentuates her bone structure. I'm pleased to see she's wearing the deep brown lipstick I bought her from a chemist in Montreuilac. Fixing her hair and make-up won't make today any less painful for her, but I hope she feels a little better about herself.

'Yes, thank you, darling. It was sublime.' Miles dabs his mouth with his napkin.

'Mrs King used to make brilliant pasta,' Vivienne says. 'Do you remember, Miles?'

'Mrs King?' I say. 'Who was she?'

'The Sinclairs' housekeeper in London.' Vivienne sips her wine. 'When he was a boy, Miles used to hang out in the kitchen with her all the time.'

'Mrs King.' Miles stares at Vivienne. 'Yes. She was an excellent cook.'

'Poor Miles used to hide out in the kitchen. Me too, when I stayed at that house. It was the only place we could get away from Bruce.'

Miles reaches for the bottle of Sancerre at the centre of the table. 'More wine, anyone?'

'Please, dearest,' Vivienne says.

I let Miles top my glass up too, resolving to drink this one more slowly. I'm already tipsy thanks to the French Gimlets Vivienne insisted we start our evening with. Tasted almost like neat gin to me.

Vivienne cups the neat ends of her bob in both hands, as if checking it's still there.

'It really suits you,' I tell her. 'You'll get used to it.'

'I'm getting used to it already,' she says. 'I'm glad you persuaded me to do it.' She picks up her full wine glass. 'What do you think, Miles? Does it suit me?'

'Vivienne, I hardly know you,' he says.

When I stand up and reach for the empty plates, Vivienne stands up too.

'Sit down, birthday girl,' I say. 'You're not doing a thing tonight.'

'I won't argue.' Vivienne sits down and picks up her wine. 'I could get used to being spoiled.'

'Miles?' I say. He pushes back his chair and gathers up our empty plates. 'Back in a minute with pudding,' I tell Vivienne.

'Miles, bring the speaker from the kitchen,' Vivienne says. 'Let's have some music.'

In the kitchen, Miles and I leave the dirty plates and bowls on the table to deal with later. I fetch the birthday cake I bought in Montreuilac this morning and slide it from its box onto a large blue ceramic serving plate. After studding it with the gold birthday candles, I present the cake to Miles with a flourish. 'What do you think?'

'Nice,' he says, his voice flat.

'Is something wrong?'

He looks at me for a moment, his face taut with tension. 'I'm just tired.' He picks up the round Bluetooth speaker from the kitchen dresser. 'Better get this out to the birthday girl.'

'Grab those too.' I point to the box of matches next to the cooker. Hosting this dinner tonight makes me feel like we're a proper couple. In the future, when we're married, maybe we will bring guests here on holiday and I will be in charge of entertaining, as I am tonight.

I carry the cake out to the terrace, where Vivienne greets me with enthusiastic applause.

'You bugger,' she says. 'I'm supposed to be a grieving widow hating my birthday. I'm not supposed to be having fun.'

'Well, obviously I never knew your husband,' I say, 'but I'm sure he'd want you to enjoy your birthday.'

Vivienne swallows. Her eyes shine with tears. Shit. I shouldn't have mentioned her husband. To distract her, I strike a match and light each of the seven candles. A random number but a lucky one.

Miles and I sing an out-of-tune rendition of 'Happy Birthday' as I place the cake in front of Vivienne. She leans in and blows out the candles in one steady exhalation.

'Wait,' she says, when I pick up the cake knife. 'Let's get some pictures before we demolish it.' She hands me her phone. 'Come on, cousin dearest. Obligatory birthday pic.'

Miles moves to the other side of the table and sits beside her. I frame the shot, the two of them with the cake between them. Viv's arm around Miles' shoulder.

'Smile,' I say. All of a sudden, Riley is there beside them, gazing into the camera. Riley in her white cocktail dress, a martini in one hand. If she hadn't died, she would be here now, celebrating Vivienne's birthday with her. The two of them closer than Vivienne and I will ever be.

I blink Riley away and take three pictures of Miles and Vivienne before handing the camera back.

'Look at us.' Vivienne shows Miles the photographs. 'How did we get so old?' She reaches for her wine and knocks back half the glass. 'Let's have some music.' She switches on the Bluetooth speaker and taps away at her phone. 'Hits of the eighties,' she declares as 'Girls Just Wanna Have Fun' blares from the tinny speaker.

Maybe a hen do with Vivienne won't be so bad after all. She can be quite good company after a few drinks.

Miles gets up and returns to sit next to me. He does look exhausted. His face is expressionless, his eyes vacant.

'We didn't always look this old, Leah,' Vivienne says. 'Wait here. I found something I want to show you.'

She leaves the table and heads into the dining room. Peering inside, I see her at the sideboard, opening a drawer and reaching inside.

I cut into the cake, separating out three small wedges of the intense, rich concoction.

'We forget plates,' I tell Miles, 'could you go and—'

'Wait until you see these.' Vivienne weaves her way back to her seat, unsteady on her feet. In her hand she clutches what looks like a wad of photographs.

'Vivienne,' Miles says. 'Must we?'

'It's my birthday and I say we must.' Her seat wobbles as she lands on it. 'Oops.'

'Be careful,' he says, a warning note to his voice.

'Some of these are priceless.' Vivienne shuffles through the photographs. 'Look at these, Leah.'

She hands me some of the pictures. Teenage Vivienne looks up at me, pale as she is now but with more flesh on her bones. Rocking a number of very eighties outfits.

'Lace-edged pinafores were all the rage then,' she says, puffing on her vape.

'Is that a ra-ra skirt?' I ask, examining a picture of Vivienne and Miles standing by the front door of the château.

'Guilty.' She laughs. 'Look at Miles in his U2 T-shirt. Wasn't he adorable?'

Miles was cute, no doubt about it, but in the picture he doesn't exude confidence. He looks shy, hesitant.

'It's hard to believe we were once so innocent,' Vivienne says.

In the next photograph, Miles is wearing a white T-shirt and pale blue jacket, sleeves rolled up to his elbows. His hair is gelled back from his face.

'That was my *Miami Vice* phase.' He smiles. 'Where did you find these, Viv?'

'There was a load of old albums up in the attic,' she says, handing me more pictures.

'Oh.' The first shot is one of Vivienne and Miles dressed in fluorescent ski outfits. They are standing almost knee-deep in snow, clutching their skis.

'Chamonix,' Vivienne says. 'Sorry, Miles. I didn't realise those were in there.'

I glance up at him. His lips are pressed tightly together. A muscle twitches at the side of his face. When I move on to the next picture, I realise why. Bruce gazes out at me from the centre of the shot, Vivienne on one side and Miles on the other. Was this the ski holiday Bruce didn't return from? I had no idea Vivienne was there.

Cyndi Lauper is replaced by a song I recognise straight away thanks to my mother's love of Duran Duran.

'"A View to a Kill",' I say. 'This was a Bond theme tune, wasn't it?'

'I was so in love with John Taylor back then,' Vivienne says wistfully. 'We had tickets to see a Duran Duran tribute band that holiday. Do you remember, Miles?'

'I remember.' He scrapes back his chair and stands up. 'I'll go and get some plates.'

'Bring wine,' Vivienne says.

'I'll make coffee,' he says sourly. 'I think we've all had enough to drink.'

'Spoilsport.' Vivienne rolls her eyes at me as he marches indoors. 'Just when we were starting to have fun.'

'You were on that holiday?' I ask. 'When Bruce died?' I don't care if my ignorance shows how little Miles has shared with me about this family tragedy. My curiosity is greater than my pride.

'I was.' She tips back the last of her wine. 'God, it was awful.'

'Did he have a skiing accident?'

She tucks her new, neat hair behind her ears. 'Miles really hasn't told you much about himself, has he?'

'I imagine it's painful for him.'

'Yes. To be fair, it will be. Very painful.'

I listen as she tells me about Bruce's demise. He died after a fall, but not on the ski slopes as I'd imagined. Instead it was a drunken fall down the stairs at the family's chalet.

'We'd all been drinking,' Vivienne says. 'Miles and I went to bed, but Bruce carried on alone. He was like that. Once he got started, he couldn't stop. Had he lived, I think he would have been an alcoholic.'

I glance over my shoulder, hoping Miles doesn't appear. I want to hear the rest of the story.

'I slept in late,' Vivienne says. 'The sound of Natalie screaming woke me up.'

'Natalie?'

'Our chalet girl. She came to make breakfast.' Vivienne blinks. 'Bruce must have gone to bed after we did and fallen down the stairs. Neither Miles nor I heard a thing.'

'That's awful.'

'Yes. Tragic.' She takes a drag of her vape pen. Soon, a cloud of exhaled smoke surrounds her. 'Natalie had been with us the previous night so she was able to confirm how drunk Bruce was.'

'Your aunt and uncle must have been devastated?'

She nods. 'And it was hard for Miles and me. For a long time, we thought it was our fault.'

'You shouldn't think—'

'They said he died instantly, though, so that was a small blessing. At least we know he didn't suffer.'

'That must have been terrible for the whole family.'

'It was.' Vivienne smiles. 'But at least Miles and I had each other. That was something.'

46

VIVIENNE

August

Happy birthday to me. I've had far too much to drink. Lying here in my lumpy bed, the curtains drawn at my side, my head is spinning. Happy birthday to me. I tried turning off my bedside lamp but the darkness made my dizziness worse.

All in all, my birthday hasn't been as bad as I feared. I've missed Dom all day, but that's only to be expected. There was a moment though, when I looked at my new haircut in the mirror in the hairdresser's and wondered if it really might be possible to start my life over again.

My bedroom door creaks open and clicks shut again. Footsteps echo on the bare floorboards. A shadow, large and bulky, falls on the curtains beside me.

'Vivienne?' Miles pulls the curtains aside. 'Are you okay?'

I nod and lift the bedcovers. 'Getting in?' When we were kids, we would spend hours cosied up in this bed, talking. Our own secret world.

Miles perches on the edge of the bed. I let the bedcovers drop.

'Where's Leah?' I ask.

'Taking a shower.'

Anger uncoils inside me. I bet she is. Afterwards, she will cover her smooth, young skin in expensive body lotion and don more of that racy underwear I saw her in. Getting herself ready to put out for money like the little tart she is.

'Thanks for a lovely birthday,' I say. 'To both of you.'

He looks down at his hands. 'I don't need to be reminded of the past, Vivienne. You didn't need to do that.'

Didn't I? Perhaps sharing those photos of Chamonix was a little careless, but Miles could so easily stray. I wanted to remind him of the bond we share, and to make sure he keeps his promise to see this through.

'Leah's just been asking me questions about Bruce,' he says.

'She's bound to be curious.' I quite enjoyed telling her our story about Bruce. The one Miles and I concocted as we sat beside his dead body in the chalet, both of us still drunk. Both of us stunned. At no time did either of us consider calling the police or trying to contact my aunt and uncle. The cover-up was mutually agreed. Each of us protecting the other.

The story still sounds convincing, even after all these years.

'Please don't bring it up in front of her again,' Miles says.

I sit up and rest my head on his shoulder. 'Are you angry with me?'

'How could I be angry with you after everything we've been through together?'

'You do seem a bit cross.'

'I'm just tired.'

I lift my head and kiss his cheek. 'Must be all the sex you're having.'

He stands up. The lamplight hollows out his cheeks and makes his eye sockets look dark and sunken.

'This will all be over soon,' I say.

'Yes,' he says. 'It will.'

* * *

When Miles leaves, I turn out my lamp and lie in the dark, my brain buzzing. The euphoria of the night is wearing off and a prickly dread is rising up in me. I see Bruce's leering face in my mind's eye. I hear his voice in my ear.

Shut up. Stop it.

I'm beginning to regret dredging up what happened in Chamonix. It took me years to block out my memories of Bruce. Years to lock them away somewhere safe. I don't want him bothering me again.

I wish Miles could have stayed with me tonight. The summer after Bruce died, when I came here to the château as usual for the holidays, he often came to me after dark. Neither of us were finding sleep easy at that time and we were relieved to be together again. Each of us finally with the only other person in the world who knew their darkest secret.

After Bruce's death, my uncle stayed at the chalet to deal with the immediate formalities and my aunt took Miles and I back to England. My mother came to meet us at Heathrow airport, and that was where Miles and I had to say goodbye. We hugged each other tight, our secret nestled deep inside us. The next time we saw each other was at the funeral, where we didn't speak of what had happened. Each of us acting out our part in the story we had created.

The reality, as much as we had been able to piece it

together, was somewhat different. After I passed out in the chalet's living room, Miles left Bruce nursing a bottle of gin and carried me upstairs and got me into bed. Then he went to the bathroom along the hallway, threw up and passed out on the bathroom floor. Soon afterwards, he heard me screaming and, when he entered my bedroom, he found Bruce on top of me.

'I wanted to kill him,' he told me as we sat beside Bruce's dead body. 'When I saw him there in your room, I wanted to kill him.'

He didn't mean that. He only wanted to protect me.

After the funeral, Miles went back to boarding school and school resumed for me as well. We didn't write to each other as we usually did, not wanting any written evidence to exist between us. We spoke on the phone though. He sometimes called me from a phone box and I listened to him weeping and whispered words of encouragement.

Only when we came here to the château that summer could either of us relax. We would fall asleep in each other's arms and Miles would creep away to his own room at dawn. My aunt and uncle were too numb with grief to care what we got up to. My mother had supported her sister through those initial hard months, although she confided to me that Bruce's death hadn't shocked her. She said he was always an accident waiting to happen. She blamed my uncle for not disciplining him more and for 'letting him get away with murder' as firstborn sons often did in families with money. She even said she thought Miles would make a much better director of Sinclair Properties than Bruce would have. All this she said, unaware she was making me feel better about what had happened. It felt right to me that Miles should be the one to come into the money. He was much more deserving.

What happened between Miles and I that summer was, with hindsight, inevitable. We were both struggling to shed our guilt about Bruce's death. We both needed to forgive ourselves and move on. One night, as we lay here, in this bed, Miles told me he didn't think he could ever have a girlfriend, not after what he'd done. He didn't think he deserved to be happy. His honesty made me open up about my own feelings of shame. I told him the sexual assault had left me feeling soiled and ugly. I said it was a terrible way to lose my virginity, and I wished I could claim it back. I wished I could lose it to someone I loved.

I kissed him first. He resisted for a while, but then he kissed me back. I asked if he would have sex with me and if we could pretend I was a virgin. That way, I would be able to look back on this significant rite of passage with affection and happiness. A bad memory would be transformed into a good one. And if Miles, who was still a virgin too, could lose his innocence to me, it might help him conquer his guilt. Love is, after all, the most important thing in any relationship.

We did it the next night, here in this bed. Miles had gone to Montreuilac to buy condoms to make sure it was safe. The act itself was gentle and sweet and meaningful. All the way through it, Miles stopped to check if I was okay. To see if I was enjoying it. He was scared him being inside me would bring back memories of the night in the chalet but nothing like that happened. It was a beautiful experience. Nothing wrong or sordid about it at all. At dawn he crept back to his bed as usual and we slept in our own beds for the rest of the summer, each of us healed by what we'd shared. We've always been able to make one another feel better. It was another secret between us but a happy one. A secret borne of love. Over the years, we would sometimes exchange a glance and smile, each of us remembering that night.

Miles gave me my innocence back. That's another reason why I've always looked out for him. Why I've always protected him.

That's why Leah Williams doesn't stand a chance against me.

47

LEAH

August

The day after Vivienne's birthday, a Tuesday, the weather takes an even hotter turn. By lunchtime the temperatures are in the early thirties. We spend all of Tuesday and Wednesday at the château, sitting by the pool, escaping the oppressive heat with regular swims. Lying on my sun lounger, eyes half-closed behind my shades, I see Riley a number of times. Floating around the pool on her Lilo, a glass of champagne in her hand.

The rest of us are not in a champagne mood. Miles is withdrawn, Vivienne subdued. Hardly a fun lead-up to a wedding for a young bride-to-be. Once again, I imagine the wedding I might have had in different circumstances. Guests arriving a week before the ceremony to make a holiday of it and to help with preparations. Caterers and wedding planners coming and going.

Even for a wedding as small as mine, there still seems a lot left to do. The wedding rings haven't arrived yet, despite assurances from Boucheron that a courier will deliver them soon.

My dress needs to be picked up from Montreuilac, and I've yet to organise even a bouquet for myself let alone flowers for the house. No way I'm going to return to *Esprit Fleurs* and risk another run-in with Naomi. We don't even have another witness for the wedding ceremony. Miles says he wants us to ask a random stranger to be our second witness. He thinks that would be romantic. Like something from a movie.

I feel flat. Low in energy. Instead of thinking about my future, I'm preoccupied by the past. By Riley and by Bruce. I think about Vivienne being present at both of those accidents. Coincidence? Probably. She seems to have spent almost all her childhood and teenage holidays with Miles and his family. Am I seeking some sinister connection between her and these tragedies as another distraction from the commitment I'm about to make?

On Thursday morning, I get round to cleaning up some of the objects Anne-Marie and I found in the barn so they can be used in the wedding pictures. I photograph the objects and send them to Anne-Marie, who is quick to reply.

OMG love these!!!!

At least someone is enthusiastic about the whole thing. In the afternoon, a gardening firm arrives to mow the front and back lawns and weed the flower beds. Watching them work, I can't help thinking of Jacques. Is he still with Estelle or has he taken off again?

On Friday morning, the bell doesn't ring for breakfast. When Miles and I go downstairs, we find the kitchen deserted. Miles goes upstairs to check on Vivienne and when he returns to the kitchen he has a grim expression on his face.

'She slept in,' he says. 'She says she took a sleeping pill last night.' He sighs. 'I thought she was doing better, but I must confess I'm worried about her.'

'In what way?'

'She seems depressed.'

She has certainly been quiet the last couple of days. 'That's a shame. She was on great form on her birthday.'

'She was.' Miles opens the fridge and pulls out a carton of orange juice. 'I thought she might be turning a corner but now I'm not so sure.'

'But she seemed so much happier.'

'A haircut can't fix everything.' He unscrews the lid from the juice carton and takes a swig. I hate it when people do that. 'I've seen her like this before,' he says. 'She puts on a happy front for a while but behind it, she's heading for the edge.'

I'm not sure I agree, but he knows her better than I do. 'Maybe the wedding is too much for her? Us being happy when she's still grieving.'

'Maybe, but I'd rather she was here with me than all alone at that house in Kent. I don't think it's safe for her to be by herself at the moment.'

Is she really that unstable?

Miles and I make our own breakfast and eat it out on the terrace. The air is hot and still. I swear the trees and walls that mark the château's boundaries are moving closer day by day. Playing grandmother's footsteps with me.

'What are your plans for the morning?' I ask Miles.

'Work meetings. My contact at Heritage Capital is keen for another face-to-face, but I've postponed that until after the wedding. Until then, online will have to do.'

The thought of the potential sale gives me an adrenalin rush. Think how much money Miles will make.

'What about this afternoon?' I say. 'Are we going to pick up the dresses?'

Miles swallows his mouthful of croissant. 'Yes, after lunch.'

'And the rings are coming today?'

He nods. 'According to the courier, they'll be here by lunchtime.'

'I still need to sort out flowers. The wedding's only five days away.'

He dabs his mouth with a napkin. 'That, my darling, I may have sorted out for you.'

'How?'

He places a warm, clammy hand on top of mine. 'I called Anne-Marie yesterday.'

'Anne-Marie?'

'She's coming over this morning.'

'Why?'

'You've seemed a bit down yourself the last couple of days. I thought you'd appreciate the company.'

'That's very sweet.'

'She's going to take you to a florist she knows in Pont-Sainte-Maxence. She promised me you'll get everything you need there.'

'Thank you.' For the first time, I feel excited about our wedding preparations.

'Go and have a coffee somewhere,' he says. 'Pont-Sainte-Maxence is not the most exciting town, but you haven't been there yet, and it will do you good to have some time away from the olds.'

'Don't say that.' I kiss his cheek. It will be good to hang out with someone closer to my own age. Not that I'd ever tell him that.

'Maybe I should invite Anne-Marie to the château for

drinks when you're with the mayor?' I say. 'She could join Vivienne and I and we could—'

'No. Sorry. That's not a good idea.'

His curt tone startles me. 'Why?'

'Anne-Marie seems a decent sort and I have no issue with you seeing her. I'm just wary of the company she keeps.'

'Who? The couple she mentioned? I thought they were friends of yours?'

'Pauline and Colin Forsyth were never friends of mine. Riley used to invite them here for drinks sometimes. I couldn't stand them. Neither could Viv.'

'Oh.'

'Pauline is an appalling gossip. I'm sure she got plenty of mileage out of Riley's death, and Vivienne would hate the thought of Pauline talking about Dom. I don't think she would be comfortable having Anne-Marie here socially, given her connection with the Forsyths.'

'Sure. Okay.'

'You don't mind, do you, darling? The last thing we want to do is upset Viv just now.'

'No,' I say, ignoring a prickle of irritation. 'I don't mind at all.'

* * *

Anne-Marie is due to arrive at ten-thirty. I've arranged to meet her at the château gates to save her the trip up the driveway. After getting dressed, I'm on my way downstairs when I meet Vivienne on the first-floor landing.

Her face is sleep-creased. Thin grips hold her bobbed hair back from her face. The buttons of her black shirt dress are out of sync, revealing a flash of white midriff.

'Why are you all dressed up?' she says.

I have made a bit of an effort for my outing. Dior linen maxi dress. Celine sunglasses and my hair in an over-the-shoulder ponytail.

Vivienne looks confused when I explain I'm spending the morning with Anne-Marie.

'But I think the plan is to go into Montreuilac this afternoon to get the dresses,' I say.

'Whatever.' I watch her descend the stairs ahead of me, her hand gripping the banister. Maybe Miles is right about her sliding into a depression. I can understand why having Anne-Marie here for drinks might be a bad idea. Vivienne seems to be in a much worse place than I thought.

* * *

Anne-Marie arrives on time, her Range Rover sweeping up in front of the château gates, which have just swung shut behind me.

'Thanks so much for doing this,' I say as I climb into the passenger seat.

'It's my pleasure. What a sweetheart Miles is for arranging this.'

We lean in and kiss each other on both cheeks.

'You look gorgeous,' Anne-Marie says.

'As do you.' Anne-Marie looks fresh and serene in a white cotton maxi dress. Her lips are scarlet as before and her light, floral perfume fills the vehicle. 'Okay. Let's do this.'

I fasten my seatbelt. She pulls out onto the road. After a few minutes I realise with relief she is a much more sedate driver than Vivienne. The Range Rover is solid and comfortable. The air conditioning effective.

'It'll take about twenty minutes to get to the florist's,' she says. 'You'll love Genevieve. Her bouquets are truly divine.'

'Can't wait.'

We chat trivia as the Range Rover travels smoothly along the narrow, winding roads, a welcome respite from the intensity of my own thoughts in recent days. A break from my changeable moods and unruly imagination.

'So,' Anne-Marie says finally, 'are you getting excited for the big day?'

'Yes. Well, today I am.'

Anne-Marie slows down as we hit the outskirts of a village. Two old men sit on a bench in front of a sandstone church.

'Run me through the itinerary for the day again,' she says.

'Pictures at the château before the ceremony,' I say. 'And then into Montreuilac to the town hall.' An idea occurs to me. I don't know why I didn't think of it before. 'Anne-Marie, would you be our second witness?'

'Oh my God, I'd love to.' She performs a drumroll on the steering wheel.

'You'll be there anyway taking the pictures so it would make sense.'

'Yes. Count me in. I might cry, though. I'm such an old romantic.'

Surely Miles and Vivienne can't object to Anne-Marie being the second witness? I've got to have some input to my wedding day. Even if it means having a woman I've only met twice as a witness to my marriage. It's not as if we'll be socialising with her after the ceremony is over.

'Who's your other witness?' she asks, the Range Rover speeding up again as we leave the village behind. 'Vivienne?'

'Of course.'

'I was having lunch with Pauline the other day, the woman I told you about and—'

'Pauline Forsyth?'

'Yes. She was surprised to hear how close you and Vivienne seemed.'

'I'm not sure we're close, but—'

'According to Pauline, Vivienne hates pretty much everyone except Miles.'

'And Riley. She thought the world of Riley.'

'That's not what I heard.' Anne-Marie slows down to let a car pull out from a junction ahead of us. 'Pauline says Vivienne hated Riley. The feeling was mutual, apparently. Vivienne thought Miles had made a huge mistake marrying her.'

'Oh.' I force a smile. 'I guess I must be more charming than I thought.'

Anne-Marie laughs. 'You *so* are. I was saying to Pauline, I really hope you'll be coming here most summers. It would be great to hang out properly. Get to know one another.'

'I'd like that.'

I look out of the window. If Vivienne and Riley hated each other, why hasn't Miles mentioned it? He has always told me the two women were close. Was he lying or just unaware of a bad dynamic between them? Did Vivienne keep her feelings about Riley hidden? Having seen Vivienne in action these past few weeks I find it hard to believe she would keep her opinions to herself. Did she lie to me about her close relationship with Riley to make me feel insecure? Or perhaps to make herself look better? No one likes to speak ill of the dead.

'Leah?' Anne-Marie says. 'Everything okay?'

'Of course.' I turn my head. 'Everything's wonderful.'

48

VIVIENNE

August

I'm sitting at the kitchen table, drinking my second espresso of the morning and vaping myself into some semblance of humanity. Taking that second sleeping pill last night wasn't the smartest move, but after taking the first one I still couldn't sleep. Talking about Bruce on the night of my birthday has left me askew. The past feels uncomfortably close. I shouldn't have poked it. My memories of Chamonix are becoming horribly vivid. This morning I woke in a panic with my sheet over my face and Bruce's voice in my ear.

Shut up. Stop it.

The château is quiet now that Leah has flounced off for a morning out with her new BFF. Why on earth would Miles arrange such a thing? We're supposed to be limiting her contact with the outside world.

Just as well this whole charade will be over next week. Not long until I get my grand finale. I've been trying to get Miles alone to discuss it, but he's been difficult to pin down. I'm glad he's delivering such a convincing performance, but at times he seems to have forgotten he's not actually getting married. I have the odd moment when I forget myself. When I think about what jewellery to wear with the green dress. Or wonder what colour lipstick would best complement it.

Never mind. I'll find another occasion to wear the dress when all this is over.

First things first. What will we eat at Leah Williams' last supper? How about slow-roasted lamb? That feels appropriately sacrificial.

We will eat it at the dining room table. Indoors will suit the occasion better. More formal. I will lay out the best set of silver cutlery, the one tucked away in the dining room sideboard. Silver serving spoons centuries old that were used by the Dumonts when they were in residence here. Every detail must be perfect so that when Miles tells Leah he's made a mistake and wants to call the wedding off, she will be totally blindsided.

I'll be there, watching her. Savouring the moment.

The trouble is, when I imagine it, when I picture the shock on her face, I don't feel as satisfied as I should. It doesn't feel like enough.

It will have to be. Leah will be upset afterwards and, hard as it will be not to tell her who I really am, not to lash out, I will remain a calm, consoling presence. I will help her pack her belongings. Maybe I should be the one to drive her to the train station. The two of us alone together, one last time.

Once all this is over, I suppose I will have to face reality and go back to what remains of my old life. I will have to get used to my empty home. To life without my husband. Perhaps I'll sell the house in Kent. How will I ever get over my grief if I stay in the place where we were once so happy?

If only I could stay here. I've no need to go back to work so why not? Once Miles has sold the company, he could stay here too. We would rub along quite happily together. As friends, companions. We could care for one another. I would look after him, unlike the woman who thinks she's marrying him in five days' time.

My phone trills in my apron pocket. I pull it out, check the screen and then turn it off. Can't be distracted. Must keep my focus.

'There you are.' Miles appears in the dining room doorway. 'How's my favourite girl?'

He comes over to the table and kisses the top of my head.

'I'm good. Yes. All good.'

He strides over to the fridge, yanks open the door and peeks inside. Is he really hungry already? Miles has always loved his snacks. At his age, he might want to cut back on the goodies.

'I'm not sure Leah being out with Anne-Marie is a good idea,' I say. 'Who knows what they might talk about.'

'Don't think it matters at this stage.' Miles reaches into the fridge and pulls out a bottle of champagne. I thought we were saving that for our final meal with Leah?

'If Anne-Marie is friends with that dreadful Pauline, she could pass on all sorts of misinformation about Riley.' I hesitate. 'And I hate the thought of them discussing Dom.'

'It'll be fine.' He wipes condensation from the front of the bottle. 'I've already made sure Leah knows Pauline is a gossip with no credibility. And anything awkward Leah might say to Anne-Marie we can easily dismiss. We can say Leah was a pathological liar, as well as a gold-digger. By the end of the summer it will all be forgotten.'

A liar as well as a gold-digger. It's good to hear him talk

about Leah like that. Underneath his bravado performance, he hasn't forgotten what she truly is.

'When I see Philippe the day before the wedding, I'll tell him things aren't going well with Leah and that I want to call the whole thing off. At least then he'll have some warning and I won't feel as bad for lying to him.'

'Good idea.'

'Now.' He holds up the champagne. 'Another reason I sent Leah off with Anne-Marie this morning is so you and I can spend some time together.'

'Champagne? It's quarter to eleven in the morning.'

'Who cares? Let's make the most of having the place to ourselves.'

'You've got to drive to Montreuilac this afternoon.'

'One glass won't hurt. I'm celebrating. Soon this whole business with Leah will be over and you and I can start living our lives.'

He looks so happy and relaxed. The best I've seen him look for a while.

'You were right about all this, Viv,' he says. 'It has helped me move on. I think it's helped you too. Look at you.' He gives me a shy smile that reminds me of the boy he once was. 'You look lovely.'

Heat stains my cheeks. I've forgotten how kind Miles can be. How tender.

'Only one last thing remains for us to do,' he says. 'After that we'll be truly free.'

'What's that?'

'Have you got your keys?'

'Of course.'

He holds out his hand. I fish in my apron pocket and pass the cold, heavy jumble of keys to him.

'Grab two champagne flutes and follow me,' he says.

Intrigued, I fetch two crystal flutes from the dresser and follow him out of the kitchen. Are we going to drink the champagne on the terrace? Instead of leading us outside, Miles heads up the first flight of stairs, clutching the champagne.

'I've been planning exactly how I'll end it with Leah,' Miles says. 'I'll say it doesn't feel right and that I've changed my mind. Maybe add in that I'm not sure she's genuine. She's only after my money, blah blah blah. I'll keep it short but I'll be tough.'

A strange quivering in my chest. When we reach the first-floor landing, I wonder if he is about to lead me to my room, where we will drink the champagne in bed together, like we did as teenagers. Instead, he continues to the attic staircase, his deck shoes echoing on the wooden stairs. He should really have his espadrilles on.

When we reach the attic landing, Miles stands beside the door to the east wing.

'What are you doing?' I ask.

My keys rattle as he searches for the right one. 'Little trip down memory lane,' he says. 'For old times' sake.'

'I don't think that's a good idea.'

The key clicks in the lock. When the door opens, my knees go soft. Silly. I've been in here recently and nothing terrible happened. Riley didn't appear. She's gone. All that is over now.

Miles steps inside. 'I thought it would smell worse than this. It feels quite fresh in here.' He looks back at me. 'Come on.'

'Where are we going?' I ask, although I already know.

He takes my free hand and leads me past the boxes and piles of debris. 'We need to move on, Vivienne. Really move on.'

'I don't want to go out there.'

'I don't want to either, but earlier I thought, fuck it. Château Clairvallon is ours, Vivienne. Not Riley's. Ours. We need to reclaim it.'

His hand is a vice around mine. I can see what he's trying to do but I don't want to.

When we reach the window at the gable end, he lets me go. After passing me the champagne to hold, he throws open the shutters, yanks up the latch and opens the window.

'Come on,' he says. 'Let's go out there and have a drink and show the past we don't give a shit about it any more.'

Panic swamps me. Sharp, stabbing pains in my chest.

'I don't want to.'

Sunlight streams through the open window. 'Why?' he says.

I put the champagne and glasses on an upturned wooden chest beside me. 'It's not safe.'

'It'll be fine. You're with me.'

'No. I can't.' I turn and stumble my way back through the attic, crying out as I hit my ankle on a discarded typewriter.

'Vivienne. Wait.'

Once I'm out of the attic, I fly down the first set of stairs to the landing. My feet are on the top step of the next set of stairs before he catches up with me.

'Vivienne.' His hand is on my shoulder. I almost lose my footing. 'I'm sorry,' he says when I turn around to face him.

'It wouldn't feel right to go there,' I say. 'It's not safe.'

'I'm sorry.' He is out of breath, his voice hoarse. 'I don't know what got into me. I just... I just sometimes wish none of it had ever happened. I thought maybe if we could act like the past didn't exist we could make it go away.'

Wishful thinking.

'It's okay,' I say. 'I understand, but it's dangerous up there, Miles. You know that.'

'I know.' He cups my face with his large, warm hands. 'You're right. That's the trouble with this place. Accidents do happen.'

He looms over me. His grip on my face grows tighter. Such a sad, haunted expression on his face. I hate to see him looking like that.

The whiny buzz of the entry phone interrupts us. A dark cloud of anger passes across Miles' face. The buzzer rings again. Whoever wants access to the château is impatient for an answer.

'It must be the courier,' I say. 'Your wedding rings have arrived.'

'Damn. I'd forgotten they were coming.'

I remove his hands from my face. 'I'll go and let them in.'

At the foot of the stairs, I glance back and see him still standing there, forlorn.

'Cheer up,' I say. 'You're not actually getting married, remember?'

49

LEAH

August

When I return from my trip out with Anne-Marie, I'm relieved to hear Miles on a work call in the study. Vivienne is in the kitchen with the radio blaring.

'Hi.' I put my head round the door. 'I'm back.'

She is sitting at the table, flicking through a recipe book, a glass of white wine in her hand. Bit early, isn't it?

'Nice time out with your friend?' she says.

'Very nice. The flowers are sorted. They should arrive the day before the wedding.'

'How lovely.' Vivienne sucks on her vape pen. 'Miles will be on his call through lunchtime. I'll leave out some bread and cheese in here and you can help yourself.'

'Thanks.' I put a hand to my forehead. 'Think I'll have a lie-down.'

'One of your headaches coming on?'

I nod. 'Think so.'

Up in my bedroom I half fold the shutters and lie down on

the bed. My morning with Anne-Marie was marred by what she told me in the car. As Genevieve the florist enthused about her homegrown flowers and her seasonal bouquets, I thought about Vivienne and Riley and whether they had really hated each other as Anne-Marie claimed. As I picked out white and pink roses and green foliage for my bridal bouquet, I wondered why Miles would lie to me about the relationship between his wife and his cousin.

Maybe the two women had a personality clash. Two strong characters butting heads. Doesn't necessarily mean they hated each other.

Half an hour later, Miles comes upstairs and finds me still curled up on the bed.

'Darling?' he says.

'I've got a splitting headache.'

He sits on the bed beside me and places a hot, sticky palm on my forehead. 'Too much sun? It is fierce out there today.'

'That and too much coffee.' I tell him Anne-Marie and I went to a coffee shop near the florist and talked so much I ended up having two cappuccinos.

'Poor thing,' he says.

I roll onto my back. 'I can't face coming into town this afternoon. Could you go with Vivienne and pick up the dresses?'

'Won't you need to try yours on?' He brushes my hair away from my forehead. 'What if they haven't made the right adjustments?'

'It'll be fine. The seamstress was very thorough.'

'I'm worried about you.'

'A rest will help. I didn't sleep well last night.'

'Pre-wedding nerves?'

'Probably.'

He kisses me tenderly on the cheek. 'Rest up, my love.'

* * *

From the corridor outside our room, I watch as the Lexus disappears into the lime trees at the end of the driveway. Once I'm certain Miles and Vivienne have gone, I hurry back to my room, pull out my suitcase from the wardrobe and retrieve Estelle's keys.

I am sure there are secrets hidden here in the château. Answers that would put my mind at rest one way or another. Whether I am pursuing truth for its own end or for the power it could give me, I'm not entirely sure. I do know I'm getting married in five days' time and I want to know as much as possible about the man I'm marrying.

Knowledge is power, Leah.

The tiles are cold beneath my bare feet as I hurry along to the landing and make my way to the east wing and to Riley's room. My hands shake as I unlock the door.

When I step inside, the room looks just as it did the first time I saw it. What exactly am I looking for? If Riley did hide secrets here then surely they would have been removed after her death?

I begin in the wardrobe. The shoeboxes on the shelf above the rail contain two pairs of strappy silver sandals and a pair of DKNY slides, all with the price tags still attached. Shoes she never got to wear.

In the chest of drawers, I find only a selection of black silk underwear and three identical white T-shirts from American Vintage.

One of the bedside cabinets is empty. The drawer of the other one, which must have been Riley's, contains a black silk blindfold, a packet of Nurofen and Chanel hand cream in a black oval container.

This is pointless. Maybe I should search Vivienne's room while I have a chance.

As a last resort, I crouch down by the bed and slide my hand between the mattress and the divan base. My fingers encounter a metal handle. This must be an ottoman bed base. I press down on the handle and the side of the bed lifts effortlessly up and back on smooth hinges, the mattress staying securely in place.

A cold tingling sensation along my spine. As if an icy finger is trailing up and down my vertebrae. For a moment I let myself imagine Riley is here with me, trying to lead me to what I need to find.

Inside the bed's storage cavity are a number of small cardboard boxes. That icy finger travels down my arm and seems to guide me towards a box with a black lid. Like that game I used to play with my father. The one where he would hide an item somewhere in the room. You're getting cold; you're getting hot. Only now, getting cold means I'm getting close.

I lift the lid of the box. Inside is a photo album with a black silk cover. I remove it from the box. I hesitate. Do I really want to see what's inside?

Don't ruin a good thing, Leah.

Leah, baby. Go take a look. Can't hurt to look, right?

My mother and Riley. Two competing ghosts pulling me in different directions.

The photograph on the first page of the album is of Riley. She is naked and she is gazing into the camera with a seductive look. Did she have one of those erotic photo shoots done? The kind women get done for their partners as a gift. In the next photo, she is not alone. She is lying in a bed with a man who is not Miles. A man with a blond buzz cut. Her arm is outstretched to take the photograph. She is looking into the camera, but the man has his lips on one of her breasts. Underneath the photograph, in her neat, angular handwriting, are the words: *Daniel, Covent Garden Hotel.* I turn the page and there is Riley with a different man. He is sitting in a black leather armchair and she is straddling him, hiding his face. He has strong thighs. His hands are gripping her waist and a wedding band glints on his ring finger. *Larry. Holiday Inn Express, Tower Bridge.* More men follow. More explicit images of Riley. In the photographs, she is unguarded and uninhibited. She seems to be enjoying herself.

Is this a record of conquests she kept for herself? A highlight reel of infidelity. Have these photographs rested here unseen since her death or, more likely and more worryingly, does Miles know about them?

The next photograph I come to makes my heart jolt. Pressure builds in my temple as I stare at it. With trembling fingers, I remove it from the album and tuck it into the pocket of my dress. Then I put the album back in the box, close the ottoman bed and, leaving the room exactly as I found it, I lock the door again.

50

LEAH

August

The bikes are leaning up against the wall of the château, next to the main entrance. I grab one, climb on and set off down the drive. The afternoon sun still has a sting to it, and I can feel it nipping at my bare legs and arms. Before coming out, I changed into a T-shirt and my denim shorts. In one of my back pockets is my phone. In the other, the photograph I found in Riley's room.

I punch the code into the keypad at the side of the gates. While waiting for them to open, I find Estelle's address in Contacts on my phone and copy and paste it into Maps. *Les Arbres. Rue des Bois.* I have a vague idea which direction to go in from here but don't want to get lost. I drop my phone in the bike's wicker basket, volume turned up high.

After the gates clang shut behind me, I turn right. Only when I see a car headed towards me do I remember I need to cycle on the opposite side of the road. The rusty bike squeaks as I pick up speed. It feels good to pedal hard. I need to get rid of some of the agitation building inside me. I don't know how long Miles and Vivienne will be away, and right now I don't care. I want answers to the questions whirling around in my head.

By the time I reach Estelle's cottage on the outskirts of the woods, I am out of breath and bathed in sweat. *Les Arbres* is a single-storey, sandstone cottage. An L-shaped building with a colourful, well-kept garden at the front. Behind it rise the tall pines that mark the entrance to the woods. It is beautiful. I don't know anything about property prices in this area but if Miles did give Estelle the cottage, it was a generous gift.

I prop the bike against the low wall surrounding the property. The black Hilux is parked in the driveway. My temples throb. There is a hard, dark knot at the pit of my stomach. I push open the plain metal gate that leads into the garden. Flower beds fringe the neat, dry grass, providing splashes of orange and pink and yellow. The air is fragrant and heady.

Jacques opens the cottage's red front door before I get a chance to knock. He is dressed only in black board shorts. His smooth, bare chest reveals a flock of small swallows.

'I told you to stay away from me,' he says.

I reach into the pocket of my shorts, take out the photograph and hold it up in front of him.

'*Merde.*' He sighs and steps back from the door. 'Come inside.'

* * *

The living room at the front of the house is small. Family photographs clutter every available surface. Pictures of Jacques and his sister at various ages. A vast widescreen TV dominates one wall. Parked in front of it is an empty brown leather recliner seat. This must be where Estelle spends most of her days.

'Is your mother in?' I ask.

'She is out with Béatrice.'

'I thought your sister was away?'

'Yesterday she came back.'

He turns away and walks out of the living room. I follow him down a hallway into a small bedroom. I leave the door open. On the narrow single bed is a rucksack and a pile of folded clothes.

'Going somewhere?' I ask.

He picks up several black T-shirts from the top of the pile, rolls them together and shoves them in his rucksack. 'I am leaving today.'

'Why?'

'Béatrice doesn't want me here. Also, I have a job to get back to.'

'Really?'

He fixes his dark eyes on me. 'Yes.'

I hold up the photograph again. 'So, you're not leaving because of this?'

'Where did you find it?'

'In Riley's room.' I don't mention the photographs of the other men. Does Jacques know he was one of many?

He snatches the picture from me and scrutinises it. The black and white image is imprinted on my mind. Riley is lying on her back with Jaques inside her. Her legs are wrapped around his waist and they are looking into each other's eyes. It is a hot, raw moment. When I saw it, I felt a tug deep inside me. The memory of what it feels like to truly connect with some-one. A feeling I've never had with Miles.

'*Putain.*' He grips the photograph with both hands. If he

decides to tear it up, there are several more of him in that photo album.

'You told me you didn't have an affair with her,' I say.

'I did not.'

'This picture says otherwise.'

He pushes his rucksack aside and sits on the bed. 'It was not an affair.'

'That's not how it looks to me.'

'Her husband knew everything.'

I stare at him. 'What?'

Impatience flashes across his face. 'Miles. He knew. They had an open relationship.'

An open relationship? Really? Never once has Miles ever hinted that his marriage to Riley was anything but conventional. 'Did he have lovers too?' I ask, struggling to grasp this turn of events.

Jacques shakes his head. 'Only Riley.'

'And Miles didn't mind?'

'Mind?' Jacques laughs. 'For him it was a big turn-on.'

The images from the photo album crowd my mind. 'Did he take the pictures?' I ask. 'Was he there?'

'No. Never.' Jacques rubs a hand back and forth across his smooth chest. 'She took the pictures to show him. He liked her to tell him everything.'

Was the photograph album a gift for Miles? Something for him to look at when he wanted to get aroused. Or did he put it together himself? Either way, it doesn't seem likely Miles would kill his wife for having affairs when he was fully aware of what was going on. I should feel relieved but doubt still whispers inside me.

'How did it start between you?' I ask. I'm supposed to be

getting married in five days. I need to know what I'm getting myself into. I need to know if I should bail out now.

And I want to know what happened to Riley.

Jacques shrugs. 'There was always something with me and Riley. When she was at Clairvallon for the holidays and I was working, we flirted.'

'Yes, Naomi told me about the flirting.'

Jacques' eyes widen with surprise. 'You know Naomi?'

'Our paths have crossed a couple of times.'

'She spoke to you about me?'

'Amongst other things. What happened? Did you screw her over?'

'No. We slept together. It was fun but I didn't want anything else.'

'Were you getting close to Riley by then?'

He nods. 'Miles could see we had an attraction for each other. He told her she should sleep with me.'

'You didn't care that he knew? You didn't mind him being in control of the situation?'

'Why care? I was having fun, she was having fun and Miles was getting what he wanted.'

'So what went wrong?'

'Vivienne. I think.'

'You think?'

'She started to get suspicious. She was always here, you know, in the holidays. Sometimes with her husband. Sometimes alone. One time, when the family was here for Christmas, I had sex with Riley in her bedroom. Miles wanted us to. After, I was coming downstairs and Vivienne was there, waiting for me at the end of the hallway. I said I had been fixing the shower in Riley's bathroom, but she did not believe me.'

'Did she say anything to Miles?'

'I don't know. Maybe. But she did not like Riley and Miles knew that.'

'Vivienne didn't know about the open relationship?'

'No. She thought Riley was cheating on him with other men.'

'So you think she had you sacked to stop you sleeping with Riley?'

'I don't know. Not for sure. But yes, I think so. I never stole anything.'

'Why didn't Riley and Miles defend you?'

He shrugs. 'Why would they? They'd had their fun. They did not want Vivienne to know the truth about how they lived their lives.'

'You could have told her.'

'I did not want to make trouble.'

'So your relationship with Riley ended the Christmas before she died?'

'You are making a timeline or something?'

'What about this cottage?'

'What about it?'

'Naomi said Miles gave it to your mother.'

'He did and also a small annual pension.'

'Why did he do that?'

'Why would he not? Maman worked for his family for decades, no?'

'Yes, but—'

'And because I lost my job, I had to go and work away. I think he owed my mother something.'

'Why did he wait until after Riley died?'

Jacques groans. 'I don't know. Maman and Riley, they were close. Riley was very upset when Maman got sick. Maybe Miles, he decides it was the right thing to do. That Riley would have wanted this for Maman.'

'But...' I trail off. But what? What exactly am I trying to say? I came here certain I was about to uncover something, but everything Jacques has said so far could easily be true. Why then do I still feel he's hiding something? 'I want to find out what happened to Riley. What really happened.'

'Her death was an accident.' Jacques springs up from the bed. I edge backwards.

'Was it?' I remember what Naomi said about the mayor's involvement with the incident and what I saw on Riley's death certificate. 'There was no proper investigation into the fall. How does anyone know?'

'You think someone killed her?' He laughs. 'That's crazy.'

'Is it?'

'Okay.' He takes a step towards me. 'I will tell you what I think.'

'Go ahead.' He is standing very close to me now. It would be easy to touch his bare chest. To trace the outlines of the birds that flit across it.

He holds up the photograph. I stare at him and Riley locked together. 'I think you are making up stories to distract yourself.'

'From what?'

His hand brushes my hair away from my shoulders. A crackle of desire runs through me. 'From the truth. You are about to marry a man you do not love because he has money and part of you knows this is wrong.'

'You don't know anything about me,' I say, even though he may well be right.

'You remind me of her.' Jacques drops the photograph on the bed. 'You are very beautiful, just like her.' His dark eyes search mine. 'You are also lonely. Just like she was.'

I try to tell him he's wrong, but when I open my mouth no

words come out. He is going to touch me. He is going to fuck me. I feel sick with anticipation. Sick with want.

'I think you are here because you want what she had,' he says. 'You want to feel what she felt.'

'No,' I whisper, but when he tells me to take off my clothes, I obey. When he takes my hand and leads me to the bed, I follow. He sweeps his rucksack, his clothes and the photograph of him and Riley onto the floor. I let him push me down on the mattress and when he dips his head between my open legs, I offer no resistance.

My body feels painfully alive as his tongue works on me. I'd forgotten what arousal like this feels like. The terrifying intensity of it.

My climax is fast and violent and then he is on the narrow bed with me, turning me over, pushing himself inside me. It is rough and sore and exquisite. My face is pressed against the mattress. His hand is at my throat. Our tangled noises are feral. Unsettling. We lose ourselves in one another. We lose ourselves in time. I am aware of nothing apart from him inside me.

'Look at me,' he says. I turn my head and watch him give in to pleasure. When he comes inside me, I feel a hot, tingling sensation.

We lie still for a few moments, his arm around my waist, his knees slotted into the back of mine. We are both breathing heavily.

He breaks away first and sits up. 'Did Miles send you here? Is this one of his games?'

'No.' I sit up. When I touch his back, he shakes me off. 'This is nothing to do with Miles,' I say.

'So he has never asked you to be with other men?'

'No.' There was the time he asked me about losing my virginity but that's hardly the same thing.

Jacques stands up. 'I have to finish packing.'

'You're really going?'

'Yes.'

Suddenly I do feel lonely. Lonelier than I've ever felt in my life.

He picks his black shorts up from the bedroom floor and puts them on before passing me my clothes. 'You have to go. Maman and Béatrice will be back soon.'

As I get dressed in silence, Jacques picks up his rucksack and stuffs his remaining clothes into it, along with the photograph of him and Riley.

'You have to go,' he says.

I nod. A hot ball of tears lodges in my throat as I follow him back through the house. I swallow it down. He opens the front door, and I step outside into the sunshine. Into the warm, fragrant air.

'Goodbye, Leah,' he says.

I hesitate. 'What did you mean when you said I didn't know what I was getting myself into?'

'What?'

'In the car that time.' I look into his dark eyes. 'You said I was too young to be engaged to Miles and I didn't know what I was getting into. Did you mean the open relationship stuff?'

He shrugs. 'They are a fucked-up family. That is all I am saying.'

'So you don't think I should marry Miles?'

'Marry him, don't marry him. It is your choice.'

'But what do you think?'

'I cannot answer this for you.' A sad smile haunts his face. 'I am just as fucked up as they are.'

51

LEAH

August

The day before our wedding, I wake early, greeted by six chimes from the grandfather clock outside our bedroom. Miles snores gently beside me, oblivious to the world. I get out of bed and tiptoe my way to the en suite.

Once inside, I pee quietly and, after flushing the toilet, commence my usual morning routine. Wiping my face and armpits. Freshening up between my legs. As I do so, I think of Jacques. Our fast and dirty sex, both of us sour with sweat.

A hollow feeling swells in my chest. Three days have passed since Jacques left. Yesterday, when Vivienne went to Grandfresnoy, she met Jacques' sister, Béatrice, in the village store. Béatrice told her Jacques had returned to his labouring job in Marseilles.

What did I expect? That he and I would fall madly in love and run off into the sunset together? No. It was a pre-wedding dalliance. A cold-feet shag. I doubt I'm the only engaged person ever to have given in to temptation before the big day.

I finish my routine. Quick lick of deodorant, teeth scrubbed clean. Lip gloss on, sharp pinch of the cheeks until they flood with colour.

Deep breath. Back into the bedroom and into bed. Thankfully, Miles does not stir. I lie still beside him, watching the morning light seep through the muslin curtains. Tomorrow, Wednesday the 16th of August, I am getting married. My dress is hanging in the bedroom wardrobe. The alterations were a success; it is a perfect fit. Today there is little left to do in terms of preparations. This afternoon, Miles is going for drinks with the mayor and Vivienne seems delighted at the prospect of the two of us having cocktails together. She says she makes a killer Negroni. Then, tonight, the three of us are going to eat a special dinner Vivienne wants to cook for us.

Her mood has picked up over the past few days. She seems genuinely excited about the wedding. Occasionally, I find myself looking at her and wondering if she and Riley really did hate each other. I've heard from more than one person about what a flirt Riley was. Did she flirt with Vivienne's husband? The affair Vivienne found out about proves he was capable of cheating. Did he cheat on her before that? With Riley? If so, did Miles know? It seems unlikely he would sanction Riley sleeping with his cousin's husband. Jacques said the Sinclairs are a fucked-up family, but I don't think they're as bad as that.

Whenever these thoughts come into my head, I remember Jacques telling me I was inventing dramas to distract myself from my upcoming marriage. Maybe he was right. Maybe Riley's death was purely an accident and neither Vivienne nor Miles had anything to do with it.

I've wondered about Miles too, of course. About his Las Vegas wedding which, if it was spontaneous, might have left him without a prenup. And even if he was a willing participant

in the open marriage, the arrangement might still have made
him jealous at times.

When I put these wild theories out of my head, what
remains? Marriage to the man lying beside me. A life of
comfort and security in return for some compromises.

You don't get something for nothing in this life.

'Morning, darling.' Miles stirs beside me and pulls off his
snore strip with the usual sticky, ripping sound. I turn on my
side to receive my morning kiss and a gust of his stale morning
breath. He pulls me close, already restless with desire.

I place a hand on his chest. 'I think we should wait until
after the wedding.'

He gives me a quizzical look. 'Seriously?'

'Yes. We should keep some part of this traditional.' I stroke
the coarse grey hairs on his chest. 'Think how much better it
will be on the wedding night.' I give him a lingering kiss.
'Think how much we'll both want it.'

He groans. 'Fine. God knows how I'll get to sleep tonight.'

'You'll manage. Unless you want us to sleep in separate
rooms? Make it even more traditional?'

'Not a chance.' He opens his arms and I dutifully snuggle
into him.

We lie silently together as the birdsong gathers volume
outside and the day beyond the curtains comes to life. It has
been hard to act normally around Miles these past few days.
When I returned to the château after my encounter with
Jacques, I was relieved to find him and Vivienne were still in
Montreuilac. Despite being hot and sweaty after the cycle ride
back, I took a long, scalding shower, sobbing as I reluctantly
washed all traces of Jacques from my body. When Miles
returned, I pretended I still had my headache and lay in bed
until dinner time, my mind spinning with everything Jacques

had told me. I realised how little I know the man I was supposed to be marrying. How could I truly know Miles when we only met less than three months ago?

I managed to put off having sex with him until the following evening. Any longer and he would have wondered why. He was moved when I cried afterwards, but I was crying because I would never experience the same intensity with him that I had with Jacques. The same intensity Riley must have felt when she was with her lover.

My lack of guilt about my infidelity is unsettling. When I was having my affair with Nick, there was always a moment, right after we finished having sex, when he would look sad and go silent. I always assumed he was grappling with guilt. He told me he'd never cheated on his wife before and I believed him.

Perhaps the fact Miles let Riley sleep with Jacques makes my actions seem less dishonourable. A poor excuse, I know. Riley had Miles' permission to sleep with another man. I did not.

I still find it hard to imagine Miles in an open relationship, but Riley sounds like the kind of woman who could have brought out something different in him. Will he expect a similar arrangement from me? Yes, he got off on my story about losing my virginity but that was just fantasy. Dirty talk. Would I enjoy being able to sleep with other men? Possibly, as long as it was my choice and I didn't feel coerced into doing it solely for Miles' pleasure. However, I don't think I'd feel comfortable sharing details of those intimacies with him. I'm not judging him for finding that a turn-on; I just don't know if it's for me.

'I thought we should take another look at the vows today,' Miles says. 'I'm nervous about messing them up.'

'You'll be fine. There isn't much to them.'

A couple of days ago, we chose a set of standard vows for

the ceremony and Miles has been rehearsing them ever since. I've hardly looked at them.

'It's mostly about honouring and cherishing,' I say. There is no mention of obedience, which is a relief.

'And forsaking all others,' he says.

I lift my head and look at him. 'Is fidelity important to you?'

'Of course.' A wounded expression comes over his face. 'Isn't it to you?'

'Sure. Yes. I assumed we would be monogamous but—'

'I don't want anyone else,' he says, 'and I don't want to share you with anyone.'

'Okay.'

'This marriage is a fresh start for me.' He plants a tender kiss on my lips. 'I want to do things differently.'

Maybe he's telling the truth. Every relationship is unique to the people involved and he may not want to repeat what he had with Riley.

Loneliness washes over me again. Marrying Miles means giving up experiences like I had with Jacques, but what kind of life would a man like Jacques be able to give me? A man with a criminal record. A man with a suspect moral compass and little thought for the consequences of his actions. A man who described himself as a fuck-up.

Horror floods through me as I realise what I risked by sleeping with Jacques. What if Miles finds out? My recklessness could cost me my safe, secure future. A future I've invested in heavily by giving up my job and my flat. If I don't marry Miles what other options await me? I'll have to go back to London, broke, and try and get another job and a place to live. Get back on the same depressing treadmill.

No thanks. I have no intention of going back to my old life. If my marriage to Miles goes the distance, I will end up a wealthy widow. If it doesn't, I'll still come out of it with a house and, if we have children, a sizeable income to raise them properly with.

'I want an honest marriage,' Miles says. 'One where we can accept each other with all our flaws and mistakes.'

I nod in agreement, even though I'm not sure Miles would be willing to accept the mistake I made with Jacques three days ago.

'If I sell Sinclair Properties, it will be really liberating for me,' Miles says. 'I want to make some big changes in my life.' He strokes my hair. 'I might even sell Clairvallon.'

'But your family have owned this place for decades.'

'Families can be stifling sometimes. All that history.' He kisses my forehead. 'Maybe it's time I set myself free.'

52

VIVIENNE

August

When I open the oven door, heat and steam and the scents of garlic and rosemary envelop me. I lift out the blackened roasting tray with the sizzling, spitting leg of lamb at its centre and place it on the hob. With a serving spoon, I baste the meat with hot fat and bloody juices before returning the tray to the oven.

Dinner is going to be delicious. Not that any of us will have time to savour it with all the difficult discussions that will take place. I wonder if Miles should wait until after the main course before he tells Leah it's over?

Today, the last day the three of us will be together, is flying by. It's already five in the afternoon and Miles will be off to have drinks with the mayor soon. Leah spent most of the morning in the bathroom, attending to what she called her 'beauty-duty'. No doubt plucking her eyebrows and removing all her body hair in preparation for tomorrow. After lunch, she headed out to the pool and is lounging around there still.

She has been somewhat subdued these past few days. Last night at dinner, she was lost in thought and hardly said a word. For a moment I worried she was having second thoughts and would call the wedding off and spoil my fun.

I'm sure she's just suffering from pre-wedding nerves. Only natural. I've reassured her everything is organised. Her dress is ready. The wedding rings are here. As chief witness I offered to take charge of them and take them with me to the ceremony tomorrow. What will Miles do with the rings when Leah is gone? I suppose we could sell them online. The flowers came just before lunchtime. Leah's bouquet is sitting in a bucket of water in the scullery. The other arrangements I found vases for and placed in the entrance hall, the drawing room and the dining room. Leah has already chosen the arrangement she thinks will go in the barn tomorrow as part of her silly tableau thing.

Miles is in the study. He said he had a long call with Chris, his manager, to get out of the way. The sale of Sinclair Properties is looking ever more likely. I'm happy for Miles and, I must admit, whatever recompense I get for my own shareholding will be very welcome.

Once Miles has left for Philippe's, Leah and I can enjoy a Negroni together. I want her to feel happy and relaxed before the dinner but not too drunk. I want her sober enough to understand she's getting dumped.

I look at my watch. Time is marching on. I should check in on Miles. Tell him to get moving. I'm planning to serve dinner at nine and I don't want him to be late.

When I reach the study, the door is closed, but I can hear Miles on the phone. He must still be talking to Chris. Maybe once he has laid the groundwork for the sale of the company, he and I can have a proper holiday here. Some time to unwind and regroup.

Not wanting to interrupt his call, I wait for a moment, expecting him to finish soon. His voice is low, and I press my ear to the door, eager to glean anything I can about the potential sale of the company.

'Yes, that's right,' he says, 'the Dulwich property. The Georgian mansion.'

The Dulwich property? Is that the one he pretended to Leah that he wanted to buy?

'Offer them the asking price to start with,' he says. 'But, between you and me, Simon, I'm willing to go up to half a million over if I have to.' He laughs. 'Yes, I'm keen. As of tomorrow I'll be a married man and I want my wife to have a home to go to.'

He's speaking to an estate agent? He's putting in an offer on the house? What the hell is he playing at?

'Great,' he says. 'Pull out all the stops. I want this house and I want it as soon as possible.'

* * *

I'm standing at my bedroom window, peering through my binoculars. From here I have a good view through the pine trees to the pool. I can see Leah's toned, tanned legs stretched out on a sun lounger. I can see Miles perched on the lounger next to hers, one hand resting on her thigh.

After he ended his phone call with the estate agent, I crept away from the study door, furious and confused. Back in the kitchen, I attacked a courgette with a sharp knife, hacking it into uneven chunks.

'Hey, you.' Miles appeared at the kitchen door in a pale

blue linen shirt and navy chinos. Smart casual attire for his drinks for the mayor. 'I'm just going to say goodbye to Leah and then I'm off to Philippe's.'

'Great.' I mustered a smile. 'How did your call with Chris go?'

'Good,' he said, avoiding my eyes. 'We're getting all our ducks in a row for Heritage Capital.'

His casual lie almost made me recoil. As if he'd punched me in the gut.

'Well,' I said, 'have a good time with Philippe. Give him my best.'

'I will.'

'Tell Leah to come in and join me for cocktails. I'll start getting the Negronis together shortly.'

'She'll love that. You girls have fun.'

I picked up the knife and another doomed courgette. 'We will.'

Now, as I watch him with Leah by the pool, I cannot shake the terrible thought that gripped me when I heard him on the phone. What if he's changed his mind? What if he thinks he can wriggle out of our plan and marry Leah and live happily ever after?

Fool. They can't have a future together. Not one that doesn't involve her finding out exactly what he and I have been up to all summer. Does he think he can persuade me to drop the plan and stay silent? No chance of that happening. If he doesn't tell her the full story of what we've been up to, I certainly will. She won't want to stay with him after that.

A shiver runs through me. What if she does? He might persuade her he only went along with the plan to please me. If she really is after his money, she could decide to overlook his deception and betrayal. Miles was worried about her finding out in case it harmed the deal with Heritage Capital, but what if she realises that keeping Miles free from scandal so the deal can go ahead is in her best interests?

Bloody Miles. He promised he was in this with me until the end. I promised him there wouldn't be any trouble. He has broken his promise so maybe I don't need to keep mine.

I've no intention of losing two men to Leah Williams. And I've no intention of letting my cousin enter into another ill-fated marriage. One lesson the past has taught me is that when all things are aligned, when you have right on your side, you can get away with anything.

53

LEAH

August

I lie back on my sun lounger, eyes shut beneath my Celine sunglasses, savouring both the sun's dwindling warmth and my last moments of solitude before joining Vivienne for cocktails. Miles promised he would only stay at Philippe's for an hour, but I suspect he may feel pressured to be polite and stay longer. Before he left, he kissed me and told me he loved me. He said he would see me at dinner and then we would talk.

'Talk?' I said. 'About what?'

'About everything.' For a moment he looked lost and scared and it worried me, but then he clapped his hands together, jumped up from his sun lounger and declared himself ready for his very tame bachelor party.

I open my eyes. Riley floats into view on the white Lilo, glass of champagne in hand. Maybe selling this place is a good idea. I can't help seeing her everywhere. In her room, when I found the photographs, I even let myself imagine her ghost had led me to them. If Miles does get rid of Clairvallon, I won't have to dwell on her tragic death. We could buy a holiday villa somewhere else. Italy or Portugal perhaps. A place Vivienne hasn't been visiting since birth and therefore can't treat as if it's her own.

With a sigh, I sit up and check my phone. It is nearly 6 p.m. Miles, who left half an hour ago, should be at the mayor's by now. Philippe apparently has a stunning farmhouse about twenty minutes' drive from here.

I pull my Missoni kaftan over my head. After pushing my feet into my Chloé slides and slinging my basket bag over my shoulder, I set off towards the château, accompanied by the languid chatter of the birds. I don't feel like an excited bride-to-be. My limbs feel heavy; my heart feels weary. Even with all the exciting financial prospects ahead, I feel only resignation. A desire to get the ceremony over with as soon as possible.

The birds go quiet, just long enough to reveal the deafening silence they mask with their song. Silence that feels like it is waiting for something. Silence like someone holding a breath.

As I reach the back terrace of the château, a movement in the distance catches my eye. A figure darts into the walled garden. Hard to tell who it is from here, but I'm sure it isn't Vivienne.

I take off my slides and move stealthily across the terrace, glancing in the kitchen window as I pass. Vivienne is standing with her back to the window, slicing something on a chopping board. Once I reach the grass, I walk faster, my bag bouncing against my side.

When I enter the garden, I have the strangest feeling I'm about to see Riley, kneeling by one of the overgrown vegetable patches. Instead, I find Estelle. She is clutching her paisley dress in her hands and staring up at the château.

'Estelle?' I say. She must have walked here again. She isn't wearing her purple bum bag today, so I doubt she has her phone on her.

She turns towards me. Tears leak from the wrinkled corners of her eyes.

'Estelle,' I say. 'I'm Leah. We met before. I'm Riley's friend.'

She shakes her head. 'Riley is dead.' She turns her attention back to the château. '*Je me souviens*. I remember.'

'What do you remember?' I stand beside her and follow her gaze. She is looking up at the roof terrace. To my surprise the attic window above it is open. Why?

'*Ce n'était pas un accident*,' she says.

'Riley's death?' My heart stutters. 'Are you saying it was an accident?'

'*Non*.' She shakes her head. 'It was *not* an accident.'

'You were here?'

'They were fighting.'

'Who? Who was fighting?'

Estelle takes a step forward, her eyes still trained on the roof terrace. '*Pas un accident*.'

'Estelle,' I say gently, 'who was fighting?'

'Vivienne,' she says, her voice so low I can barely hear it. 'Vivienne *et* Riley.'

A chill spreads across my chest. 'What happened?' I ask, aware that, given her condition, anything Estelle says could be dismissed as unreliable. 'What did you see?'

Her eyes dart from one side of the roof terrace to the other, as if she is seeing the events of that day again. A strangled sob rises up from within her.

'It's okay,' I say. 'You can tell me.'

'They argue. They shout.' Estelle turns and lands a sharp slap on my arm.

'Jesus.' I recoil. 'Estelle.'

'They hit, they fight.' She pulls at her hair. 'They do this.'

'Stop. Don't hurt yourself.'

'They push each other and Riley, she is up against the railings and Vivienne, she holds her like this.' Estelle reaches towards my chest, grabs hold of my kaftan and pulls me to her. 'Then everything falls down.'

'The railings?' I let her hold on to me, not wanting to sever the memory she is reliving.

'Yes. Everything falling and Riley, she screams and Vivienne...' Estelle shoves me away. 'She pushes her.'

My heart batters against my ribs. My throat is dry. Is this true or am I listening to the delusions of a sick woman? 'Did you tell anyone else?' I ask. 'Does anyone else know?'

Her head jerks towards me. Her face is twisted with terror. '*Tu vas me mettre dans une maison de retraite*?' she says.

'Sorry, I don't understand.'

'No care home. Please.' Her hands curl into fists. 'Jacques says if I tell anyone what I see, Vivienne will put me in a home.'

'Jacques? Does he know what you saw?'

'*Mais, bien sûr.*' She looks at me as if I am stupid. 'He was here. With me.'

'He saw Vivienne and Riley fighting?'

Estelle smacks a fist against her head. 'My Jacques is a good boy.'

'Estelle... don't... don't hit yourself.'

She thumps her head again. Harder this time. 'I want to go home.'

'Estelle, stop it.'

She turns and bolts. She moves fast for a woman her age. I follow her out of the garden. She heads across the grass towards the outbuildings. Towards the woods she came through to get here.

'Estelle,' calls a voice behind us. '*Arrête. Maintenant.*'

I turn and see Vivienne running across the grass towards us, a dark vision in her black shirt dress, her black apron flapping up and down. Estelle stops. She lets out a whimper. She seems to deflate, as if the sight of Vivienne has punctured her.

'I heard shouting,' Vivienne says. 'I came to see what was going on.'

Did she hear Estelle and I or did she see us? I think of the binoculars lying on the desk in her bedroom. Did she spy on us when we were in the walled garden? Did she see Estelle gazing up at the roof terrace? Did she watch as Estelle acted out her version of Riley's death?

'I want to go home,' Estelle says, when Vivienne reaches us. '*Je t'en prie.*'

'Well come on then.' Vivienne's voice is brisk and authoritative. She holds out her hand. Estelle hesitates. 'Come on,' Vivienne says, firmer this time.

Estelle sidles up to me and clasps my hand.

'Fine.' Vivienne sighs. 'We'll all go.'

* * *

Vivienne drives Dolly the 2CV more carefully than she did the day she and I went to Grandfresnoy. Estelle is in the back, her seatbelt fastened, a chastened expression on her face like a child about to get into trouble. I'm cramped in the passenger seat with my bag between my legs. I didn't have time to change out of my bikini and kaftan before we left.

'Honestly,' Vivienne says, flicking ash from her cigarette out of the window. 'Béatrice is going to have to keep a closer eye on her mother.' She takes another drag on the cigarette. 'Estelle looked upset. What was she saying to you?'

'Nonsense, mostly.' My heart is still darting around my chest. 'She was upset because the garden was a mess. She said Riley would be angry.'

'Poor thing literally doesn't know what day it is.' Vivienne exhales smoke out of the open window but the breeze blows it straight back into the car.

Vivienne is right. Estelle is very unwell. Yet she convinced me that she saw what she said she saw. Or perhaps she just believes in a false memory so strongly she has made me believe it too. I sneak a glance at Vivienne. Did she do it? Is she really capable of that? Until recently, I believed she loved Riley, and I have only heard otherwise from less than reliable sources.

In the car, it only takes us five minutes to reach *Les Arbres*. My stomach twists when we pull up in front of the low sandstone cottage. I know Jacques has gone but my memories of being here with him are still fresh and raw.

Béatrice is waiting for us at the garden gate. Vivienne called her before we left the château. She has dark hair, like her brother, only hers is cropped short. Her hands are tucked into the pockets of her jade-green sundress.

'*Bonjour*,' Vivienne calls through the window.

Béatrice opens the gate. 'Vivienne, *je suis vraiment désolée.*'

'*C'est bon,*' Vivienne says. '*Pas de problème.*'

Vivienne steps out of the car and folds the driver's seat forward. 'Come on, Estelle.'

Glancing in the rear-view mirror, I see Estelle shrink back against the seat as Vivienne leans over to unclip her seatbelt.

'Hello.' Béatrice appears at my window. 'You must be Leah?'

'Yes. Hi.' Béatrice gives me an intense once-over. I doubt Jacques told her anything about me, but she has probably heard rumours about Miles Sinclair's much younger fiancée.

'Béatrice, can you give me a hand?' Vivienne says. Béatrice scuttles round to the other side of the car.

'Maman,' she says. '*Ça doit s'arrêter.*'

While the two women coax Estelle out of the car, I reach into my bag, pull out my phone and send Miles a text.

> Can you come back? Need to talk about Vivienne.

I can't be certain if what Estelle said was true, but I would prefer not to be alone in the château with Vivienne right now. She and Béatrice are chatting away in French as they guide a meek and silent Estelle through the garden gate.

I stare at my phone, but no reply from Miles appears. He might have turned his phone on to silent out of politeness. My eyes stay fixed on the screen, willing a message to materialise.

'Who are you texting?' Vivienne is suddenly back at the car, flinging the driver's door open.

My pulse thrums. 'Just Miles. Checking when he'll be back.'

'He'll be a while yet.' Vivienne slams the car door and puts her seatbelt on. 'Philippe loves to talk, and he's bound to have opened a bottle of something expensive they'll have to savour.'

She crunches the 2CV into gear and executes a jerky three-point turn. As we pull away, I glance back at the cottage. Estelle stands alone at the garden gate. When I wave goodbye, she presses a finger against her lips. A warning to stay silent.

'I told Béatrice she should get a carer in more often,' Vivienne says as the car picks up speed. Without our infirm passenger, her driving has reverted to erratic bordering on dangerous.

While she rambles on about the failings of the French social care system, I try to think logically. Vivienne told me that on the day Riley died, she was in Compiègne and that Riley was already dead by the time she got back. Either she is lying about that or Estelle has mixed up two separate events. She could have seen Vivienne and Riley fighting on another occasion and in her decaying mind has merged that memory with Riley's death.

If Jacques was here, I could ask him, although I doubt he would tell me the truth. When I was with him a few days ago, he gave no hint he and his mother had witnessed Riley's death. Either they didn't, or Jacques lied to my face. Both options are possible. If Jacques did witness what Estelle described to me, did he confront Vivienne with it?

'Here we are.' Vivienne swerves sharply into the entrance to the château. 'And we've still got plenty of time for cocktails.'

She springs out of the car and taps the entry code into the keypad. I check my phone. Still nothing from Miles. As the gates groan open, I have a sudden urge to get out of the car and run.

Vivienne jumps back into the driver's seat and shuts her door. 'Let's do this, as the young folk say.'

The 2CV lurches forward. The gates clang shut behind us. I wait for Vivienne to speed up the drive, but instead the car remains stationary.

'So,' she says, 'I've been researching how we can make this hen do thing a bit special.'

'I don't think we need to make—'

'Apparently the thing nowadays is to have a ritual of some kind.'

'A ritual?'

'Something that symbolises a new beginning.'

'Right.' The air seeping into the car is thick and warm. Oppressive.

'With that in mind, I think you and I should drink our cocktails up on the roof terrace.'

'What?' So that's why the attic window is open. The shock on my face must show because she laughs and lays a hand on my arm.

'Think about it. If you really want to be happy with Miles, you need to blow Riley away. Get her out of your system.'

'She isn't in my system.' My weak voice betrays my lie. Riley is everywhere.

'What happened to her was awful,' Vivienne says, 'and I think about her every day.'

I think about her too. And now I'm wondering if Vivienne was responsible for her death.

'But we have to move on,' she says. 'So I propose drinks on the roof terrace, like we used to before all this happened. We can give Riley a send-off and welcome you to the family at the same time.'

Before I can reply, she jams her foot on the accelerator and the car lurches forward.

'It's a lovely idea,' I say, 'and I'm very grateful, but it isn't safe up there.'

'We'll be careful.' She smiles at me. 'It'll be fun.'

No way am I going up there with her. I need to put her off until Miles gets back. I'll say I need to freshen up. A long shower will eat into our time together.

We speed up the driveway. Nausea swills in my stomach. As we approach the château, I see a car parked outside it.

'Who on earth is that?' Vivienne says.

Relief spreads through me. The car doesn't belong to Miles, but I'm grateful for any visitor right now.

The 2CV screeches to a halt. Vivienne flings off her seatbelt and gets out of the car. The car in the driveway is a black VW Golf with English licence plates.

The door to the château is wide open.

'Who is it?' I ask Vivienne as I pick up my bag from the car floor.

'Oh dear.' Her face is ashen. One hand clutches at the neck of her shirt dress.

'Vivienne?' A man appears at the château doors. 'I thought I heard a car. Sorry to barge in like this but I keep calling and you won't answer so you gave me no choice. I even tried calling the landline here.'

I open the car door and step out onto the gravel driveway.

'The code for the gates was the same as before so I let myself in,' the man says. 'I hope I...' He trails off when he catches sight of me. 'Leah?' he says.

I stare at the visitor. It takes a moment for me to place him. 'Nick?' I say finally. I laugh, unable to make sense of what I'm seeing. 'What are you doing here?'

54

LEAH

August

We stare at each other. Nick? Here at Château Clairvallon? He looks different. Still lean and rangy but he has shaved off his thinning hair and a grey beard now frames his thin lips. I only ever saw him in business suits and winter clothes but here he has on grey chinos and a white linen shirt.

'Vivienne,' he says, 'what's going on? Why is *she* here?'

Why am I here? Why is *he* here? Is he friends with Miles? That would be awkward.

'Hello, Dom,' Vivienne says wearily.

Dom? As in Vivienne's husband Dom?

'What's going on?' Nick says.

Ignoring his question, Vivienne climbs the steps up to the château, pushes past him and disappears indoors.

'Who are you?' I ask Nick. Dom. My thigh muscles soften. Black dots dance in front of my eyes.

'I'm Dominic,' he says. 'That's my full name. I should have

told you my real name, but I liked the secrecy at first. I liked pretending to be someone different.'

'Is... is Vivienne your wife?'

'Soon-to-be ex-wife. If she ever signs the bloody divorce papers.'

The driveway feels like it is tilting beneath me.

'But you're... you're dead,' I say.

'What?' A short, caustic laugh. 'I'm sure Vivienne would prefer it if I was but no, I'm very much alive, thank you.'

'You died in a car accident.'

'I can assure you I didn't. Although that's a miracle with Vivienne's driving.'

My head pounds as I try to absorb what I'm hearing. Vivienne's husband isn't dead.

'Shit.' Dominic stares at me. 'Are you helping her with the divorce in some way?'

'What?'

'Is that why you're here? Did her lawyer suggest this?'

'No. Jesus. I don't understand any of this. I didn't know she was your wife. I swear.'

A grim expression settles over his face. 'I've had enough of her bloody game-playing. Let's get to the bottom of this.'

* * *

We find Vivienne in the kitchen, standing at the table, slicing a large orange into thin circles.

'Negroni?' she asks in a light, chirpy voice. As if nothing has happened. As if she is a hostess welcoming old friends. 'I made them earlier.' She taps the blade of her knife against the large jug of ruby red liquid in front of her. 'They're a touch strong but really delicious.'

Her eyes have a glazed, vacant look. I wonder if she is in shock. She's not the only one. My blood roars in my ears. My bag is still slung over my shoulder and I'm gripping it so tightly the straps are digging into my fingers.

'Why is Leah here?' Dominic asks. 'What have you done?'

'Calm down, darling,' Vivienne says. 'It's all a bit of fun. A game. Women like Leah know all about games.'

Games? What is she talking about?

'You told her I was dead,' he says. 'Why would you do that?'

'It was true. Sort of.' Vivienne rests the knife on the chopping board. Her eyes fill with tears. 'You left. You were gone. It was like a death.'

'It's not the same thing,' I say. 'Not even close.'

'Really, Leah?' she replies. 'Your father's alive but you tell everyone he's dead.'

A tremor runs down my spine. This woman knows everything about me.

'Anyway, I thought I'd sound more pitiful if I claimed my husband was actually dead,' she tells me. 'I was fairly certain Dom hadn't told you anything about his family but I couldn't be 100 per cent sure.'

'I never told her anything about you,' Dominic says. 'Or Nathan.'

'So honourable,' Vivienne says. 'A real gentleman.'

'Did you tell her about me?' I ask Dominic. 'About our affair?'

He shakes his head. 'I didn't need to. She'd had a private detective on to me for weeks. I bet she had him look into you as well.'

'Nothing gets past me, Dominic.' Vivienne drops ice from a bowl into the three squat tumblers next to the jug of Negroni. 'I knew you were up to something from the start.'

'The last time I saw her, we had a huge row,' Dominic tells me. 'She showed me all the evidence she'd collected. I thought she was going to use it to try and make me settle for less in the divorce. I had no idea she would try to get to you in some way.'

A stab of pain behind my forehead. My reality is fracturing, and I can't keep a grip on the pieces.

'I made it clear I wasn't leaving you for Leah,' Dominic says to Vivienne. 'You know that. She didn't want me.' He turns to me. 'Which I totally get, by the way. Why would you, at your age?'

'Touching as this lovers' reunion is,' Vivienne says, 'the fact remains that *she* ruined our marriage.'

'No.' Dominic shakes his head. 'I was unhappy in our marriage long before Leah came along.'

Vivienne ignores him, focusing instead on dropping a slice of orange into each of the tumblers.

'Did she get in touch with you?' Dominic asks me. 'Did she befriend you in some way?'

'Miles,' I say, holding up my left hand so he can see my engagement ring. 'I'm here with Miles.'

'Fuck.' Dominic looks from me to Vivienne, who is pouring the Negroni mixture into the tumblers with a disturbingly steady hand.

Miles. He told me more than once that Dominic was dead. Whatever is going on here, he's part of it. 'That night in the Mandarin Oriental, when I met Miles. That wasn't by chance, was it?' I ask.

'Of course not, you silly girl.' Vivienne takes a swig of the Negroni. Puckers her lips. 'Punchy. Very punchy.' She gestures to the other two tumblers. 'Care to try?'

Goosebumps rise up along my arms. Miles and Vivienne have been playing me all along. Fear surges through me. If

Vivienne has gone to such lengths to get me here, if she hates me that much, what else is she capable of? If what Estelle told me earlier is true, then this château is not a safe place for me to be. Thank God Dominic is here.

'Where is Miles?' he asks.

'Having drinks with Philippe.' Vivienne takes another swig of her cocktail. 'Who knows how long he'll be.'

'I texted him earlier,' I tell Dominic. 'Hopefully he's on his way back.' I ease my bag off my shoulder and retrieve my phone. I'm not sure whether to be relieved or scared when I see Miles has replied to my message.

Has something happened?

I text him back.

DOM IS HERE!

The ceaseless churning of my thoughts is making my head throb. Miles has been so loving these past few days. So excited about the wedding and our future together. None of this makes any sense.

'I should have guessed Miles would be involved in this somehow,' Dominic says to Vivienne. 'You and he have always had something strange going on.'

Vivienne's expression hardens. 'Don't talk about him like that.'

'There's something not right about the two of you,' he says.

'Shut up,' she snarls.

'I'm not the only one who noticed it. Riley did too. We spoke about it once. She said—'

'Shut the fuck up.' Vivienne hurls her glass at Dominic. He

dodges it just in time and it shatters against the wooden dresser.

'Let's get out of here.' He puts an arm around my shoulder. 'I'm not hanging around to see Miles. We'll go somewhere and regroup and decide what to do.'

'Good idea,' I say.

He steers me out of the kitchen. 'I'm so sorry you got mixed up in all this.'

'It's okay. It's not your fault.'

My phone pings. A reply from Miles.

On my way. Can explain everything.

'Don't you walk away from me!' Vivienne screams.

We get as far as the hallway before she catches up with us. She launches herself at Dominic's back, as if by hanging on to him she can stop him from leaving. He lets go of me and cries out as she punches him in the side three times. Three quick jabs. Only when she steps away do I see the knife in her hand.

'No.' Dominic gasps as blood soaks into the back of his white shirt. He falls to his knees and then collapses onto his front, his body blocking the château door.

'Dominic?' Vivienne drops to her knees beside him. 'It's okay, my darling, I'm here.'

55

VIVIENNE

August

'Dominic?' My husband is making a strange, gurgling noise. 'Dom?'

In my right hand is a knife. It is covered in blood. I don't recall picking the knife up from the chopping board. I do recall the vicious pain in my heart when I saw my husband put his arm around Leah. The way they looked at me as if I was crazy. The way they turned their backs on me and walked away. As if they were walking into the future together.

'Vivienne.' Leah's voice is distant. Muffled. As if a bomb has gone off nearby and now everything sounds like it is under-water and there is a strange ringing in my ears.

'Vivienne,' she says. 'What have you done?'

I would have thought that was obvious. She really isn't the sharpest knife in the drawer.

The knife. The sharp one in my hand. My hands are also covered in blood. There is blood everywhere. Seeping into the black and white tiles. These old tiles are cracked and porous. Scrubbing the blood off them is going to be a hell of a job.

Leah steps closer. 'We need to stop the bleeding. Tie something around his waist.'

The ringing in my ears stops. Every sound is now sharp and clear. My husband's moans, the shrill birdsong outside, Leah's footsteps.

'Back off.' I jab the knife towards her. 'This is your fault. You did this.'

'I'll call an ambulance.' Her phone is in her hand. She is tapping at the screen.

'No.' I lurch to my feet, the knife outstretched in front of me. 'He's my husband. I'll deal with this.'

'Vivienne, please. He needs help.' She is too busy with her phone to notice me lunging at her. When the blade of the knife slashes her right forearm, she cries out in pain. The phone drops from her hand. Her bag falls to the floor. She backs away from me, terror in her eyes.

'I won't be long, Dom,' I say over my shoulder. 'I'm just going to sort things out with Leah.'

If Leah Williams had never existed, none of this would be happening. Perhaps if she ceased to exist, all of this would stop.

Her eyes dart left and right. She is deciding which way to bolt. She heads right, towards the dining room, but I block her way. She stumbles backwards out of the entrance hall, clutching her arm, desperate to avoid the blade that glints in front of me.

Under the archway we go. Delicious gasps of fear escape her lips. Drops of blood trail in her wake. She makes a run for the kitchen but I catch her just in time, yanking her back by that long, thick hair of hers.

She screams and wriggles from my clutches. Towards the stairs we go. Inevitable, really.

'Up you go,' I say.

She scrambles away from me, tripping every now and then on the hem of her stupid designer kaftan. One of her expensive shoes falls off.

'Please, Vivienne,' she says.

When we reach the first-floor landing, she veers towards the west wing, but I grab her floaty kaftan and slash at the colourful material. She stumbles again, taking me down with her. The knife misses her by millimetres. She rolls onto her back and kicks me hard in the stomach.

'Bitch,' I say, through winded breath.

She hauls herself to her feet and shakes her other shoe off. She runs towards the east wing but I am there again, knife outstretched and she makes for the attic staircase, as I knew she would. A song pops into my head. That chirpy, eighties number about the only way being up.

Up and up we go and the only door open is the one that leads to the east side of the attic and once Leah is through it she slams it in my face but there is no key in the lock, and when I throw my weight against it the door gives way and there she is, veering through the dusty old crap that means nothing to anyone any more and I am after her and soon she is at the open window and she is hauling herself up and over the sill.

I don't get to the window in time to see her land on the roof terrace, but from the agonising howl she emits, I assume her landing was not a gainly one.

When I look down at the roof terrace she is on her back, clutching her left ankle. When she sees my legs dangling over the windowsill, she hauls herself up but can do nothing to stop my smooth descent and safe landing. Wielding the knife, I walk towards her. She limps away into a corner of the terrace, blood still dripping from the slash on her arm.

Looks like we're going to have our rooftop party after all.

'Vivienne,' she says, all doe-eyed and pitiful. 'This has gone far enough.'

'I disagree.'

'We have to get help for Dominic. He was losing a lot of blood.'

I glance at my hands. They are stained red with my husband. I think about my son and what he would make of all this. *No. Do not think about Nathan.* A sob tries to push its way up my throat, but I swallow it down and look out over the château grounds. The light is taking on a rose-gold tint. The air is soft and warm. It is a beautiful evening. How lovely it would be to sit here alone, with one of those delicious Negronis to sip on.

'Vivienne.'

Look at her trembling and cowering. As if she is the injured party here. 'This is all your fault,' I say.

'All we have to do is go downstairs and call for an ambulance,' she says. 'People will understand. I know you haven't had it easy since your marriage ended.'

'Thanks to you.'

'I know you haven't been well. Miles told me about your suicide attempt.'

'Suicide attempt?' I wipe my bloody hands on my apron. 'I may have had a minor breakdown after Dominic left but I never tried to take my own life.'

Why would Miles say that? A dark thought crawls into my head. I remember him trying to get me to come up here with him that morning Leah was out with Anne-Marie. The same way I planned to lure Leah up here earlier today. He was so insistent. Was he going to hurt me? Did he intend to push me off the roof and make it look as though I'd killed myself?

No. Miles wouldn't do that. He is the one man who has always looked out for me.

'I'm sorry, Vivienne.' Leah's face twists with pain as she tries to put weight on her left foot. 'I'm sorry I slept with your husband. I had no intention of taking him away from his family. When he said he wanted things to get serious, I ended it. You know that.'

'Yes, yes, you're a saint, but actions have consequences.'

'Did you bring me to the château to kill me?' she says.

'That wasn't the original plan.' I tap the blade of the knife against my thigh. 'But plans do change, don't they?'

56

LEAH

August

Eyes fixed on the blood-smeared knife tapping against Vivienne's thigh, I press myself further into my corner. There are railings on both sides of me and, beyond them, a dizzying drop to the ground.

The gash on my arm is not as deep as I feared but it is still bleeding. My left ankle throbs and every time I shift my leg, a searing pain shoots up it. There is no way I can get myself up and run back to the window without her catching me. I need to stay still and stay calm. I need to keep her talking in the hope Miles returns before she decides to execute her revised plan.

'What was your original plan?' I ask. 'You obviously put a lot of thought into it.'

Vivienne scrapes the knife back and forth along the railings. The grating sound of metal-on-metal rings out into the warm evening air. I shudder. My body is still buzzing with adrenaline. From the terror of her chasing me. From the awful realisation I had nowhere to go but the roof terrace. The place where Riley met her end.

The metallic scraping stops. 'Yes,' she says. 'A *lot* of thought.'

She looks almost proud as she tells me about the scheme she and Miles concocted. I think back to that first meeting in the Mandarin Oriental. How I had no clue what I was getting myself into. Blinded by my quest for money, I thought I'd spotted an easy prey.

'That Cartier necklace he gave you,' she says, 'the one that got you into his bed, I chose that. And your engagement ring.'

'You have excellent taste.'

As she continues to detail her exploits, I tear a strip of fabric from the hem of my kaftan and tie it around the wound on my arm.

'Why?' I ask, after she has finished describing all she did to get me here. All she has done since I arrived. 'Why go to all this trouble?'

'To humiliate you,' she says. 'To stop you ruining other men's lives. Someone has to protect men from women like you.'

She tells me how it was supposed to end. Miles announcing over dinner tonight that the wedding was off. Me shipped back to London, hurt and confused. My dreams of an easy life shattered.

'I was doing you a favour,' she says. 'You might have learned a valuable lesson.'

My right hand tingles. My palm is ice cold. Logically I know this is because my arm is injured and bleeding, but I can't help imagining a ghost-hand sliding itself into mine. As if Riley is here, beside me. An ally urging me on.

'Is that why you killed Riley?' I ask. 'To teach her a lesson?'

Vivienne recoils and takes a step away from me, her knuckles white around the handle of the knife.

'Estelle told me everything,' I say. 'You were up here and you were fighting. You pushed Riley and she fell.'

'Estelle is hardly a credible witness.'

'Jacques was with her.'

Vivienne lets out a deep, weary sigh. 'Yes. He was.'

My guts clench. Is Vivienne about to share the events of that day with me, and, if so, does that mean she will ensure I don't share the story with anyone else?

Stay calm. Keep her talking.

'Did he blackmail you?' I say. 'Is that why Estelle got the cottage and her pension?'

'He took a photograph.' She reaches into her apron pocket and pulls out her vape pen. 'What kind of person does that? What kind of man watches his lover plunge to her death and then takes a fucking photograph?' She sucks on her vape pen, exhales a cloud of smoke. 'Even from that distance you could tell it was me looking over the edge.' She points to where the roof terrace has crumbled away. 'Just there.'

A calculating move from Jacques. Did he ever consider going to the police with the picture or did he always have blackmail in mind? He warned me he was fucked up. He wasn't lying about that.

'Two days after it happened, when I'd already given my statement to the police, he came to see me,' she says. 'He showed me the photograph, and of course the date and time were on it. He threatened to go to the police. By then, I'd already lied about where I was that day. I was in a bit of a bind.'

'So he asked you for money?'

'Yes. Not for himself, but for his mother. So she would be

safe and looked after. He said he wouldn't ask for anything more than that and, to his credit, he never has.'

Jacques' concern for his mother hardly justifies what he did, but he at least has some redeeming qualities. 'What about Béatrice?' I ask. 'Was she in on it?'

'No. She knows nothing.' Another deep drag on the vape pen. 'I suggested to Miles we should give Estelle the cottage and a small annual payment. He was such a mess at that point, I think he'd have agreed to anything.'

'So he knows nothing about any of this?'

Vivienne shakes her head. Stares at her bloody hands. I strain to pick up any hint of an approaching car. *Where are you, Miles?* I'm furious with him right now and I don't trust him, but I am also certain he wouldn't do me any physical harm.

'Why did you kill Riley?' I say.

'It was an accident.' Her tone is irritable, as if I am one of her former pupils who cannot grasp a simple concept. She marches across the terrace to the gap in the railings. 'We were fighting. I can't remember who started it. I think I may have slapped her; anyway, we were grappling with each other.' She puts her vape pen back in her apron pocket. 'We got to here,' she says. 'She was clawing at me, so I pushed her against the railings. I was shouting at her to stop. There was this awful sound. The stone crumbled beneath her feet. She started to fall, and I had to let her go. Otherwise, she would have taken me with her.'

'If it was an accident, why didn't you tell the police what happened? You could have explained. Instead, you left her there and drove away.'

Vivienne stares at the spot where Riley fell. 'Why make something terrible even worse? I didn't want Miles to know her last moments had been ones of conflict. I wanted to spare him that.'

'Very noble.' Gritting my teeth against the shooting pain in my leg, I shift my body out of the safety of my corner, intending to move closer to the window, but Vivienne wheels around and storms back towards me.

'It was an accident,' she says, the knife outstretched. 'Do you understand?'

'Yes.' My legs are shaking. 'I understand.' It is possible she had to let Riley fall to save her own life, but I also know that Vivienne, who stabbed her husband in the heat of the moment, is capable of having pushed her. If she was angry enough. If she had a good enough reason.

I clear my throat. 'What I don't understand is why you were fighting. Did you always hate her?'

'Of course. That Vegas wedding was her idea. She swept Miles off his feet and, bloody fool that he is, he didn't get her to sign a prenup.'

'They must have been very much in love.'

'Don't give me that crap. She blinded him with sex. She had a hold over him. I told him to make her sign a post-nuptial agreement or a consent form to protect his future earnings, but she refused and it turns out it's difficult to force someone to sign anything like that once you've tied the knot.'

Sounds like Riley played this game a lot better than I have.

'Miles was trapped,' Vivienne says. 'He had several companies desperate to buy Sinclair Properties, but he couldn't sell it in case she decided to divorce him and waltz off with half of the money.'

'I suppose a sale would have suited you?'

She frowns. 'What?'

'You told me Dominic lost money on his business ventures.

Your money. Were you angry because Riley was blocking the sale of the company and stopping you getting money for your shares?'

'Don't be vulgar.' Her nose wrinkles in distaste. 'Not everyone is motivated by money like you. Yes, a windfall would have been welcome, but I did what I did out of love. To protect my cousin.'

'From what?'

'From a life of misery. Riley treated him terribly. Promising to have children and then changing her mind, not to mention all the affairs. She was using Miles for money and sleeping with any man she wanted to.'

Vivienne clearly has no idea Miles and Riley had an open relationship. Telling her now might only enrage her further.

'And when she started with Jacques.' Vivienne shudders. 'It was so obvious to everyone. She was hardly what you'd call a subtle flirt.'

'Is that why you had him sacked?'

'Someone had to do something.' She scrapes the knife back and forth along the railings. 'I thought that would put an end to it, but a few months later they were at it again and Miles wouldn't take me seriously when I told him.'

I almost feel sorry for Vivienne, being lied to like that. Miles misled her. He let her be angry on his behalf and that anger had fatal consequences.

In the distance, I hear what might be the sound of a car engine. I glance at Vivienne, who is lost in thought and doesn't seem to have noticed it.

'Were you fighting about Jacques that day?' I ask.

She nods. 'We were all here for Easter,' she says, 'but after the Easter weekend, Dom had to go back to London for work. I had a longer holiday so I decided to stay.' She presses the back of her hand against her forehead and when she removes it, a dark red stain remains.

I listen out for the car as she talks about the day of Riley's death. How Miles had left for Paris that morning and how she had decided to go to Compiègne for the day to do some sightseeing.

'After Miles left, I heard Riley on the phone to Jacques, begging him to come over after lunch,' she says. 'I pretended to leave for Compiègne, but then I came back. I parked my car near the woods and walked to the château. I wanted to catch them at it. I wanted proof to show Miles. I wanted him to see the truth.'

I think of the photographs hidden under Riley's bed. Miles would hardly have been shocked by anything Vivienne had to show him.

I hear the car again. It must be at the bottom of the driveway.

'When I got to the château, Riley was up here.' She taps the knife against her thigh. 'I thought Jacques would be with her, but when I got up here, it was just the two of us. He was late. He always was an appalling timekeeper.'

'And then you argued?' *Keep her talking. Keep her talking.*

'I told her the affair with Jacques was unacceptable and that it had to end. She just laughed. She laughed in my face and then she said terrible things.'

'What things?' I ask.

'She was always flirting with Dom, just like she did with every man, but she told me she was going to make a play for him.' The knife blade twitches by Vivienne's side. 'She said he would sleep with her in a heartbeat.'

Maybe he would have. The Dominic I knew was desperate to be wanted.

'He would never have done it,' Vivienne says. 'He was a good man. Faithful.' Her face contorts with rage. 'Until he met you.'

The noise of the car gathers into a roar as it accelerates towards the house. Vivienne's head jerks up.

A screech of brakes. A car door slamming.

'Miles to the rescue.' Vivienne moves towards me, the blood-smeared knife pointed at me. 'The idiot thinks he's in love with you.'

In love with me? After what I've heard I doubt that's possible.

'He likes to save women,' she says. 'Another of his strengths that is also a weakness.'

'What did he save Riley from?'

Vivienne shakes her head as if to say, no more questions. No more delays.

A bitter chill spreads through me. 'Please, Vivienne.' I try to get to my knees but she launches herself at me. I kick out at her with my injured leg. The pain makes me scream. I collapse onto my back. She straddles me and raises the knife up high. My hand shoots up to grab her wrist. She may be small, but her strength is ferocious. We grapple, the knife poised above us.

'Please,' I say. 'Stop.'

'It's over,' she says. 'I killed Riley and now I'm going to kill you.'

'Vivienne.' Miles is crouched on the attic windowsill, ready to pounce. 'No.'

57

LEAH

August

A thud as Miles lands on the rooftop. 'Enough,' he says. 'This stops now.'

Vivienne freezes. Lowers the knife to her side.

'Dominic is dead,' Miles says.

Vivienne folds in on herself and releases a soft, low moan before springing to her feet, the blood-smeared knife hanging limply by her side. For a moment I think it is all over and she will give in without a fight, but when Miles edges towards her, she thrusts the knife into the space between them and he retreats. He looks from her to me and back again. He can see that she is nearer to me than he is to her. She could reach me before he could get to her.

I sit up and press my back against the railings, trying to ignore the drop behind me.

'Leah, are you okay?' Miles asks, his eyes wild with panic. He spots my bandaged arm. 'Christ.'

'It's okay.' The gash still stings like hell and blood is still soaking into my makeshift bandage. 'I twisted my ankle getting down here.'

There are streaks of blood on Miles' pale blue shirt. Blood on his hands.

'Did you call an ambulance for Dominic?' I say. 'Just in case he's—'

'There was no time,' he says. 'I had to get to you.'

'It's her fault.' Vivienne points the blade in my direction. 'She took Dom from me. She was going to take you as well.'

'That's not true,' Miles says.

'You were going to betray me,' Vivienne says. 'I heard you putting in an offer on a house. You were going to marry her tomorrow.'

'Leah, I can explain everything,' he says.

Vivienne's laughter is off-pitch, verging on hysteria. 'I'd like to see you try.'

'Leah, I was going to tell you everything tonight,' he says. 'All about... all about Vivienne's ridiculous plan. I was going to tell her it was over and that I wanted to be with you.'

'And what did you think would happen?' Vivienne says. 'Did you think she would forgive you and marry you anyway?' She sighs. 'Let's face it, she might have done. She's only in it for the money. Just like Riley.'

Anger darkens Miles' face. 'You really killed her? You killed Riley?'

'What you heard me say was out of context. As I've already explained to Leah, it was technically an accident.'

'Why did you do it?' he says.

'To protect you.' She leans towards me. I cry out as she grabs a handful of my hair and twists it tight. 'From women like this.'

'Let her go, Vivienne,' Miles says.

'Everyone knew Riley was sleeping with Jacques,' she says. 'Everyone except you. You wouldn't listen.'

'He did know.' My voice is raw with pain and fear. 'He knew they were sleeping together.'

'What?' Vivienne releases me. 'What are you talking about?'

'He knew about all her men,' I say. 'He and Riley had an open relationship.'

'Miles?' Vivienne rests one hand on the metal railings. 'Is that true?'

Now that her attention is on Miles, I manage to edge away from her. Just a little. I feel bad for deflecting her wrath in his direction, but he's better equipped to deal with her than I am right now. If her focus isn't on me, I might be able to put more distance between us.

'Who told you that?' Miles asks me.

'Jacques.' I stare defiantly at him. 'I've seen him a few times. He had some interesting things to say.'

'Did you hear that, Miles?' Vivienne laughs. 'She's *seen* him a few times. History repeating itself.'

Miles has the nerve to look hurt.

Vivienne moves towards him. 'Why didn't you tell me about this... this open relationship?'

Miles stands his ground. 'It was none of your business.'

'You said sex was a sacred bond between two people who loved each other.' Vivienne's voice is frail and girlish. 'That's what you said.'

'Sometimes it is,' he says gently. 'With certain people.'

That icy ghost-hand in mine. Riley, urging me on.

'He liked Riley to tell him about her encounters with other men,' I say. 'It turned him on. It was their thing, Vivienne. Jacques told me.'

'You're both making it sound sordid,' Miles says.

'Did you know about Dom?' Vivienne says. 'You saw Riley flirting with him. Did she tell you she was going to try and seduce him?'

'No.' Miles shakes his head. 'I would never have condoned that.'

'Don't pretend you had any control over her.' Vivienne sneers. 'She was a law unto herself.'

'I would never have let her hurt you like that,' he says.

'You were the one man I thought I could totally trust,' she says. 'The one man.'

A pained silence stretches between the two of them. Putting my weight on my hands, I shift my body further away from Vivienne. Closer to Miles and to the window.

'We're supposed to share our secrets, Miles,' she says, 'not keep them from one another.'

'My marriage was *my* business,' he says.

'I thought I knew everything about you.' The knife twitches by Vivienne's side. 'Then I hear all this about Riley and tonight you were going to betray me. To choose *her* over me.' The look she shoots me is pure hatred. 'Why did you tell her I tried to kill myself? Why would you say that?'

'To make our story more credible,' Miles says, a desperate edge to his voice. 'I thought if I made you sound unstable and in need of help, it would explain why I wanted you here all summer.'

I edge further away from Vivienne and her blood-smeared knife.

'You know, Leah,' she says, bringing me to a halt. 'I'm not the only person Miles has kept secrets from. There's a lot you don't know about him.'

'Vivienne, please,' he says.

'I feel like an idiot now,' she says. 'I was doing all I could to protect you from Riley and you didn't even want me to.' She shakes her head. 'I thought I owed it to you. I was trying to save you, like you once saved me.'

'That wasn't the same,' he says.

'He killed Bruce.' Vivienne's tortured eyes turn to me. 'He killed his brother.'

'Miles?' A tightness in my chest. 'What is she talking about?'

'It's true.' His shoulders sag. 'I was going to tell you about that too. I wanted you to know everything.'

'Liar,' Vivienne says. 'It's our secret. You would never have told her.'

'Bruce didn't fall down the stairs,' Miles says. 'We were fighting. He'd attacked Vivienne.'

'Don't.' She shakes her head. 'I don't want to hear it.'

'I'm sick of carrying it around,' he says. 'I'm done.'

I listen as, in a trembling voice, he tells me about his brother's sexual assault on Vivienne when they were teenagers. He describes the fight that happened when he intervened and the tragic way it ended. What a mess. I feel sorry for the teenage Vivienne, subjected to an attack like that and sorry for Miles too. His drunken attempt to do the right thing and protect his cousin has haunted him ever since.

'I never meant to kill him,' he said. 'We decided the best thing to do was cover it up. We thought we were doing the right thing.'

'We were,' Vivienne says. 'Bruce deserved what happened to him.'

'And you've held it over me ever since. I've never been able to shake you.'

'Don't say that.' Vivienne jabs the knife in his direction. 'Don't.'

'But you saved her,' I say to Miles. 'Why do you still feel you owe her something?'

'I killed my brother,' he says. 'Guilt changes everything. You're never free of it.'

Thanks to Miles' guilt, Vivienne had power over him for years.

All relationships are based on power, not love.

'It's over.' Miles is shaking with fury. 'I want out, Vivienne. Every time I look at you I'm filled with guilt and shame.'

'How can you say that?' Tears gather in her eyes. 'After everything we've been through together. After all I've done for you.'

She moves fast, a dark blur, the knife glinting in her hand. Miles dodges her and flees to the edge of the terrace. Close to the railings.

She turns and comes for him again. When she thrusts the knife at him, he steps aside and then darts behind her.

'No!' she screams.

With one hand he grabs her apron and pulls it up over her face, blinding and disorientating her. The knife flails around as she tries to drive it into him. He grabs her wrist and wrenches it until she howls and drops the knife to the floor. He kicks it in my direction. Ignoring the pain in my leg, I scrabble forwards, grab the knife and retreat back against the railings.

'I did it all for you,' she says. 'I loved you and you—'

'Shut up.' He pulls the black fabric of the apron tight across her face. 'Stop it.'

Without warning, her body goes limp.

'Miles, let her breathe,' I say.

When he lets go of the apron, she surges back to life and

breaks away from him. Her face is a mask of shock and fear as she staggers towards the edge of the terrace. To the gap between the railings. To the precipice of crumbling stone.

'I remember,' she says. 'I remember about Bruce.'

'So do I.' He strides over to her, grabs her by the shoulders and shakes her. 'You never let me forget it.'

'I remember everything.' She lashes out at him, scratching his face.

'Shut up,' he says. 'Stop it.'

'Watch out,' I say. They are both dangerously near the edge now. Vivienne thrashes in his arms, edging them closer, her arms clasped around his waist.

Then she is tipping backwards, over the edge. Miles is trying to loosen her grip on him, but she won't let go.

'Please,' he says. 'Stop.'

She tilts and for a moment I think they are going to fall together but, at the last moment, Miles frees himself from her embrace and staggers back to safety.

Vivienne hovers for a few seconds, her pale arms reaching for the heavens, and then she falls. When she disappears from view, her final scream lingers in the still evening air.

Then, silence. Even the birds cease their singing.

She hits the ground with a dull, crumpled thud.

58

LEAH

August

The journey downstairs is arduous. Miles helps me back into the attic and, with one arm around my waist, takes my weight so I can hobble my way through the piles of dusty memorabilia.

'I'm sorry,' he says as we spill out onto the landing. An apology he keeps repeating as we negotiate the stairs down to the first floor. I say nothing. My body is shaking. My heart rate is out of control. On the first-floor landing, I see one of my Chloé slides. I remember Vivienne slashing at my clothes with the knife. The knife I left out on the roof terrace.

The pain in my left leg is intense as we manoeuvre down the next set of stairs to the entrance hall. I pass my other discarded shoe.

'She might survive,' Miles says. 'People can survive a fall like that.'

Unlikely.

When we reach the entrance hall, I press my hand to my

mouth. Dominic is lying by the door, where he fell. His head is turned towards me and his vacant eyes confirm what Miles said. It is too late. He is gone.

Blood everywhere. So much blood. In the deep red pool of it I see my bag and my phone.

Miles lets me go. After rummaging behind one of the coat stands, he produces a sturdy walking stick. 'Can you manage with this?' he says.

I nod.

He squeezes my hand. 'I need to go to her.'

'Go.'

I stare at Dominic's lifeless body. Ours was a short affair, our time spent only in bars and hotel rooms. I hardly knew him, but I remember he had a mole beneath his left shoulder blade and that whenever we met, his breath was always minty. As if he'd just cleaned his teeth or eaten chewing gum, which showed he'd taken time to prepare himself for me. It was a small detail, but I always found it touching.

When I reach the back terrace, I find Miles kneeling beside Vivienne's body. She landed on her back. Blood trickles from her shattered skull onto the mossy flagstones. Her arms and legs are splayed out at odd angles. Like a starfish with a missing limb.

Her open eyes are vacant. Just like Dominic's.

'I didn't want her to fall.' Miles looks at me, his eyes dark with grief and fear. 'You saw what happened. She would have taken me with her.'

The birds have started singing again, Vivienne's demise a brief interruption to their normal service. The rose-gold evening light is flattering everything. It gives Vivienne's lifeless body an almost holy glow.

'I've called the police,' I say, leaning my weight on the walking stick. 'They won't be long.' In the entrance hall, I plucked my phone out of the blood, wiped the screen and looked up the number for the French emergency services. The operator spoke good English. Before the call ended, I gave her the code for the château gates. 'They told me they'll send an ambulance.' I look at Vivienne's corpse. 'But...'

Miles shoots me a desperate look. 'We need to work out what to tell the police.'

'We?'

'Leah. Please.' He presses his hands together as if praying. 'I love you. I still think we can—'

'None of it was real,' I say. 'You were lying to me from the start.'

'No.' A pleading look in his eyes. 'At first, I thought this game would make me feel better. Help me get over Riley's death and the way she treated me. Then I got to know you and it became real.'

'Why would you need to get over how Riley treated you? Sounds like you had exactly the arrangement you wanted.'

'It wasn't like that.' He runs a hand through his thinning hair. He looks suddenly old. Or maybe he just looks his age. 'Plenty of people have healthy open relationships; ours was anything but.'

'I thought you enjoyed it?'

'It was never my idea.' He holds his head in his hands. 'After she told me she didn't want children, she said she wanted to sleep with other men.'

'Why didn't you divorce her?'

He looks up. 'I didn't want to. I couldn't let her go.'

'Because you didn't have a prenup? Vivienne said you got married without one.'

'That was part of it.' He looks at his dead cousin. 'She told me I was an idiot marrying in haste and she was right.' He touches her pale face. 'She was right about a lot of things.'

'So it was just about the money?'

'No.' He wraps his arms around himself. 'I was trapped. It was toxic. Riley knew I got a thrill from her being with other men. We discussed it once as a fantasy and when she suggested making it real, I went along with it. She knew how to tap into my weaknesses. How to manipulate my desires.'

Vivienne was right when she said Riley had a hold over him. A hold just as powerful as money.

I listen out for the sound of approaching sirens, but there is still only birdsong.

'Seems to me you were a willing participant.' I glance at Vivienne. 'Why were you so ready to believe Riley's death was an accident? You knew Vivienne hated her.'

'Yes, but I never thought she would hurt her. I didn't think she was capable of that.'

'What about Jacques? It didn't occur to you that her ex-convict lover could have been involved?'

He sighs. 'If we're being honest, and I want to be honest with you, I was glad Riley was dead. I was heartbroken and I was sad, but part of me was relieved. I felt free.'

The distant wail of sirens drifts in on the warm, evening air.

'Did Philippe help you?' I ask.

'What?'

'Did you ask the mayor to prevent a full investigation into Riley's death?'

'I didn't have to. Her death looked like an accident, and everyone was happy with that verdict. But Philippe did use his influence to get the matter concluded quickly. He knew I didn't want the pain and inconvenience of an investigation. As a friend, he wanted to spare me any more trauma.'

I look at Miles' sad, haunted face. It is not a pretty story, but instinct tells me it is a true one.

'I love you, Leah,' he says. 'I know this is a mess, but I think we can get through it.'

'Love?' I say.

'Yes.' He looks into my eyes. 'I love you. Can you say the same about me, or has it always been about the money?'

No. I can't say the same. I did think we could be happy together and that our marriage could be mutually beneficial.

'It's okay if it is just about the money,' he says. 'That doesn't mean we can't turn this into something real.'

He looks so earnest. As if he really thinks we could have a future together.

'I want to start again,' he says. 'I *need* to start again.'

The wailing sirens are growing louder now. The police are closing in.

'All we need to do is give them the right story,' he says.

I think back to the day Vivienne and I met Philippe in Montreuilac. *A sad story about your husband. I was sorry to hear it.* 'But you told the mayor Dominic was dead.'

'I told him Dominic had left her. I knew I couldn't lie to him about that. All Vivienne and I had to do was make sure you never spent any time alone with him.'

I misinterpreted what Philippe said that day. Ever since I arrived at Clairvallon, I've been living in a false reality.

'Listen,' Miles says. 'We tell them Vivienne and Dom were in the middle of a bitter divorce, which is true. Dom turned up here to persuade her to sign the divorce papers. You walked in on them arguing and saw her stab him. You tried to intervene, but she attacked you and chased you up to the roof terrace. When you got up there, she realised what she'd done and threatened to jump. I arrived and we tried to stop her, but she threw herself off the roof. A murder-suicide. End of story.'

'That's one version.' I look at him. 'Or I could easily tell them another.' His face crumples as I outline a different story. The story of how I was tricked into a relationship with him. How I was lured here under false pretences by both him and Vivienne. She wanted to kill me, and I could easily argue that he was her accomplice. 'It doesn't look good,' I say. 'If the press get hold of that story, you can say goodbye to the sale of Sinclair Properties.'

The sirens come closer.

'If I really wanted to make life hard for you,' I say, 'I could even claim you pushed Vivienne off the roof.'

'No.' He looks horrified.

I feel it now. The power. Once it was his, but now it is mine.

'Please, Leah,' he says. 'I'll agree to whatever terms you want.'

'You'll make changes to the prenup?'

'Yes.'

'No ring-fencing of assets? If we split up, I'll be entitled to money from the sale of Sinclair Properties?'

I hear cars speeding up the driveway, sirens blaring.

'Yes,' Miles says. 'Anything.'

'And I can have other men? Like Riley did.'

'If that's what it takes.' He looks exhausted. Resigned. 'I'll do anything, Leah. Anything.'

PART IV

59

LEAH

Five Months Later, February, London

It is 7 p.m. on a cold February night. I'm sitting alone at a table in the Beaufort bar at the Savoy Hotel, a vodka martini in front of me. My red dress is low-cut, my black stilettos dangerously high. My eye make-up is dark and dramatic, my lips crimson. I look like *that* kind of woman.

I'm attracting a lot of attention, which is good. Cold, disparaging looks from the wives in the room. Admiring glances from the men that are with them, as well as the men sitting alone.

I ignore them all. My date hasn't appeared yet, but when he does, he'll have my full attention. I check the picture of him I have on my phone. Tousled sandy hair, pale blue eyes, cheeky smile. The smile of a man who knows he's handsome.

When he finally appears, he is even better-looking in the flesh. He recognises me from the picture I sent him and, with a broad smile on his face, comes over to the table.

'Hello, Will,' I say.

'Hello, Martina.' He bends down and kisses me on both cheeks before seating himself opposite me. He glances at my left hand and looks pleased to see my engagement ring and wedding band there.

Alex, the barman, comes over. Will and I both order vodka martinis. Alex winks at me. He knows to make mine non-alcoholic and I've tipped him for his discretion.

When the drinks arrive, Will and I clink our glasses together and make small talk. The weather, yesterday's Tube strike, his work as a hedge fund manager. I tell him I work in fashion, but he doesn't press for details. He wants this part of the evening over with.

As soon as we finish our drinks, he suggests we go up to our room. The one he has booked for our night of casual, no-strings sex. In the lift, he leans in for a kiss. I usually try to avoid the kissing but tonight, curiosity gets the better of me. He smells good. Woody-scented soap. Subtle, musky aftershave. His kiss leaves me tingling.

The room, a junior suite, has been turned down for the evening. One corner of the bedding folded back, a small square chocolate on each pillow. Will removes my faux fur coat for me and drapes it over a chair.

'I'm just going to use the bathroom,' I say.

He smiles. 'Be my guest.'

In the gleaming marble bathroom, I take my phone from my Chanel clutch and send a text.

> All ready. Room 352.

Five minutes later, I emerge from the bathroom. Will is lying on the bed in a pair of black boxer shorts and looks puzzled to see me still dressed. He looks even more confused when the knock on the door comes.

'I'll get that.' I pick up my coat from the chair. 'Thanks for the drink.'

When I open the door, I find Sabrina, his fiancée, glowering in the corridor, phone clutched to her chest. In her skinny black jeans and black polo neck, she looks like an assassin. A woman ready for action. 'He's in there,' I say.

Hurt flashes across her face as she looks me up and down. 'Thanks.' She pushes past me into the room. 'You lying piece of shit,' she screams at Will. The shock on his face is priceless.

I close the door behind me as I leave. In the corridor, a satisfied smile spreads across my face. Time to go home.

* * *

The view from the floor-to-ceiling windows in the living room of my Dulwich penthouse is spectacular. This side of the apartment looks across the river to the city. I can see the lights twinkling on the London Eye.

My phone pings in my coat pocket. When I look at the screen, I see a text from Pete, my boss.

Great job, Leah!

After texting him back, I shrug off my coat and drop it on the cream corner couch. Jobs like tonight leave me feeling both satisfied and slightly soiled.

The centrepiece of my sleek, designer bathroom is a clawfoot bath, like the one I was banned from using at Château Clairvallon. I turn on the gold taps. While the bath fills, I undress and leave my clothes and my phone on the white wicker chair in the corner of the room. Next I remove my rings.

The extravagant diamond engagement ring Miles bought me and the cheap, platinum-plated wedding band I got from Amazon. I did think about selling the Boucheron diamond but decided to keep it. Along with the thin, silvery scar on my right arm, the ring is a warning of what could have been.

When the bath is full, I add a scoop of luxury salts, climb into it and sink back with a sigh. I wonder what Will and Sabrina are doing now. They might still be arguing in the hotel suite. I hope she's giving him hell.

I've been working as an assistant at Bond Investigators for three months now and Sabrina's case is, sadly, a typical one. She wanted to find out if Will was cheating on her. She'd discovered he was using Hidden Flame, a website that connects people in relationships looking to have discreet affairs. My work at Bond's is mostly boring research and admin duties and will remain so until I qualify as a private investigator, but I do get the occasional honeytrap job like tonight. I had to make a fake profile on the website and then contact Will to arrange a date.

Strange, to be catching out the unfaithful when I once had sex with a married man in hotel rooms. I thought about Vivienne earlier, when I was in the suite with Will. How crushed she must have felt when she found out about her husband's affair. How her understandable hatred of me turned into an obsession.

I thought about Miles too. How odd it is that I once trawled hotel bars for rich men like him. The old me, just looking to take what I could get. The new me felt a strong connection to Sabrina tonight. I know what it's like to be engaged and to doubt the man you are about to commit to. An engagement is a tenuous time. A limbo in which you can discover all sorts of things you'd rather not know.

As my limbs soften in the hot, fragrant water, my mind drifts back to Château Clairvallon. Sometimes I dream about it. Sometimes those dreams are unpleasant ones. I don't often look Miles up online, but a few days ago I succumbed to temptation and found an article in *The Financial Times* announcing that Sinclair Properties had been bought by Heritage Capital. Miles will be even richer now.

Will that make him happy? I have no desire to know. Once our business affairs were concluded, I warned him never to contact me again. Not that I expected him to. I would only remind him of everything he wants to forget.

When I think back to that last, terrible day at Clairvallon, it still amazes me that Miles thought we had a chance together. That we might still marry. When he said he loved me, I believed him. His desperation to start again, to erase the past and pretend he could feel young and untainted and in love, was pitiful.

I could have said yes. As the police cars sped up the drive towards the château, I considered it. I had power now. Miles was prepared to agree to any terms I wanted. Financial security for life as well as sexual freedom.

You won't get a better deal than that, Leah.

My mother made her feelings clear, but I knew I couldn't go through with it. I didn't want to spend my life in a toxic marriage with a man I didn't love, just for money. I wanted to be able to look after myself. I wanted my freedom.

As I stood on the terrace with Miles, waiting for the police cars to reach us, my mind raced through a number of options.

'This is what we're going to do,' I said. Miles almost smiled with relief when I agreed we would tell the police his version of events. A tragic murder-suicide.

374 T. J. EMERSON

'What about Riley's death?' he asked. 'What will we tell them?'

What would Riley want me to do? I waited for some sort of sign, but there was nothing. I knew for certain then that the strange sensations I'd experienced, those sudden chills and icy shudders, had never signalled the presence of a ghost. They were my gut instinct trying to communicate with me. Trying to warn me I was in danger.

'We say nothing,' I told him. Vivienne was dead. The score was settled. I had never known Riley, but I got the impression she was a woman who would appreciate vengeance more than justice.

Miles and I looked at each other. I weighed up what he had done. He hadn't killed his wife and his unconventional sexual relationship with her was not a crime. Yes, he killed his brother all those years ago, but that was an accident and he was trying to stop his brother from attacking his cousin. Besides, there was no evidence to prove his guilt. Vivienne was gone and Miles could deny any involvement in Bruce's death. That crime was too far in the past.

In the present, he had deceived me and put me in a dangerous position, but I had survived, and I wasn't sure the law would be able to help me or would even look favourably on me.

As the police cars screeched to a halt on the other side of the château, I laid out my terms for my continued co-operation. As I spoke, Miles looked more and more dejected, but he agreed. He didn't have much choice.

Knowledge *is* power. My mother was right about that. Knowing the truth gave me leverage that day. Seeing the whole picture set me free.

The mayor came soon after the police arrived. He was

shocked and sympathetic. What a terrible end for Dominic and for Vivienne, he said. Terrible to have an incident like this at the château so soon after Riley.

Miles couldn't avoid an investigation this time. I was concerned the police would find out about my affair with Dominic, but whatever evidence Vivienne had on us was not at Château Clairvallon and, as Miles explained, the investigation was being conducted by the French authorities and would only deal with what had happened in France. As far as the police were concerned, there was no need to search beyond the story we told them. Vivienne did kill Dominic and she did fall from the roof terrace. The lawyers acting for the couple confirmed their divorce proceedings were ugly and complicated and the stash of medication in Vivienne's bathroom added to the image of her as a troubled and unstable woman. Her son, shattered by the loss of both parents in such disturbing circumstances, had no desire to complicate proceedings. He wanted the matter resolved quickly and with as little publicity as possible.

In the first chaotic days after Vivienne's and Dominic's deaths, I wondered if Estelle might cause us problems. Would news of the fresh tragedies at Clairvallon prompt her to tell Béatrice what she knew about Riley's death? I reasoned that even if she did, her story would probably be dismissed as a delusion. Béatrice did visit the château during that time to pass on condolences, but that was the only contact Miles and I had with the Framboust family. Jacques did not come back, and I didn't expect him to. I knew he would never speak about Riley's death to anyone, and I knew I would never see him again. That was fine with me. I had no desire to see him and still don't. I am, however, oddly grateful to him. He was right when he told me I was marrying Miles for the wrong reasons. Perhaps he helped me see that more clearly.

In the end, Miles and I got away with our official story. Everything outside of it is a secret he and I will carry forever.

He was grateful for my discretion. Grateful enough to buy me this penthouse and give me a one-off payment of £250,000. I had to sign an NDA for him, but I didn't mind. I came out of a nightmare situation with a home and a decent nest-egg.

Don't judge me. I'm only human.

From the wicker chair comes the soft ping of an incoming text. I get out of the bath, bubbles sliding down my body, and pad across the room to retrieve my phone. Once settled back in the bath, I read the latest text from Freddie.

> Just meet me, Leah. That's all I ask. Just to talk. Fxxx

Freddie and Florence split up last month and he has been texting me ever since. Telling me how much he regrets ending our relationship. Begging me to give him another chance.

I stare at his message, my thumb hovering over the phone's keypad.

No. Not a chance. I drop the phone onto the bathroom floor and sink back onto a pillow of bubbles. The hold Freddie once had over me is gone. We're done.

All relationships are based on power, not love.

Not *all* relationships. My mother was wrong about that. She never had a relationship with herself, as I am trying to do. Learning to love myself, as the famous song goes. Unfortunately, she was right about the majority of relationships. That is why I enjoyed tonight's assignment and want to do more like that. I want to help other women get all the knowledge they need. There is nothing more powerful than a woman who sees the whole picture.

EPILOGUE

There is a new ghost at Château Clairvallon. Vivienne drifts around its dusty rooms in the same black dress and apron she met her end in. She remembers how when she was a child she dreamt about living here forever. The irony of this memory is not lost on her.

In those first moments after her death, when she realised she was no longer in her body, she glanced up at the roof terrace and saw Riley looking down at her, triumphant. She worried the two of them would be stuck together for eternity, but the moment turned out to be a brief, ghostly handover. As she watched, Riley faded away, never to be seen again.

Those early months were lonely. Clairvallon was closed up again after its latest tragedy. Miles was back in London. The winter was long and harsh and lonely. She sensed the presence of the château's other lost souls, but they never fraternised.

She had a lot of time to replay that final, fatal row with Miles on the roof terrace. The moment when he pulled the black fabric of her apron over her face. His words in her ear.

Shut up. Stop it.

At that moment, knowledge sure and true exploded within her. A knowledge she must have always had. A knowledge that had lain muddled and dormant within her since the night she was raped in Chamonix.

It was Miles, not Bruce. Miles who had spoken those words in her ear as he forced himself inside her.

Not Bruce. Miles.

She remembered lying on her bed in the ski chalet in Chamonix, her intoxicated mind coming in and out of consciousness. She saw Miles looming over her. Miles bruising her lips with clumsy kisses. Miles pulling her jumper over her head.

When she screamed at him on the roof terrace – I remember everything – she saw terror in his eyes. He knew exactly what she meant.

Now she is dead, she can think clearly. She understands the events of her life in the way only the dead can. She knows exactly what happened between her and her cousin that night. She knows that shortly after Miles put her to bed, he and Bruce carried on drinking downstairs. She knows Bruce passed out and that is when Miles crept back up to her room. Miles, a confused tangle of teenage hormones, his frustrated urges for the chalet girl mingling with the familiarity of his cousin's flesh. Miles, at first curious and then unable to contain himself.

Miles interrupted by his older brother.

What the fuck are you doing? Miles screamed those words as Bruce pulled him off her. Poor Bruce. Dumb and arrogant he may have been, but a rapist he was not.

If only she had understood this sooner.

* * *

It is summer now. Almost a year since Vivienne's death. Still she lingers at Château Clairvallon. Still she drifts from room to room, a cold, invisible presence.

Miles is back. He could have sold the place. Cut himself off from all the dark memories. Instead he is with her. He wants to punish himself. Sometimes he goes up to the roof terrace and sits cross-legged, like he did when he was a boy. He cries. His grief is real and now and then she pities the sad, confused boy still trapped inside him.

Her anger, however, outweighs her sympathy and she refuses to pity him for long. Sometimes, when he is on the roof terrace, he steps close to the edge and looks down at the drop. She remembers how she tried to take him with her when she fell. Sometimes she puts an icy hand around his throat and whispers in his ear.

Jump. Go on, do it. Jump.

There is someone keeping him tethered to the living. The new girl. Her name is Tegan and she is a year younger than Leah. Miles asked her to marry him and she said yes.

Of course she did. Miles is even wealthier since he sold Sinclair Properties and Tegan is out for what she can get. Vivienne even has days when she wishes Leah would return to the château. Vivienne still hates her, even in death, but this Tegan is in another league altogether.

Tegan is shallow and cold and calculating. Miles thinks they are trying for a baby together, but she has yet to stop taking the pill. Tegan, as Vivienne has discovered, is predisposed to scheming. As Tegan lies on a sun lounger by the pool, watching Miles drink too much, repulsed by how old and bloated he is looking, she often fantasises about him dying shortly after their wedding. She fantasises about the money she would inherit – substantial thanks to the generous prenup she has negotiated – and she fantasises about how she would spend it.

At these moments, Vivienne is there. Perched on the edge of the sun lounger in her black dress. Whispering words of encouragement to Tegan. Warning her about the kind of man Miles is. Fanning the young girl's dreams about the life she could have if she one day decides to take matters into her own hands.

After all, Château Clairvallon is a place where accidents do happen.

* * *

MORE FROM T. J. EMERSON

Another book from T. J. Emerson, *Dying to be Here*, is available to order now here:

https://mybook.to/BeHereBackAd

ACKNOWLEDGEMENTS

Writing a novel is a team effort. Yes, I'm the one sitting alone for hours in my sweatpants putting the words on the page, but I'm only able to do that because of all the people who contribute to and facilitate that process. Turning those words into the book you're now reading takes even more dedicated folk.

Thanks as ever to my agent, Charlie Brotherstone, for his continued support and input. Charlie, I'm lucky to have you. To Rachel Faulkner-Willcocks, my editor at Boldwood Books, my gratitude. Once again you were a calm, insightful guide throughout the writing and editing process and, when I was stuck, you encouraged me to write the story I wanted to write. It was great to have the freedom to do that. Thanks to Helena Newton for her perceptive and transformative copy-edit and to Gary Jukes for the thorough and invaluable proofreading. I'd like to thank the skilled and talented team at Boldwood Books for getting this book to print and putting it out into the world. You are all so friendly, communicative and enthusiastic and make what can often be a daunting process very easy.

Huge thanks to Louise Dean and everyone at the Novelry. Their Advanced Course was an indispensable guide while I was writing this book. My coaching sessions with the brilliant Amanda Reynolds were the spark that brought this story to life. Thanks, Amanda, for your encouragement and all credit to you for more than one of the twisty moments in this book. Thanks also to the authors who, despite being ridiculously busy, put time aside to read an advance copy and provide a quote. My beloved friend, Liz, I'm so grateful you took time out from your hectic life to read a draft and, as always, give superb advice.

Château Clairvallon is fictional, but I was lucky enough to spend a week at Château de Sacy, an arts retreat an hour north of Paris. Spending time there gave me so many ideas for the setting of *The Last Mrs Sinclair*. I'm indebted to Murphy Williams for allowing me to roam her fascinating home and make it mine for the week. She also took the time to drive me around the area and show me different locations, and the snippets of local stories she shared were inspiring on lots of levels. Thanks also to Aditi and Kathy, fellow retreat guests. Being able to share my first chapter with you and get your feedback made me feel confident I'd at last found the right narrative voice for Leah.

As usual, expert help on all things police-related came from Stuart Gibbon of the Gib Consultancy. Much appreciated, Stuart. Heartfelt thanks to Rachael Noble and Nadia Sirc for advice on legal and financial matters. Apologies to anyone who helped with research that I've forgotten here.

To my family, thanks as always for your love and support. Thanks Dad, for everything, and thanks Susan for being a great sounding board and such a merciless reader!

To my friends, thanks for the light relief, the chat, and for being one of the best resources any writer could wish for.

To Susie and Mary, my greatest collaborators, all the thanks. Without your support and inspiration, I wouldn't be able to write books. I'm so very lucky to have you.

ABOUT THE AUTHOR

T. J. Emerson's first psychological thriller for Boldwood, *The Perfect Holiday*, was an Amazon bestseller and received brilliant reviews. Her short stories and features have been widely published in anthologies and magazines, and she works as a literary consultant and writing tutor. She lives in Scotland.

For an exclusive deleted scene from The Last Mrs Sinclair, sign up for T.J. Emerson's newsletter here!

Visit T. J. Emerson's Website: www.traceyemerson.com

Follow T. J. Emerson on social media here:

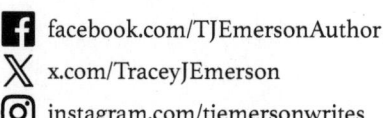

facebook.com/TJEmersonAuthor

x.com/TraceyJEmerson

instagram.com/tjemersonwrites

ALSO BY T. J. EMERSON

The Perfect Holiday

The Ideal Man

Mother's Day

Dying to be Here

The Last Mrs Sinclair

THE Murder LIST

THE MURDER LIST IS A NEWSLETTER DEDICATED TO SPINE-CHILLING FICTION AND GRIPPING PAGE-TURNERS!

SIGN UP TO MAKE SURE YOU'RE ON OUR HIT LIST FOR EXCLUSIVE DEALS, AUTHOR CONTENT, AND COMPETITIONS.

SIGN UP TO OUR NEWSLETTER

BIT.LY/THEMURDERLISTNEWS

Boldw**oo**d

Printed in Dunstable, United Kingdom

70376300R10225